SOMEWHERE BEHIND THE MORNING

In working-class Leeds of 1914, sisters Julia and Margaret Wood are struggling to rise above devastating poverty. War seems inevitable and their German-Jewish father's search for work proves hopeless. It is self-educated, entrepreneurial Julia who keeps the family afloat by hawking homemade pies on the streets of Leeds, while Margaret, an apprentice milliner and new member of the suffragette set, pins her hopes on a rich suffragette, Mrs Turner, and her journalist son Tom. As war rages, Julia discovers for herself the meaning of courage, and looks forward to that fresh, magical start – somewhere behind the morning.

Somewhere Behind The Morning

by

Frances McNeil

Magna Large Print Books
Long Preston, North Yorkshire,
BD23 4ND, England.

British Library Cataloguing in Publication Data.

McNeil, Frances
    Somewhere behind the morning.

    A catalogue record of this book is
    available from the British Library

    ISBN   0-7505-2515-0

First published in Great Britain 2005 by Orion
an imprint of the Orion Publishing Group

Copyright © Frances McNeil 2005

Cover illustration © Getty Images by arrangement with
Orion Book Publishing

The right of Frances McNeil to be identified as the author of this work
has been asserted by her in accordance with the Copyright, Designs
and Patents Act, 1988

Published in Large Print 2006 by arrangement with
Orion Publishing Group

Magna Large Print is an imprint of Library Magna Books Ltd.

Printed and bound in Great Britain by
T.J. (International) Ltd., Cornwall, PL28 8RW

For my mother

I have always been delighted at the prospect
of a new day, a fresh try, one more start,
with perhaps a bit of magic waiting
somewhere behind the morning.

J.B. PRIESTLEY

ACKNOWLEDGEMENTS

Somewhere Behind The Morning draws on *Sisters On Bread Street*, published in a limited edition (Pavan Press, 2003) to mark my mother's hundredth birthday.

Tom Maguire's poems from *Machine-Room Chants*, 1895. *The Iliad* quotations from Simone Weil's *The Iliad, a Poem of Force* in *The Pacifist Conscience*, edited by Peter Mayer, 1966. Charlotte Perkins Gilman's 'The Socialist and the Suffragist', *Suffrage Songs and Verses*, New York, 1911 (and in *One Hand Tied Behind Us*, Liddington and Norris, 1978). *Leeds Pals*, Laurie Milner, 1991, and *Cowards*, Marcus Sedgwick, 2003, provided useful background detail.

Thanks to Bill Featherstone (Master Butcher) and Audrey Featherstone. Sylvia Gill, Patricia McNeil and Peter McNeil gave unfailing support throughout.

SPRING
AND
SUMMER
1914

ONE

On Pollard Street, our little look-out gave the warning whistle that usually meant 'Coppers chasing Sunday street-traders! Scarper!'

Today it meant something else, but I didn't know that.

Fast as I could, I gathered the pies into the centre of the beef sheeting, knotted the corners and rushed the lot to Mrs O'Malley. She took the bundle from me and shut the door, as Dad tipped the handcart to run it into the alley out of sight.

'Get the Yid!' came the yell.

They came out of nowhere, three lads, the skinniest waving a cricket bat. Two of them would have blown away in a strong wind but together they caught Dad off-guard as he came out of the alley. Later, he said they'd tripped him, but all I saw was Dad fall and boots flying at his ribs, belly and head.

I tugged at a collar and a lump of shirt, pulling at the biggest bruiser, a ginger-haired lad covered in freckles. I couldn't drag him off. The white-haired one, rat-eyed, caught my wrist and shoulder with a kind of sneering grunt, and flung me against the wall, but not before I yanked at his hair fit to split his scalp. He would have throttled me but let go when the scabby boy with the cricket bat yelled, 'Don't heed her, get the Yid's money.'

The ginger bruiser stopped kicking and bent down over Dad to rifle his pockets. I thought they'd killed him. The scabby lad thought that, too. I could tell by his scared look. His nose started to bleed then, and he rubbed the back of his hand against his nose. Blood poured through his fingers. While he looked at it, sort of surprised, he relaxed his hold on the cricket bat. I grabbed the bat from him and swung it at his knees. His legs buckled and he gasped in pain.

I swung out again and bashed the bruiser on the head and shoulders while he was still trying to rifle Dad's pockets (having no luck, as I'm the one who keeps the cash). I belted out with the bat, walloping White Rat and Ginger Bruiser, then dancing out of the way as I've seen Frank do in the boxing ring.

I don't know how Dad managed to get up. He tried to land a punch but fell against White Rat and sent him sprawling.

Mrs O'Malley opened the door, shouting to her husband to come, and charged out, waving her rolling pin.

The three ran. At the end of the street, White Rat turned and yelled, 'We'll get you for this, Yid. You too, Yiddess.'

I have the same jet-black hair Dad once had; his now has streaks of white. He has a weather-beaten face and hazel eyes. My skin is fair and my eyes true blue, though I felt them blazing with hurt and anger. Dad took my hand between his finger and thumb, asking was I hurt. I told him I thought we'd hurt them more. But I don't believe that because there is more than one kind of hurt.

Calling names doesn't hurt, people say. That's not true.

I'm not a Yiddess. I'm not even Jewish. My mother was Margaret Lynch and that's about as Jewish as soda bread. But I wished at that moment I was Jewish *and* German, then I would be like my father.

Dad took a few breaths, shallow and noisy, as if the air hurt him. He squeezed my hand. 'Is all right, Julia. We see them off.'

He gave a gasp as if something jabbed his chest, then reached out to the O'Malley's window sill to steady himself. Mrs O'Malley took one arm and I took the other to lead him inside.

Little Mr O'Malley, blinking sleep out of his eyes, pulling his braces onto his shoulders, flung the door wide open and tried to look gigantic. The smell of cabbage and sweaty feet hit me full on. By this time all the little O'Malleys appeared from indoors and out, and the eldest boy, Steven, picked up the abandoned cricket bat.

When Mr O'Malley realized what had happened, he wanted to go rushing up Pollard Street, looking for our attackers. I told him they could be the other side of Leeds by now. Mrs O'Malley seemed grateful for that and patted my arm.

Dad sat on the one O'Malley chair, clutching a cracked mug of tea. I crouched near the door, drinking sweet tea from a jam jar. Mr O'Malley leaned against the mantelpiece, snapping his braces and saying he would go after the blethering attackers and I must give him a categorical description.

Dad held his hand up and shook his head.

17

'They know no better. Pity their ignorance.'

Mrs O'Malley started to say something about Dad being a finer Christian than most, even though he's a Jew.

When Mr O'Malley moves, I imagine that's how a pixie dances. His blue eyes shone with excitement when I said that a little help would be worth a lot of sympathy, and if he would finish our pie round for us and bring the cart back to Bread Street afterwards, we'd pay him for his trouble.

He rolled up his striped shirt-sleeves, bobbed down and thrust an arm under my nose. 'See that bicep, young lady? Charge your man wi' pushing two carts twice round Leeds and I'll do it and fend off an army.'

It hurt Dad to speak, so I made Mr O'Malley say back to me which streets he would cover and in what order. After Balaclava and Alma Street he should cut across Beckett Street to the Workhouse Infirmary where the overseer, Mr Shepherd, buys from us.

It turned into an outing and six little O'Malleys went along with their daddy, to keep a look-out for police who like to pounce on Sunday street-traders. I went with them as far as Beckett Street, while Dad rested in Mr O'Malley's chair.

It felt strange watching the O'Malley clan head up Granville Place with our handcart, Mr O'Malley singing out, 'Come and buy yer meat-an-tater pies.' I wondered how many pies would be left to sell by the time the clan rounded the corner.

I stood on Beckett Street with my back to the recreation ground. An April shower started and I turned my face to the rain. It felt cool and calming. Only then did I realize that, from my toes to my head, I felt turned to lead inside, heavy and tense, but exhilarated because we'd seen off our attackers and they hadn't got a penny.

Behind me on the recreation ground, children played and called out to each other, but their voices seemed far away, unreal. The exhilaration turned to anger. I wanted to yell and scream at someone. Maybe that was why the first horse and cart didn't stop. Then a brown mare trotted into view, a small cart behind. I waved at the driver. He had a lined and lived-in round face and wore a brown suit, shiny with age. He told me that the last time anyone waved at him that alarmingly it was to alert him that a cart wheel threatened to spin loose. He agreed to pick up Dad and take us back to Bread Street, refusing to take payment for his trouble.

Now Dad has a lump on his head the size of a crab apple. Aunty Amy (our next-door neighbour, no relation) heard the horse and cart, and looked through the window of her corner-house-shop. But I caught her eye and she nodded. Dad hates a fuss and it would mortify him to be helped indoors by his daughter and an old woman. She's a herbalist – though some children who don't know any better call her a witch.

Five minutes later she tapped on our door and came in with witch hazel, and beef sheeting cut into bandage strips for Dad's ribs and head, and my arm. She says she's sure he has at least one broken rib and must rest. Dad pretended his grimace of pain was a smile and said she was making a fuss. He would lie still and be 'reet as rain' tomorrow. He likes to say little phrases in a Leeds accent as though he is an Englishman. But he never really pulls it off.

I unfolded Dad's bedchair, but he wouldn't lie down. We sat side by side while Aunty Amy made a pot of tea. While it was mashing, she nodded for me to go to the bottom of the stairs. Then she marched me upstairs, saying that she'd bring my tea up and I'd be doing the right thing by resting for an hour because then Dad could get some shut-eye on his bedchair.

So I lay on my bed, shut my eyes tightly and conjured up those three evil faces.

Ginger Bruiser with wide cheekbones and eyebrows that met; White Rat who'd blow away in a strong wind; Scabby Lad with the cricket bat and the nervous nosebleed. I'd lost my shawl from my shoulders in the scuffle, and the blood from his nose had stained my blouse.

Dad can say 'Pity their ignorance' all he likes. I say different. I don't believe in turning the other cheek.

It annoys me that these events have turned out to be my first entry in this journal, which is really an old accounts book Dad had when he kept his own butcher's shop. I rescued it from the bureau. He said I could tear out the accounts and use the book. I cut the used pages out carefully, so as not to loosen the corresponding pages at the back of the book. (It is a great pity Dad had to give up the shop. Business was not bad.) For my birthday

Dad bought me a pen, inkpot, pencil and a ruler. With the ruler I will underline important entries.

I decided to keep this journal because I was fifteen on 15 April and <u>this year of 1914 will be the only time my birth date and my age coincide</u>. I am doing tiny writing or I shall soon use up the pages. I have discovered that if I miss out vowels I can still read back what I have written as well as get it down faster.

I had meant to write my opinions about something important. Perhaps Tom Maguire's poetry. I am infuriated to end up writing about the blooming pie round and the three great stoits who think they can just come and beat you up for your hard-earned cash.

TWO

I watched Dad limp out to his work this morning, still hurting from the kicking he took. He came home less than an hour later. I had just carried a basket of washing up from the cellar.

Dad's shoulders stooped. He wouldn't look at me. I went up to him and asked, 'What's wrong?' I made him look at me.

He has this little trick, where he lifts his left eyebrow and turns down the right corner of his mouth – as if his face is shrugging. He half-closed his eyes and looked away from me, as if he couldn't bear the effect of his words. 'Boss says I'm not fit. Not fit to slaughter beasts. They give me the sack.'

'We'll think of something,' I said.

I straight away came up with a Good Plan. Dad must have guessed what was in my mind because he made me promise not to tell the cousins or Uncle Lloyd about the attack. It was as if he thought that being attacked was somehow his own fault. I promised not to tell. Though it's likely to come out one way or another.

Cousin Bernard nodded to me as I gave our salute and walked through the lounge bar of the Dragon. He couldn't salute back as he was playing Schubert. Uncle does not allow his first-born to lower himself by playing the piano during opening hours. He wants to keep a quiet and orderly public house. This means that Bernard has to work behind the bar, which he hates, while the pub piano player pounds away and is a constant torment to Bernard. Not that it is hard to torment Bernard. He is the finest complainer in the world, though usually only to me because we are each other's favourite cousin. If he has nothing new to complain about, he will resurrect some old grievance from last week, last month or his fourth birthday when his twin brothers, Kevin and Johnny, didn't give him a chance to blow out the candles on his own cake.

The cellar trapdoor stood open. I heard Uncle calling, 'Bernard! Get yer features down here! Lend a hand!'

The Dragon's cellar steps have a steep rise. I reached out for the wall, feeling my way down in the dim light from Uncle's lantern, which he'd hung from a ceiling beam in the centre of the cellar. The cold comes up to meet you with the malty smell, hops and sour barley from the beer barrels. I hate that stench, worse than rancid butter.

When my eyes adjusted to the gloom, I saw Uncle Lloyd. Stooped over, sleeves rolled up, he was rolling a barrel off the gantry. His gold watch on its chain swayed close to the barrel, looking as though it would smash against it.

We were never supposed to play in the cellar as children and only got to sneak down there when the pub was busy and no one noticed us. I get a sick, dizzy feeling down there, as if some ghost will materialize and draw me into the damp walls.

The cold of the cellar flags seeped through the soles of my feet, reminding me that the cardboard insoles in my shoes needed replacing, or I'd wear out my stockings.

Uncle heard me before he saw me. He straightened up, saying, 'About time.' Then he realized I wasn't Bernard. 'Oh, it's you, lass. I thought it too good to be true that Bernard had condescended to come and put his spoke in't wheel.'

I said, 'He's needed in the lounge bar. Piano doesn't play itself.'

Then I felt mean at making a joke about Bernard. It was like joining sides with Uncle against him. I went to help Uncle with the barrel but he said, 'Nay, lass. I can't have you heaving a barrel, though you frame yerself better than that great stoit upstairs. If you want owt doing, do it yoursen, that's my motto, and it's just as well with a cellarman who takes all day on an errand

and a son who wants to do nowt more than thump the ivories morning till night.'

When I told him I had hit upon a good idea, Uncle grinned. His two gold teeth looked black in the gloom. 'Go on then, Julia, lass,' he said. 'I'm a man of many parts. I can lend you an ear and connect up the barrel at the same time without toppling over.'

I told him my plan. Instead of me and Dad going out selling our pies on Sunday mornings, I should bring the pies to the Dragon on Saturday night, straight from Scarborough Lizzie's ovens, and Uncle could sell them to his customers.

Uncle Lloyd finished attaching a pipe to the barrel. Then he eyed me up and down, as if doing a few calculations. 'What's brought this idea into your pretty little noggin, Julia? Your dad wearying of pushing the old handcart? And you? Lost your yen to be a hawker?'

The answer came out more haughty than I meant. I said, 'Selling pies on a Sunday doesn't make me a hawker any more than it makes Dad a pie man, or me a pie man's daughter.'

Uncle reached for the mop and dabbed at a puddle of beer on the flagged floor. Bending over the barrel had made his breath come hard. Even in spring his chest wheezes. 'So what's behind this, then? Ist thah hankering after the easy life?'

I didn't like the mocking edge to his voice. I know he thinks himself a cut above Dad, just because he's a landlord. Sometimes I wonder what it would have been like if my mam and her sister had lived. Uncle Lloyd wouldn't have spoken to me like that. I wouldn't have needed to ask a

24

favour. This conversation wasn't going how I had heard it in my head when I thought of the Good Plan. Uncle was supposed to leap at the chance of selling our pies.

In future I must remember never to ask a favour of someone in a pub cellar. Stink, damp and gloom put you at a disadvantage.

I took a deep breath and started again. 'It's just that with us being family... All the pies would sell in one place. I could bring them here straight from the ovens, on Saturday night. Piping hot pies one penny.'

Uncle perched on a barrel, getting his breath. 'One penny to who?'

I took a deep breath and made myself sound very patient. It came out like Miss Blanchard from Standard Two explaining whole numbers and fractions. 'That's what we charge, Uncle. A penny a pie.'

He pulled out a big red handkerchief and wiped his hands. 'Then I can't charge tuppence, can I? Not for penny pies. What do I get out of it?' He dabbed at his forehead with the hanky.

I hadn't expected to be asked for anything, given how well-off Uncle is. The words toppled out before I even thought what I might answer. 'Well, you can have half a dozen pies for yourself.'

Uncle slid off the barrel and stood legs apart, hands on his hips. He nodded his head a couple of times, as if he might agree with me. Then he let out a rollicking laugh. It was not the kind of laugh you would join in with, but a mean, false laugh that came from his throat not his belly. He just laughed and laughed until finally I gave in and asked, 'What's so funny?'

He said, 'Nay, lass, do I look like a man in need of half a dozen penny pies? What passes as a good arrangement with young Fisticuffs Frank White-lock, or your little lookers-out posted on street corners to whistle when the coppers come, doesn't hold good here. Frank doesn't help you and your dad for the pies he takes home to his mam. He pushes that handcart because he's sweet on you. Now if you want to make a business pro-position, I suggest you talk it through with your dad and come up with summat sensible.'

I was glad for the gloom of the cellar because I felt myself turn hot and prickly. I didn't bother to say that Frank hadn't helped us on Sunday because of his boxing tournament. If he had been with us, no one in Leeds would have dared attack us.

Uncle twisted his small gold signet ring, which gets back to front on his pinkie finger. 'Be a good lass, run upstairs and make a pot of tea.'

I walked back up the cellar steps slowly, touching the cold wall with my fingertips. I wondered whether my mam or aunty had ever walked up from this cellar with a heavy heart, trailing a hand along the wall in just the same places as me. Uncle should have known I wouldn't have asked him if it wasn't important. Even worse, I couldn't stop hurt, angry tears pricking their way into my eyes. I have never asked Uncle for anything before.

Bernard stopped playing. 'What's up, cuz?'

I didn't answer.

He ran his fingers across the piano keys, shut

the lid and pushed his stool back a little way from the piano. 'If my name was above the door of this public house, you'd only have to ask, cuz. Anything. You know that, don't you?'

He didn't even know what I wanted and he was saying he couldn't do it. I thought if I spoke I'd cry. If you only have a few people in the world who you think will be on your side and then one of them isn't, that's enough to make you want to cry.

Cousin Bernard walked me through the lounge bar, to the Peter Street door, without another word. He intended to open the door for me but I got in first and pushed the brass handle with both hands. He watched me all the way to the corner. I knew that if I turned back and waved, he would shade his eyes against the sun with his left hand and raise his right hand in our salute. But I didn't turn round.

One thing worse than someone who could do you a favour refusing to do it, is someone who says that they would it they could but they can't.

Dad has his pride. I have mine.

There's more ways than one to put meat in a pie.

THREE

Revenge.

Frank did not waste time.

It was 6.30 p.m. and still light, but I had drawn the blind because the sink is by the window and

27

my sister Margaret, who is three and a half years older than me, demanded to have her hair washed. Her hair is light-brown and what people would call luxurious. Every time it is washed she has a vinegar rinse, which has worked wonders to bring out the red tones.

The vinegar rinse, with an infusion of rosemary, has been so successful that we have made a decent quantity and bottled it. We sell it in Aunty Amy's shop in pretty bottles with handwritten labels that say 'Wood Sisters Rosemary Rinse for Red Highlights', not mentioning the vinegar. (Though you can smell vinegar over and above the rosemary if I'm not careful.) It has begun to sell almost as well as our 'Wood Sisters Beer Shampoo', which is made with soft soap and the mild beer slops that Bernard saves for us.

Just as I poured the vinegar rinse, a loud rap on the window made me jump. Margaret makes such a fuss if a drop goes down her neck. She told me not to dare raise the blind till she had wrapped the towel around her hair.

Tap-tap again, rattling the pane. Frank's voice called me to come and look.

I raised the blind and stared at a squashed-up, freckled face against the window pane. Then the face pulled back and took on a different shape. Beyond the face stood Frank, holding a terrified lad by the scruff of the neck. Frank said, 'This one o' the poxes what had a go at thee and thah dad on Sunday?'

I nodded at the same time as Margaret said, 'Say no!'

In spite of his dire peril of a throttling by Frank,

28

the boy couldn't take his eyes off Margaret. Even with a grotty, worn-out towel around her head, Margaret is a beauty with her ivory skin, high cheekbones and eyes the colour of amber.

Frank squared up, dancing into a boxing stance, and gave Ginger Bruiser the same chance. Margaret groaned. Frank threw a punch and dodged, as Ginger Bruiser tried to land a punch back. He had no chance. Blood mingled with freckles beneath his nose and by his lip. Ginger Bruiser put his hand to his mouth to check his teeth, but Frank punched him again, in the chest this time.

Margaret said, 'What? What?'

'He's one of them who attacked Dad,' I told her. 'On Sunday.'

'Very clever of Frank,' Margaret said sarcastically. She pulled the blind down angrily. 'Now they know where we live. And we have the distinction of sinking to their level. A fight outside our house.'

'It's not a fight,' I said. 'It's revenge.'

I went to the door. Frank had stopped hitting the lad, but held onto his collar as if he didn't know what to do next. 'Does thah want to thump him thissen, Julia?' he asked.

I shook my head. 'Let him go, Frank. He's not worth the trouble.'

FOUR

Mr Fischer was serving a customer, as I fastened the cord around the sack of poultry feathers. Between serving customers and plucking chickens I didn't have a minute to think today. I couldn't decide what to ask Mr Fischer first. If he would give me four days' work a week instead of two, that would be a great improvement for our – ha, ha – budget. Mr Fischer is the one person Dad would accept help from because years ago, when Dad had his butcher shop, he helped Mr Fischer through some bad times. So I knew I could tell Mr Fischer about Dad losing his job, and how we are in a bit of a difficulty. But I am not good at asking favours.

I had decided to wait till Mr Fischer's son, Alec, went to make some deliveries. Mr Fischer likes me but he wants a Jewish girl for Alec. I do not say too much to Alec and never smile at him. But twice today I had to be very busy or hurry to serve someone because of the way Alec came so close to me, building up ready to speak. It got so poor Mr Fischer hardly dared answer a call of nature because he did not want to leave us alone together. He stepped from one foot to the other for so long that in the end I made the excuse of going back to the bookstall to swap my book, to give him chance to go to the Gents.

Alec had finally gone to make his deliveries. I

had just decided that the most pressing question was how we would get meat for our pies. I took a deep breath, ready to speak, but before I had chance, I saw Mr Fischer frowning at someone over my shoulder. Alec had done an unexpected about-turn and wheeled the handcart back to the stall with the poultry orders still undelivered.

Alec glared at his dad. 'I have to tell her.'

Mr Fischer glanced at the handcart, quickly checking that all the parcels were still intact.

Alec looked at me, kind and sorry at the same time. 'I'm getting engaged to Sophie Solomons. After we're wed, we'll open our own shop in Chapeltown. I wanted to tell you myself.'

I made myself look pleased and congratulated him. He seemed surprised. I managed a big smile. 'You needn't have come back specially to tell me. I don't know the poor girl so I shan't spend the weekend pitying her.'

Mr Fischer went to serve Mrs Goldman who always buys a pigeon on Thursdays.

I picked up the sack of feathers and lobbed it across the stall to Alec. 'You might as well take these.'

Alec held the sack in his arms. He looked at me as he always looked at me, in that way that annoys me. He said in a low voice, 'There's a Thomas Hardy poem about a young woman who marries someone not good enough for her because she doesn't know about her own beauty. She says, "Nobody told me I was a peach." You're a peach, Julia. Don't forget it. You won't be on this stall long. But I'll always think of you.'

He turned and squeaked off with his handcart

that needed oiling.

I felt humiliated. Did they both think I'd set my sights on Alec? After that I couldn't ask Mr Fischer for a favour.

FIVE

Dad looks a greyish colour and seems to have shrunk since last Sunday. He has been out tramping for work – a waste of time. No one will employ a man who looks so bruised and ill. He said that this is the first Friday night he has not put a guinea on the mantelpiece. He did not offer to light the candles as he usually does on a Friday, so I lit two. I put pickled herring on plates while Margaret sliced bread. Dad took a mouthful of herring. I knew he was wondering whether Mr Fischer had given it to me yesterday, but he did not ask.

After supper, Margaret was singing as she rinsed the plates under the tap. I asked her if she would give me and Dad a hand with the potatoes for the pies, cutting them up after Dad and me peeled them – I know she would never want to peel the spuds and dirty her hands, or cut up meat and get blood under her nails. But she told me she could not help with cutting up potatoes either. She had promised to go round to Miss Mason's house. Apparently, Miss Mason needs Margaret's opinion on the shades of thread for her new tapestry in Berlin wool. I could have said something but I didn't, for Dad's sake.

When Margaret shut the door behind her, Dad said, 'What's that little thing Mrs O'Malley say?'

I smiled and did my best Mrs O'Malley voice. 'You make a foine pie, lass, and allus a tasty morsel o' meat.'

Dad rolled up his trouser leg and looked at his hairy calf. 'How many pies that make, you think?'

'Dad!'

We knew without putting it into words what we had to do.

Dad brought up the pram from the cellar. I took the small key from the fruit dish in the bureau. He 'borrowed' that key months ago and had it copied. This would be the first time we had used it since he got the sack. We set off for the meat market, with a candle and Dad's butchery tools tucked in the pram.

I always wear Mam's big old black shawl when we do this job. It covers my head and I hide inside it, fastening it at my chin with a safety pin to keep my hands free. We never go the same way twice. We walked along Little Lemon Street and got to the Lemon Tree pub just as a pair of drunks, locked in a tomcats' embrace, hurtled through the doors in a swirl of stale beer and curses. We looked away and hurried on, not speaking, not wanting to attract attention. Too many young men hate foreigners, especially Jews. That's how Dad lost the butcher's shop he once had, before I was born. Bricks through the window.

'This the last time,' Dad said, as we crossed Harper Street.

A high-stepping, sleek black horse pulling a polished cab raced out of nowhere, the driver shouting and cracking his whip.

'Why should tonight be our last time?' I asked.

'Because I must joint a beast. It will be missed.'

It dawned on me. Before Dad lost his job, he could tuck some meat away in a corner to come back later. Other workers got away with taking a joint out under their overalls, but not Dad, not the foreigner.

We walked past the cattle pens towards the massive pair of wooden doors, with the smaller entrance set into the main doors just above ground level. I slid the key into the lock, and stepped into pitch darkness, a black void that seemed to press against me. With my eyes closed I would know where I was, breathing in the smell of sweet blood, sour flesh and fear. Dad lifted the pram across the threshold. The sawdust on the stone floor muffled the sound of its wheels.

Dad closed the door behind him. Once you get used to the darkness, it isn't quite so black. The vaulted roof has some glass panes that let in the moonlight. Some of them are broken, and a disturbed pigeon fluttered across, the sound of its wings startling me.

The first match went out. I took the candle from Dad; he lit it with the second match. We walked through the slaughterhouse. Dad slid back the bolt on the door leading to the cooling alley. Someone had laid sacks in the doorway.

We could have made do with a bit of offal, liver and lights or a brain. But the vats were empty. Dad muttered under his breath that the offal had all gone to Wildblood and Whites. As my eyes got used to the dim light, I focused on the shapes hanging row after row from hooks on the rails that ran the breadth of the cooling hall.

There wasn't a sheep or beef carcass to be seen, just pigs, nothing but pigs.

In the candlelight, our shadows loomed against the far wall of the cooling hall.

'We don't have to do it, Dad. I'll get some leeks. Leek and potato pies.'

Dad squeezed my shoulder and kept hold of my arm as we walked to the end of the hall where we could climb to the next level to reach the rail. 'Even a Jew must provide for his family.'

I started to say something else but Dad shushed me. I know that he has had to slaughter pigs, but he had never taken one home.

We carried the heavy wooden stepladder across from its place by the wall. Dad unclipped the hook from the rail, not wanting to leave a reminder that the smallest carcass had gone missing. Gently, we lowered the pig onto the sacking. The effort hurt Dad's chest and he had to stop for a moment to catch his breath.

I took the cleaver, he took the saw. We jointed the pig quickly and roughly, only as much as we had to to make it fit in the pram. We lay the tools in the bottom of the pram, the meat on top. I covered it with the old red eiderdown as carefully as I'd tuck in a baby. It didn't all fit. Dad put the rest in a sack.

I have never had to push home so much stolen meat. I seemed to hover above myself, looking down on the shapeless bundle of a creature in Mam's shawl, trying to make itself invisible.

We carried the partly jointed meat into the

cellar. Dad hooked the fore loin to the ceiling beam. I passed him the hind loin and watched as he expertly hooked that, too. I must have looked worried, because he leaned against the cellar slab and said, 'Is all right.'

I wasn't sure I believed him. I know he has to work with pigs, but not by choice. When he had his own shop, he never sold pork. We have never used pork for our pies.

He put his hand on my shoulder. 'When I was boy, if you said pig, I would cover my ears and run. But I met your mam. Your mam kept pigs as a girl. What did your mam say? "Never eat pork if there is no 'r' in the month." Never in warm weather months. In hot countries, we Jews never had "r" in the month. Always warm weather months. That is why we said eat no pigs. Is all right, *liebling*. We make pies. Nothing wrong with that.'

Margaret thinks I'm mad that I like our cellar. I like the cool flagged floor, the ceiling beams and the stone slabs that we scrub clean. I set out Dad's butchery tools on a strip of beef sheeting: saw; steak knife; boning knife; cleaver; and butcher's steel for sharpening knives.

Dad lit the set pot. I could see that his chest still hurt and so I said that I would do the work.

You have to be careful with pork; cut it clean and straight. I picked up the saw, setting the blade just above the halfway point to separate the knuckle. I sawed steadily through to the bone then chopped through with the cleaver. It takes skill more than strength. I cut loin chops, spare-rib chops from the blade, spare ribs from the belly.

We keep the saltpetre upstairs where it's not quite so damp, but I had brought some down. Dad dropped a quarter of a pound into the simmering water of the set pot, to keep the meat pink. Everything that we could boil or salt we would, and quickly. The trotters slid into the water first. I lifted the tin bucket into the flat stone sink and turned on the tap. We watched the bucket fill.

'I can do this,' I said. 'Just tell me what pieces to salt and how much salt I need.'

Dad smiled. 'Enough salt to float an egg.'

'Tell me properly!' We didn't have an egg in the house and if we did, I wouldn't use it to test whether I had enough salt in my tin bucket.

'Watch!' He took the cover from the rock salt and chipped some off. He placed the chunk of salt on a board. I picked up the rolling pin, but he took it from me and began to roll the salt, asking me, testing me. 'Which cuts then? Which cuts we salt, which use for the pies?'

I have never made as many pies as on that Saturday. Mincing the pork, rolling the pastry. I swear the Garretty children smell it when we have meat in our cellar, or else it comes to them in a dream. Gregory and Sarah called to me through the cellar grate at eight o'clock on Saturday morning. Did I want any errands running? I gave them a note to take to Scarborough Lizzie, at the ovens. I asked Lizzie for rusk, bottom-of-the-oven crumbs or stale bread – as much as she could supply. I have never made pork pies before and didn't have a recipe. But nobody expects pure pork in a pork pie.

SIX

Dad hated missing the pie round, but I said that if he rested just one more day, to recover his strength, perhaps he would be all right to go back to work on Monday. That convinced him. Frank and I did the round on our own.

Street after street of porridge smells, fatty bacon and slops, and skinny, snotty kids, big eyes, hoping for a free pie. I hate it. I hate women in flowered pinnies telling me I make the tastiest pie in Leeds and allus a tender morsel of meat. I hate being called the pie man's daughter, as if I live in a nursery rhyme. Dad's not a pie man. Just because we lickety split round with the handcart every Sunday, that doesn't make us hawkers. Twice as bad today with double the pies to sell. But twice as good, too, with no worries about this week's rent.

Usually, Mrs diClementi says to Dad, 'You gotta fine-a girl there, pie man.' I thought I'd have a rest from that today. No such luck. 'You gotta fine-a girl there, Frank. You'll be marrying soon.'

I'll make her a special dirty toenail pie, just to show her how fine-a I am.

While Frank wheeled the cart back to the stable, I stashed our takings behind the brick in the cellar wall, feeling rich from the large number of pork pies I'd sold.

Dad lay on his bedchair, so quiet, a pint of cold

tea on the floor beside him. 'I'm mending my rib,' he said, and winked at me. He said that he wanted nothing more, just peace and quiet.

Frank and me caught the tram to Roundhay Park.

The gardens swayed with daffodils. That rich, powdery daffodil scent clutches the back of your nose like sweet baking powder.

Frank's hair seems glossier when it's washed. He still had a tidemark on his neck, but I didn't have the heart to tell him. Not till he annoyed me by swinging me round and round after I told him to stop. This is the first time the two of us have done the pie round without Dad, and the first time we have ever taken ourselves on a proper outing.

To describe him: medium height; seventeen years old; stocky build; dark hair that curls onto his forehead. He'll bend his arm and say, 'Feel that bicep.' Or he'll stand square up in front of you and say, 'Hit me, go on, hit me in the solar plexus.' He will do this in any spare moment, such as when Dad exchanges a word with a customer and we are standing slap-bang in the middle of the cobbles with the cart.

I have a party trick of my own. I root myself to the spot, elbows bent, arms tight by my side. I make myself a dead weight and say, 'Go on, lift me. Just try.' He can't. No one can.

Frank's light on his feet but says he will only dance in the boxing ring. Broad hands, big fists, grazed knuckles and short, stubby fingers. I wish he wouldn't bite his nails.

The most important thing about him, he claims, is his determination. Boxing Danny Hescott recruits lots of lads to put on shows, some in booths, some open air. Charges plenty, too. Gents sixpence, ladies threepence. But Frank's the cream of the crop and has never lost a fight. He would like to do well enough at the boxing to give up his job at the furriers. He says some exhibition boxers earn good money and everyone knows their names. I don't.

As we sprawled on the grass looking up at the sky, he reeled off these boxers' names, their techniques and bouts lost and won. Next time he won a prize himself, he said he'd like to treat me to a new frock. I told him when the pork ran out, he could buy me a clod of mutton.

After I'd said that we had such a laugh because all the clouds took on the shapes not just of animals but offal and we couldn't agree whether the fastest cloud was a pig's trotter or an ox tongue. Our hands were very close. He stretched out a stubby finger and tapped my palm.

He said, 'I'm that 'appy. I've never been this 'appy.'

I said, 'Me too,' which wasn't exactly true. The best day of my life was going to Mother Shipton's cave at Knaresborough with Mam, Dad and Margaret. We all made a wish. Mam put her hand on her belly and said, 'Wishing the best for all five of us.'

I had got scared and said that she shouldn't tell a wish. But Mam just laughed and said it wasn't her wish, that it was just a thought, an expression.

Frank started to move closer towards me, so I rolled away, leaped up and raced him to the lake, brushing the grass from my skirt as I ran. I just kept talking and talking. And got him talking and talking. I got the feeling he had started to moon over me and wanted to kiss me. I needed time to think. I'm fond of Frank, but he is more like family or a good friend. I just can't see me mooning over him at all.

Dad spoilt everything when I came home. I stood at the sink filling a jam jar with water. Through the window I watched a couple of bairns playing with gas tar in the gutter, but everything looked bright to me, bright and real. Dad tapped ash from the bowl of his briar's pipe in an irritated way that usually means he's out of tobacco, but as he had a good two ounces of Cut Cavendish in his baccy pouch, it meant something else. He watched me arrange the daffodils in the jar. He tapped his pipe so hard that the bowl snapped from the stem. Then he said that when Mam spotted Frank in the street, playing with gas tar and the arse hanging out of his trousers, she brought him in out of pity to patch his clothes, not so he could take up with me and interfere with my future.

When I took no notice, Dad started yelling. He said I'm too smart for Frank. In a few years' time, Frank will be an even bigger Dummkopf than he is now, because of the blows from boxing.

Just because Dad's not well doesn't mean I have to put up with his yelling. I told him that me and Frank are friends and if it wasn't for Frank, how would we have managed today?

That just made Dad worse because he said he *could* have pushed the cart this morning. He only stayed at home because me and Margaret kept saying over and over that he should rest. I left him to his rage, went to see Aunty Amy and gave her half the daffodils.

SEVEN

When I opened my eyes this morning the first thing I saw was the damp brown patch on the bedroom ceiling. It used to look like Asia. Now that it's dried out a little, it's shaped like America. If Dad had got to America instead of being put off the boat in Liverpool, he wouldn't have met Mam. Me and Margaret wouldn't be on earth, much less sharing this bed and her flinging her arms about and taking up most of it.

I tried to remember when we swapped places. I used to sleep on the inside of our bed, near the wall. Margaret slept on the outside, the big sister, so I wouldn't fall out. Now I'm on the outside, because I'm always last to bed and first up. Being on the outside means I am in charge of the candle. This makes it easier for me to write in my journal.

I woke up knowing that if Frank asks me to go to Roundhay Park again I will have to say no. He obviously cares for me, very much more than I guessed, and everyone saw it before I did, including Margaret, Dad and Aunty Amy, which is surprising because I am the most observant of all of us.

I am ashamed to admit that part of me is glad he moons over me. It cheers me to realize I *am* moon-able over. But I feel bad because it is not fair to Frank when I don't moon back. I cannot even say he is like a cousin to me or 'the brother I never had' as I already have cousins. Frank is a helper and a friend. I don't want to get into a worry over him as I have Dad to think about, and Margaret. She doesn't earn a penny, but by some twisting turn that only she could set us on, we are drawn onto a stony path where we pay for her millinery apprenticeship. Who but Margaret would work somewhere where we pay the employer for the privilege? If she had read as many novels as me, she would know that most poor milliners end up on the streets. Of course, Margaret's dreams lead to a high-class establishment in Mayfair where society ladies pay vast sums for the honour of plonking Margaret's stunning creations on their bonces.

Now she is complaining that my pencil scratching on the page has woken her, started her day with a headache, and she must have a cup of tea in bed. I have told her to climb over me but she has decided to have five more minutes and says it is up to me not to let her fall asleep, and that if the positions were reversed (which they never are) she would certainly bring me a cup of tea. She has put me off writing.

I am writing in the one place I get some peace and sympathy: the stable at the Dragon. The sympathy is from Solomon, when he is not out working in his cart. Solomon is a roan cob. Uncle brought him home on my tenth birthday, and so I named him.

43

He whinnies as soon as he hears my footsteps, and nuzzles against my skirt pocket, to see what I've brought. I love his smell of straw and adventure. I groom him, or just talk to him and stroke his neck. I'm sure he understands what I say. Telling something to a horse is a good way to calm your feelings, but it does not help me to find a way round our difficulties.

I shall begin on Sunday, after the pie round, when I refused to go to Roundhay Park with Frank. I should have said 'No thank you', and not added a reason. That was my mistake. I told him that Margaret would be speaking at the Votes for Women meeting at the Town Hall and I was going to listen. He said suffragettes are trouble-makers, that they only do it to get in the newspapers, and if he did half of what they got up to he would be thrown in gaol and no one would give a tinker's damn. I explained that Margaret's group do not chain themselves to railings or set fire to pillar boxes, as he likes to think. They produce pamphlets, write letters, hold meetings and give speeches. Some of them are affiliated to the Independent Labour Party. He gave a huge yawn and said they sounded even worse. Breaking windows and setting fire to things at least showed a bit of spunk. Then he said he did not want to come. It was not his idea of how to spend a Sunday. I told him that I had not asked him to be there.

I wish he had kept his word and stayed away. It would have been duller, but with less bloodshed.

A small crowd had gathered. I saw Margaret on the Town Hall steps, near the stone lion. She wore her green skirt, frilled white blouse (a plain thing until yesterday when she sewed on the antique lace), the fine silk Indian shawl Aunty Amy's nephew brought home from his travels and a small pale-green hat with an appliqué velvet apple. Sometimes Miss Mason's customers pass on this or that, a blouse or skirt. Margaret is a great one for making improvements and creating a wonderful item of clothing out of a cast-off. As she moved, I caught the sheen of the amber brooch she wore at her throat.

Seeing her there gave me a small jolt, as if she did not belong to me any more, was someone else's sister. I drew closer, half-wanting her to see me, but something got in the way. It was as if I had caught her out in another life and would spoil it if I barged in. The tall man beside her seemed just as striking, with thick, straight blond hair that fell over his forehead, and a slightly bronzed skin that made him look healthier than everyone else. He pushed back his hair with his hand as he listened to Margaret. I wondered if she was admitting her nervousness, which I knew about well enough. They were both smiling. The man wore a good-quality dark blazer and twill trousers. The other men round about wore suits; some fine, some shabby. Those who didn't own suits sported parts of suits put together – like the slightly drunken man with long, ape-like arms who stood near me. He wore a patched shiny jacket, hitched-up trousers and an old waistcoat with odd buttons.

The man with Margaret stood out from the crowd for another reason. There was only one other man who was part of the Votes for Women crowd – an elderly chap, somebody's husband.

The first speaker took her place. Margaret listened attentively, then turned to the man beside her and said something. They looked at the stone lion. Margaret shook her head and laughed. Then she whispered to him. He smiled. I'd made my way closer to them, but didn't get chance to speak. He hitched her up beside the stone lion. Anyone a bit fatter wouldn't have kept their balance so well, but she is slender and graceful. She leaned against the lion as if she'd known it all her life and there was not a more comfortable place to be in the world. Margaret didn't look in my direction. She was listening to the first speaker – a stout, fierce-looking woman – and I guessed it must be Mrs Turner, whose house they meet in once a week.

Mrs Turner finished to applause and catcalls. I edged closer and closer to Margaret and her stone lion, so that if she forgot her speech I could say the words loudly in my head and will her to remember.

I stood quite close to the young man who'd helped her up beside the lion. I liked the look of him from the first because his eyes were honest and steady. He listened to Margaret with so much attention, as if he knew the speech, too. I guessed that he was Mrs Turner's son, Thomas. Margaret had described all of the group to me.

'Thank you for coming here today to listen to why I believe women must be granted the vote,' Margaret said. 'Once women have the vote, Parliament will be forced to take notice of what is important for women and children, and the concerns of people who up to now have had no power in our land. People like you and me, our

46

mothers and our grandmothers.'

She stopped there and her face went blank. If someone had said to her, 'What's your name? What day is it? What town are we in?' she would not have been able to answer. After what seemed a long long time, she remembered.

'Parliament will never give priority to the needs of women, children – and men – who need decent housing, nourishing food, wages above starvation level and a reasonable education. Why? Because Parliament is made up of privileged men who have taken these things for granted all their lives. They are voted for by other privileged men who have never had to give these matters a moment's thought or consideration.'

I knew her speech by heart. She had made me listen while she practised it over and over, sitting up in bed. It lasted a full four minutes, timed by Dad's fob watch before he pawned it.

She had started quietly but then spoke up so her voice carried all the way across the Town Hall steps to the Upper Headrow. She has a fine pair of lungs. You know the minute you open our door if Margaret is in because if she is awake, the chances are she is singing. She doesn't know she does it. Mrs Turner had coached her on how to speak up in public. I know that they had wanted her to wear her black woollen shawl because Mrs Turner's lot are mostly middle-class ladies and like to show Margaret off, to prove that they are not snobs. But Margaret wouldn't wear that old thing. Good for her.

She looked neat and spoke calmly. Margaret rarely gets agitated (except with me) but when she does her hands won't stay still, so she had added large pockets into that skirt using remnants of unbleached linen. She had slid her hands into her pockets, which meant she felt more nervous than she looked.

She missed more out of that speech than she put in, but only I noticed that. I had to smile to myself when she said about food for the working classes. I am the one who bakes all the pies and goes out selling. She only ever complains that I take over the house on Saturdays. She won't even come to St Peter's Square with me to take the trays of pies to Scarborough Lizzie's ovens. She doesn't want to be seen doing lowly tasks. The only time she ever came with me, she accident-ally-on-purpose dropped the tray.

I wish Dad could have seen Margaret speak today. But she had said not to tell him till later, in case he got anxious about her being looked at in public and making a show.

As she made her speech, the sun came out and the grey sky turned pure blue. When she stopped speaking, a cloud came over the sun – and that is the honest truth. I clapped like anything.

The man next to me had taken off his jacket and rolled up his striped shirt-sleeves. He stank of beer and sweat. 'Stop yer caterwauling,' he yelled at Margaret. Then he turned on me and said, 'And thah should be home, helping your ma wi't dinner.'

That got my mad up. He just thought he could say anything, because he was a man and me a girl. There was nothing I would have liked better than to go home to my mam, but I never will.

I told him that he was talking rot. Of course, he didn't like that and pushed into me saying if I was his he'd show me a thing or two. I told him if he were mine he'd wake up and find his throat cut. I could feel things getting dangerous, but there were police nearby. I'd just deny everything. He pushed into me again and said I'd stood on his foot. If I did, it was only because I was too angry to notice his damn foot and because I wouldn't budge for him, though the stench of him made me want to move away. I told him that he shouldn't be there. Someone like him wasn't fit to have a vote because it should only be given to people who can reason, not to dumb apes.

He raised his hand to hit me. I ducked out of the way. Next thing I knew, the chap who'd helped Margaret up onto the stone lion was standing beside us, saying in this calm, educated voice, 'I'm sure we can sort out any differences.' (He is very handsome close-up.) I said I very much doubted that and I didn't know why some ignoramuses bothered to come to hear a lady speak. Unless it was because they'd spent their beer money and had nowhere else to go.

Then the ape started to curse, and Thomas Turner (it was him) came between us, which seemed to infuriate the ape even more and he swung out, catching Thomas on his closely shaved chin. Thomas looked surprised and touched his fingers gently to his jaw.

One minute Frank wasn't there and the next he was. He must have followed me and been spying from across the Upper Headrow. He landed three or four quick Frank specials – upper-cuts and jabs on the ape's jaw and chest.

Thomas took the ape gently by the arm, helping him to get his balance and said, 'On your way, eh? Sorry about this.'

The ape didn't need telling twice.

Then Thomas turned to Frank. 'We don't want violence here.'

Frank grabbed him by the lapels of his blazer, pulled him close and snarled, 'And you keep your face out of my Sunday afternoon.' Then, as if he just couldn't resist the opportunity, he nutted him on the nose and grabbed my hand.

The crowd parted as we made our way back to the Upper Headrow. I was beside myself. 'You needn't have interfered!' I said.

I drew Frank well away. We walked towards the cathedral. My face was still burning with embarrassment. He kept tight hold of my hand as we walked, saying over and over, 'See what happens. You can't trust 'em. Out for theirsens, the lot of 'em.'

'Who is?' I sat down on the cathedral steps.

'Feller in't blazer, the whole lot of 'em. Posh buggers.'

'The ape wasn't posh.'

'Well, I sorted him out, didn't I? Don't mix with 'em. It'll only lead to trouble.'

'Apes? Don't mix with apes?'

'Posh buggers. You can't trust 'em.'

I took a few deep breaths. I knew that he meant well. I said, 'I didn't need you to come in punching. You're too ready with your fists. The fellow in the blazer,' (I didn't let on I knew who he was), 'was trying to calm the situation.'

'I had to get in first. I had yon's measure. I'll not take no chances where thah's concerned.'

'Frank, you're always spoiling for a scrap. There's never a weekend goes by that you're not in some street corner punch-up. You're too old for that now. You need to curb your temper.'

Don't ask me why, but he seemed pleased to be told off. I didn't want him to be pleased.

I added, 'And don't follow me about. I don't need an escort.'

He ignored that. 'I know I'm sometimes a bit hasty, Julia, lass. But it's what's inside me. Summat builds up, like a scream, like a fury, and I lash out. But it's nowt. It's done and over. D'you want me to be like yon pansy in't blazer?'

I didn't answer him. I felt too unsure of myself. I hated hearing him call one of Margaret's friends a pansy. Thomas seemed a nice man, kind and well-meaning. Thanks to me, he'd taken a powerful blow. I had wanted to deal with that ape myself. I could have outclevered him. It's not for nothing that I'm known on the market stalls as Miss Repartee.

When I didn't answer, Frank said, 'All right. I'll try to be more steady-like in future. Will that suit?'

'It's for your own good not mine,' I said. I felt uncomfortable. I had started the day meaning to keep him at arm's length. Instead the punch-up and my criticizing him had led us where I didn't want to be. I stood up and set off home, not waiting to see whether he was with me or not. He was, of course. I kept my hand well out of his way so he couldn't take hold of it.

It was bad luck and bad timing that we saw

White Rat on the Lower Headrow, coming out of the Three Legs. He had just asked an old chap in a greasy checked jacket and cap for a light. Leaning against the wall, White Rat puffed on his ciggie and blew out a smoke-ring. I stopped short when I saw him. He recognized me straight away, and I'd described the white hair, pale face and pink-rimmed eyes to Frank all too well.

'That him?' Frank said.

I nodded.

'I know him an' all,' Frank said.

The lad looked from me to Frank. A terrible realization came over him.

Frank slipped off his jacket and handed it to me. As if remembering what I'd said about not losing his rag, he squared up to the lad, boxing fashion and said, 'You and me have got a bone to pick.'

'It weren't how it looked, Frank!' The lad looked round, as if seeing whether he could escape, or get back into the pub where he probably had pals. I stood by the pub door, blocking his way.

'No 'arm was meant to the lass,' he said.

I said, 'No harm in bashing me against a wall?'

That was the trigger for Frank. White Rat put his fists up but had no chance. He squirmed on the ground, hands protecting his face, crying out, 'I give up, don't put boot in.'

Just then the parade came by.

I heard the singing and turned to stare. Margaret and another girl about her age walked at the front with a banner embroidered in the suffragette colours – green, white and violet –

'Give Women the Vote'. Fortunately, Margaret didn't see us (I thought). Bustling Mrs Turner and her cronies strode behind. Thomas and the older man came along in the rear.

Please, Frank, I thought, as Thomas Turner looked at us in amazement, me holding the jacket and Frank standing over the pathetic figure, *please Frank, don't put the boot in.*

The procession went past. Frank held out a hand and pulled the lad to his feet. The beaten rat put his fingers to the side of his mouth, wiping the blood. He checked his jaw for broken teeth. 'Sorry, sorry. I didn't know the Yid and his lass were owt to do with thee, Frank, or I wouldn't have gone near.'

That made me mad. I wanted to punch him myself for calling Dad the Yid. But he won't bother me or Dad again.

Of course, Margaret *had* seen. She had seen everything. That evening she was sitting at the table, sewing new ivory buttons onto her cream blouse, giving me the cold shoulder. But she couldn't keep it up. She pricked her finger on the needle, then acted as if it was all my fault. Dad lay sleeping in the chair so she hissed at me quietly, not wanting to wake him. 'What a spectacle you made of yourself today. No lady holds a jacket for someone fist-fighting in the street. What a disgrace!'

I told her I'd rather get my own back and be a spectacle and a disgrace than stay a victim.

She said that some day she might introduce me to Mrs Turner and Thomas and then what would happen? They regarded her as a civilized person.

How could a civilized person have a wild thing for a sister?

I told her that I have no desire to meet either of them, and that they all looked very silly walking in a procession through the town. I was the one who should feel embarrassed by her.

Apparently, according to Margaret, that is because I have no desire to better myself and would not be able to even if I wished, because I am wild and do not know how to behave.

Then I realized Dad had woken up and started to listen, trying to hear what we were arguing about.

Margaret spotted it, too. She said, 'If you bring your blue blouse down, I'll stitch that seam.'

I went upstairs to get my blouse, but she was right behind me. She shut the bedroom door and grabbed my wrist. 'Just answer me this: Did you tell Thomas Turner you're my sister?'

I didn't answer her. I pulled free and picked up my blouse to hand it to her.

She grabbed it and flung it across the room. 'Did you? Did you?' She caught my wrist with both hands and started to do a first-degree Chinese burn.

'*You* call *me* wild!' I said. Both of us were speaking quietly, so as not to let Dad hear. 'You're mad.'

Her face turned red. 'Just answer me.'

'Let go then!' I pulled myself free. 'Thomas Turner just wanted to see if everything was all right. Then Frank appeared. There was no more talking. Your precious Thomas doesn't know I'm your sister.'

She looked shamefaced then and spoke more

softly. 'Just don't spoil things for me. They're my friends. They think well of me.'

'More fool them,' I said. She wouldn't get round me that easily.

She picked up my blouse. 'Is there anything else you want mending?'

I wanted to say no there wasn't, but actually my stocking had a hole in the toe. I knew she wouldn't want to mend it without it being washed, but since she had twisted my wrist, I said that there was something else and peeled off my stocking.

She took it, and sighed. 'All right, all right. I'm sorry I hurt you. You're too young to understand why some things are very important.'

Then she was off down the stairs, singing. She's like that. She doesn't stay angry long, unlike me who can fester a bit. But it is hard to stay mad at her when she is singing so I had to put my mind to it.

'We're not the Wood Sisters any more,' I hissed at her as we sat at the table and she handed me my mended blouse. 'Just because it says Wood Sisters on the shampoo and hair rinse bottles in Aunty Amy's shop. Just because Dad's our dad. You're not my sister any more.'

'We'll always be the Wood Sisters.' She mussed up my hair. 'When I marry you'll be my bridesmaid and when you marry I'll be your maid of honour. Even when we have different names, we'll always be the Wood Sisters.'

'I'm never going to get married,' I said. 'I'm going to get a job in an office.'

She smiled in a way that anyone who doesn't know her would describe as sweetly. 'Of course you are,' she said. 'Miss Wood the younger will produce the neatest ledger copy and anyone in the office who says different will feel her swift, sharp upper-cut.'

I wanted to hit her.

EIGHT

If Margaret hadn't been so blooming superior and ready to criticize, I probably wouldn't have tried to show her how I'm the one that gets things done. I'm the one who baked double and triple quantities of pies, sold the chops to the market café and joints to Uncle Lloyd and Mrs Shepherd at the Workhouse Infirmary. (For Mr and Mrs Shepherd, not for the poor inmates.) I'm the one who managed the money well enough to have some tucked away behind the brick in the cellar. But I now regret how much cash I handed over to Miss Mason.

Miss Mason seemed surprised to see me. She was fitting a customer with a small felt hat trimmed with bright yellow lace. Margaret had told us about the hideous yellow lace hat. So I had all on not to stare at the sharp-nosed young woman who tried it on. She was smiling at her own reflection, turning her head this way and that to see all sides of herself in the new creation.

I dived into the back room where Margaret was measuring ribbon to decorate a straw boater. She let the ribbon fall onto the table. 'Is Dad all right?'

I slipped my hand through the false pocket of my skirt to get to my money belt. I took the loose shillings, tied in my best embroidered handkerchief, and swung the hanky round and round. I told her that I'd brought the money to cover the last payments for her apprenticeship, and to do it in advance so it was finished and settled.

She whispered so Miss Mason wouldn't hear. 'Why didn't you give it to me? It looks silly for you to come when I'm the older sister.'

She would have said more but Miss Mason bustled in, her black taffeta skirt swishing. She set her plump pasty face to give a smile and a little frown both at once, just to let me know that although she is always glad to see me, it is not the done thing for her apprentice's sister to come in for an idle chat. Even if you did not know her history, you would look at Miss Mason and say to yourself that here was a woman who had come down in the world. To save Margaret's embarrassment, I told Miss Mason that Dad had meant to give Margaret money this morning, to cover the next four weeks of her apprenticeship fees.

'How vairy thortful,' Miss Mason said, her hand twitching for the cash. She pronounces 't' in a very definite way and puts a long 'a' and a letter 'r' in as many words as she can. This is because she is educated and genteel. Margaret can speak in an almost vairy thortful way herself when she is with Miss Mason and the suffragette set. Margaret says that if you want to survive and prosper in the world you have to be able to speak like the people who survive and prosper. I have tried this way of speaking and I can do it.

57

Sometimes it is very useful in shops. (But I have to keep my hands out of sight or wear gloves.)

Miss Mason practically grabbed the money, but I held onto it and said (pronouncing my t's very carefully), 'You'll want to give me a receipt as this will be the final payment.'

Margaret stared. She picked up the scissors but didn't trust herself to cut. Usually we have paid one week at a time. Occasionally we got behind and had to catch up, like when the slaughter-house closed for a week last summer.

My hands were shaking. I have never handed over so much money and I wondered had I done the right thing. But like the rent, it had to be paid. I had checked Margaret's indentures, and her apprenticeship had only four weeks to run. After that we could expect some decent money from her, and not before time.

Even the smoke from all the factory chimneys in Leeds did not entirely blot out the blue sky, as Margaret and me walked to the Dragon together, arm in arm. (We always go to the Dragon for our bath.) We stopped to look in the draper's shop window at some bales of material on display. Margaret said it made her feel cheered up to have Miss Mason think that we did not have to scrimp and scrape and could pay her fees in advance. I knew she wanted to ask me if Dad realized I had given Miss Mason money, and if I had this week's rent. I acted very confident, determined not to mention the flutters in my stomach. Even though she's almost four years older than me, I've managed the money since I don't know when. She and Dad trust me to get it right.

To put her off, I said that it would be worth it when she's proprietress of her own high-class millinery establishment and makes lots of money. I asked if she had thought of a name for it yet. But she changed the subject.

The George & Dragon sits bang on the corner of Peter Street, just a short walk from the Woolman Street flats where Cissie Garretty lives. When I was little, I used to think that 'the Dragon' really was a dragon, so big and squat with many window eyes looking towards Kirkgate Market, as if seeing who and what it could swallow up. Inside the Dragon seemed scary, too, because our house has just one room up, one down and the cellar, and the Dragon goes on for ever and ever. Even the yard has stables and surprises, and although it does not seem big to me now, it felt huge when I was little. One morning when I stayed there, I think it must have been when Mam got poorly, Bernard said to come to the back door. There was an elephant in the yard having a shower under the hose pipe. It threw its trunk and head back, appeared to smile and fixed its little eyes on me. Uncle Lloyd had told the circus man that he could hose the elephants down in the Dragon yard. We got free tickets for the circus and all the circus people came in for their drinks to the Dragon. It is that kind of place – a bit respectable but with theatrical and political patrons, too.

But the best thing about it is the bathroom. A large bathtub stands by the far wall near the sink and it has two taps, one cold, one hot. (The hot one even works.)

I wished I hadn't remembered about the

elephants. Perhaps that's how Uncle Lloyd regards us. Two exotic circus creatures, coming for their weekly hose-down.

We tossed a coin for who would have first bath and I won. She was being especially nice to me by not trying to do me out of going first. Of course, the water was very hot and turned my skin red, and out of consideration I didn't put cold in so as to keep it hot for her. She washed my back. There's no escape when you're in a bath if someone wants to go on at you. I had to listen to how there are different ways to get on in the world. Some girls get paid work in the political groups, sending out magazines for the suffragettes and answering letters and so on.

I slipped down under the water, so that it covered me completely. I shut my eyes. It would be just like her to stop talking about being a milliner in Mayfair now that her apprenticeship was almost up. I held my breath till I thought I would burst. Did she now expect us to pay for her to write give-women-the-vote letters, lick envelopes and sell magazines?

'What is it? What are you doing?' she said.

I came up for air. 'I hope we haven't been paying out hard-earned cash money for your apprenticeship for nothing.'

'Course not,' she said, forgetting to talk refined. 'And don't keep mithering on about money. It's vulgar, and saying "cash money" is doubly vulgar.'

I slid under the water again. When I had counted to forty and Margaret had still not nagged me to get out of the bathtub and let her climb in before the water turned entirely cold, I knew she was up

60

to something.

I dried myself while she soaked. At the Dragon we have a towel each. At home we all share a towel, so whoever gets it last finds it wet.

I washed Margaret's back. Then she decided to wash her hair.

I filled the jug from the sink tap to rinse her hair. When I turned round, she wasn't there. Usually it is me who slides under the water.

She came up for air. 'Some things only happen if a person is exceptional. Am I exceptional? Or do I only think I am exceptional?' She screwed her eyes up tight as I poured the water over her hair. 'One more rinse.'

I poured some vinegar rinse into the jug, then held it under the tap. We'd used all the hot water.

'It'll cool your scalp,' I said, before she got chance to complain that it was cold.

Margaret took my towel to wrap round her hair, so that she could have the dry towel for her body. She pulled out the plug. 'I wish we had dressing gowns. Then you could just slip yours on and walk along the landing to the upstairs lounge, leaving me to have the bathroom to myself for once.'

'I'll go now,' I said. My legs were too damp to bother with stockings but I pulled on my skirt and blouse. 'It's you to clean the bath then.'

She stepped out of the bath, tucking the towel around herself. 'Oh no. You had the benefit of first bath. You have to clean it.'

So we tossed the coin again. I won. I don't think Margaret minded. She did not put up much of an argument. Of course, when the next unpleasant thing has to be done, it will be my turn. Nothing new about that. I guessed that she wanted to have the bathroom to herself, to look at herself in the long looking-glass – and it is true she is something to look at. She is trying to decide something. I have a feeling I know what it is.

I am sitting in the window seat in the upstairs parlour at the Dragon. A few trains have passed by. Normally I would look out and try to make some young man on the London train wave to me, and imagine that as he sped by he was wishing that he could get to know me. He would be filled with impossible longings all the way to at least Wakefield.

But today I have not waved to anyone. I am considering Margaret's question. Is she exceptional? Am I exceptional? Is it a good thing to be exceptional or is it just a way of making life hard for yourself? If we are exceptional, these are the reasons why:

Margaret: a fine singing voice; beauty that turns heads; a way of walking that makes her look as if she owns the world; amazing cleverness with a needle; the confidence to get up and speak in public; neat hand-writing.

Julia: I will come back to this.

If we are exceptional, how did this come about?

Looking smart: This is due to Margaret and her clever needle and passed-on clothes from Miss Mason's customers.

Reading: some people only read the same book over and over, like Aunty Amy with the Bible and *Pilgrim's Progress*. Because Dad cannot read English, we have always read to him. Margaret reads the newspaper, and I read whatever book I am reading, and he does not mind if I miss out a few chapters because I have read it myself in between. He is happy for me to sum up the story so far. We have both read non-stop since we could read and that was at the age of three or four. Dad has heard the whole of Jane Austen, the whole of Thomas Hardy, lots of mysteries, murders, *Hamlet* in its entirety, and much more besides, from the lending library and the bookstall in the market where you can take one book back in part-exchange against the next.

Discussing: Dad and Aunty Amy have always talked to us as if we were grown-up. I notice this is not true of other people, for instance, in Cissie's and Frank's families.

Writing: Margaret, with my help, can compose good letters and speeches. I can do this because I paid attention at school and have taught myself after that.

Speaking: Margaret has been taught how to speak well by Miss Mason, who feels it makes a better impression on the customers. She has also had lessons in breathing (yes, breathing) from an actress customer of Miss Mason, although she is not an actress any longer, having married well and had six children. These lessons have been passed on to me so that I can talk properly or normally, depending on where I am and who I am with.

Wanting to improve our lot: This is part of being exceptional because so many people round where we live seem satisfied with what they have got. They have no thought or hopes of things ever getting better for them.

Those are the ways we are different from the girls we were at school with. Though when I say that I have to think of Clarice at the Wheatsheaf, who was at school with Margaret. She is also very smartly turned out, but that is because her parents keep a public house.

I can hear Margaret on the landing. She has been a long time so I hope she has cleaned the bath. I do not know whether she will tell me what it is she is hoping for. I can guess. She wants to make Thomas Turner fall in love with her.

NINE

For once, I have the bed to myself and am sitting with Margaret's pillow under my knees. I had to come up here to be as far away from the cellar as possible. Dad is still down there, emery-papering the hooks and greasing them; oiling the saw and sharpening the knives on his butcher's steel. He enjoys that work and especially prizes his butcher's steel, as it belonged to his father.

I no longer work for the Fischers. After making the biggest number of pork pies the world has ever seen, I couldn't go back to their stall, it wouldn't be fair. Their stall's not exactly Kosher, or they wouldn't have employed me, but they like to think it is. I didn't want to ruin their trade. Someone would be bound to have seen me selling pork and it could have got back to them. Besides, I didn't want to hear any more about the blissfully

64

happy Alec Fischer and his new wife, Sophie.

Old Mr Fischer was very good about it. I chat to him whenever I go to the market. Today he gave me a beast's head. As Dad still hasn't found work and we daren't risk going back to the meat market at night, that head will be our life-saver. I placed the sack on the stone slab. Dad had followed me down to the cellar. I laid out the tools, saw, steak knife, boning knife and cleaver, while he unwrapped the head.

Lately, Dad leaves too much to me. Also, he goes over everything he has ever told me. He asks me questions, to be sure I have understood. Without meaning to, I have learned his trade.

'Take the cheeks off,' he said, handing me the knife.

He knows I hate heads. 'Just do it, Julia.' I hadn't realized my palms were clenched. He opened my right hand and put the knife handle against my palm. He closed my fingers round it. 'Don't think. Do. You vill do vorse than this in your life. This is nothing.'

I placed three fingers on top of the beast's head and pointed my knife. The head rocked. I held it steady with the palm of my left hand and sliced. We set the slices aside, ready to mince. Dad nodded at me to go on.

Dad removed the eyes. The brain came out all of a piece. I slid it into the bucket of cold water.

'Now the tongue,' Dad said.

The thick tongue pointed at me. The skin felt rough to the touch. I thought of the beast in the field, slurping grass around its mouth, moving the green blades down into its throat; I saw it drinking from a trough, the sun on its back; I thought of the dry tongue pressing against the roof of its mouth as it took its last walk into the slaughterhouse.

'Don't think,' Dad said. 'Cut it out.'

I sliced at the base, surprised at how easily it gave way under the knife. I picked up the heavy tongue, weighing it in my hands; it must have been 4 or 5lbs. Dad nodded his approval.

We had decided to pickle it in rock salt and to press it. It would keep well and we could sell it by the slice.

'The date,' Dad said.

'Why? We know the date.'

'You must learn everything.'

'I'm just helping. I'm not a butcher.'

He put his hand on my shoulder. 'You are butcher. Write the date.'

I turned away from him, suddenly feeling cold. I looked towards the window; someone in clogs clattered by the cellar grate.

'You like to write,' Dad said. 'You write with a knife, that is all.'

Slowly, I picked up the smallest knife. He must have thought I didn't know the date. He raised an eyebrow. 'I write date in pencil?'

'I know the date, and I know the numerals.' Why was it so important to him that I do this? I asked myself. But I knew why. Slowly and neatly as I could, I began to carve the date on the beast's tongue in Roman numerals: VI VI MCMXIV.

'I have teached you all I know,' Dad said, as I carved the final V.

I put down the knife and rubbed my hands

along my arms.

He grabbed me in a bear hug. It was his way of not letting me see his eyes. He knew that I had understood. He has taught me everything, so that I can manage without him.

I couldn't think of anything to say. I just hugged him back, then rushed upstairs. For a long time I heard the sounds of knives being sharpened against his butcher's steel. Now the house is quiet.

TEN

One week Aunty Amy does our washing, the next week I do hers. As she tied her washing into a bundle, I suddenly noticed how the veins stand out from the back of her hands. It gave me a little shock. I can't imagine getting to be so very old. She is sixty-six and doesn't seem to mind. I have a feeling I would mind very much.

In the cellar, Dad had the wooden tongs in his hand, lifting a sheet from the set pot into the sink for rinsing. I dropped Aunty Amy's bundle and went to help but he glared at me. 'If I cannot vash sheets and save my daughter's hands it's a poor thing.'

When he'd rinsed the sheet he wrung it tightly, twisting until his knuckles turned white. We each took two corners and folded the sheet. I fed it into the mangle while he turned. He'd placed the mangle well away from the cellar window so that no one would see him. He glanced up quickly as

67

a pair of boots passed by our cellar grating. That made me laugh. He laughed, too, which made his poor ribs hurt again.

'Is bad enough being the foreigner and the Jew. But vasherman!'

Pegging sheets on the line across the street always puts me in mind of Mam. I like to hoist the sheets high like a brave flag in the dirty breeze.

One sheet I hung out today has a large patch in the middle and two small darns near the top. I remember Mam lying back in her bed, resting her hand on the sheet, her thumb stroking the stitches as if half-remembering the day she had darned it.

She lay there, pale, with a smell like something rotting coming off her. She seemed so tired and could barely lift her hand. 'Margaret, Julia, you're going to be all right.'

Neither of us spoke.

Mam took Margaret's hand. 'Tell me you'll be all right.' Her voice was a whisper. 'You're the Wood Sisters, strong as your name, strong as an oak tree. Remember that.'

Margaret said, 'We'll be all right, Mam. We're the Wood Sisters. We're strong.'

Mam reached for my hand. I kept it from her. She scared me.

'Julia?'

Margaret prodded me. I said, 'We'll be all right.'

I thought afterwards that if we had said no, no, we will not be all right, no, we are not strong, she would have managed not to die. It makes no sense, but something you believe as a child has such a power that it never stops being true, even when you know it's not sensible. After that, we were stuck with being strong.

I try to make sure Dad gets that sheet with the patch and the two darns, because if I sleep on it, I wake up crying. Sometimes I dream that I took her hand.

'Look after each other,' Mam had said. 'Look after your dad.'

After that Dad took me and Margaret next door to Aunty Amy.

Mam was right. Dad takes some looking after. I have known that since the night he came into the bedroom when he thought me and Margaret were asleep. She was asleep, fast asleep as usual. I was alert, as usual.

I must have been about seven and Margaret nearly eleven. I pretended to sleep, peeping at him. The moon shone through the window and he stood over us, rocking back and forth, clutching at the old pillow with the striped ticking cover. I knew how the little princes in the tower must have felt.

A feather burst from the cover and floated towards me and I thought: *If I can watch that feather and not lose it from my sight, he won't kill us. If I can push the bed-warmer, which had gone cold, away with my foot without him noticing, he won't kill us.* Margaret lay warm and close up next to me, smelling of her nighty, cotton and moth-balls, and her skin smelled of carbolic soap. Her nighty had ridden up, and her warm leg touched my leg. I felt scared when I saw Dad. I felt the scaredness in my whole body and thought she would, too, through me. But she didn't wake up.

That feather from the old pillow came floating so slowly that it seemed to stop in the air on the way down. After an age of Dad's moaning, it landed on my nose. I daren't breathe in case I sent it away out of sight, or snuffled it up my nose and choked, or in case I sneezed. The feather went to my mouth like a fairy kiss, and tickled me. Then it blew off out of sight when I let air from my lips. So I took a chance and opened my eyes. Dad just rocked back and forth, and still a kind of moaning came from somewhere deep inside him.

I don't remember if I made him go away by thinking it, or if I told him that if he tried to smother me I'd scream the house down.

The sheets on the washing-line got in the way of my noticing that Dad had left the house. By the time I saw him, he was turning the corner into Great Garden Street. Out tramping. Tramp, tramp, tramping for work.

He didn't tell me he was going because I would have said not to. He is not in a fit state to work. Anyone can see that.

ELEVEN

Mrs Garretty never usually sets foot outside her door and doesn't own a pair of shoes. There she stood in the doorway, smiling and showing all her gums, Baby Jimmy on her hip. She shuffled to meet me, trying to keep a floppy pair of men's slippers on her feet and saying, 'The donkey, the donkey.'

I looked across the road and saw a gentleman gypsy hawker, with a worn-out donkey that had almost disappeared under the rattle of pots and pans strapped to its body. The gypsy, his shoulders thrown back, breathed his tummy in and stuck his chest out. He wore a striped shirt, sleeves rolled up, sturdy boots and a gold cross on a chain. Grinning, he called over, saying what high-class pots and pans he had – practically to give away. Pans and pots as rattled and used in the finest houses in the land. All the time he spoke, I could feel his gypsy eyes darting over my body.

Mrs Garretty shifted Baby Jimmy to her shoulder and took my arm to cross the street, whispering, 'The baby hasn't shook off his hacking cough. Happen passing him under the donkey will do some good.'

I didn't want to join in with her superstition but she dug her bony fingers into my arm till I thought she'd rip my flesh if I tried to escape.

She asked the gypsy if he minded. Before he had chance to answer she slid round the other side of the donkey, bobbed down and passed Baby Jimmy under the donkey, just as it raised its hind leg to give a good kick. The gypsy stood very close to me while I bent down to grasp Jimmy. It's not easy passing a wriggling, coughing infant back and forth three times under a threatening donkey with a gypsy trying to look through your clothes. I nearly dropped Jimmy. What if I'd been responsible for that little head cracking open on the cobbles? That'd cure his cough all right.

The gentleman gypsy let his shoulders slacken and didn't bother to stick out his chest. He glared at me and told me that the donkey had to be fed. I gave him a penny.

Mrs Garretty asked me to come in and see Cissie. The truth is I didn't want to because of this scream of worry going on inside me about what we'd do if Dad doesn't get work.

But Cissie is my best friend, so I went inside with Mrs Garretty, practically falling over Sol and Sarah as we made our way to their first-floor flat. Whenever they see me, all the hungry little Garrettys think it's Saturday and that I've brought pies.

Cissie lay back on the one big chair, her feet propped up on an orange box. It's strange how healthy people and sick people both get red cheeks. She waved her arm towards the floor where her drink sat. I handed her the jam jar with her medicine that smells of camphor and aniseed and has opium against the pain. Dad tells me not to visit her and if I must go to cover my face when she coughs. But Cissie and me sat next to each other on our first day at school. When Ann Dobson snatched my pencil, Cissie snatched it back.

After she had taken a sip of her medicine, she looked straight at me and said, 'Spit it out, lass. Summat's mithering thee.'

I told her Dad had no work just now.

She put her hand on mine. 'Summat'll turn up.'

I didn't say how terrible I would feel if I couldn't give the Garrettys pies on Saturday. My pies make the difference between them clemming and staying alive.

Cissie likes to talk about food and she asked me what recipe I used for the pork pies. She said I must write it down so that I don't forget, and that when we open our restaurant, pork pie and peas can be an item on the menu. I said that it might not be a very classy item for our posh restaurant, but she thought it would be very classy if made to my recipe. She always cheers me up. We discussed the menus, not just what food would be on the menus, but the style. Should we write individual cards for each table, or chalk the food on a board like in the market café? We decided on individual cards, to be hand written every morning. The tablecloths will be white, with embroidered flowers around the edge. Each table will have a tiny glass vase with a paper flower. We will charge a lot for a three-course meal, but people will be glad to come because it will be famous for its food and clientele. Because of high takings, it will be easy for us to feed any poor children or hungry people who come to the door. They can come to the big room off the kitchen and eat just as well – for a penny – but without the tablecloths. We had a long discussion about what to do if people had no penny. Cissie thinks anyone can manage to get a penny and we cannot feed people for nothing. She is probably right. I could not leave before agreeing the first menu: oxtail soup; pork chop, mashed potatoes and cabbage; jam pudding and custard.

Mrs Garretty wants to be the first customer. She would need to buy a pair of shoes, but I didn't mention that.

Dad and I worked through the night. May Clements in the market café will always buy my soup. We took it to her by six, while she was still serving breakfasts. Dad wheeled the pot of soup on the cart. I did the talking because Dad's too soft about money. Kept a pot back for the Garrettys.

Out cleaning today. I took down all the curtains for Alec's granny, old Mrs Fischer. I washed her windows and put up fresh curtains. Only, as soon as the sun came out, all the streaks showed up on the windows. She took a couple of newspaper pages, made a scrunched-up ball of them and got me to put a bit of elbow grease in, polishing every window again. It worked and got rid of the streaks, but my arms hurt. Rain started as I left. She gave me an old brolly and the tram fare on top of my pay.

I have shifted myself into 'hell' to write this, so that Margaret can have the table to herself.

When I was small and first heard about hell-fire, I used to think that the inner red circle on our rag rug must be it because it was made of little red wool tongues. Also, burning sparks from the fire sometimes shot onto it. I would sit in 'hell', as a dare to myself. When we were told about hell-fire and eternal damnation at school, it did not make an impression on me as I had already grown fond of my rag-rug hell.

Dad does not believe in hell. He once said that hell is when you lose the wife you love and the baby boy you never got to know. Hell is when your little girls lose their mam. That was the time he took us away from the Catholic school. We had come home with a note that our pinafores were dirty and that we had failed to donate a penny for the holy souls. After that we went to the Board School and became, according to Uncle Lloyd, heathens.

So here I am, sitting in hell, with my feet by the coal scuttle, while Margaret sews on the table. She had to push aside my sheet of figures as I sat for an age this afternoon, not writing in my journal but trying to make the figures add up. Outgoings: rent; flour; potatoes; charge for ovens; candles; coal; burial club. Dad looked over my shoulder. He says I am very good at making figures do as I tell them. Not today I wasn't.

In some moods he sends out invisible spikes. He started walking about, muttering to himself, 'I'm finished, finished.' He knocked his bedchair flying, and said, 'You have the chair. You the one who earns money.'

He went out and slammed the door so hard that the window rattled. Next thing I heard the cart outside. He had wheeled it round from the stables. He came back inside, emptied the bureau, putting the contents on the floor, then took the bureau outside, tied it onto the cart and wheeled it away.

When Margaret came home, she couldn't bear the mess of everything scattered about on the stone floor and across the table. We wrapped the glass dishes in newspaper to store them in a box from the cellar. Then Margaret pulled the box away from the wall, so it wouldn't get damp. I told her that if the box got damp, perhaps we wouldn't.

She is hemming a pair of curtains for Mrs Turner, who has praised her needlework. 'She puffs me up all the time,' Margaret said.

I wanted to say that if you made curtains for someone, free of charge, they probably would puff you up. Cheaper than paying you. But I kept that thought to myself.

Margaret re-threaded her needle. 'She doesn't have a daughter, only Thomas. Do you think she regards me as the daughter she never had?'

I recognized this line from a book I had read to Dad a little while ago. But I just said, 'I don't know, do I? Why doesn't she offer you money?'

Of course, that was just me being vulgar again. Margaret said, 'Some things are more important than money.'

'Do you mean some things like getting in Mrs Turner's good books?' I asked.

She blushed. That's when I knew I was right.

TWELVE

Coming back from the park, we sat upstairs at the back of the tram, open to the sky. As the tram jolted, we were thrown together. The slats of the seats pressed through my skirt, so I had to keep shifting to get comfy. Each time I did, Frank seemed to get nearer, and then I edged away and he edged closer. I looked at my hand lying on the seat next to his and he looked at his hand. One of us would only have had to move our fingers a fraction of an inch for our hands to touch. But we didn't.

When we got off the tram, he held out his hand and helped me down. It might be different, but we have known each other since I was five years old. He is my second oldest friend, after Cissie.

But that doesn't stop the comments. Why they've started saying this and that after all these years I don't know. Last time, Dad. This time, Aunty Amy.

I'd turned red as a beetroot from sitting in the sun. When we walked back, Aunty Amy was looking out of the window and called us in. She made us put camomile lotion on our faces and said she thought I had more sense than to take too much sun. Next time I want to go gallivanting, I am to remember that she has a parasol brought from India by her nephew Malcolm and I must get some use of it.

After Frank had gone, Aunty Amy said he is not a bad lad, and a great help with the pies. I could do far worse in her view, but I could also do a great deal better.

I said, 'We've been to the park, that's all. We're not walking out.'

She asked who paid the tram fare. I said that Frank did. She asked who bought the ice cream. I said Frank. She said, 'Well, if that's not walking out, I'll go to our house.'

I'd simmered all day but wasn't able to do anything about it until I'd finished my jobs, by which time children were coming back from school.

I'm glad I bashed on Mad Hatter Mason's door

77

and told her what I think. What low-down meanness. For years and years she has snatched our money for Margaret's apprenticeship. Then, just as Margaret should be earning proper money, goodbye.

How dare she sack Margaret? After such fine, such beautiful styling and making.

Miss Mason reckoned without a visit from me. She opened the door a fraction and gave her miserable little attempt at a smile, moving the cracked corners of her dried-out mouth, touching at the bow on her blouse to puff it out and disguise her flat chest, trying to push me out: 'It's nothing personal, just business.'

I pushed the door wide open and told her just what I thought of her.

One feeble excuse after another: 'Not enough work to keep Margaret busy.'

I looked round at all the hats Margaret had made, and said, 'There was enough work to keep her busy for the seven years we were handing over money to you.'

She told me not to shout like a common fishwife. I told her not to steal like a common thief – to take money week after week, to take Margaret's time and good ideas and her willingness.

She started to move hats and hat stands, as if I was going to tear and smash them, saying, 'Margaret was a bad timekeeper. She had a day off once a month with cramps. No business woman could afford to put up with that.'

I wanted to rip her felt hats to shreds and shove them down her throat, false cherries and all. If I'd kept that money I gave her a month ago, we wouldn't have got behind with the rent. I asked her for it back. She said no. I can't remember what else I said. I left in such a rage because I feared I'd hit her.

Guessed right that Margaret would be at the Dragon. Thought she would be in the kitchen, making herself useful, sewing on Uncle's shirt buttons. But no, she was in the upstairs parlour, and not alone. Bernard stood by the sideboard, and I got the whiff of burnt sugar and rum. He was doing the measuring and what-not that he does for Uncle. Margaret sat in the window seat, half-turned from me. Someone sat beside her. They leaned towards each other, so close that their heads touched: his fair; hers vinegary-red.

A train streamed past, along the bridge, just a foot or so away from the window. Bernard nodded to me, with that martyr's look on his face, asking for my sympathy because he was doing one of his hated jobs. Neither Margaret nor Thomas Turner noticed me until I called her name.

She looked round, and so did he. A sheet of ruled foolscap slipped from her hand. She put her pencil behind her ear and shot me a look that wished me anywhere but there. 'Julia!'

'I've just been to see Miss Mason.'

Margaret got up and came towards me. Bernard had stopped what he was doing and looked at both of us. Smiling, Margaret grabbed my wrist threateningly. 'I don't think you've met Mr Turner properly.' She spoke through gritted teeth. 'Julia, Thomas Turner. Thomas, my sister, Julia.'

Thomas leaped up and crossed the room. He

took my hand and shook it firmly. 'How do you do, Julia.' Then a flicker of recognition told me that he remembered me from the day of Margaret's speech. For a moment I thought he was going to make a joke.

I heard myself say, 'How do you do' in such an angry voice that he dropped my hand as if it were a burning coal.

'Let's go organize a pot of tea,' Margaret said. She turned to Thomas. 'We'll be back in a shake.'

She practically pushed me out of the room and onto the stairs towards the kitchen.

'What's he doing here?' I asked.

'Keep your voice down,' she said. 'He's visiting me. The editor on the *Leeds Mercury* asked him to write an article about the conditions of working women. He values my opinion.'

'Huh! What would you know about the conditions of working women?'

We got to the kitchen. She filled the kettle. Even the water hitting the kettle sounded angry. I didn't offer to help. She set the teapot to warm in the oven.

I told her that I'd had it out with Miss Mason. Did Margaret say thank you? No. Did she say I'd done the right thing? No. Margaret got angry with *me*. She said it was bad enough that Miss Mason did not need her any more, without me making a public show. She was mortified.

Typical. All speeches and no fight when it comes to something real. I watched her wiping a damp cloth across the tray decorated with pansies.

'Why didn't you stick up for yourself and ask for some of the apprenticeship money back?' I asked her.

She just sighed as if I'd asked a really silly question. 'Perhaps it will turn out for the best,' she said, spooning tea into the pot. 'And don't worry, I won't trouble you and Dad to keep me any more. Uncle has said he is very pleased for me to stay here. As long as I like.'

I never usually cry. But what a way to find out that your sister is leaving you in the lurch. I started to cry and I couldn't stop. I could hardly get the words out. 'We're supposed to be the Wood Sisters. Two branches on one tree, you said.'

She looked impressed. 'Did I say that? It's very poetic.' She put her arm around me then and said, 'Don't, don't. I'm thinking of you and Dad. We've been poor too long. You and Dad do your best, but it's no good. Don't you see? You have to lift yourself out of it another way. Don't think I'll ever leave you. I'm going to improve myself – perhaps marry well. I can't do that out of Bread Street. Stop crying.'

She gave me her hanky. As I dabbed at my eyes, she said, 'Open the biscuit tin. Put some biscuits on that pretty plate with the cherry pattern.'

'Why didn't you stick up for yourself with Miss Mason?' I asked again. 'You're good at making speeches, why didn't you make one to her and ask for some of the money back?'

'I understand her predicament, that's why.'

'I wish you'd understand our predicament of being behind with the rent.'

'Isn't there anything left to sell?' she asked.

'Your sewing machine,' I said, expecting her to

say no.

'Good idea,' she said. 'I prefer Aunty's machine and Uncle says no one else uses it.'

I think she was relieved when I said I wouldn't go back up with her for tea. 'Hold the door open for me,' she ordered, standing there with her tray.

I flattened myself against the door. 'What about Dad? What will Dad say about your moving out?'

'I told him this morning,' she said. 'He won't stand in my way, so don't you. Now move! This tray's heavy.'

I opened the door and let her go upstairs.

THIRTEEN

I feel like breaking into Miss Mason's shop and taking goods to the value of all the money we paid for Margaret's apprenticeship. Seven years, and it started out at five shillings a week, then reduced to two shillings and sixpence. There cannot be enough goods in that shop to repay us. Those damn hats are worth nothing to me but I could take them round certain areas on a handcart and see what they would fetch.

When I went back and said that I had seen Margaret, Dad said something in German or Yiddish. He couldn't or wouldn't translate it properly but I didn't need the dictionary to work out that it meant rats leaving a sinking ship. I told him that Margaret isn't a rat and we're nowhere near sinking yet. He said that I may not be, but he is.

Once upon a time Dad would have noticed how upset I am. But now he notices nothing. He goes out and walks and walks and comes back and plays Patience till his arm hurts. His boots are past mending. Although I was ready to burst, I decided not to tell him about Miss Mason giving Margaret the sack. He'd probably forgotten her indentures were up. But it just came out.

And all Dad did was sigh. Just sigh.

Something else, too. The reason I cannot sleep. Dad went into the cellar and was there a long time. I went down to see what he was doing.

He had tied the washing-line to a hook in the ceiling and was tugging at it, as if testing it for strength. I pretended not to notice and just said, 'I can't seem to stop the window rattling.'

While he was fixing my bedroom window, I went back into the cellar. I have hidden the wash-ing-line under my bed, and undone the noose. I would speak to him, but my mouth feels dry and I don't know what to say.

The market café serves tea in thick mugs. Frank swapped his for mine because my mug had a crack. He has only half an hour for dinner, and usually takes something with him to eat at work. I felt awkward munching my cheese sandwich while he spooned sugar into his tea.

'Thah munna take this the wrong way,' he said, and at first I thought he was talking about his spoon clunking round the mug. He pulled out an opened wage packet and slipped the little brown envelope under my plate.

I said, 'Why are you giving me this?'

He tapped the spoon on his mug. 'Put it in thah money belt. It's nobbut some of mi boxing winnings. To tide thee over, no obligations.'

Before I had chance to answer, he drank down his tea in two gulps, slid his chair back and left.

I watched him go. A skinny old woman, clutching a moth-eaten shawl with one hand and holding a rattling cup and saucer in the other, asked if he was coming back. When I said no she took his seat and started talking to me, complaining about something. Under the table, I put my fingers into the pay packet Frank had handed me and felt the coins – a sovereign and a crown.

I stayed in the café a while and took my time over the cheese sandwich. I'd been hungry for hours and started to feel my strength coming back and some hope to my heart. At first the feeling about the money was just relief. But some other feelings came next, like a stab of warning in my chest.

Aunty Amy reckons you're walking out with a lad if he pays the tram fare and buys the ice cream. This was different. Whatever he said, this put me under an obligation. He had given me money but taken something away. It wasn't an accident that he'd put the money in an old wage packet. He wanted me to know what he earned. He had told me before that only the best furriers are kept on all year round. Now it is out in the open without him having to speak a word.

Frank had noticed that Miss Mason never shuts the small window above her shop door. Margaret told me ages ago that on Wednesday nights Miss

Mason plays whist in the Ladies' Room at the Liberal Club and drinks two glasses of fortified wine. That's why we chose a Wednesday. With the nights so light, we had to wait until we thought she'd be home in bed, sleeping soundly after her tots of tawny.

When I heard Frank's signal, I pulled Mam's shawl around me, slipped on her old soft shoes and crept downstairs to the sound of Dad's snoring. The noisiest part was opening our outside door.

In the shop doorway, Frank bobbed down for me to sit on his shoulders. The small top window was open, as Frank had said. 'Stretch thy arms in first. See to't shop bell.'

I had to feel my way blindly for the bell, then wind a strip of cloth around the clapper. 'What now?'

'Gerrin feet first, Julia, or thah'll be jammed like a rat in a trap.'

I felt like a contortionist, getting first one leg then the other through the tiny space. My bum was practically on Frank's head. He wriggled till I could lever myself onto the window frame and push the window open as far as it would go. Then I couldn't budge. I could imagine the article in the paper, and the humiliation of being arrested while stuck in a little window. But Frank kept saying, 'Slither for'ard, thah's breakin' mi neck. Slither thi'sen down.'

I jutted my legs forward, leaned my body backwards, making myself skinny as possible, and pushed. I hurt my back on the window frame, and cried out as I dropped to the floor with a thump. I thought the whole street would hear me.

I daren't look at the lock, thinking she may have taken the key upstairs. But it was in the lock. I turned it, drew back the bottom bolt then brought the stool from behind the counter and climbed up to draw back the top bolt.

Frank struck a match, lit a candle and stood it on the floor. Something about the way he did it told me this wasn't his first time breaking into a shop. He pulled a sack from under his jacket and thrust it into my hands. I held it open, my hands shaking, and he grabbed hat after hat, dropping them into the sack.

I wanted to change my mind when he tossed a bride's headdress and a couple of wedding hats into the sack. I suddenly felt sorry for Miss Mason because she's old and ugly and makes hats for other people's weddings. I whispered, 'Miss Mason isn't rich. We shouldn't.'

Frank grabbed the last few hats. 'Put a sock in thah gob. She's richer'n thee, and she'd see thah clem.'

We left the shop and I wanted to run. Frank said to wait in the doorway because the copper on his midnight round had to pass the end of the street where he'd rat-a-tat-tat with his night-stick to tell the sergeant patrolling Regent Street that all was peaceful.

The parish church clock struck one. We waited. Shortly after came the beat copper's rat-a-tat-tat.

We separated at the top of Bread Street, Frank carrying the sack of hats.

On Thursday morning, we met at the railway station, in time for me to get the first train to Wakefield, with directions from Frank on how to get to the markets area. I arranged myself in the railway carriage, the sack of hats at my feet and the hawker's basket on my knees.

I can't remember anything about the day because it passed in fear. I kept expecting to be arrested, some Wakefield policeman having a description of stolen millinery. I sold all but one hat. I felt so sad, dumping that one small black felt hat, made by Margaret, into the waste bin in the ladies' waiting room at Wakefield station, so as not to be caught red-handed on my return to Leeds.

FOURTEEN

Saw Bernard on York Street and could not believe my eyes. Usually he walks with his back rounded, shoulders hunched, examining the cracks in the pavement. Today he walked with a straight back and seemed to float a foot above the flags, grinning like some music hall comic who has just told a very funny joke. He saluted in his usual fashion and immediately came out with this great flood of news. He had applied to be a pianist on an ocean-going liner and has been accepted. He should soon hear what ship and what port. If it should be Liverpool, we must all go to see him off.

I asked him what Uncle Lloyd has to say about it.

Bernard grinned and his eyes lit up. 'Dad's furious,' he said. He swung his brown-paper parcel round and round till the string tightened and hurt his finger. 'The atmosphere tends towards abominable, that's why I've come out for a stroll.'

Well, he is twenty-one, and what can Uncle do? I wish it were me. I wish I could do something exciting.

Bernard has bought six new shirts and twelve collars, and we are all invited to his party.

Bernard was still brimming over with joy about the job on the liner. He played music hall songs on the baby grand in the Dragon's upstairs sitting room. A huge vase of lilies and roses sat on the piano, their scent filling the room. Of course, the McAndrews do everything in style. They had a maid trotting about, bringing in trays of sandwiches and jugs of ginger beer.

Thomas Turner, wearing his blazer with its cricket team badge, turned the pages of the sheet music for him. Margaret, wearing a pale-green dress trimmed with roses, stood beside Thomas, singing with delicate gusto as only she can. I'm sure she didn't need to read the music as she knew all the songs by heart, but she leaned close in to Thomas, as if she might miss a note.

When Bernard stopping playing and stretched his fingers, Thomas turned to look at Margaret with utter admiration. She made as if not to notice she had captivated him and came over to greet me. I asked her whatever got into Uncle that he allowed Bernard a party.

She said that she and Kevin and Johnny had

persuaded Uncle to let Bernard have the celebration. Of the three brothers, Bernard has always been the least favourite of his father even though he is the eldest, which I think strange. Kevin and Johnny, the twins, they're a year younger than Bernard and have the same black hair and blue eyes, but they have a kind of glow and the good looks poor Bernard missed out on. It seems cruel that such small things like sallow skin and ears that make him look ready to fly should get in the way of good looks.

But when he plays he comes to life. He looks like part of the piano, all black and white: well-oiled black hair; pale face; white fingers racing along the keys; dressed in black with a bright white shirt. Part human, part musical instrument. He started to play again, and Thomas asked Margaret to dance. I could tell they had been practising – very much in tune with each other. I wondered whether he had cleaned his teeth with soot or something to make them so white. He smiled and smiled at her, and she at him. I wandered about with my ginger beer and started to chat with Clarice from the Wheatsheaf. She has always had an eye for Kevin but he doesn't seem to notice her. Johnny, who once confided in me that he likes plump girls, cares for Clarice very much. He can't understand how she of all people, well able to tell all the differences between himself and Kevin, prefers his brother. Clarice was eyeing Kevin and stuffing a meat sandwich into her mouth when Johnny asked her to dance.

That left me talking to Jean from Edinburgh who had come straight from work and wore a creased fawn costume. She's twenty-two, works in a legal office and sells the suffragette paper on Saturday afternoons. She sat on the window seat, sipping her ginger ale.

'I wonder if Mrs Turner knows her precious son has fallen for your sister,' she said. 'She won't like that.'

'What do you mean?'

'There are great plans for that laddo.' Jean budged up on the seat to make room for me. 'And I don't think bonny Maggie Wood is part of 'em.'

I would have asked her to explain but a train steamed by noisily, and everyone went on dancing to the music in their heads, unable to hear the piano. I glanced at the passengers on the train, and one young, smiling fellow waved and looked as if he envied our huge enjoyment. I waved back and wished he could be here. I wonder if I'll ever see that smiling face again.

While Thomas played a waltz, Clarice and Jean danced with Kevin and Johnny, and lanky Willie Maguire pirouetted Margaret about the room.

Me and Bernard sat in the window seat. Bernard said he's never been so happy. Working in the pub has been hateful to him. Helping his dad, counting barrels and bottles, checking orders against delivery notes and brewery invoices, adding columns of figures and bringing up crates from the cellar – it makes him want to tear his hair out. He dragged me over to the sideboard and brought out a small, blue, velvet-lined case containing weights and a scale. I had to watch him as he explained to me what tedious tasks Uncle orders him to do. It's Bernard's job to dilute the rum. He demonstrated how he weighs burnt sugar, which he pours into a big stone jar with rum. It can be spot-checked by Customs and Excise officers and heaven help him if he makes a mistake. Bernard says that it is tedious beyond belief, and all for the sake of profit. I told him I'd swap him jobs any day. If he wants to pluck fowl till his fingers turn numb, do two lots of washing and ironing, clean for a pernickety old lady, peel potatoes, bake pies, carry heavy trays of pies to the ovens every Saturday, and lickety split a handcart round the streets every Sunday to let me know.

He put little weights on the scales, so that they balanced evenly, and said that his life had been stolen from him measure by measure. When that letter came, offering him the job on the liner, it changed everything. Now he can start to live. When he knew he would never be a top-class pianist, never first-rate, he had thought there was no hope for him. But now he'll be earning his living doing what he loves to do, and not many people get that chance. I agreed with that. He said he danced a jig when the letter came, which I couldn't imagine and I asked him to do it again, but he escaped by edging Thomas off the piano stool and taking over.

I'm sure Margaret went on dancing with Willie deliberately to keep Thomas on the hop, hoping for a dance. I wished she hadn't because she knows all the dances and I don't, and when Thomas held out his hand to me and asked for the pleasure of a spin around the room, I didn't know the steps.

'If you're half as light on your feet as your sister

you'll float across the floor,' he said.

I have never had time to learn to dance. Margaret says this is my own fault and I should spend less time scribbling and sitting in the stables talking to Solomon, and more time paying attention to the things that matter. Bernard kindly started a Strauss waltz, probably guessing that I wouldn't manage anything fancier than that. Thomas took my hand, placed his hand loosely on my waist and started to count quietly as he guided me round the room: 'Step two three, step two three, turn and step and step. You've got it!'

And I had. It was so easy to dance with him. I expected him to be looking at Margaret because, as she danced with Willie Maguire, they both laughed a great deal. But Thomas did not look at Margaret once. He danced with me as if there was no one else in the room. I think we would have gone on dancing if Margaret hadn't told Bernard to play something more lively. When we stopped, Thomas lifted my hand to his lips in a slightly mocking way but not unkind. Then he stroked a finger across the back of my hand, seeming to test its roughness, as I had with the beast's tongue.

He led me back to the window seat. 'What do you do?' he asked. 'What do you do for a living?'

Before I had chance to answer, two things happened. Margaret took up her position by the piano, nudged Bernard and started to sing 'Cherry Ripe'. Thomas forgot I existed. At the same time, Uncle appeared in the doorway, glanced round the room and spotted me.

Naturally Uncle waited, not wishing to interrupt Margaret's song. He stood with his back to the fireplace in that usual way of his, legs apart, taking all the heat from the room winter or summer, fingering his watch absent-mindedly. Margaret has that effect on people. Even Clarice, who's almost entirely wrapped up in herself and tone-deaf to boot, whispered to me that when Margaret sings, you forget to breathe.

As soon as Margaret's song ended, Uncle beckoned me over and whispered that I'd better take Dad home because he was becoming a right misery in the downstairs bar. I must have looked surprised because why shouldn't Dad feel down-hearted? He has plenty to be miserable about. We have not been able to keep a secret of the fact he lost his job.

Uncle said the trouble was that after a couple of drinks, Dad goes into German and Yiddish, and not all the customers like it, especially when he seems to be complaining. And even when Dad speaks English, he makes remarks such as 'All men are brothers' and 'There is neither English nor German, Christian, Turk nor Jew but only humankind.' Uncle said that men who have had a few drinks can take that kind of philosophical remark very well or very badly, depending upon their interpretation. A market trader in fine linens had taken exception to being dubbed a Turk.

Uncle started to manoeuvre me downstairs by the elbow, telling me that he likes to nip trouble in the bud.

Margaret thinks it's bad luck to pass on the stairs and if you do it, one person must say "salt" and the other "pepper".

'Salz,' said a voice, and there was Dad, swaying

93

slightly at the bottom of the stairs.

'Pepper,' I groaned.

Uncle squeezed flat against the wall, as Dad lumbered towards us. 'Joseph old chap, sorry about this, but your little Julia needs you to take her home. She isn't feeling one hundred per cent.'

'Julia?' Dad said, full of concern. 'Julia poorly?'

'No,' I said. 'You're drunk and going on about universal whatnot and internationalist thing-ummyjig. You're causing bother, Dad.'

Dad slapped his hand to his mouth. 'I shut up. I shut up now. I just go hear my eldest *Tochter* zing.' He lumbered past us, towards the upstairs parlour.

Uncle glared at me. 'Thank you. Just keep him up there, out of the way of my customers.'

I sighed and followed Dad up the stairs. Margaret would not be pleased. She had sworn me to be on my best behaviour and I'm sure didn't want her precious Thomas to meet her tipsy dad.

I caught up with Dad and we went in together, winding our way through the dancers. Johnny grabbed me and whirled me round the room before I had chance to get Dad to the window seat.

But Dad couldn't be faulted. He sat in the window seat, drinking ginger beer and nibbling on a cucumber sandwich. 'Is like the old days,' he said, as I waltzed past.

It was Clarice's turn by the piano. She belted out a couple of music hall songs, embarrassing Kevin by mooning at him and driving Johnny to distraction by not catching his eye at all. As soon as we'd applauded her, dear Bernard called for me to recite, knowing that I can't hold a tune.

Margaret smiled encouragingly, and mouthed, 'Shelley.' She wanted the family to make a good impression on Thomas. But after Clarice had just sung the plaster off the ceiling with 'Look What Percy's Picked Up in the Park', reciting 'To a Skylark' didn't seem to fit the party mood. I realized that Margaret thought if Dad ate enough cucumber sandwiches, he might sober up a bit.

As I walked towards the piano, Bernard gave me a few notes of dramatic introduction. I smiled around the room, as Margaret does before she announces her song. I said, 'There's a wonderful Leeds poet who died not so many years ago and who's buried in Beckett Street cemetery. Last autumn I planted daffodils on his grave and sure enough they came up beautifully in the spring. His name's Tom Maguire and this is one of his poems.'

Margaret mouthed, 'What about Shelley?'

I pretended not to see her. Before I even started, Dad gave me a round of applause. I took a deep breath, and began.

The firm gave us a holiday.
Our fines made up expenses
For railway fare, for breakfast and for tea;
And hadn't we a jolly day?
We took leave of our senses!
And laughed and carried on like mad,
At Scarboro' by the sea.
And O! the sea was new to me

95

At Scarboro', at Scarboro',
A-shining and a-shimmering through a veil of misty
  grey;
Its face was fair – but ah! Its lips
Were fringed with foam, at Scarboro'–
That curled about my feet in scorn and spattered me
  with spray.

Dad put down his ginger beer and clapped and clapped.

Thomas beamed. 'I love Tom Maguire, too.' And he quoted: '"When men learn to love one another as heartily as they have learnt to hate one another, they will probably be able to differ in opinion without descending into slander and vituperation".'

Dad applauded Thomas. The cucumber sandwiches had not done the sobering trick.

I felt very pleased that Thomas appreciated Tom Maguire. I pretend he's my favourite poet and he is not, but because he lived near us, as I walk about, I imagine him in the same streets as me, turning up his collar against the rain, running for a tram, hoping for glory and better days.

Margaret came over and said, 'Well done, Julia, but I thought you'd perhaps recite Shelley for us.'

Of course Thomas had to agree with her, urging me to recite some Shelley. They were standing so close, their ankles, knees and hips touched. She moved her arm towards me, but brushed his arm as she did so, and he sort of caught his breath as if he'd been winded. Then he concentrated very hard on me and said, 'Tom Maguire's sympathies were in the right place, but he had a lot to learn as a poet.'

I didn't get chance to contradict him, as Margaret smiled and said, 'No one comes close to Shelley.'

'Well, why don't you recite then?' I said, knowing full well she never troubles to learn poetry and can just about remember a few nursery rhymes.

Margaret turns everything to her advantage. 'Thomas,' she said, turning to him and smiling, 'I'm sure you'll give us some Shelley.'

Clarice's face! She glanced at Kevin and Johnny for moral support. This wasn't her idea of a good time.

Thomas didn't notice. 'You'll know "The Revolt of Islam",' he said to Margaret. 'Cyntha pleads with her poet-lover to let her play her part in the future revolution, and says, "Can man be free and woman still a slave?" That's why I joined the suffrage group.'

'Bravo,' Dad called. He raised his ginger-beer glass. 'To Shelley.'

I could see what Margaret was thinking. She needed to introduce Thomas to Dad, but not let Dad take over in his tipsy state. She took the plunge and made the introduction.

They shook hands solemnly.

'I'm so pleased to meet you, Mr Wood.'

Dad smiled. '*Hallo*, Thomas. *Wie gehts?*'

'*Gut, danke*,' Thomas said as if he hadn't noticed Dad had forgotten to speak English.

Bernard struck up another tune just as the door opened and some of Kevin and Johnny's friends from work came in, followed by Clarice's sister and cousin.

I could see that Dad had suddenly realized this was a young persons' party. He looked tired. Margaret and Thomas were dancing again, laughing together.

'Shall you and me go home, Dad?' I asked him.

'You stay, *liebling*.'

'No. I'll come home with you. I've had enough.'

I watched Margaret and Thomas dancing round the room, gazing into each other's eyes.

On the way home I told Dad Margaret's good news. Miss Mason, without a hat left in her shop, has taken Margaret on for three days a week and is paying her. Margaret has given me a few shillings. She said she would willingly give me all her money but needs to save for her trousseau. I didn't tell Dad that part, because he would be sure to ask more questions than I had answers for.

FIFTEEN

Dad was snoozing in his chair when Frank got back from his boxing and came to the door, so I didn't ask him in. We sat on the doorstep and he showed me the medal he'd won last night in Sheffield. He said that he'd thought of us this morning and worried about us, wondering had the pie round gone off all right. It had. No trouble.

Opposite, Mr Hardiman was yelling at Mrs Hardiman. Their door opened and all the kids tumbled out onto the street in a rush as if they'd been thrown out.

We walked to the tusky as the sun started to set, and for a while we sat on a felled tree and just watched. The wild rhubarb isn't ready for picking yet, but some children were walking through, checking to see which stalks were turning red, not wanting to miss the moment of ripeness. I'd never seen the sun so huge and red. It would be a good place to write my journal on a fine day. As we watched the sun dipping, I thought, I'll always remember this moment.

Frank said that all the Leeds lads had won their bouts, including Willie Maguire, though only just. Danny Hescott, their promoter, had been in a great mood. Frank took a cigarette packet from his pocket and handed it to me to read the name and address he'd written on the back. The name was Ted Hescott, Danny Hescott's cousin, and the boss of a building site in Holbeck. If Dad goes to him and mentions Danny's name, there'll be a job.

I didn't know what to say. I can't picture Dad working on a building site. Frank took my silence the wrong way. He said, 'Thah don't have to say it came from me.'

'Why not?' I asked.

'Thah knows why. I'm not good enough for thee. That's his view, and I expect Aunty Amy and your Margaret feel't same.' Before I got chance to answer he added, 'And thee. Or thah'd have invited me to Bernard's party on Friday night.'

'I thought you'd be training,' I said.

'I were. But I'd have come for a look-in.'

I got up with a shiver. We walked back in silence. I don't know what it is. When I'm with him, we're both that happy. No one makes me as happy as him and no one makes me as sad. I know he feels the same.

But when he's not there, something inside me says a big no. I feel that once I get tied up with him, I'll never get untied, and I can't be sure. Who is it in me that says yes to him? Who is it that says no?

It was a dry Monday morning, a good washing day. I took the sheet from the mangle as Dad turned. I told him to leave me to get on and that he should go to Holbeck about the job.

He picked up another sheet. 'Nothing for me in Holbeck. Just wear out shoe leather.'

I thought of the rope I'd taken and hidden under my bed. 'None of us'll have shoes at all if you don't do something.' I grabbed the posser and flung it across the stone floor. 'Why should you just give up? I don't need you to wash sheets; I can do that myself. I need you to bring in some money.'

'Tramp, tramp, tramp. I sick of tramping.'

I explained for the umpteenth time that this was a tip-off from Frank who was owed a favour by Boxing Danny. I felt like screaming.

He said, 'All right. I tramp. Tramp, tramp out of Leeds, out of your way. I hold you back.'

If Margaret had been there that moment I'd have hit her with the posser and wound her hair through the mangle. I felt angry with him and angry with Margaret for moving out. At least with Margaret in the house it had felt like the three of us, pulling together. I looked at the beam in the ceiling, thinking of the rope. He saw me looking. For a moment neither of us spoke. Then I said, 'At least try for the job. They need a night-watchman. Nobody would bother you.'

He wiped the sweat from his forehead with the back of his hand. 'Do they know I'm a Yid? Do they know I'm bloody foreigner?'

I said, 'Maybe they'll know that "There is neither English nor German, Christian, Turk nor Jew but only humankind" — and you're it.'

He put his hand on my shoulder. 'All right. Give me the address.'

Funny how quickly things can change. One piece of good luck and you think, yes, everything will be all right.

Ted Hescott gave Dad a start. He patrols the building site through the night and in-between sits in his hut. He gave me a full account, including a description of the battered old black kettle that he kept on the boil all night, and filled in good time for the site foreman this morning.

To the Varieties. What a great show! How we laughed. And the songs – so cheeky!

A shower on the way home, and we snuggled together under my umbrella, singing 'My Old Man'. Frank remembered the comic's patter and kept me in stitches. He even remembered where to pause for the laughs. I wished Margaret could have heard. She wouldn't call him two notes short of a melody if she heard that he can remember a whole comic routine.

Also, he brought me a pair of boxing gloves and

two thick overcoats, so that when we spar he can land a punch without hurting me. We pushed Dad's chair against the wall, took up the rag rug and sparred. He showed me how to hold my arms and hands, right hand protecting my face, left arm protecting my body. We each had a 'corner' and came out of our corners on my 'ding dong'. I can land a right hook and a left jab and dance out of reach. Boxing is about skill, timing and weighing up your opponent. It is not about mean feelings and boiling over inside. Though if you have mean feelings and are boiling over inside, it is a very useful sport. He has hung a punchbag in the cellar for me. (I chose the spot where Dad placed his noose.)

When he left, the rain was sheeting down, but he wouldn't take the brolly. I stood on the step and watched him to the end of the street. He did a sort of hop, skip and jump before he got to the corner, turned and waved.

Mrs Hardiman was peeping through her curtains. Let her look, let them all look. We're friends, that's all. People can be friends. Of course, the disadvantage is I feel obliged to help out because Frank's mother is badly. She had asked him to ask me if I would fill in for her and do her early-morning cleaning at the Workhouse Infirmary. I never say no to work, but I would have said no to this if it hadn't been for Frank getting Dad the job and all. The reason I would say no is that Mrs Whitelock takes half the money and I'm sure stays 'badly' much longer than she would if I weren't doing her shifts.

I hated doing it. Mrs Whitelock is supposed to

be in charge of the women from the Workhouse who are well enough to clean, and mostly they are the same ones each day and know what to do. Today a new woman joined in. She was about thirty. I had to explain how to go about things. A strand of fair hair, streaked with grey, kept falling from under her cap. Instead of tucking the hair under her cap, she'd comb it back with her fingers and down it would fall again. In the end I took a clip from my own hair and went across to her and said, 'Here.'

But the woman just looked at me blankly, so I pinned her hair back for her and when I did that she started to cry. I did not know where to look.

She said, 'Thank you, miss,' as if I'd done her a great service.

I had a cup of tea with Mr and Mrs Shepherd when I had finished the work. Mr Shepherd says that when he was in Africa, he noticed that in the tribes, whichever man or woman did the cooking did not do any other work. They kept their hands clean for that one job. Here in England decent folk work harder than any heathen would be expected to. I told him that I always scrub my hands before I make the pies. He said he did not mean that, he was sure I was very clean, but he was thinking how sad it was that girls got wore out so early. I felt myself blush at that. Straight away I thought of Dad. I know Dad wanted better for me, wanted me to stay on at school. It was not to be. But who knows? I have not given up hope and never will.

SIXTEEN

Glorious evening – sky streaked red, promising a grand day tomorrow. Dad and me had tea at the Dragon, and then walked Margaret to the Turners's – a big house on Roundhay Road with a long garden full of wallflowers and geraniums.

Dad said Margaret mixes with a good class of person in the Votes for Women movement. He wanted me to go in with her. Margaret's face! She needn't have worried. I can't be bothered with all that jawing and sewing banners.

We left her at the Turners' gate and got the tram back to town. Dad went to his job and I went to the Dragon stables to see Solomon. The poor weary fellow had been out in the cart all day long.

The sky came over grey and cloudy today and stayed that way but it didn't bother me. Mrs diClementi had sent Marco and Anna with a sack of rabbits to skin. (Their Carlo had been out in the country with a rifle.) I showed Marco and Anna how to slit the belly and lift the rabbit out of its skin. Marco did not want to do it at first, but once you have done one and have blood under your fingernails, the next is not so hard to do. Anna would not try, or stay to watch. But Marco should be able to do it himself in future.

When Marco had gone, I bundled up the skins. Mr Ferrett's 'High Class Furs' is a grand-looking shop in Kirkgate. You get to the cellar workshop through the yard round the back. I tapped on the window to get Frank's attention. He grinned up at me then went to open the door, and motioned for me to come down the steps.

'What about Mr Ferrett?' I asked.

'He's out.'

I showed him the parcel. 'I've got some rabbit fur.'

Frank held the door open for me. 'Come and tek a look round.'

I went inside. Men worked at long tables. I recognized Reg Greaves, Frank's ginger-haired workmate. He nodded to me and kept on cutting a skin to shape. 'Persian lamb. Some old dear'll be warm this winter, but it'd look finer on thee, lass.'

'Come and see Ferrett's office,' Frank said.

Mr Ferrett's office is built out from the cellar wall. From about waist height it is entirely of glass, so that he can see all around the workshop. Frank tried the door. 'He's forgot to lock it.'

'Frank!' I looked round to see if anyone was watching.

'No one'll say owt. He won't be back much afore dinner.'

A wild cat with fierce glass eyes stood ready to pounce from one corner of the desk to the other. A dirty blotter with green leather edging sat squarely on the desk, and a matching green leather holder held a couple of pencils.

Frank picked up a pencil, rubbed it along the bottom of his shoe and replaced it in the holder. 'Why are you doing that?' I asked.

'Because Ferrett stirs his tea with it.'

I stopped myself from doing any more than groan at him, and handed him the rabbit skins.

He inspected them quickly. 'These are grand. If the skin had blue marks inside, see, it'd be in moult. But this is clean. Good quality.'

'We'll go fifty-fifty,' I said, feeling eyes watching us from the shop floor and wanting to be out of there.

When he brought me to the door, he slipped a parcel into my hands, and I thought at first he was returning the rabbit skins. I kept it close and didn't look until I was well past the market. A muff. He has given me a beautiful Persian lamb muff.

Gregory, Sol, Sarah and Essie Garretty were leaning over their balcony railing and came running down the steps to meet me. Then they ran up ahead of me to tell Mrs Garretty and Cissie I'd brought rabbit stew. Poor Cissie couldn't manage more than a couple of spoonfuls of stew but she enjoyed watching the others eat and never stopped smiling. The bairns finished every morsel and licked the dish. Mrs Garretty was in the family way again, so said she'd take some, too. You hardly ever see her eat otherwise, just tea and bread and butter.

Me and Cissie talked about what we will do when she gets better, how we will find ourselves a couple of lads and go to Kirkstall Abbey. She has a quick smile and a way of tilting her head on one side as if to get you to tell her all your secrets.

I straightened Cissie's cover and plumped her

pillow as best I could because all movement pains her. As Cissie leaned forward and I made her comfy, she said, 'These two lads, you better keep your eyes off my lad and pay heed to your own.'

I told her that I wouldn't look at hers. Mine would be much better-looking and have a few bob in his pocket. She started to laugh but it made her chest hurt.

Mrs Garretty ordered Sol to go out onto the landing and come back in. She asked could he smell rabbit stew. Sol said no he could not. All the little Garrettys became anxious and went in and out of the door to the landing, commenting on smells.

Cissie saw my puzzled look and whispered, 'Dad'll know we've been eating and want to know where it's come from and why he didn't get the lion's share.'

I passed her her jam jar of medicine and she drank, then reached for my hand. Her hand feels light as a paper hat but full of life.

Cissie said, 'Don't be sad for me. Just think that I'll never be mithered with a drunken feller and too many babies. I'll never get old and fat nor look in the glass one day and see my hair turned grey and my teeth gone. When someone says "Cissie", the picture in their mind will be young.'

'And lovely,' I said, and I stroked her hair.

'Give over,' she said, pushing my hand away and laughing. 'I'm not lovely now and never likely to be. That's your neck of the woods. But we do have one thing in common.'

'What's that?' I asked.

'Patience.'

'Me, patient?' It was my turn to laugh. 'What gave you that bright idea? And you were never patient.'

'There are different kinds of patience, Julia. I've learned the patience to endure, because I have no choice in the matter. You have the patience to persevere, no matter what goes wrong for you and your dad.'

'I have no choice either,' I said quietly.

'You do though. You could take the choice your Margaret makes, and leave your dad to it. No one would blame you.'

But of course I couldn't. You can't help what you're made of. Margaret can't, and nor can I.

Cissie watched me. 'That's how I know I can ask you.' She took my hand.

'Ask me what?'

'Never let my sisters and brothers starve.'

I heard the breath go out of me. 'Why do you think they'll starve, Cissie?'

'You know why,' she said. 'They would have starved already if not for thee.'

I didn't get chance to answer as Mrs Garretty came, saying that young Sol had given the whistle. Mr Garretty was here.

I kissed Cissie and left. I never know when it will be the last time, and I felt bad that her question had so taken me by surprise I hadn't been able to answer.

Who should I meet on the stairs but soot-black Mr Garretty, his miner's lamp still on his head, stinking of beer. We came face to face and did a little dance to avoid each other. He glared at me. We could hear the children on the landing.

'Yon's lively,' he said. 'As thah been feeding my bairns?'

I looked him straight in the eye and said, 'No. Have you?'

He stood aside and let me pass. Then he let out a grunt and the children on the landing went silent.

SEVENTEEN

Now that Dad works nights and Margaret has gone to the Dragon, it feels strange to be in the house alone. So quiet, without Margaret singing and bossing me, without Dad tap-tapping his pipe and asking to be read to. Until a little while ago, the street was full of children playing but now they have all gone indoors. Mrs Grundy has been to the door calling their Dennis and Mr Barker, whistling for whichever little Barker hadn't returned home.

I suppose I should be glad that I have the table to myself now that it's not spread with Margaret's sewing. At night I have the bed to myself and can sleep on the outside, the inside or slide into the middle.

LATER

So strange that as I was feeling lonely and wishing Margaret was here, she arrived. I felt so happy to see her. She had a surprise for me, and came in all smiles, carrying a brown-paper package tied with string. I placed it on the table and she watched me untie it, interrupting when I tried to hurry and use the scissors because she said all the bows and knots could be undone and the string saved.

She has made me a motoring hat, the colour of bluebells, with a generous amount of material in the scarf. I put it on and she tied a bow under my chin and held up the glass. The scarf drapes beautifully. Then she helped me on with my old blue jacket, which she has altered. The shiny pearl buttons, dark pleat and new collar make it look new. I didn't try on the skirt but the pleat on the hem brightens it up well enough. What's more, she has patched the tear so carefully you cannot see the mend unless you look for it.

She asked am I all right on my own, with Dad on his night job, because, if not, I could come to the Dragon. I told her I am just fine. I almost told her about seeing Dad in the cellar with the noose and my fears for him. She was waiting for me to say something else, but I know she's happy to be at the Dragon and I don't want to spoil it for her.

I hung my skirt and jacket on the back of the bedroom door so that it wouldn't crease. It looks almost like a proper costume. Margaret said that her wardrobe at the Dragon has plenty of space and that she is sure Dad would be glad for me to move in there. He could lodge with Aunty Amy now that her lodger, Dorothy, has moved out to get married.

'Stop going on!' I told her. 'We're managing.'

She took my hand. 'Come on! Back downstairs.'

At the table, she plunged my hands, which were rough from cleaning old Mrs Fischer's stair rods, into a bowl of cucumber water. 'I want you to stop skivvying. Mam would be furious if she knew.'

'Mam always worked hard,' I said, miffed.

'Yes. Baking sausage rolls, helping Dad, dress-making. You're letting us down, Julia. You won't ever make anything of yourself with a scrubbing brush in your hands.'

The best thing about her visit was that we came up with a Wood Sisters plan to make our own hand cream using lanolin and whatever we can get through Aunty Amy to make it sweet-smelling and posh. Of course, our only trouble is that round here no one has much money to buy anything fancy, but we keep the price low and summat's better than nowt.

One moment Margaret is full of confidence and bossy ideas, the next moment she can collapse into a great misery. The collapse came as she finished manicuring my hands: 'Thomas will be going back to work on a newspaper in London. He's been offered a job. His mother says he may even go abroad. You know he covered some war or other for a newspaper a couple of years back.'

I hadn't known. 'Did Thomas say for sure that he'll be going away?'

'He mentioned something. And then Mrs Turner went on and on about good oppor-tunities.' She crossed her arms on the kitchen table and leaned forward as if she had a pain in her stomach. 'I think it's because of me. I'm not good enough for her, Julia. I can't bear to be looked down on. And not just me. Us.'

I knew what she meant. Dad. His foreignness, and because he is a Jew. And Mam was Irish and we started out as Catholics before we turned into

111

heathens. Now we're nothing at all. Only ourselves.

'Of course, we live in the wrong place, too,' Margaret said. 'I know I've moved into the Dragon and that should chalk one up to me, but I'm not sure if it does in Mrs Turner's eye. If only Dad had been able to hold onto his butcher's shop. That would have given us a peg up.'

I tried to be encouraging, but I thought that Margaret could bring me motoring hats and costumes to fill a shop and Mrs Turner would still look down on us. I said, 'Thomas obviously likes you. If it matters that much that you're from the wrong family in the wrong street, he's not worth it.'

'He's not conventional, like Mrs Turner. He liked Dad.'

I waited to hear whether he had liked me, but she didn't say.

'Does he love me?' she asked. 'Does he care for me enough not to mind differences?'

I thought of the way Thomas had looked at her at the party. 'I'd say so. And I'd say you're good enough for him, or anyone.'

'I'm going to try and make him marry me.'

I must have looked alarmed because she added, 'Don't worry. I'm not stupid. I won't do anything daft.'

She has gone now and I feel so sad again. We are a funny little family and always have been. Not as hard-up as some other people on this street, but we have got this determination that we won't put up with poverty. We have had that feeling as long as I can remember, though it took a big blow when Mam died. What if we are kidding ourselves and never get the good luck or the chance to change things? You see so many people who think something will turn up, and it never does.

When Margaret left she took my precious copy of Shelley, as she intends to learn a couple of poems to recite if called upon. I offered to write out the shortest for her, 'A Hate-Song':

A Hater he came and sat by a ditch,
And he took an old cracked lute;
And he sang a song which was more of a screech
'Gainst a woman that was a brute.

I told her to recite 'A Hate-Song' and Thomas Turner would hear that my Tom Maguire sounds like Shakespeare by comparison. Margaret says I am very peculiar to make a love figure of a dead tubercular, socialist, photographer's assistant who wrote indifferent verses. She thought that wouldn't do at all and wanted something romantic and idealistic.

I walked her to the end of the street. She kissed me on the cheek and said, 'If I marry well, you will, too. I'll improve your chances, and make life easier for Dad.'

She turned and waved. I watched her walk along York Road, full of herself again and swinging her velvet bag. I wondered whether she loved Thomas. She had never said so.

What a shock I got when I saw the blind pulled down at Cissie's flat. I rushed in, expecting the worst. But it was Mr Garretty, killed in the mine.

He had been brought home on a cart, laid on the floor and covered with a sheet.

Mrs Garretty knelt on the floor beside him, counting out his wages, crying and blethering to his corpse, saying, 'Eh Dan, lad, it's the first time thah's ever tipped up thah wages.'

His workmates had taken a collection, too, so a lot of counting and re-counting went on. Coins arranged and re-arranged in piles. Sol and Sarah set out the coins one by one alongside Mr Garretty so that they ran the full length of him and round the top of his head. Baby Jimmy was given a penny to roll but he would chew it, which didn't seem to me a good idea. When they had grown tired of playing with the coins, Sol and Sarah perched on their haunches by the corpse, watching to see if he would come back to life and start thumping and cursing.

Sol answered a tap-tap on the door and a red-faced man came in unsteadily. 'I'm sorry for yer trouble, missis. We took a collection at Miners' Arms.'

He handed her the money and shuffled about till she thanked him and offered him a cup of tea. He shook his head. 'I won't trouble yer, missis. We – the Miners' Arms regulars – we just wanted yer to know.'

When he had gone, Mrs Garretty said, 'If the landlord of the Miners' Arms give me back half the brass poor Dan handed over, I'd be rich as a pawnbroker.'

Cissie whispered to me, 'Anyone'd think he'd been forced into supping and pissing his wages away.'

I asked had anyone sent for Aunty Amy, but Mrs Garretty hadn't. I said that I would go, just so as not to have to watch Sol and Sarah re-arrange the coins and create a complete frame for the corpse. But Cissie grabbed my hand and said, 'Don't go!' She seemed scared.

Sol and Sarah went instead.

When Aunty Amy came with her bundle, Mrs Garretty took the children outside. I expected her to come back, but she didn't.

Aunty Amy looked at me. 'Someone'll have to help me.'

I poured water from the kettle into the tin basin and added cold water from the tap. Aunty Amy had brought her own soap and cloths.

'I'll go find your mam,' I said to Cissie, and again she called to me not to go, but I pretended I didn't hear.

Mrs Garretty was in the courtyard downstairs, holding Baby Jimmy, surrounded by a group of ooh-ing and aah-ing neighbours. She came over to me and whispered, 'Tell Dan I'm sorry but I can't bring meself to lay him out.'

I looked across at the huddle of women, arms folded against their breasts. Mrs Garretty wrung her hands and gave me a pleading look. 'Don't ask them. I'd be that ashamed for 'em to know I can't see to me own man.'

I went back upstairs. Aunty Amy had washed Mr Garretty's hair. 'They should have fetched in the table for him,' she said. 'My poor knees.'

I answered her unspoken question about Mrs Garretty with a shake of my head. Cissie lay very still, staring at the wall, deliberately not looking in our direction.

Aunty Amy whispered to me, 'Thah'll have to help me.'

I didn't move. I had been taken to kiss Mam goodbye when she died, otherwise I have never touched a dead person.

'He can't hurt thee now,' Aunty Amy said.

She undid his shirt and held him up while I slipped it off him. Then she took a cloth and began to wash the coal dust from his skin. Aunty Amy washed his face, tracing the cloth along the deep lines that ran from his nose to his mouth. Things always seem more terrible in my thoughts than in life. I washed his arms and hands, lathering up his shaving brush to try and get his hands clean and the grit from under his nails. Thinking about the dirt on his hands made it seem less scary. It took a long while to get him something like clean. It no longer seemed like Mr Garretty, even when we had finished and he lay there wearing a newly ironed shirt that smelled of scorch from the iron, pennies on his eyes, hands folded on his chest.

We washed our hands. Aunty Amy said, 'I'm sorry you had to do that, lass. But it'll stand you in good stead.'

I had forgotten about Cissie, lying there, watching now. A movement from her chair made me turn round. Cissie was trying to stand. 'Help me, Julia.'

Aunty Amy gave me a quick look and said to Cissie, 'Stay put, lass. Don't strain thissen.'

But Cissie would come over and so we helped her, Aunty Amy on one side and me on the other.

Cissie looked down at her dad, and then spat on his face.

In her shock, Aunty Amy let go of Cissie. 'Show respect for the dead!'

But Cissie just said, 'You don't know.'

I helped Cissie back to her chair.

Now I am home in bed, writing in almost-darkness. Essie Garretty lies in Margaret's place. At the bottom of my bed, Sol's by the wall and Sarah on the outside, having all come back to spend the night. Gregory, although he has left school and thinks of himself as the big boy who can look after himself, has gone to Aunty Amy's. Only Mrs Garretty, Cissie and Baby Jimmy are in the flat with Mr Garretty. I'm sure that Cissie will not sleep at all. Aunty Amy says that Baby Jimmy is not long for this world.

Cissie said that some day she would tell me why she hated her dad more than the 'normal sort of hate'.

EIGHTEEN

Dad tired out, so Frank pushing the cart.

Frank huffy. Very huffy. Says he is sorry Mr Garretty died but what was Mr Garretty to me that I couldn't come and meet him last night as arranged, or even bother to send word?

I told him that Cissie is my best friend and meeting him just went right out of my head.

That got him even huffier. He says in all these

years he has only ever missed two Sundays coming out with me and Dad and pushing the handcart, but I think nothing of leaving him standing by the Corn Exchange like a wheel that wants greasing. Everyone comes before him in my regard, he says, including Mr Garretty, who I never had a good word to say about.

All this goes on in a big whisper, as if Dad's not supposed to know we've fallen out.

Big baby! I told him me and Dad do not need him to come out with us, and that I am sorry I left him standing there but he is not the centre of the world. He opened his mouth to speak but no words came out; we just stood there and looked at each other. Then he turned and marched off. I nearly called after him but stopped myself. I just don't like the way he tries to pin me down. He tries to make everything so definite and unchangeable.

He thought better of it and caught us up on Recovery Street to push the cart, but didn't speak to me, only to Dad.

When we got home, Dad said, 'Maybe it is time to give up the pie round.'

I would love to give it up, especially now we are using horse meat. But we need the money.

Dad said I should move into the Dragon with Margaret and he would lodge somewhere. This made me see red. Something inside me snapped. I yelled and yelled at him. All these years we have kept going and now he wants to give up.

He said that it is not giving up. Things change.

I said that we can't give up now. Frank would think he had got the better of us. Dad looked as

118

if he wanted to argue, but didn't.

But I was thinking of the rope, tied to the beam in the cellar. I was thinking of him lodging in some strange place, without me.

All the Garrettys except Cissie were at the funeral for Mr Garretty and Baby Jimmy, who died the day after his dad. I sat with Cissie on her balcony, looking down onto the street, watching the hawkers and the carts go by. I started to brush her hair. We felt so sad about little Jimmy. Cissie had an upset and strange feeling. She had always pictured her dad at *her* funeral, looking down and fighting back tears and feeling very sorry not to have been more kind to her. Now he has gone before, and that feels like a big cheat. She wants to yell at him, and wishes she had yelled at him, but only ever did it inside her head because of not wanting a thump or a thick ear. When I asked what it was she had been going to tell me, she just looked away and said that I was lucky to have a dad who loved me. She did not even like the thought of Baby Jimmy being in the same grave. She might have said more but a voice called up to us from the street. Frank. Cissie waved him to come up.

It was his dinner break. 'I thought thah'd be here,' he said to me. He said sorry about our falling out, and how miserable he had been. He thinks of me all the time. He told me and Cissie to close our eyes and open our mouths. Then he popped a piece of chocolate into my mouth. Poor Cissie still sat with her mouth open and her eyes closed, and he popped a piece of chocolate into

119

her mouth, too.

He took my hand and held my fingers to his lips, kissing each finger in turn, then put the rest of the chocolate in my hand and turned to go, saying, 'I have to get back or I'll be late.'

'Don't you want some chocolate?' I asked.

'All I wanted were to see thee, Julia.' Then he whispered, 'I'd meant to kiss you but I didn't dare.'

Cissie thought it was more romantic than anything in a book. 'He loves thee. That's obvious.'

'I don't love him,' I said quietly.

We watched him as he got to the end of the street. He turned and waved. 'Poor Frank,' Cissie said. 'Thah going to break his heart.'

I didn't ask him to be in love with me. To be in love, you have to be able to see yourself going on through life together. I don't see myself being with Frank. I don't see it at all.

I thought I had better tell him straight away and so went to meet him after work. But then I realized that if I met him, he'd take it the wrong way. He has helped us so much, I feel obliged to him, and it makes it very awkward.

On Saturday, very early – Dad had got home from work and gone up to my bed, done in and his eyes half-shut with sleep – I'd just tied my pinafore and tipped flour into the bowl, when Frank came to the door. He was on his way to work and wanted me to come as far as the market. He had something to show me and wouldn't say what, but it was urgent. Wrongly guessing it was something to do with cheap flour or a cut of meat, I took off my pinafore and picked up my shawl, determined that at some point on the way to the market I'd tell him the truth.

At first when he pointed, I didn't know what I was supposed to be looking at. A row of horses and carts jostled for places by the kerb, some carters delivering to the market, others coming to buy.

Then I saw him. The lad struggled with a sack of potatoes, tottering as he half-ran to Mrs Walsh's handcart and dropped his burden.

'He'd blow away in a strong wind. Isn't that what thah said?'

The lad had a sack of his own that he kept an eye on. After he pocketed the coin Mrs Walsh gave him, he picked up a few loose cabbage leaves and a stray spud and put them in his sack.

'He's scabby an' all, like thah said. Only I haven't seen him loiterin' with the other two beggars who attacked thee and thah dad. I didn't want to give him a thrashing needless, like.'

When I didn't answer, Frank strode over to the lad and spoke to him. The lad looked across and saw me. Frank marched him towards me. He had a gaunt, hungry face and wore a floppy old check cap. Frank pulled off the cap. Scabby Lad's lank straight hair fell over his face. 'Push the hair out yer eyes,' Frank ordered. Scabby Lad trembled. Frank gave him a shove. 'Says his name's Harold Wragg and he lives on Mushroom Street. This him?'

It felt uncanny that of all the runtish, half-starved lads, Frank should pick on the very one. The lad put the back of his hand to his nose as if it might start to bleed. I looked at the fresh scabs on his face. One of them opened and bled a little.

I shook my head. 'No. It's not him.'

As we turned away from the boy, I said to Frank, 'I don't want you to beat people up for me. I know you mean well.'

He started to answer me, but I stopped him. I said, 'And I don't love you, Frank. I thought I'd best say.'

For a minute he was quiet and in the deafening noise of the carts and the shouts of the market workers I only just caught his words when he did speak. 'I know that. But I love thee enough not to mind, like. And I know you'll come to love me in time.'

He didn't wait for me to contradict him, just kissed me on the cheek and hurried away to work.

NINETEEN

I have a new place to sit and write, and perhaps it marks a huge change in my whole life. I am in Aunty Amy's shop, sitting behind the counter on a tall stool. I have always liked this shop, though it used to scare me a little when I was small. With the blinds down it seemed dark and threatening, because the shelves against the wall go all the way to the ceiling and are stacked with hundreds of jars in different sizes, all with labels neatly written in tiny script.

For a house-shop it is well fitted out, with a fumed oak counter. In the window there's a special display of Wood Sisters Beer Shampoo,

Wood Sisters Rosemary Rinse and Wood Sisters Mystery Hand and Body Cream (whatever herb we can get our hands on mixed with sheep fat and water). The drawers are labelled in Aunty Amy's small, bold writing, the ink brown and faded. Aunty Amy has been writing neat labels since she was a young woman. Now her writing seems less definite and more shaky.

Bunches of herbs hang upside-down from the shop ceiling, some with paper bags attached to catch the florets. The lavender is special for me. Mam had lavender-scented talcum powder and I still keep the empty container. Aunty Amy had introduced me to the herbs long ago, as if they were people – 'This is rosemary. Sage, parsley, rue.' But she introduced me again today as I could not remember which name went with which herb, like when you start school and hear the children's names but don't know who is who, except for the person sitting next to you. Miss Lavender.

Being the end house, hers is bigger than ours. Of course, I know this house almost as well as my own. You go through the shop to the downstairs room at the back, her kitchen-cum-parlour. She has a big, velvety sofa, given to her by a grateful customer whose ringworm she cured. Between the shop and the downstairs room, the stone staircase goes up on the left. We always have booby traps halfway up our stairs: an Oxo tin; black leading; a pair of old boots. Aunty Amy's steps are clear. She says that at her age it would be too easy to trip and come a cropper. On the opposite wall from the shop counter is a tall, glass-fronted cabinet, full of books. I have been reading a leather-bound book about herbs and wild flowers, leafing through, looking at the illustrations. Already I have helped her today, making the dandelion and burdock drink, which she sells at a penny and in this warm weather goes very well.

But I need to put this down in order. Dad, Aunty Amy and I had been invited to Sunday dinner at the Dragon, along with Miss Mason. Margaret was there already, of course. Uncle welcomed us at the door. He wore his brown suit and brown brogues polished to perfection. Dad says when you look at a person's shoes, you see their place in life and attitude to it. Life has treated Uncle well, and he expects it to go on doing so. Dad had polished his boots, too, and wore his blue knitted tie. I had worried in case Dad felt bad about Margaret moving out, and especially since it might seem that Dad cannot provide for her. I need not have worried. Dad was all right about it and seems glad that Margaret has chosen to stay at the Dragon, as at one time we thought she would move in with Miss Mason. She is with family, Dad says, and she has a new horizon.

Anyhow, this Sunday dinner event came about because Margaret wanted to show off her room. She'd always wanted her own bed. Now she has a bedroom with two single beds. This room was sometimes rented out to commercial travellers and has been newly decorated in silver-striped and rose-patterned wallpaper, with new dusky tapestry curtains on wooden rails with loops. Margaret pointed out that the colours bring out the pinky wavy lines that thread through the grey and black in the marble of her fireplace. She has filled the mantleshelf with ornaments: a china retriever dog; two china tortoiseshell cats; a crinoline lady; and a trinket box that won't close because it's crammed with all our dead Aunty Mary's paste jewellery. Margaret whispered to me that Aunty Mary's best jewellery is in Uncle's safe, and something may come to us or not, depending on how much goes to our cousins' wives when they marry. (I hardly remember our aunty, so feel only a little bit sorry that she is no longer around to enjoy her own jewellery.)

Margaret keeps her collection of thimbles in the carved cedarwood box on her chest of drawers, in front of her miniature cheval mirror. (I suppose one advantage of being out of Bread Street is that her things are not at risk of being pawned or sold.) A china dish, decorated with roses and filled with rose petals, sits beside the mirror.

She had begun work on a tapestry wall-hanging: a medieval pastoral scene. This was draped on a stand in front of the fireplace. Miss Mason went around the room, clapping her hands and exclaiming, 'My, my!' and 'What an exemplary model of style!' over everything.

Aunty Amy and I were supposed to make the same kind of fuss, but Aunty Amy would not make a fuss if the roof fell in. She said, 'In my young day, bedrooms were for sleeping in, if thah was fortunate enough to get any sleep and lucky enough to have a bed.'

I laughed but Margaret beamed pityingly at Aunty Amy, as if to say that this was our day now,

125

and Aunty Amy's day was gone. She turned to me. 'That spare bed's yours if you want it. There's an empty drawer in the dressing table and space in the wardrobe.'

She doesn't give up easily! The bed did look inviting, with a clean embroidered counterpane, smoothly tucked around the pillow. But she knows I won't leave Dad. One of us has to stay with him.

Aunty Amy and me left Margaret and Miss Mason discussing the tapestry wall-hanging and the best shades of green wool for the forest.

I took Aunty Amy out to the stable, to see Solomon. Charley was with him, and Solomon had a bandage on his hind leg.

Charley is a tiny man with a wispy beard. He holds himself very straight and tall. He has a creased-up little face and wears lots of clothes, winter or summer. He once confided in me why he has a beard. As a young man he worked as a carter for the railroad, transporting goods from the station to their destination. A horse kicked him and left a scar on his chin. The beard is to hide his scar. The smell off Charley can be strong, but he's good with Solomon and so I am fond of him. He told us that Solomon had slipped on cobbles by the brewery, where some fool had spilt beer.

Aunty Amy bent down to look at Solomon's hind leg. He lifted it for her, as if he knew she meant well. She unwrapped the bandage carefully and probed gently. 'I think he's pulled the cruciate ligament. Painful. I have that problem meself sometimes.'

She sent me back to the shop for a preparation

126

she had made for herself. I ran all the way there and back. Poor Solomon.

Solomon stood very still, his hurt hind leg raised, while I gently massaged the oil above, below and around the sore place. I will note the remedy here, in case I need it in the future:

Rubbing oil – people or animals.

Uses: for calluses, painful joints and swellings.

Steep one ounce of dried camomile flowers in olive oil for twenty-four hours.

Strain before using.

Uncle came out to see. I'll say this for Uncle, he will never work a lame horse, so I hope to see Solomon on the mend soon.

Aunty Amy and me sat on the bench in the yard, looking across at Solomon, who looked across at us. Not much sun comes into the yard. I realized how cleverly Charley had placed the bench, as we were sitting in the last patch of evening sunlight.

Aunty Amy said, 'You know I've always done my best to look out for you two girls, since your mam died.'

'I know.'

'You could do worse than join Margaret here. Your dad'd be pleased to see you set up well.' When I groaned at her instead of answering, she said, 'I thought not.' After a long time, she put her bony hand on mine. 'When your mam died, your Margaret asked who would do her hair. You asked how you'd be fixed, without Mam dressmaking and baking sausage rolls.'

'I don't remember.'

'No. I didn't think so. But you see, yon was always set on turning herself into a lady, and thah were never scared by hard work.'

'She's going to marry well,' I said. 'That's her plan.'

'And thee?' Aunty Amy asked. 'What's thah plan?'

'To look after Dad.'

'Look, lass, thah's blowing with the wind, nay, blowing with the breeze. Doing too much and going nowhere.'

That's when she asked me to come and work with her. I said that I don't want to help her lay out the dead, and I won't help her deliver babies. She laughed and said she hoped I wouldn't. It's in the shop with the remedies and the drinks that I could help her.

So now I am sitting at Aunty Amy's counter, waiting for customers, and hoping that I don't give out the wrong items.

One more thing I must set down, about Margaret.

The reason she invited us on Sunday was not just to show off her room. After tea, she got me on my own for a few minutes in the kitchen while Aunty Amy and Miss Mason chatted over second and third cups of tea, sitting on the bench in the yard. Uncle had gone into the bar, and Dad with him.

Margaret seemed glad when I mentioned Thomas's name. I did it jokingly really. He had written an article about Margaret, 'the milliner suffragette', which I had read aloud to everyone before tea. I picked up the article and said that

I'd like to keep a copy of it.

Margaret burst into tears and ran upstairs. I followed her. We went in her room and she shut the door behind us, standing with her back to it. 'I only organized today because I'd intended to ask Thomas and Mrs Turner for tea.'

'Couldn't they come?'

'I didn't pluck up the courage to ask.' Margaret pulled a lace hanky from her sleeve, dabbing at her eyes. 'I almost invited the whole group – the Misses Reeves, Mrs Walsh, Jean and everyone – thinking that would be one way of doing it. But Uncle doesn't agree with women having the vote so I thought it might be a disaster.'

'Is that why you didn't ask Mrs Turner and Thomas?'

'I didn't ask because I'm afraid she would have refused. She could see me working up to it, she's clever like that. She knew I was about to ask her something personal and put me off asking.'

'How?'

'Women like her can do that. Let you know that they're deliberately changing the subject. She won't accept me, Julia. I know she won't.'

'What about Thomas? Isn't it up to him?'

'I think he cares for me. But perhaps I'm just a novelty. *The milliner suffragette.*'

'Do you love him?'

'I don't know if I can let myself love him. I don't want to make an idiot of myself.'

'Does he loves you?'

'I thought so, but honestly I just don't know anything any more.'

'I thought you were hoping to marry him.'

'Not if his mother can help it. Some London friend of the family, a top newspaper man, has got him an assignment in Paris. He's bound to meet some French girl. I'm sure Mrs Turner arranged it because she knows he likes me and I'm not good enough.'

'Of course he likes you! If she'd seen you two dancing together, she'd give up on sending him to Paris, or anywhere else. And you're more than good enough.'

That seemed to cheer her up. She smiled and threw her shoulders back. 'You're right. He's promised to write to me every day.'

We didn't have time to talk much more about it after that, because Miss Mason came up to say that she was leaving.

I have been thinking it over. I'm sure Margaret's right. Mrs Turner won't accept her as a daughter-in-law, even though she's moved from Bread Street to the George & Dragon. In Mrs Turner's book a publican's niece will be no better than a butcher's daughter. No matter how well-decorated that girl's bedroom is!

I am picking up my pencil again after a visit to the shop from Margaret, who stood at the far side of the shop grinning and waving envelopes at me while I was serving a ha'penny drink. She has had two letters from Thomas, one written before he left London, and another from Paris. She got very mysterious and would only say that they contain endearments. That made me very annoyed. Endearments. She should tell me what he says or shut up about it.

TWENTY

I carried Cissie's chair onto the balcony. She was that happy, watching folk walking along the street and seeing their shadows, like a child seeing a shadow for the first time.

She asked me what dress I will wear when I marry. Will I invite a chimney sweep to the wedding for luck? Will I have a boy first or a girl? She asked how I will look after my first baby if it gets sick. Then she turned spiteful and said what will I do when I have too many mouths to feed and no money and Frank gets drunk, calls me a fat lazy cow and kicks me about.

That was when I told her I couldn't see myself walking up the aisle with Frank and staying round here. Then she changed her tune and spoke up for him, saying he'd never hurt me, that he loves my bones. I said if I had one drudgy self that could marry Frank and not mind the course my life would take, working my fingers to the bone, shopping, cooking, cleaning, having babies, I might just take a chance on doing that. But only if I had another self that I could send off into the world to do great things and have adventures. She started to cry, saying that she'd like a life of working, shopping, cooking, cleaning and having babies, and never will.

I got her off the topic by telling her one of our stories:

131

Cissie Garretty and Julia Wood sail down the Nile on a barge rowed by twenty-four young men. Twelve worship Cissie and twelve adore Julia. At each stop, on the way down the Nile, Cissie and Julia take turns to set a task for the young men to fulful. Task one: scale the steep and slippery golden pyramid. Twelve of them succeed and twelve fail. At the second stop they must fetch a glass of creamy milk from the two-headed ass on the other side of the quicksand. Six succeed, six fail. At the third stop they must slay the many-headed serpent. Four succeed and two fail. Finally they must rescue the bewitched, saucer-eyed cat from the land of portly, boil-ridden giants. All succeed. Cissie and Julia must judge the young men's performances on agility, good grace, eagerness and handsome visage, and bestow favours accordingly. The grief-stricken, unchosen suitors fall on their swords, pine away, jump in the Nile with a pyramid slab tied to their waists, or leap onto a funeral pyre.

She said I'd missed a bit. The part where one of the suitors slips on the glass pyramid and breaks his ankle. He would be the one I loved. I told her she was being silly. She said I'd only been happy with Frank when he was a scruffy lad coming round with us for a free pie. Now he was his own man, he scared me. I told her she was being ridiculous, but she wouldn't stop going on.

In the end it turned cold. Her mam and me helped her back inside and hauled the chair in from the balcony. As I got up to go, she pulled me back. Her fingers are so thin now they felt like claws on my arm. 'Promise,' she said, 'promise you won't go off adventuring and forget about our Gregory, Sol, Sarah and Essie. Mam's never managed that well. Mine's a bad enough way to die, but I can't bear to think of our bairns dying of hunger.'

'They won't,' I said. 'Not while I'm here and can do something about it.'

'But will you be here?' She wouldn't let go.

'I'll see them through, Cissie. I promise.'

She shut her eyes then, seeming very tired, and her fingers slid from my arm. I picked up her hand and placed under the thin blanket, as she didn't seem to have the strength to move.

I hope this promise only binds me to her lot for their childhood. I don't want to spend the rest of my life being responsible for the Garretty clan.

Utterly beside myself with rage. Cannot believe even Frank Whitelock would stoop so low, especially after coming round this morning and saying he would like me and Dad to have a rest today, because of me starting the job with Aunty Amy and Dad looking done in. This last he said in a whisper. But it's true. Dad and me both appreciated the offer.

Frank said he and his brother would take the handcart out and sell the pies for us.

I waited for him to come back.

One o'clock, no Frank. Two o'clock, no Frank. Three o'clock, no Frank.

I heard his footsteps, but slow for once and no rattle of the handcart.

133

He stood on our doorstep, looking at his boots and did not offer to come in. 'I will make it up to thee, Julia, I promise,' he said.

'Make what up to me?'

It turns out that after he sold all the pies he had the good idea to treble the money for us because of our troubles. He put it on a dog called Bruiser that was sure to win its fight. But it did not. He knows I hate dog fights. I could not believe Frank's stupidity. What made him think the dog would win? He just stood there, shifting his weight from one foot to the other and polishing the toe of his boot on the back of his trousers.

'Someone must have got to that dog,' he said. 'Bruiser was a sure thing.'

When I asked him where was our handcart, he got all huffy and said that was definitely not his fault. His cousin Eric was supposed to be watching it and he doesn't know how it went missing.

I told him I did not believe him. That cart rattling along would wake the dead.

'Not if thah's caught up watching a dog fight,' he said.

That made me hear the horrible noise of hurt animals and violent, greedy men goading the dogs to tear into each other.

I just looked at Frank standing there, running stubby, nail-bitten fingers through his nondescript hair. It was as if I was seeing him for the first time. His brow, between hairline and eyebrows, is narrow. Uncle said that is a sign of low intelligence. Frank's eyebrows are close together with a fine line of hair joining them. Margaret said that is the sign of a violent man. I should never have been friends with him, but when we met at the age of five I did not notice such things. Besides he sometimes has such a graceful way about him that you forget his imperfections. But today I noticed everything, seeing him in his true light.

'I'm sorry,' he said, and he really did look sorry. His mouth turned down. 'I'll mek it up to thee.'

'Sorry's no good,' I said. I shut the door in his face.

Dad is too kind and forgiving. He said it is bad, but Frank is young and young men do silly things. He said that because we would not finish with the pies, the pies had finished with us. This was Fate speaking.

TWENTY-ONE

At last! I am on a train bound for London and my writing is too scrawly for words. Our luggage was taken into the van by porters and we brought only a basket with some provisions into the carriage. The most exciting moment for me, so far, was waving to Bernard. For years, I have looked through the Dragon sitting-room window, waving to people on the train, and now I am the person on the train. I had arranged with Bernard to be in the window seat as we passed. Margaret waved, too, and even Mrs Turner joined in after I explained that I had always wished to be the one on the train, flying past the window, faster than a smile.

I would be very disappointed if there was an appalling accident, say a bridge freakishly collapsed on our carriage, or something like that, and we were tragically killed in the spring of our years (at least, Margaret and I would be in the spring; Mrs Turner must be about forty-five, as Thomas is twenty-three). But if I die today, I will have achieved one of my ambitions: to be the person on the train waving to the person on the window seat. I wonder how Bernard felt as he watched us hurtle past. Did he feel a longing inside, mixed with sorrow, sadness and envy, as he caught a glimpse of us just for a few seconds? Of course, he won't wonder too much about our lives, as he knows who we are and where and why we are going. But he has no idea what it will be like. No more do I.

I will stop writing, gobble up the view from the carriage window and experience the adventure of a journey to London.

I have not had time to write until now and must make myself begin at the beginning or it will make no sense, but I do not think I will get a moment's sleep tonight after what I have just overheard.

Margaret's speaking engagement at the Votes for Women Rally in the East End of London was arranged many months ago. (Had it not been, I think Mrs Turner would have tried to get out of it.) We came from the railway station yesterday, by hansom cab, to a tall house on a square with quite a large area of greenery in the centre of the square – well-trimmed grass and lilac trees, the paths set with park benches, the whole surrounded by wrought-iron fencing and gates. The house itself has high rooms and old but good furniture. Margaret thought the furniture a little too old and if she had such a house, she would go for new. The owner was not at home but we were welcomed by servants. Margaret and I were shown to a room on the second floor, with two long windows that overlook the square. Mrs Turner is on the first floor, immediately below us.

Yesterday evening we went for a walk about the area, admiring the houses and listening to the chatter of the servants, who all seem to live below ground and sit about on stone steps, gossiping and ogling passers-by. The Londoners do speak funny, though we heard a few northern and Scottish voices coming up from basements and chatting on street corners.

This morning we saw Buckingham Palace and the Houses of Parliament. It was so exciting to see places that I have only ever seen in books, though none of it felt real. I think for a place to feel real, you have to know something about the people who live there and whether they have had a good breakfast or haven't eaten for days and what they do when they get up in the morning.

Margaret was a huge success at the meeting tonight. I see now why she was invited. There was another girl from a humble background who spoke, a young woman who had worked in the cotton mills in Lancashire. I got the impression that the main point of the meeting was to discuss the division between people who want to promote the vote for women and those who say that it must be for all – for the working classes, men and women. Someone like Margaret and the Lancashire girl seem to be able to argue both ends against the middle. Margaret pulled off a great trick, which even Mrs Turner hadn't expected. Until the last minute she did not know whether to do it but I said yes, because when Margaret sings, does she sing! Her song was written by an American woman called Charlotte Perkins Gilman. And Margaret says that when she marries, if she has a girl, she will call her Charlotte. I can't remember every verse but it went:

Said the Socialist to the Suffragist:
'My cause is greater than yours!
You only work for a Special Class,
We for the gain of the General Mass,
Which every good ensures!'

Said the Suffragist to the Socialist:
'You underrate my Cause!
While women remain a Subject Class,
You never can move the General Mass,
With your Economic Laws!'

'A lifted world lifts women up,'
The Socialist explained.
'You cannot lift the world at all
While half of it is kept so small,'
The Suffragist maintained.

The world awoke, and tartly spoke:
'Your work is all the same:

Work together or work apart,
Work, each of you, with all your heart–
Just get into the game!'

I got the impression that speakers at these occasions do not usually sing. The audience went wild. I could just imagine Margaret on the stage, at the City Varieties. She could hold her own anywhere. She looked all around the audience, so that everyone felt she caught their eye. Only I knew that she was searching for Thomas, hoping he would come back from Paris and walk into the hall at the last moment. No such luck.

Mrs Turner looked so proud and clapped and clapped. I felt sure that any objections she might have to Margaret as a daughter-in-law must have disappeared in a cloud of admiration.

We met so many people that I shall have to set aside some time just to describe them all and what impression they made on me. I have asked Margaret to make a special effort to remember, so that between us we can capture the memory of the smart young women and the earnest young men with moustaches and bright eyes. I didn't notice the older people quite so much. Margaret was introduced to the famous Mrs Pankhurst, who complimented her on her singing. I was introduced too – 'and this is her sister' – but got not so much as a nod!

I have not set down my account of the meeting in as much detail as I would have liked. This is because the most extraordinary thing happened after we got home.

The man of the house, Mr Mitchell, came from

139

his study to greet us, and shake hands all round. He seemed familiar, though could not have been. Even if he had been to Leeds, I'm sure he is too high-class for the Dragon. I wondered whether he was famous and I had seen his picture somewhere. He is fair, though his hair is receding, and has a moustache and small beard, not unlike the King's. Perhaps that's why he was familiar. He did seem a little 'royal' in his courtesy and his insistence that we have some cowslip wine, which was very sweet. I could have drunk a lot more if it had been offered. (Actually, it was offered, but Margaret declined for me, saying we had had quite enough.) He listened to Mrs Turner's account of Margaret's triumph, his head a little on one side, his mouth amused (what I could see of it under the moustache) and a twinkle in his eye. 'You don't change, my dear,' he said to Mrs Turner. 'Still the enthusiast.'

For some reason this seemed to upset her. She took a deep breath and I thought she was going to launch into a speech, but she said very softly, 'You look at me beside two beautiful young girls and you say that I don't change!'

He looked away and stood up. That's when he offered more wine and Margaret said that she was tired and we would go upstairs if they'd excuse us.

Of course, I wasn't a bit tired. She manages to sleep whether she's tired or not.

We came upstairs together. I wanted to talk, but Margaret was in bed in a trice and fast asleep. I decided to write this journal, and that's when I realized I didn't have it in the room. I had gone out to sit in the square earlier, intending to try and sketch the house. John Ruskin says you never truly see a thing unless you try to draw it. But I spent so much time watching the people who came and went in the square that I didn't write or draw a thing. When I came back inside I put my journal on the hall table.

I could have left it there till morning but I had a fear of someone, Mrs Turner to be truthful, picking it up and reading it. It strikes me as the kind of thing she would do. That's why I tip-toed downstairs to retrieve it.

At the bottom of the stairs, I could see my journal. I could also hear Mrs Turner and our host having an argument. The drawing-room door was open a little. Could I get past and retrieve my book without attracting attention? The trouble with a strange house is that you don't know which bits of the floor might creak and groan. At home, with stone stairs and stone floors, nothing creaks and groans. Our house just tries to murder you with the cold sometimes but doesn't have much to say for itself except in the rattling window, squeaking door and wind down the chimney department.

I didn't hear what they said as I tip-toed towards the table for my book. They were having the kind of argument where they moved around the room. By the time I wanted to get back upstairs they seemed dangerously near the door. I stayed beside the umbrella stand, trying not to breathe too loudly.

'I blame you for his politics,' Mr Mitchell said.

She said, 'How dare you blame me for anything? You paid for the liberal education, blame that. Who wanted to send him to a Quaker school?'

'Huh!' he said. 'You could have something to say had I not paid his school fees. Anyway, have you forgotten? We chose the school together.'

For a moment they went quiet. Mrs Turner said, in a tired voice, 'He seems to be finding his way. I don't want to quarrel.'

They were talking about Thomas. Mrs Turner has a certain tone to her voice when she talks about him. It has made me dislike her less, because I hear the love. It is like when Dad talks to one of us about the other.

Mr Mitchell said, 'I'd like to see him settled properly. He could get a job with one of the national newspapers.'

'Yours, you mean!' There was something like scorn in her voice. Or perhaps it was spite. It can be hard to tell what an emotion is when you don't see a person's face. She said, 'You want him now. Now that he's grown-up.'

He must have gone close to her. His voice seemed to come from the same part of the room. This was my chance to get back to the bottom of the stairs without being noticed.

'Constance, we want the best for him. Freelancing's no good for a career. If you want him with you, and that's where he wants to be, let me get him onto a northern newspaper. All I need do is pick up the telephone–'

'Career, career. He won't have a career if he marries badly.'

'What do you mean?' he said.

'There's something else,' Mrs Turner said. 'That's why I don't want to fall out. Something you can do.'

142

His voice was very soft now. 'I'll do whatever I can. You know that.'

I waited at the bottom of the stairs. I know that it is considered disgraceful to eavesdrop and that ear-wiggers never hear anything good about themselves, but in my opinion it would be more of a disgrace not to find out something that could affect your sister's future happiness.

I heard the chink of glass and a drink being poured.

Mrs Turner said, 'He's in love. And this *is* my fault. I introduced them. He's in love with Margaret.'

The notebook slipped from my hand but fell onto my foot and did not make much of a noise, though it made me jump. When I heard him laugh, I almost gave myself away. He let out a loud cackle.

'Constance, Constance, my love! You are not telling me that he's in love with a singing suffragette milliner?'

Mrs Turner's voice was flat, with no emotion, like someone defeated before she has begun. 'The daughter of a slaughterhouse man.'

I wanted to interrupt and tell them that Dad was really a butcher and had once had his own shop and could read and write Hebrew and speak three languages: German, Yiddish and English.

Mrs Turner added, 'She's a lovely girl. But not suitable. He needs the right kind of wife.'

'Of course he does, my dear. Leave it to me. When he comes back from Paris, I shall arrange for him to be swept off his feet by the most suitable girls in London.'

I can't tell Margaret what I overheard. It would upset her too much.

She is sleeping peacefully, and smiling in her dreams.

TWENTY-TWO

On the journey back, Mrs Turner and Margaret chatted away. I could not bring myself to join in, knowing that Mrs Turner was so treacherous.

I was dusting jars in the shop. Aunty Amy flicked through one of her books, looking for a remedy. When she had noted the page, I told her what had been said about Margaret being an unsuitable match. I asked what she thought I should do.

'Leave well alone,' she said, then asked, 'What's he like, this top chap, this newspaper owner of Mrs Turner's?'

'Thomas's godfather? You'd think him very pleasant if you met him.'

Aunty Amy laughed. 'I wouldn't meet him though, would I? Because he'd never meet me. What's he look like?'

'Like...' I hesitated. 'He looks like Thomas but older and with a beard like the King's.'

Aunty Amy corrected me saying that the correct way of saying it is to say that the younger man looks like the older man, not the other way around, then she asked me to get the stepladder. She pointed to the red clover flowers that hung from a hook in the ceiling. 'Can you reach? My shoulder's giving me gyp today.'

'You don't seem very interested in this topic,' I said as I climbed the ladder and unhooked the red clover.

'Oh, I am.' She took the clover from me. 'It's just that I need to be on with an ointment for a lady who has lymphatic swellings.'

As I put the ladder away, she asked me what else I'd heard. She said we might as well know what we were up against. Interference wouldn't help, but having your guard up never hurts. That's when I told her the rest of the conversation I had overheard, and she asked me if I had heard the phrase, 'The wrong side of the blanket.'

I had but did not know what it meant.

Now I do. Much as I would like to tell Margaret, we decided it was better not to just at present because we could be wrong. Aunty Amy said that Margaret is 'guileless and appealing' (I laughed at that!) and to tell her our suspicions would be like deliberately pulling the thread from her needle.

The good thing is that Thomas has gone on writing to Margaret and looks forward to seeing her. But of course he would hardly inform her if he has been 'swept off his feet' by half a dozen suitable girls. Or, even worse, by one suitable girl.

The pot of red clover flowers simmered on the kitchen range. When the water had cooled I held the jug, a piece of muslin tied securely to its rim. Aunty Amy strained the flowers through the muslin. As we waited for the stuff to dry a little, I lit the gas ring and heated some water in a saucepan. I scooped sheep fat into the bowl, to melt above the saucepan. The amount of fat and the flower residue must be equal. When you have been doing it a little while it becomes easier to judge. I still can't judge. I had too much fat and needed to drain some into a smaller container. When it had melted, I took the wooden spoon and stirred in the red clover flowers.

I stirred the mixture for a good long while, then strained it into the jug, through the muslin, squeezing tightly to get as much of the mixture out as possible.

Aunty Amy gave me a fresh piece of muslin, which I placed over the clean jug, then wound the string tightly round the jug and knotted it, to make the muslin secure. Aunty Amy snipped it with the scissors. 'Has thah father been following't news in't papers?'

I felt myself go prickly and uncomfortable. Since Margaret had gone to the Dragon, reading the newspapers to him had become my job.

Aunty Amy asked me to look for jars in the cupboard. While I had my back to her, she said, 'I've known thah dad years and years, but I've never known, and maybe you don't – is he a British citizen?'

'He's German.'

'Some foreign folk they take on the nationhood of the land they live in.'

I found two clean jars and set them on the table.

'Some folk come into the country without the authorities knowing their names.' She took the lids from the jars. 'For such-like, it would be safer for them to be Belgian, at present. Unless their name is already on an official list.'

I had to concentrate very hard to keep my hands from shaking. I think what shocked me most was that Aunty Amy was coming at this through me. It made me realize that she knows how much I look out for my dad. He has a kind of helplessness about him these days, since the attack. She's saying to me that we have to watch out for him. Take care of him. How am I supposed to do that? I just hope nothing bad will happen in the world.

Margaret came round today.

There we sat, the three of us, like old times on a Sunday afternoon. I was sitting in the red circle in the middle of the hearth rug. Dad half-dozed in his chair.

Margaret took up most of the table, as she read the newspaper to Dad. At first I took no notice as I had got to the good part in *The Hand of Ethelberta,* where Picotee tells Ethelberta that she used to meet Mr Julian on the road. I am good at blotting everything out when I read, but today I couldn't. Margaret sometimes reads half to herself, almost as though Dad isn't there, and he can fall asleep easily as blink. Today she read differently. I kept losing my place. That's why I closed my book and listened to her.

She read about English children at school in Germany being ordered to leave. I wondered why English children go all the way to Germany to school in the first place. Dad said they would be the children of the ambassador and other officials.

147

She read about continental travellers tumbling over each other in the rush to return home. I pictured them clutching valises and holding onto their hats. A few Bank Holiday excursionists had set off across the Channel and had been turned back.

I asked who had turned them back. Margaret scanned the story, but it didn't say. She sipped at her water and said she had a frog in her throat. Dad kept saying, 'Go on.'

Margaret read about Prussian militarism and tyrannous intentions, Belgium integrity and French colonies.

The more she read, the less I understood.

She read that the newspaper editor 'hoped against hope' that there will not be a war.

Dad forgot to re-light his pipe. He took it from his mouth and said, 'Hope against hope. *Hoffnung gegen Hoffnung.*'

Margaret read something to herself, gave a little gasp and said, 'Poor Bernard.'

Dad opened his eyes. 'Cousin Bernard in the paper?'

Margaret folded the paper. She had had enough. Her voice was very quiet. 'Bernard isn't in the paper, no. But all ocean liners are being recalled. If they're in the middle of the ocean, they have to turn around and come back.'

This week Bernard was to have joined his liner, to start his job as a ship's piano player.

It's not that I don't know what the word means. But it's such a little word for such a big thing. War. In the wars. I've always been in the wars. Everyone round here is in the wars all the time.

So what does it mean? What will it mean? You go around telling yourself things will get better. War sounds too much like 'worse' to me. Just from a word point of view. War, worse. Peace, sense. I looked up war in the dictionary to see if it sounds the same in German. It doesn't. *Der Krieg.* Peace doesn't sound the same either. *Der Friede.* The fact that the words aren't even similar doesn't give me much *Hoffnung gegen Hoffnung.*

What a mess. School reports, birth certificates, marriage lines, Mam's funeral card, holy pictures, string, bits of candle, used gas mantles, old bills, a card from Dad's sister in New York dated 1909 — everything flung together in the box in the corner. A few nails, picture hooks, two stubby pencils and an old razor blade. Receipt for a mirror dated November 1905. More funeral cards and holy pictures.

Dad came in from his shift. I stopped and poured us both a cup of tea. He asked me what I had been looking for.

'Naturalization papers.'

He held his hands around the mug of tea. 'I like to have a daughter who look for things that do not exist. It is a good sign.'

TWENTY-THREE

If that suffragette meeting was politics, I'd rather skin a rabbit. You'd think with all her money, Mrs Turner would lay on an egg and cress sandwich. But I expect that's how rich people stay rich – by laying on weak tea and finger biscuits.

We were shown into the drawing room by Maisie, the maid. Margaret said that the style of the room is Moorish. There were richly coloured covers and cushions on the chairs and sofa – gold, amber, burnt orange – in geometric patterns. I sat on a dark-red leather pouffe tooled with gold, planting my feet on the Persian rug. Next to me, an inlaid octagonal table was set with a cedarwood box of Turkish cigarettes. I helped myself to a couple.

The Misses Reeves arrived soon after us. As we heard them come into the hall, Margaret whispered. 'They're school teachers and strict vegetarians. Don't talk about meat.'

Why would I talk about meat? She never stops telling me how to behave, as if I'm likely to disgrace her.

Because the elder Miss Reeves has a deformed spine, she curves forward. It gives the impression of her being very interested in whatever you have to say. The younger one angles herself forward as well, as if in sympathy.

Still no Mrs Turner.

The Misses Reeves are very good at keeping a conversation going. Margaret excels in that department, too, telling a story about how I once lost her favourite umbrella. Strange how her polite conversation so often revolves around me doing something wrong.

Jean arrived next, like a breath of fresh air. I love her hair – very dark, sleek and short. I liked the fact that her skirt and jacket looked crumpled as if she'd dropped them on the floor last night and just picked them up this morning. She carries herself with great style. Though she has lived in Leeds since the age of nine, her Scottish accent's thick as barm cake. She told a funny story about her boss reading the letters column in his newspaper and finding a letter from her – his typist – on the suffrage question.

One more person arrived, an extremely elegant, smiling lady of forty-something, expensively dressed and with beautifully manicured hands – Mrs Walsh. She snapped open a tapestry bag and pulled out a huge, mud-coloured piece of knitting, long enough to circle the earth three times and be back in time to trip you up before breakfast. I thought I was good at dropping stitches, but Mrs Walsh drops stitches like Bernard drops hints about his birthday – extravagantly, frequently, remorselessly.

Jean asked, 'What are you knitting, Mrs Walsh?'

Mrs Walsh dropped a few more stitches. 'A scarf. For the troops.'

Jean pulled an impressed face. 'Will it be shared by a whole regiment, or shall they cut it up between them?'

I laughed. Margaret stepped on my foot to shut me up.

Mrs Walsh said that war was no joking matter, clickety-clicking her needles.

Jean lit another cigarette. 'Surely it's not too late to stop it? It's madness. How many people will be killed?' She suddenly noticed the crumples in her skirt and tried to smooth it.

The older Miss Reeves leaned even further forward into the room. 'We can't let the Germans get away with it. They're the aggressors.'

Mrs Turner made a grand entrance at this point. She wore a red skirt, white silk blouse and blue embroidered waistcoat. She wears her hair piled high in elaborate rolls and had stuck little paper Union flags in her hair, the type children wave when there's a royal visitor.

Everyone in the room forgot their good manners and stared in amazement. Mrs Turner filled the doorway. 'So sorry to keep you waiting, ladies. Poor Thomas. Unwell.'

Margaret kept her composure. No one but me saw that she was agitated. Just for a moment she made fists of her hands, then relaxed again. She hadn't known Thomas was back.

Since Margaret and I had heard raised voices upstairs when we arrived, I didn't believe for one moment that poor Thomas was unwell. I wondered whether his not coming downstairs was connected with Margaret and whether he was reluctant to face her, perhaps having become attached to someone else.

Maisie sidled in behind Mrs Turner, carrying a tea tray.

Mrs Turner strode across the room, checked the weight of the teapot and started to pour. As the cups were passed round, she said, 'I have a proposal to make.' Teacups stopped clattering while everyone listened. 'I propose that we halt our suffrage actions for the duration of the national struggle. With the nation at war, in a battle of light against darkness, we must stand in the light and be counted.'

Jean's cup started to rattle against the saucer and she forgot to tip the long stretch of ash from her cigarette. 'We canna give up our fight for the vote. Not after all these years, all our hard work. Why should we stop, because governments run by old men decide that young men have to go out and kill one another? We women must hold our tongues?'

The older Miss Reeves said, 'We must defend our future, Jean, my dear.'

The younger Miss Reeves put an arm around Jean, but in an awkward way, and Jean dropped her cup and spilt tea all over the Persian rug. Mrs Turner rang the bell for Maisie, who had just left.

Jean said, 'I'm sorry.' She stood up suddenly. 'No, no, I'm not sorry.' She rushed out into the hall. 'I'd rather spill tea than blood.'

Mrs Walsh stopped knitting. 'Poor girl, she works so hard.'

The younger Miss Reeves went after Jean. Everyone was quiet while Maisie picked up the cup and saucer, and mopped the tea.

I looked out of the window. Jean was crying. She and Miss Reeves stood by the gate a moment. Jean wiped her sleeve across her face, patted Miss Reeves's arm and crossed the road to the tram stop. Miss Reeves watched her go, then came back inside.

I don't know what made me say it. It wasn't a good moment. But I suddenly knew. Things could get bad for Dad, and a little extra money always makes a good cushion. I put my cup and saucer down very carefully. 'Our Margaret's come across some lovely maroon felt with matching antique lace. Would any of you ladies like a new hat? She could create four very different styles.'

They stared at me – Mrs Turner, the Misses Reeves and Mrs Walsh. Margaret turned scarlet and looked at her shoes critically, turning her right foot so that she could see the sole.

Mrs Turner said, 'I don't think any of us will be thinking about new hats. Not while there's a war on.'

Sometimes I think lots of things at once. I thought if they'd all said yes we could have had cash by the end of the week. At the same time I was thinking: *There really is a war on; what am I doing here?*

I wanted to smash everything in that room, rip the scarf from Mrs Walsh's knitting needles and choke her with it.

Margaret stood up. 'Thanks for the tea.'

Thomas must have been watching from an upstairs window. He came charging up the path before we got to the gate, his face dark with anger, his mouth tightly drawn. He took a deep breath as if he hardly trusted himself to speak. He put his hand on the gate as I made to open it. 'You'd do me a great service if you'd let me escort you home. I need to get out of the house or I'll explode.'

He had left the door ajar and a dog came charging out, wagging its tail. 'Come on then, old girl,' Thomas said. 'You've had enough, too.'

As we walked round the back of the house to where the motor car stood, Thomas explained that he had just today come back from London and would have called to see Margaret but did not like to drop in.

Our very first ride in a motor car. Margaret and me had the good fortune to be wearing our motoring hats, as if today was meant. What an excitement, what speed! As we passed the Penny Bank, Thomas yelled, 'I can't stomach it. Mother in red, white and blue like a living, breathing bunting. She wants me to go off and be a soldier. Anyone less soldier material than myself I can't imagine.' He shouted at us over the noise of the engine about the brotherhood of man.

I shouted back, 'There's neither English nor German, Christian, Turk or Jew,' and Margaret joined in to cry, 'only humankind.'

Thomas shouted, 'Three human beings and a dog in a motor car.'

We caused a sensation on Bread Street. Every curtain twitched back, every blind raised. People opened their doors to gawp and children dashed out in their nightshirts.

Once we got there, the question was, should we ask him in? Or should we let him go straight on to the Dragon and deliver Margaret back there? Margaret and I are good at guessing each other's thoughts in this kind of situation. I knew that she was thinking: If we ask him in, he'll see for himself how poor we are, but I can't let him leave Julia at the door and let him drive me back to the Dragon. It wouldn't look right.

'You'd better come in, Thomas,' I said, climbing out of the motor car, as he went round to give Margaret his hand. 'There's something we need to ask you.'

Margaret gave me a quick look, asking was the house at least clean and tidy. She followed my gaze to the window. I'd collected devil's blossom from the tusky. I don't put flowers on the window sill unless I've cleaned the house. Margaret looked both pleased and upset. Pleased that the house would be clean, upset that I put weeds in a jam jar, and that Thomas would see how poor we are. I thought it a good thing. At least Margaret won't be hiding anything from him. He won't be able to accuse her of keeping secrets. Unless it's to do with having pretended to have read more books than she has and understand politics more than she does.

We let him have the stool. Margaret sat on Dad's bedchair, and I took up my post on the rag rug. Thomas's dog, Sheba, sat beside me. I left it to Margaret to ask. 'Thomas, we want to know what will happen to Dad, now that England and Germany are at war.'

His annoyance with his mother had gone and he seemed calm again. He tapped his fingers on the table, as if he didn't want to answer. 'Germans – all foreign nationals – will be detained. It's happened in some parts of the country already. Leeds won't be any different. It's just a matter of time.'

Margaret stood up and stretched out her hand, very formally. 'Thank you. And thank you for bringing us home.'

He stood up and a look of alarm flitted across his face as he tried to think whether he had annoyed her. 'Truly, I have only just come back from London today, Margaret. Minutes before you arrived at our house. I do want to see you. Soon.'

Margaret smiled. 'You'll have to excuse us. Julia and I have a lot to talk about.'

He looked as if he wanted to say something else, but just nodded. 'Of course.'

Aunty Amy came to her door as we waved Thomas Turner down the road. She said what a good thing Dad was out of the house and not here to witness this spectacle. What will people think, some young man bringing us home in a motor car?

Margaret went inside but I asked Aunty Amy, 'What will people think?'

Apparently, they will think me and Margaret are no better than we ought to be. Aunty Amy has never been in a motor car in her life, and hopes and prays she never will.

Margaret sat on the stool, in the exact position Thomas had taken, drumming her fingers on the table.

'What are we to do?' I asked.

'About Dad?'

'Of course about Dad.'

'Hope that the war doesn't last long. Hope no one comes for him yet. There's nothing else we can do.'

Then she leaned forward onto the table, her head resting on her arms, and burst into tears.

I went to her and put my hand on her shoulder. 'What's the matter?'

She pushed me away, her sobs getting louder and louder, and making her whole body tremble. All I could do was stand and watch. I couldn't even sit down beside her because I'd left the other stool in the cellar. I hitched myself up on to the table and put my hand on her silky hair.

'It's all going wrong,' she said between sobs.

As I stroked her hair, she gradually grew quiet and her sobs grew less. I went to the sink and let the water run a moment before filling a cup. 'Here, take a sip.'

She sipped the water. 'He'll never marry me,' she said. 'I hadn't intended him to see this house. He'll know I just want a way out.'

Her hanky had fallen onto the floor. I handed it to her, and she blew her nose.

I asked, 'Don't you love him?'

'Probably I do. But I love the idea of escaping more. Is that terrible?'

'You have escaped. You're living at the Dragon.'

'On Uncle's charity. I want a proper home of my own.'

I must have looked shocked.

She said, 'I do care for him. But I don't see the point of letting myself fall in love till I know if he means to marry me.'

I thought of a book we'd seen on the stall in the market, when looking for something suitable for Margaret to impress Thomas. The book was called *Marriage as a Trade*. We had laughed about it at the time, as you could see from a glance that the writer regarded 'Marriage as a Trade' as a bad thing. Margaret had said that she didn't see anything so terrible about it. Tailoring as a Trade seemed to her a lot worse. I said that Skivvying as a Trade left a lot to be desired, too.

I decided to tell her what I had overheard between Mrs Turner and Mr Mitchell when we had stayed at his house in London.

I gave her a not-exact account of the conversation. 'So you see, Mrs Turner believes he loves you. And Mr Mitchell's strategy didn't work. If Thomas had been "swept off his feet" by the most suitable girls in London, he wouldn't be here.'

'We don't know that.' Margaret looked as if she would start to cry again. 'Perhaps that's why he wants to talk to me. To tell me he's engaged to someone else.'

'Does he know you care for him?'

Margaret had her back to me, splashing tap water on her face. She didn't answer my question. 'Am I a complete fool for trying for him?' she asked as she dabbed her face dry with the corner of the towel.

'No. And if I were you, I'd love Thomas.'

She handed me the mirror to hold and looked critically at herself. 'I hope no one sees me in this state on the way back to the Dragon.'

'You'd better have a cup of tea then, and talk about something else for five minutes.'

Margaret stirred her tea. She told me about Clarice's elder sister, Hilda, who had been meant

159

to do better than she did. 'I saw her today,' Margaret said. 'She's twenty-two years old and looks forty. Her hair's all greasy and pulled back. Two children were hanging onto her apron strings, and another in her belly. I could hear a baby crying in the house. She was carrying a bucket of slops to the privy. One of the children got under her feet and she stumbled. The slops tipped onto the street. What a stink! She looks ancient, Julia. She's utterly worn-out, and her face – such misery when the slops spilt.'

'We're not like her,' I said. 'We won't let ourselves be trapped.'

'Then what shall I do? I thought I could win Mrs Turner round.'

'I'm sure you will. Once she knows it's inevitable.'

'But is it? And how am I to tread a line between Thomas and his mother? They've taken such different sides over this war.'

'Which side are you on?' I waited but she didn't answer. 'I'd be on his side, if he was the one I loved.'

'You keep talking about love,' Margaret said. 'I will love him if he marries me. But if he doesn't, that'll be humiliation enough without me having fallen for him.'

I'm sure she loves him, but won't admit it to herself, and certainly not to me. She looked more herself by the time she set off to go back to the Dragon. I went downstairs to my punchbag in the cellar. I put on my boxing gloves and tried out a few right hooks and left upper-cuts. I thought of Margaret walking back through the streets on her own.

Perhaps she hasn't realized that posh people don't let their daughters go walking about alone. Once that penny drops I suppose she'll expect me to tag along with her more. Why doesn't she just let herself love him? I would. If she's hurt, she's hurt. That's what happens in all the ballads. But life's not like ballads. She'd get over it. I could let her take it out on my punchbag.

The McAndrews tried to join the army this morning. Kevin and Johnny had been let off their work at the Town Hall so they could sign up. They queued from nine till twelve to see the recruiters, then got hungry and decided to try again tomorrow.

Uncle Lloyd has told Bernard to hold his horses until he can find a replacement barman.

TWENTY-FOUR

Cissie, Cissie, Cissie. Dear Cissie. Goodbye.

Cissie, Cissie, Cissie. I cannot write it. I must write it and see the terrible words that I hear over and over in my head.

I wish it had rained, stormed, blown. The sun shone hot on my face as I watched Cissie's coffin lowered deep into the clay of her pauper grave. I asked Mrs Garretty where her husband was buried. Cissie would rather be with a hundred strangers than lie near her dad.

161

I imagine her sailing along the River Lethe towards heaven, rowed by beautiful young men ready to do her bidding and to cross burning sand barefoot to fetch her fresh asses' milk from the far side of the golden mountain.

Cissie, my Cissie, you will never grow old and grey. Cissie, I remember the first day we met at school. I held your hand and forgot my own scaredness. Now I hate this life with you not in it.

My last gift to Cissie, a silent prayer for your soul. May every young man in heaven fall in love with you. But don't make a best friend. Wait for me.

I thought I would never want to help lay out another person who had died, but I did it for Mr Garretty; how could I not do it for my Cissie? I dressed her in my best blue skirt and jacket, and motoring hat.

Aunty Amy said that when she was my age, she did this last kindness for her own best friend. She says that your heart never mends, but it heals over. I don't see how it can.

Margaret the miracle worker! No one else could have pulled it off. I went with her to the Turners's under strict orders to keep shtum and give her moral support.

Mrs Turner called it a 'bandaging class'. How can you have a class without anyone teaching it? Mrs Turner tried showing us how to bandage, but since she does not know how to do it herself we did not get very far with that. Mrs Walsh did not do much better. Miss Mason preferred not to try, saying that as a milliner, used to trimming hats, she would rise to the occasion in any emergency that required bandaging.

The elder Miss Reeves had to wear her reading glasses for the job and said because she cannot easily raise her arms she will only be able to bandage in a downward direction, never up. Nobody asked what she meant by this, probably thinking it best not to know. Unfortunately I was the person to be bandaged in a downward direction by Miss Reeves and she stopped the blood in my arm so that my hand turned white. The bandage had to be cut off by Margaret as Miss Reeves had managed to knot it continually on the way down. Margaret was as careful as possible with the scissors. Aunty Amy would say what a terrible waste of a bandage. I have two cuts on my arm to prove that Miss Reeves should be sent to bandage the enemy.

Her sister was otherwise occupied and unable to attend. Good for her. No Jean, either, of course. And no sign of Thomas Turner – not at the beginning.

Margaret must have arranged it with him beforehand. She got up from her seat on the dark-red leather pouffe and announced that she would give a demonstration of how to bandage a man with a broken rib.

Mrs Turner smiled and said that was a good idea, but since we had no man and none of *us* had a broken rib or could strip off, not very practical.

Thomas appeared in the doorway. 'Perhaps Thomas could help?' Margaret said demurely, and explained the problem to him.

Thomas stripped off his shirt. He was not wearing a vest. He has hairs on his chest, but just enough to make him attractive, not like a hairy ape.

Margaret took an Aunty Amy bandage from her bag. She placed the end of the bandage on his midriff. 'Hold it, please.'

His finger brushed hers as he placed it on the end of the bandage. Lightly and deftly, Margaret wound the bandage round and round his torso, touching him ever so slightly and only as much as necessary as she held the bandage in place, pressing her forefinger and middle finger gently on his chest. He gazed at a point above the mantelpiece, his arms slightly raised to give her room to wind the bandage.

When she had finished, she touched him gently with the flat of her hand, to show that he must hold the bandage in place until she pinned it. His hand covered hers, then she drew her hand away. Taking a safety pin from her pocket, she pinned the bandage firmly.

'Excellent!' Mrs Turner said. I don't know what was excellent, whether it was Margaret's bandaging or the fact that Thomas had agreed to take part. I saw the hope in Mrs Turner's eyes. Did this mean that Thomas might change his attitude and see his duty to support the war?

I hoped Miss Reeves would ask Margaret how she learned to bandage so well. Margaret would have the opportunity to say that Dad had been knocked to the ground and kicked for being German and a Jew, and his ribs broken. We both learned to bandage him. But no one asked.

People take Margaret's accomplishments for granted. She is that kind of person.

Thomas picked up his shirt and turned to go. 'Ladies,' he said. Then he looked at Margaret. 'I'll need some help undoing this bandage.'

Margaret looked at Mrs Turner. Mrs Turner nodded thoughtfully, giving Margaret permission to go.

'Julia,' Margaret said, 'bring my bag, please.'

I picked up her bag and followed them down the hall and into the next room, the dining room that looked out onto the long back garden. I thought they'd disappeared but then heard a sigh. Margaret stood by the wall, Thomas holding her, kissing her.

'I adore you,' he said. 'You drive me mad.'

Margaret freed herself. 'Thomas! What will people think?'

'I don't care,' he said. 'I love you.'

I went out again, without either of them noticing me. I felt such a fool, standing outside the door on chaperone-sentry duty. Then Margaret called me in, and I watched as she unwound the bandage from his chest and rolled and tucked the end in the top, as Aunty Amy did. She handed it to me as Thomas put on his shirt.

'Thank you for letting me bandage you,' she said. 'I'd better join the others.' But before she did, she fastened the buttons on his shirt for him and he leaned against the wall, his eyes closed and a look of ecstasy on his face.

He caught her wrist. 'Margaret! When shall I see you? May I take you home?'

She shook her head. 'That's not a good idea.'

165

'Tomorrow then?'

'Yes. Tomorrow.'

Before he had chance to ask when, Margaret had gone. He looked at me, but I just shrugged and followed her.

Miss Mason sat on the window seat, her boots off and one leg outstretched on a stool, her skirt hitched to her knees. Mrs Walsh knelt beside her, bandaging her calf.

Mrs Turner smiled at us. She said to Margaret, 'You know, my dear, it may be that you can succeed where I have failed. I should like Thomas to go for a commission in the Prince of Wales's Regiment. If he doesn't go soon, the war could be over and he'll miss his chance for distinguished service.'

Margaret looked surprised. Her mouth opened and she took a breath before answering. 'But Mrs Turner, how could I try to influence your son? It's not as if we're close, or related. I don't see that it would be proper.'

Mrs Turner had no answer to that. I chalked up a victory to Margaret.

'How's that?' Mrs Walsh said triumphantly when she had encased Miss Mason's tender, arthritic knee in bandages.

'Do you know,' Miss Mason stood up, held the chair arm and swung her bandaged leg back and forth vigorously, 'I think I should wear a bandage on my knee joints all the time. It feels vairy, vairy comforting.'

We walked back along Roundhay Road together, Margaret, Miss Mason and me. I was glad Margaret didn't cut off and go to the Dragon, leaving me to deal with Miss Mason and see her to her door.

She asked us in. It felt strange walking through the shop I had burgled. I looked round and saw lots of hats around the shelves. She bolted the shop door behind us. (She never leaves that top window open now.)

In the airless back room, she poured three glasses of sherry, leaving very little in the bottle. It was the first time I had tasted a fortified wine.

We thanked her but did not stay long, giving the excuse of needing to get home.

'I feel sorry for her,' Margaret said. 'Since the war began, not a single person has bought a hat. If it doesn't end soon, she could lose her business.'

We parted at the end of the street, Margaret going back to the Dragon and me coming home, to write this account at the table. The night has grown dark and the candle splutters. It should see me up the stairs.

TWENTY-FIVE

It has rained all day and I'm alone in the shop, as Aunty Amy has gone upstairs to rest. I have almost filled this old accounts book so must make my writing even tinier. I have got good at new abbreviations, too. I met Jean in town and asked her about shorthand since she works in an office, and she told me the words 'the' and 'a' are dots on or above the line.

I have only one good thing to write about, which means I can creep up on the bad thing and not let it take over every scrap of space.

The good thing: Aunty Amy said she'd hire a horse and trap. What a surprise when the horse turned out to be Solomon, and Charley agreed that I could take the reins.

Aunty Amy talked about the plants we'd collect. She talks about herbs and flowers as though they are her friends, and says whatever ills we have, Nature could cure them if we let her. If we all learned to work with Nature, we would be healthy and happy. I did not remind her how many remedies poor Cissie tried.

Of course, most people don't get chance to be friends with Nature, cooped up in damp houses in dirty, smelly streets where the sun never shines.

You do not have to go very far up York Road before coming to a meadow, just a turning down a winding lane. We let Solomon loose to wander about and drink from the stream. Aunty Amy looked as though she belonged outdoors. She seemed younger and more able to bend and get about. What a meadow! I can't remember the names of half that we saw. But our main purpose today: dandelions – flowers, leaves and roots, also young nettles. When you are in a meadow and the sun shines, you forget about war and meanness and that people can be cruel. Nettles might sting you if you are not careful, but never on purpose.

I know that Aunty Amy definitely did want dandelions and nettles. But there may have been another reason for her arranging a trip to the countryside. She is trying to help me forget what happened last Saturday. But I never will.

I had been dreaming about the war and thought the sound was Germans attacking. I woke thinking of Margaret and Dad. But Margaret was at the Dragon and Dad on his watchman's night shift.

I lay there frozen, wondering had someone broken in. I got the shivers as I walked to the window to look. The street was quiet. I opened the window. The cardboard we'd put in to stop the rattling fell onto my foot. Even that made me jump. I leaned out, but saw no one. I lit my candle and slipped on my shoes, as the stone steps are so cold. I'm glad I did have something on my feet.

When I got downstairs there was glass everywhere, in the sink, on the floor, in the rag rug. My hands shook as I lit the gas mantle. I could feel my heart pounding as I took the brush and started to sweep. I didn't see the brick straight away. It was by the table leg.

The old potato sacks are in the cellar and I needed one for the broken glass. I've never felt shaky about going into our cellar before. In case there were any little animals I didn't want to see, I clapped my hands and made a lot of noise going down the steps. Even my own sounds scared me. It wasn't until I got into the cellar that I wondered if someone might be lurking there.

Aunty Amy slept through, or she would have come to see. I couldn't go back to bed. I wrapped myself in a blanket and sat on Dad's bedchair, looking at the broken window pane, keeping the sweeping brush by me as a weapon. That night was the loneliest night of my life. Who did it? Why? I think I can guess the second but not the first.

When Dad came home from work he took me in his arms and hugged me as if he'd never let go. He didn't seem surprised about the brick through the window, only shocked at my dithering state. I pulled myself together and told him I was all right. He said he wishes he didn't have to work nights. He says I mustn't be on my own any more and must stay with Aunty Amy or at the Dragon.

Dad went for his Hungarian friend, who lives on Cloth Street in the Leylands area. I don't know where they got glass and putty on a Sunday. They replaced the worn sash, too.

Henryk stayed and ate with us. He is very polite, even sombre, and leaped to attention every time I moved from my stool. He said that many people from the Leylands district had been taken away. The police had swooped and arrested everyone who wasn't a British citizen. Henryk had been missed, but expected to be picked up any day. He was only glad he had been able to help us.

After he had gone, I went upstairs and just laid on my bed, my head against the bedpost, and cried and cried.

Dad came upstairs and sat on the bed. *'Liebling, liebling.* Come down. Come see.'

He had lit the fire. He held up a battered old brown leather boot, hard and stiff as if it had been left out in the rain. Its sole had come away from the upper, like a sad gawping mouth on a hungry dog. 'Go on. Burn the boot.'

We sat side by side on the bedchair and watched the boot burn. So many colours. Blue, green, yellow, orange – all the colours of the rainbow shot from that crackling, sparking boot. Sparks hit the black chimney-back. Sparks shot out, landing near me, one on my skirt. I bashed it with my hand. I couldn't take my eyes off the boot. It smelled like boiling vinegar and smouldering rubber, sweet and bitter at the same time. The flames died. The boot had turned into a statue of grey and molten ash, a more perfect boot than it had ever been in its previous life.

Dad handed me the poker. 'Go on.'

I waited, knowing I would only have a brief moment before the boot disintegrated. I poked the ash boot, and watched it collapse.

TWENTY-SIX

On my dinner break, I had walked through the outside market. I know it's weeks off, but I wanted to look for a birthday present for Margaret. I heard a commotion near Mr Fischer's stall and went to see. Two large men wearing suits and bowler hats stood by his stall. I knew they hadn't come to buy poultry. Mr Fischer stood behind the counter, looking hot and uncertain. A uniformed policeman ordered the small crowd to disperse, but he didn't sound as if he meant it, and the crowd took no notice. Mr Fischer took off his apron very slowly and held it in his hand, not quite knowing what to do with it. One of the bowler-hatted men went behind the counter, watching as Mr Fischer reached for his jacket.

I walked over, feeling strange, as if I saw myself from above. I wanted to say 'What's going on?' or something like that, but I don't think any words came out. Mr Fischer still held onto his apron. I reached out and he handed the apron to me.

He turned and looked up at the bowler-hatted man on his side of the counter and said, 'Is all right if I ask this young lady keep an eye on the stall, till my assistant gets back?'

The bowler hat nodded.

A big brute of a man in the little knot of lookers-on shouted, 'Fritz Fischer! Send him back to Kaiser Bill!'

An old woman waved her walking stick very close to Mr Fischer's head and shouted in an ugly, peevish voice, 'He'd like to see Leeds market running with English blood.'

Mr Fischer squeezed my hand tightly. He said, 'Julia, I have to go with these gentlemen.' He clapped his hat on his head and stood up very straight, trying to look tall and to ignore the insults and jeering.

As he strode off, head high, I looked at the back of his neck, fleshy and red, between his stiff collar and the neat line of his hair. I don't know what made me dash after him, calling his name. I think I wanted to drown out the sound of insults.

Somebody shouted, 'Bloody Hun.'

A boy spat at him.

Mr Fischer pulled out a white handkerchief and wiped his cheek.

I caught up with him, and the policeman and the men in bowler hats stared at me.

I had no idea what to say or do. We seemed to stay there for ages, waiting. I put my hand in my pocket where I had a bag with a few sweets. I took one between my finger and thumb, and said, 'Have a pear drop, Mr Fischer.' Then I popped it into his mouth.

People called me names as I walked back to the stall. I said nothing. I didn't feel as if I could see or speak. I'd only turned my back on the stall a moment before, but every morsel of poultry was gone, and the till cleared.

Is there a bigger idiot's delight in Leeds than Julia Wood? I don't think so.

AUTUMN
AND
WINTER
1914

TWENTY-SEVEN

Margaret has gone stark raving mad. She came to the shop this afternoon. Would I go for a walk with her after work? Aunty Amy came back from visiting the lady with dropsy and said for me to get myself off and that she would shut up shop.

We walked together as far as Mabgate Mills, then Margaret came out with it. Would I go with her to a lecture on fevers and infections? With the war on, we needed to know all about these things, according to her. We have to be able to do something.

Everyone was clattering out of the mill by then, and the pavement was crowded. I said, 'You go, and tell me about it afterwards.'

Listening to some professor drone on about fevers and injections didn't seem the best possible way to take your mind off war, panic and shortages. Unless it's just the relief of not having typhoid fever or diphtheria yourself. But in the end I agreed, just to shut her up. I'd had no tea and we walked all the way up to the Town Hall to some meeting room, crowded mostly with well-dressed women.

We didn't find out much, or stay long. The doctor giving the talk brought out a huge hypodermic needle as part of his lecture about inoculation against typhoid fever and diphtheria.

At the sight of the needle Margaret fainted on the spot and had to be carried out.

A kind young doctor stopped a cab and put us in it. He paid, too. We asked to be taken to the Dragon, where I finally had something to eat. Margaret was very sick and spent a long time in the bathroom. She came out looking so pale she was almost green.

I went into her room with her. She flopped on the bed. I unbuttoned her boots and took them off.

'Undo my dress,' she said. 'I've no strength.'

It's not like Margaret to get ill. I helped her undress and tucked her up in bed. She still has the china dish filled with rose petals on her dresser, and I asked whether she wanted me to run a bath for her and sprinkle the petals on, even though it's not bath night. She said that she had no strength for that. I suggested a nettle tonic. I know that Aunty Amy has one bottle left that she made in the spring. Margaret agreed to that, but said that she didn't want to put me to any trouble, and tomorrow would be soon enough for the nettle tonic.

I climbed onto the bed and sat at the bottom, my knees pulled up to my chest. It's a very comfortable bed; the mattress doesn't even dip in the middle.

Margaret can get very touchy if she thinks I am prying. But I risked it and said, 'Is this to do with Thomas?' I know that he has gone back to London. She has not said whether anything is settled between them.

She lay motionless for ages. Then she raised

one hand after the other, swiping the counter-pane angrily, as if it had bitten her. 'Yes, it's to do with Thomas. And this damn war. How can a person know what to do for the best?'

'In what way?' I asked.

She sighed and spoke to the ceiling. 'If we could talk more, if I knew what he was thinking. He wants me to get engaged. I've been holding him off.'

'Don't you love him?' I asked again.

She sighed.

I tried again. 'I'm sure Mrs Turner will accept you once you're married.'

'He says he won't enlist. But I'm sure he will.'

'He'll have to do what he thinks best.'

'Julia, what if I marry him, and he goes to war and gets blown to bits?'

There was no answer to that, so I said nothing. Then she got onto what was really worrying her.

'If he goes to war, he could be maimed. I couldn't live with a disfigured cripple.'

I remembered the bandaging practice, when Margaret was perfectly happy to bandage the unblemished Thomas, but averted her eyes from Miss Mason's swollen arthritic joints.

'No, you couldn't,' I agreed.

'Did you see that young soldier at the back of the hall tonight as we went in? Did you see his appalling shot-up face? Thomas is so, so beautiful.'

It was an odd word to use about a man, but I knew what she meant. He has a kind of radiance about him, and a real grace.

'But there's nothing any of us can do about the

war.' I had slipped off my shoes. I tucked my feet under the eiderdown.

She sat up and fixed me with that look that says she is going to explain something difficult and I had better pay attention. I paid attention.

'Mrs Turner knows that I know that she doesn't want Thomas and me to marry. Without saying it, she's trying to make me enter a bargain.'

This was getting interesting. 'What kind of bargain?' I asked.

'To do with how Thomas says he opposes war.' She sighed and lowered her head. 'Well, I don't. Oh, I did at first, but now we're in it, we might as well win. Beat the Germans.'

I made myself concentrate. I had never really thought about being 'for' or 'against', not seeing that my opinion made the least difference. But since it had come up, I said, 'If I were you I'd agree with Thomas. How can we not be against it when we believe that there's no Christian, no Jew, no Turk and no Greek, only humankind? You can't believe that and support a war.'

'Julia, they're just words. We only believe them because Dad has said them over and over since we learned to talk, and even before probably. If everyone believed that there'd be no difficulty. But everyone doesn't. Only fools like us.'

'But if you believe it–'

'It makes no difference. We have to work in the world as it is. Oh, I don't have this argument with Thomas. But perhaps I should. That's what Mrs Turner wants of me. She wants me to persuade him to "do his duty" and join the army.'

The cheek of the woman took my breath away.

'Then she'll agree to have you as a daughter-in-law?'

Margaret nodded.

I swung my legs off the bed. 'Could you trust her to keep a bargain?' I asked. 'In any case, Thomas believes what he believes on principle. If you care for him, you won't want to change his mind. You won't want to "bargain" over him.'

'That's your opinion.' She spoke very quietly. 'Julia, you and me have to be able to disagree and still be on each other's side. I can't go on otherwise. I have to know you're with me. Whatever happens, we're the Wood Sisters, standing together.'

I think if she hadn't looked so poorly I might have argued longer. I said that of course I was with her, but that I didn't think she should try to change Thomas's mind.

'Perhaps I won't,' she said. 'But there's something else. Another dilemma. Thomas can't get back for my birthday. He's invited us – you and me – to stay in a hotel in London. He wanted to celebrate my birthday with him.'

'He invited me, too?'

'He's a gentleman, isn't he? He wouldn't invite me on my own. But Mrs Turner's complicated things. When I told her she said she would come as well, and we must all stay at Mr Mitchell's house. She won't hear of us staying in a hotel. Family's important. I had to pretend to be delighted. If I started out by coming between a mother and her son, no good would come of it.'

'So we're going back to Mr Mitchell's house?' I asked.

181

She sat bolt upright and seemed to have recovered from her sudden illness. 'You'll come? You said you hated it there. But I couldn't bear to be on my own with them all. I'd be outnumbered.'

'Yes. I'll come.' I had never got to walk across London Bridge and was very keen to do that. But I didn't say so.

I still wasn't sure whether Margaret would try to persuade Thomas to join the army. She wasn't sure herself. She said that if she did persuade him, perhaps she'd end up looking after a cripple. If he went on opposing the war, then their life would be impossible.

Aunty Amy baked a cake and I made blackcurrant jelly. Since we're to be in London for Margaret's birthday, we had to have an advance party.

Margaret loved my present: some scent bags – cotton squares filled with lavender, tied in little bundles and threaded through with narrow pink ribbon – no sewing involved.

Aunty Amy gave her a silver thimble in a case and said, 'Oh to be nineteen.'

Margaret said it would be better to be nineteen and no war. It is true you can hardly forget it for a moment with call-to-arms posters and Union Jacks everywhere. Gelder's the Drapers have a notice displayed in the window saying 'Business as usual during hostilities.' That made me and Margaret laugh. The men in Gelder's are so doddery that we're surprised they've even heard about the war.

Dad gave Margaret a box of seven different

shades of blue thread – Powder-blue, Sky-blue, Sapphire, Aqua Marine, Turquoise, Oxford-blue and Navy – and wished her happy birthday. He said it almost without an accent, but even so, no one could be mistaken. He tries hard but it is no use; everything about him gives him away. After Mr Fischer was taken into custody, we waited for the knock on the door, but none came. Dad says that no one in authority knows about him. I hope he is right.

I tried to hide my anxiety about going away and leaving him, but he guessed and said, 'You go. Take all your chances, take them for me.'

I'm not sure what chances he thinks there may be for me in London, except to see the sights and play my only musical instrument – second fiddle to Margaret.

I am a little embarrassed by the look of this journal and have made a brown paper cover for it, with my name and the word PRIVATE in capital letters. Margaret says I should not have put my name on the front. If I leave it on the train and someone finds it, they will know whose innermost thoughts they are reading and whose father is an enemy alien. I got annoyed with her, thinking she had read it. She claims she has not touched it but says it does not take a genius to guess what I write about.

I am pleased to say, though, that I will be leaving this almost-filled-up journal at home. Aunty Amy has given me a lovely notebook that she found in her cupboard. It has a stiff cover with a swirly pattern in purple and mauve, and coloured edges to the sheets. The first entry should be a fascinating account of our visit to London, including a walk across London Bridge.

TWENTY-EIGHT

So that's what the dawn chorus means. I always thought it meant the knocker-up banging on folks' windows and workers setting off for their early shift, clogging it along the street, complaining and calling out to each other.

The dawn chorus means birds.

I woke up thinking someone must have brought a cageful of budgerigars into the room until I realized they were free birds, welcoming the London morning, out in the green square. It's almost worth all the pain of what's happened to find that out. I could have gone through my whole life reading in novels about the dawn chorus and misunderstanding it. Last time I came to London I heard that same racket. I had meant to ask who kept canaries. I'm glad I didn't. They would have found out sooner that I am an idiot. Now they will be sure of it.

Down in the square there's a milk cart. I'm tempted to pick up my bag, go down there and ask directions to the railway station. Nothing has gone right.

When it came to dressing for the journey, I was in the wrong. Margaret said I should wear my blue skirt and jacket, and the straw hat with little flowers that I'd bought from Miss Mason. I told Margaret that Cissie was wearing my blue outfit. She said, 'But Cissie's dead.' Then she realized what I had done and wouldn't give me a minute's peace until I was newly fitted out with a dress and matching cape made from an outfit that had belonged to a dead cousin of Uncle's. So poor Cissie in her cold grave wears the clothes of the living and I wear the clothes of the dead. Margaret said it was a good thing she left nothing to chance in the outfits department, or I would have let myself down, and her, too. My new regalia is heavy serge, which Margaret claims is navy-blue but I would call inkpot-sludge. We travelled on the train to London on the hottest day of the year and Margaret said it was my own fault and I should think cool thoughts, picture a mountain stream perhaps. So I did. But for all I know, since I have never seen a mountain stream, I may have imagined it as poorly as I previously imagined the dawn chorus, and that is why I stayed so damned hot.

But that was nothing.

I really don't know why I agreed to come. I'm sure I have only made things worse. Mr Mitchell greeted us when our cab arrived from the station. Our cases were carried upstairs for us.

We were taken into a drawing room full of heavy furniture that I don't remember from last time. Sun shone through the window, lighting up dust motes. There was something comforting about that. Dust makes no favourites and will fly anywhere. The room smelled of lavender polish and fresh flowers.

Mr Mitchell stood by the fireplace, asking us

185

about our journey in a booming, friendly voice. A maid brought in a tea tray, with pretty china cups that had red flowers. Mrs Turner poured and Mr Mitchell passed round the cups with lots of 'my dears', especially to Margaret. She and I sat on a chaise longue, facing him. Mrs Turner settled herself slightly to one side, on a large sofa. Mr Mitchell explained that Thomas would be here for dinner in the evening.

Margaret was pretending to listen but I knew that her attention was on the room. She was admiring the colour scheme and the tall aspidistra. If she wasn't listening, I thought I had better pay attention.

Mr Mitchell poured himself a whisky and offered one to Mrs Turner. Surprisingly, she said yes. Margaret and I stuck to tea. Mrs Turner poured water into her whisky and said, 'Tell me, Walter, what's my boy been up to?'

Apparently, Thomas is writing freelance articles for various newspapers, including Mr Mitchell's newspaper, but I was not very sure what he was writing about.

Mr Mitchell does not seem so certain as Mrs Turner that Thomas should volunteer for the army and become an officer. 'Have you seen the casualty lists, Constance?'

Constance blushed. 'Our son is not a coward,' she said quickly, then realized her slip.

Margaret hadn't noticed. She was checking the origins of the china, turning her cup over to read the writing underneath while she thought no one was looking. I concentrated on choosing a digestive biscuit.

'Let's not be hasty about the boy,' Mr Mitchell said. He poured himself another whisky. 'You're worrying unnecessarily.'

'He's not a boy, Walter. He's a man. He has a duty to fight for his country. His honour and virtue are at stake. What kind of future will he have in years to come if he shirks his duty at the time when everything his country stands for is under attack?'

Margaret got up and excused herself, saying she'd go upstairs and rest for a while. I know she expected me to go with her, but she never looks to see if I've finished my cup of tea and I hadn't. So I said I'd follow her up.

It was the way in which Mrs Turner and Mr Mitchell sat there, sipping tea, sipping whisky and talking about Thomas, as if they could decide for him what he should do.

'For goodness' sake,' Mrs Turner said, 'I'm sure he wouldn't want a girl he admires to hand him a coward's white feather.'

She took an envelope from her pocket, and I saw that it contained white feathers. Was she going to give her own son a feather? I could see that Mr Mitchell was wondering the same thing.

'Surely it's happened to him already,' Mrs Turner said. 'And if not, it should.'

I hoped that she did not expect Margaret or me to do her dirty work. But then, that was why Margaret was there. Even Margaret would baulk at handing out a white feather. We hate people who do that since Bernard gets enough to fill an eiderdown and he would love to join up. Mrs Turner looked at me sharply, no doubt wishing I would

187

be as tactful as Margaret and disappear upstairs. She placed the envelope of white feathers on the low table by the tea tray.

'Someone gave my cousin Bernard a white feather,' I told her. 'It made him want to put stones in his pocket and jump in the River Aire.'

'That's different,' Mrs Turner said. 'Your cousin is unfit.'

I felt myself going red with anger. I said, 'Surely a person must decide for himself what's the right thing to do.'

'In times of peace,' Mrs Turner said patiently. 'But in time of war, when a struggle is virtuous, we must all take part.'

'You talk about your son as if it's your *right* to send him to war. I hope you don't think Margaret or I would give him a white feather.'

'Of course not,' Mrs Turner smiled. 'He'll see where his duty lies without that.'

I know that I am not very reasonable and when I open my mouth I do not always know what is going to come out. I thought someone else's words might be more measured than my own. Tom Maguire. Dead poet. I took a deep breath and said, 'There's a Leeds poet that I admire, and I think Thomas admires him, too. His name's Tom Maguire and he says that when people learn to love as heartily as they presently hate, they'll find ways of resolving their difficulties without killing each other.'

Mr Mitchell chuckled and said, 'I think this young lady should be writing for the *Daily Herald*.'

That he laughed at me made me furious. I

snatched the envelope of white feathers. 'I don't know Thomas as well as you do, or as Margaret does, but I know that he's a good, kind human being and he would no more want to go off and kill a German than he would want to kill an Englishman.'

I threw the envelope of feathers onto the fire.

Mrs Turner had stopped staring at me. She looked past me to the doorway. I heard the slow clapping of hands, and Thomas walked into the room.

'Bravo,' he said. 'What a speech, little one, what a speech!'

I ran past him into the hall and up the wide staircase.

Margaret sat in her shift, brushing her hair. 'I'm glad you've left them alone. They must have a lot to talk about.'

I unfastened my shoes, which had got very tight. My feet felt as hot as the rest of me. 'Thomas has arrived.'

Her breathing changed, and she turned to me. 'I wish just one thing was different. That we were more their equals. Or that there was no war. Or that Thomas was in Leeds and I could see more of him and not have to depend on letters. Any one of those would make it easier.'

Make what easier? I wanted to ask. The path of true love?

When I didn't answer, she put her brush down. 'Do they despise us? I couldn't bear it if they did.'

I pulled off the serge dress, vowing never to wear it again as long as I lived. 'They've no right to despise us.'

189

'That wouldn't stop them.'

'Thomas was born on the wrong side of the blanket,' I told her. 'Is that the one thing that'll make it easier?'

'*What?*' She lowered her voice. 'Mr Mitchell's his godfather. Don't be saying things like that.'

I stared hard at her, trying to work out whether she really had not heard Mrs Turner's slip of the tongue – being too busy daydreaming about her beautiful future – or was pretending ignorance as she sometimes did.

'For heaven's sake, Margaret, look at the two of them together.'

'But Mr Mitchell's a widower, with grown-up daughters.'

'Perhaps that's why he never married Mrs Turner.'

Margaret looked at me through the mirror. 'Do you know, I think you must be right.' She stared at me, as if I were the oracle. 'But if he's a widower and she's a widow–'

'*If* she is,' I said.

'Why don't they marry?'

'Because Mr Mitchell's more interested in Thomas's future than in his own past with Mrs Turner. But what I'm saying is they have no right to look down on us.'

She strode around the room, tidying our things, searching for her sponge bag. 'Do you think Thomas knows?'

I shrugged. 'Don't know.'

'You look like Dad when you do that,' she said.

I thought of telling her what had happened downstairs, but I didn't.

We went to the bathroom. She had to have first bath, of course, and then I got into her water. We spoke in whispers, speculating about how Walter Mitchell and Constance Turner met.

'Are you going to try and persuade Thomas to join the army?' I asked.

'Wait and see.'

I peered round the bathroom door, to make sure the way was clear for Margaret to dash back to our room without being seen. I followed.

I brushed and combed her hair, and arranged it in loops. She brushed mine and said for me to wear it just as it was, falling down past my shoulders, caught with bows at the back. I'm glad that she had found some spectacular material to make herself a flowing dress in a blue that was almost green. She knows how to cut material on the bias and how much to use to make the dress move with her body but not swirl or float. Uncle had given her a choker that had belonged to our aunt, a sapphire on a black ribbon. I fastened it for her. My dress was cream, with leg-of-mutton sleeves, a high waist and a lot of tiny, irritating buttons.

She was just about to help me fasten the buttons, when we heard a tap at the door.

I remembered the big-boned maid with the grey bun on top of her head from our previous visit. How someone with a button for a nose could look down her snitch at you I don't know, but she had perfected the art. I'm sure she was supposed to come and see if we needed anything, but had decided not to. She held out a silver tray, with an envelope that said 'Margaret' in a neat sloping hand. I took it, thanked her, then shut the door.

My hand shook as I looked at the envelope. What if we were being asked to leave because of my outburst? I handed her the note.

She read it. 'Thomas wants to see me in the drawing room before dinner. He has a birthday present for me.' She looked at herself in the long mirror, pleased with what she saw. 'What if it's a necklace? I'd better take this off.' She fumbled with the fastening and I helped her undo it.

'But what if it's not a necklace?' I said. 'This one looks just right with your dress.'

She thought about it. 'Come down in a few minutes. If I show you a present and it's not a necklace, say that I'd forgotten my choker and give it to me. If I am wearing a necklace, say you want me to fasten the choker for you.'

I didn't really want to wear a choker on top of a leg-of-mutton sleeve dress with a high collar, but I agreed.

Sitting on the bed, I began to count backwards from 300, which should be five minutes and long enough for Thomas to give her the present. Then I lost count and thought that perhaps five minutes wouldn't be long enough.

The supercilious maid was just coming out of Mrs Turner's room. She half-smiled at me and said in a snooty voice, 'Gong hasn't sounded yet, miss.'

I half-smiled back and said, 'Trumpet hasn't blown, drum hasn't beat, whistle hasn't blown and hooter hasn't sounded.' I walked slowly down the stairs, clutching my dead aunt's choker in my hand.

No sound came from the drawing room, but

the door was just a little ajar. I peeked in. They stood by the fireplace in an embrace. Thomas kissed Margaret, and she kissed him back and looked up at him. I didn't dare breathe in case they heard me.

'Answer me, Margaret. Put me out of my misery. Do you want me to go down on my knees? Because I will.' There was a pause, and Margaret made some small sound that might have been a no or a sigh. There was a gulp to his voice as he said, 'Will you? Will you marry me?'

I held my breath till I thought I would burst. There was a long silence. Margaret spoke. 'Yes, Thomas. I will marry you. Thank you.'

I breathed then because I thought they wouldn't notice. At that moment, I heard Mrs Turner on the landing. I ducked into the dining-room doorway. The butler was by the sideboard, polishing a glass. He pretended not to see me. After a moment I went back into the hall.

Mrs Turner wasn't in the drawing room with Margaret and Thomas. I guessed she had gone into Mr Mitchell's study. I decided to try and make amends for yelling at them both. After all, Thomas was their son. They were more entitled than me to an opinion about whether he should go off and murder people. I took a deep breath and went to the study door, with a very brief apology ready on my tongue. I opened the door and immediately pushed it closed. They were arguing again. Mrs Turner must have seen Margaret and Thomas and drawn her own conclusions. She said to Mr Mitchell, her voice sarcastic, 'So much for finding a suitable girl for him.'

Mr Mitchell said, 'Huh!' He seemed to say that a lot. 'Huh! The only girl he took a shine to was my own daughter. His half-sister. Anyway you're the one who brought Margaret here.'

I was glad to hear he called her Margaret now and not 'the milliner suffragette'.

Mrs Turner said, 'Yes, because I thought she might talk him into seeing his way clear to accept a commission.'

I hurried back into the drawing room, dashed straight in regardless and said, 'Margaret, what about this choker? Who's wearing it, you or me?'

Thomas turned and smiled at me. He crossed the room, took my hand and drew me across to Margaret. I know they say this in books and it sounds silly, but his eyes danced. 'With Margaret by my side and you *on* my side, I can't go wrong.' But he said it mockingly, and I felt silly. 'Tell her, Margaret.'

'We're going to be married,' Margaret said.

I said, 'Congratulations. I hope you'll both be very happy.'

'It won't be yet,' Margaret said. 'We could be engaged for some time.' She held out her hand. 'Diamonds and sapphires,' she said. Just in case I didn't recognize the stones.

That answered my question about the sapphire choker. I admired the ring and gave her the choker. Thomas fastened it and kissed the back of her neck.

Just in that moment, I wished I were beautiful.

The gong struck.

A huge candelabra lit the dining room. Dozens of candles sat on a great oak sideboard carved

194

with flowers and fruits. I caught sight of the five of us in the big gilt mirror above the fireplace. We seemed like strangers in a dream of a palace. An enormous bowl of roses sat in the centre of the table; a few petals had fallen onto the white damask cloth. The butler poured champagne into my glittering glass.

Mr Mitchell, sitting at the top end of the table, hid his surprise at the champagne. 'My request, sir,' said Thomas.

Mrs Turner sat at the bottom end of the table. She frowned as Mr Mitchell got to his feet. The candlelight caught the glitter as he raised his glass.

'A toast,' Mr Mitchell said, 'to all the gallant and courageous young people. May they find their way through this war with honour.'

No one could object to that.

We raised our glasses and drank to ourselves and all our generation.

'I have an announcement to make.' Thomas stood and spread his fingers on the white cloth. 'Margaret has consented to be my wife.' He raised his glass. 'To Margaret.'

Mrs Turner's face! The colour drained away. For goodness' sake, what did she expect? Margaret's beautiful, talented, exceptional! And Mrs Turner introduced them. Anyone else would have seen it coming. She must have been annoyed that Margaret had got the engagement ring without persuading Thomas to join up. Mr Mitchell raised his glass and proposed a toast to the happy couple. I saw Mrs Turner's throat contract as she gulped before taking a drink.

The others had sipped. I'd taken rather big gulps. The butler re-filled my glass.

I looked at my sparkling plate, wondering when someone would spoon a mouthful of food onto it. Someone did. I smelled herring but it was a kind of paste with bits of toast around it. I picked up the heaviest knife and fork I have ever held in my hands, about to tuck in, but not for long.

'I have another announcement,' Thomas smiled around the table.

I began to see that if you are poor, at least you are allowed to get on with your supper. I put my knife and fork down and picked up my glass.

'I had a meeting with a Government press officer. I have put in my application – the strongest application I can make – to be a war correspondent. I'm hopeful of acceptance.'

'Well done, m'boy,' Mr Mitchell said. I thought his surprise seemed put on. I guessed that he must have known about it.

Mrs Turner looked from Thomas to Mr Mitchell to Margaret. I could see what she was thinking. All her plans to persuade Thomas to join up, or to have Margaret persuade him, were unnecessary. Her son had arrived at a conclusion on his own without her interference.

I waited for the toast. It came from Margaret. She obviously thought she had better get the hang of this kind of thing, though I'm not sure females are supposed to do it. She raised her glass. 'To Thomas, and to his journey to the engines of war, to finding the truth and telling that truth from his heart, as only he can.'

We raised our glasses and we all drank.

Mrs Turner picked up her knife and fork. I did, too.

I was glad to concentrate on getting some food in my belly, though I did have to chit-chat to Mrs Turner. She seemed to think she had to talk to me, as though we hadn't spent most of the day on the train together and as though I hadn't put my foot in my mouth earlier.

Margaret sat on my left and was talking to Thomas, who sat opposite us, and to Mr Mitchell, who sat on her left.

It wasn't until we were eating beef in a posh stew that I got chance to say to Thomas that I didn't understand how someone who disagreed with a war could go off and report it.

I was put right by both Thomas and his mother. Another kind of wine had been poured into another kind of glass and I probably should have left it well alone. Then I may have been able to see why going off to be a war correspondent is quite a Different Thing Altogether than fighting a war, but equally Deeply Honourable.

It seems that Thomas has reported on a war before. A couple of years ago he was with the Balkans army in Bulgaria, or it may have been the Bulgarian army in the Balkans. He says that he will now take part in what is the most crucial experience of his generation and he will be a witness. He will tell the truth for his own generation and for posterity. I think it was something like that.

I started to feel sick. It was not the drink. It was not through eating a sort of fancy beef stew after herring. It was them, sitting with them. Mr

Mitchell and Mrs Turner. Little looks they exchanged. I'm sure Thomas was persuaded to apply for that job by his dad to please his mother. I wish Margaret was marrying into a family that was more straightforward, I really do.

As the butler took the plates away, I thought of walking down Bread Street with our handcart full of pies, covered with beef sheeting to keep the flies off, hungry children watching us pass.

I excused myself as the pudding came and said I had a headache. I walked in a very straight line to the door and up the stairs, holding onto the bannister, not missing a footing. I went very slowly. It wasn't till I got to the landing that I was sick. I would have got to the bathroom if I could have remembered which way it was.

I am all right now. I had to sleep with one leg out of the bed, anchoring it onto a chair to keep the room from spinning. But I got up in the night and was sick again, this time into the bowl on the washstand. After that I felt all right.

I woke to the dawn chorus.

Of course, I don't know if I pulled it off and they thought I really did just have a headache. I expect that nasty maid will have found a snide way of telling everyone how I puked all over the landing. I don't care.

I dread the thought of going home with Mrs Turner on the train. Poor Margaret will be trying to ingratiate herself and she will never do it. It should not be hard for me to close my eyes, sleep all the way and pretend this whole horrible business never happened.

Even the thought of walking across London

Bridge seems too much for me to contemplate today. But I shall if it's the last thing I do. I suppose I could be sick in the Thames if necessary.

TWENTY-NINE

Cruel Fate. If I heard those words once from Cousin Bernard, I heard them twenty times.

Margaret, Bernard and me had boarded the special train laid on by North-eastern Railways for families and friends to visit their soldier relatives training in Colsterdale. We were off to see Kevin and Johnny.

I loved the journey through the Yorkshire Dales. Rapidly shifting clouds changed shape in the bright, clear sky. You'd think some invisible magician constantly waved a wand. Cloud shadows chased each other across fields.

Margaret had her own umbrella. I shared with Bernard. I can see why any right-thinking person would not want him holding a gun. He waved the brolly constantly as we walked from the railway station to the camp, letting raindrops run down my neck as he ranted about Cruel Fate.

People started saying that there was no one waiting at the camp to meet us. Margaret said they were probably out hopping in the fields, as that is part of their training, according to Kevin's letter. They hop on one leg around the field, then hop on the other leg in the opposite direction. Bernard says it is to prove you can balance. But why should you have to go on proving that?

Hundreds of us waited in the rain outside the army camp. For hours. I do feel sorry for Bernard. But I feel sorrier for myself for having to listen to him. 'The point is, Julia, the point is...' He has complained for weeks about Cruel Fate denying him the chance to be a pianist on the liners. Now Cruel Fate has delivered him another blow. 'The point is, Julia, the point is...'

He had gone with the others to sign up for the Leeds Pals. Everybody knew how many men they needed to recruit. The illuminated light bulbs on the side of the recruiting tram under 'GOD SAVE THE KING' announced 5,000 recruits were wanted. But they didn't want Bernard McAndrew. He claims he intends to pay for a tram illumination. It will say 'GOD SAVE THE KING, 5,000 recruits wanted, but not Bernard McAndrew'.

There he had stood, in the recruitment hall, in his trousers and socks, feeling silly but putting up with it. A quarter of an inch short of 5ft 6½in, but then so are plenty of others. Bernard's breathing proved sound and his molars satisfactory. He stepped onto a sheet of green baize and hopped across the floor to prove that his feet are not flat. Just because he couldn't read the letters on an optician's card from a distance of 20ft, he was pronounced unfit for service.

Margaret interrupted to say Bernard's chest was only 50 per cent sound. He has a weak lung. Bernard sneered at her ignorance. He has one perfectly good lung and if it is good enough for him it is good enough for the army.

Rain dripping down my collar. Muddy shoes and skirt. Wet, dirty stockings. Bernard going on and on, oblivious of grey sky and teeming rain. How what he found out afterwards just takes the blooming biscuit and all the crumbs. It seems that Kevin couldn't make out all the letters on the optician's card either, but listened to Johnny and memorized the letters. That's how Kevin got in.

I took the umbrella from him in the end. He didn't notice. Rain streamed down his hair, his face and his clothes. He said, 'Just tell me, Julia, is that fair?'

Each time I tried to change the subject, Cruel Fate sprang to his lips and I had no means of escape. They should put him in the front line. Let him exhaust the Germans into submission. After half an hour of Cousin Bernard and Cruel Fate, the Huns would turn and hop back to Germany as fast as their legs would carry them.

The skin on Bernard's face looks tighter than ever. His ears have grown. They move of their own accord when he gets indignant.

I tried to make him see a good side to it. 'I could say it's bad luck, Bernard, but we never know how things are going to turn out. Just think, if you'd gone, Uncle Lloyd would have all his sons in the war. He might not want that.'

'Kevin and Johnny are favourites,' Bernard said really quietly, his ears bright red, dripping rain and very still. 'I'm the one Dad least likes to have about the place.'

I couldn't contradict him because I know that is true. So I said that parents shouldn't have favourites and that I won't, when I have children.

Of course, he only ever gets worse in that sort of mood. 'No woman will ever marry me, so the question of favourites and unfavourites won't come up.'

I could have tried to reassure him and told him that of course someone will marry him. The most unlikely men find wives. Instead I tried to change the subject again. I asked him if he knew how many things you can do with a dandelion. Surprisingly, he did.

By which time we all had to go back to the station and get the train home, disappointed. No sign of our boys.

Some people said they'd already set off for France.

Received this letter from Cousin Kevin today:

Dear Margaret and Julia

It was good of you to come up last Saturday. Johnny and me fed up at not seeing you. Everyone got hopping mad when we knew hundreds of relatives and friends waited in the rain for hours. Our colonel knew fine well about the train bringing our families and friends. But they like to let you know that once you are in the army you are not your own man. Where were we? Being marched over to Lord Masham's Swinton Estate. He gave rabbits – vermin to him – to our battalion to 'supplement our diet'. We marched six miles over there, gave three cheers to him for the contribution of his big furry rats, and marched back. Three cheers! I tell you, hurray wasn't what some of us were saying. I don't blame Lord Masham. Our colonel was invited to dinner there and simply had a mind to put on a show.

Enough of that. There are fine chaps here and though there is a lot of exercising and parading we make our fun, too. One chap has had his gramophone sent up from home and so we imagine we are back in Leeds in the Grand Theatre or the Varieties listening to Our Miss Gibbs, Maid of the Mountains and Gilbert and Sullivan operas.

Johnny sends his best. Regards to Uncle Joe.
Your cousin
Kevin

P.S. Julia – when we come home on leave we hope to have a party and want to invite the girl who sits in Brownlaw's chemist shop window advertising hair lotion. She has long wavy hair all the way down to her – to the chair seat. Someone said she is the sister of a friend of yours. We can't ask her, but you can. In haste, K.

THIRTY

Grey, drizzly afternoon. Took an apple round for Solomon, who had just been out pulling the cart. Solomon always seems pleased with himself when he has been out working, even on a horrible day like today.

Margaret asked if I fancied a walk round town. I didn't intend to go into Brownlaw's chemists and do Kevin and Johnny's bidding regarding the girl who sits in the window advertising hair lotion. We were nearby, on Briggate, and went to look out of curiosity.

She sits with her back to you, so still that she could be a statue. Her red-gold wavy hair reaches past her bum and fringes out around the stool. A card propped by the stool says that she once lost her hair through illness and worry, but Feather's Supreme Hair Lotion restored her tresses to their former glory. You think: Who is she?

Of course, we had to go in, and take a look at her face. Truly she is most striking, with looks that belong on a picture postcard. Light, honey-coloured skin, hazel eyes and perfectly arched brows. Her lips – no one has such red lips in real life – form a bow. And she has a dimple on her chin. How she stares so long without appearing to blink, I do not know. Her hands lay still in her lap, so you would believe her to be a dummy except for the slight rise and fall of her chest. The very air around her feels mysterious and tragic so that we could almost believe she had lost her hair through illness and worry. 'The sister of a friend of yours,' Kevin had said. I wanted to know her name.

Mr Brownlaw swaggered to the counter himself. He's a small man with shiny pop eyes, a plump, red, closely shaven face and a handlebar moustache. He served Margaret peppermints, popping them into a little cone-shaped bag with his fat, pale fingers. He has beautifully manicured nails and I'm sure he must run a white pencil under them. All the while he kept staring at Margaret and shaking his head. She blushed. He was trying to place her, he said, and then he did.

Seemingly, the night I left Bernard's party early, to take Dad home, Mr Brownlaw came along. Kevin and Johnny had very clumsily tried to invite the girl in the window to their party, but they got tongue-tied and left the shop having invited Mr Brownlaw instead. Because he sometimes drinks in the small bar at the Dragon, he hadn't taken the invitation as anything but friendly and his entitlement.

Now he remembered Margaret from the party. Margaret, polite as ever, asked Mr Brownlaw about his children. He frowned and acted surprised that she knew about his 'poor motherless boys' as he called them. She reminded him that he had shown her their photograph.

All the while he shook his head, which seems to be his favourite mannerism. Then he took another cone bag and filled that with mints, too. With a very grand gesture, like presenting a book on school prize day, he handed over the second ha'penny bag, with his compliments to me.

He said, 'One for you, Miss Wood, and one for your friend.'

Margaret said thank you and that I was her sister.

He said he would not have had us down as coming out of the same stable. I hated him. And I hated Margaret, too. Margaret had dressed in her best green skirt, with her green hat and veil and white gloves. I had been out delivering for Aunty Amy, having learned to ride the bicycle, and my hair was all straggly and frizzed because I'd had no time to do anything with it. Besides that, I'd tumbled off the bike as I tried to bring it to a stop at 29 Valley Street and I'd torn my blouse and scraped my wrist.

Suddenly from me going along with Margaret for a walk-about, to cheer her up, I felt very very low myself. Margaret's the lady and I'm the work-horse. But I don't care two figs for Mr Brownlaw's opinion.

As we left the shop, he walked us to the door and said, 'You remind Bernard that I still owe him a ride in my motor car. Tell him it won't be a huge jaunt, wouldn't do with a war on.'

Margaret said she'd pass on the message. I ignored him.

Once we were outside, I asked Margaret what she thought of the girl in the window. I said that I can see why she fascinated Kevin and Johnny, but is she beautiful?

Sometimes Margaret makes sharp, observant remarks. She said that men like women who look good, sit still and say nothing.

She also solved the mystery. The silent beauty is Annie Garretty.

'I know her by her hair,' Margaret said.

'Why didn't I know about her?' I asked.

'She disappeared when she was very little. Someone at school said she'd been taken by the gypsies. It scared us to think about her.'

I don't understand why no one in the Garretty family ever spoke of her. I thought Cissie told me everything.

I have seen the exact moment when a person falls in love. Now I know that I have never been in love because I stood two yards away and felt the emotion rolling off Bernard like steam out of a kettle. He even passed out, which could be dangerous.

Kevin and Johnny are due home on leave and wrote to Bernard saying that they are desperate to invite 'the girl in Brownlaw's window' to the theatre. My presence was supposed to make all seem proper and above board. Not that I could count on things being proper and above board where Kevin and Johnny are concerned.

They instructed Bernard to take flowers, which are not plentiful at this time of year. Bernard spent more than he intended on a spray of chrysanthemums, which I carried since Bernard refused to be seen with them. I gave him a little push into the shop doorway and thrust the bouquet into his hands. She really is quite beautiful, with wide cheekbones and startled eyes like a wild animal.

Bernard sort of licked his lips in the way you do if your mouth goes dry. He laid the flowers at her feet and said that he was presenting this bouquet from his soldier brothers. Mr Brownlaw must have told her never to speak or blink. She didn't budge. Bernard held out his hand and said, 'I'm Bernard McAndrew.'

She gulped slightly as if being silent for so long made speech difficult for her. She ran her tongue over her lips and said, 'Annie.'

Bernard took her hand. When he let her hand go he put his own hand to his head as if he had terrible pain behind his eyes. Then his hand went to his chest, like an actor in the melodrama or in the moving pictures. I thought he was trying to be comical, but he couldn't take his eyes off

Annie and I couldn't take my eyes off him. Then he fainted.

But that wasn't the moment he fell in love.

Mr Brownlaw led him into the back room and I went, too. Mr Brownlaw gave Bernard a glass of water and then something else, a reviving powder to sniff.

After that, I just sat with Bernard, waiting for him to say when he felt better. And I don't know what it was but Bernard's headache disappeared as quickly as it had come. He started to talk about how he felt. Sitting on a spindly straight chair, he said he didn't mind that he'd been turned down by the army. Because now he saw that the world had a pattern to it, shape, colour, meaning. It was a place where it was possible to live and to be happy. He stared at his own bony knees in his twill trousers as if he'd never seen knees or twill trousers before.

Annie glided in while he was speaking, stood over him and put her hand on his forehead. He looked up at her and they just gazed at each other. I saw two people fall in love. They didn't even know I was there.

Mr Brownlaw did not appear to notice. He fussed a little over Bernard and then instructed Annie to leave the window and take up her post at the counter. She must be used to stillness for, as she took her place behind the counter, I thought of a story where a statue came to life and then became stone again.

As we were about to leave the shop, Mr Brownlaw said to Bernard, 'Now, young McAndrew. Let's settle on that outing. I have some medical supplies to deliver. You can enjoy the thrill of a motor car ride with me. That'll bring the colour back into your cheeks.'

What excitement! The motor car lurched and jolted along the cobbles. It is not like a horse that you must give instructions. Mr Brownlaw's motor car belches and bumps with a life of its own. He hit his horn, ordering pedestrians and carts out of the way. Bernard whispered to me, 'The man's mad when he gets behind a wheel.'

As we got to the Dragon, we saw Margaret on the corner. Bernard jumped out, and Mr Brownlaw invited her to come along for the ride. The four of us sped all the way to Chapel Allerton where unfortunately we ran aground on the hospital lawn, with heaps of earth thrown up behind us and smoke belching from the exhaust.

Mr Brownlaw switched off just before we came to a halt by a tree, then leaped out and delivered his packages to the hospital. Several men helped us get started again and we came home in great style, but a little shook up.

'What a pity we didn't wear our motoring hats,' Margaret said after she had thanked him very much.

I felt a little sick but managed to keep it down until he had gone.

THIRTY-ONE

I hadn't expected him. The gas mantle was threatening to give up on me. It spluttered and flared. I wanted to go on reading as I'd got to the part in *Caleb Williams* where Caleb opens the forbidden box.

A few weeks ago I wouldn't have jumped out of my skin at a tap-tap on the door. Now I feel as if it's not just the country at war – me and Dad are in the wars, too.

I slid off the chain when I heard Frank's voice. He stood on the step, clutching something under his jacket, and asked if he could come in. He looked at the open novel on the table and it seemed to upset him. I think it's because he never picks up a book and doesn't understand how I can lose myself in one.

He took a brown-paper parcel from under his jacket and handed it to me. It weighed soft in my hands. 'Go on, open it. It's for thee.'

I slid the string off and slipped my fingers onto something warm that felt alive. I pulled my hand away.

Frank laughed and said, 'It won't bite thee, lass. It's a jacket.'

As I opened the brown paper, an envelope fell onto the floor. Frank picked it up and set it on the table. 'It's the brass I owe thee for losing thah pie money on't dogs. And a bit more, to cover the loss of thy handcart.'

He said he would have come sooner, but he wanted to pay us properly, in full, and for the cart, and to say sorry about losing everything for us.

I'd been angry at the time, out of fear that we wouldn't manage. Now I was glad. Once and for all I'd stopped being the pie man's daughter.

I smoothed the fur jacket and held it up. 'I can't accept this.'

Frank took both of my hands in his. He has a lot of small cuts on his hands, from working with the skins, and bruises from his fights. 'It's ocelot,' he said, about the jacket, as if I'd asked.

'I still can't take it.' But he held the jacket and I tried it on. It fitted.

'Wear it, pawn it, flog it or chuck it on't fireback. It's thine, Julia. There won't be any more till after't war.'

'If there won't be any more, what'll happen to all the furriers?'

He shrugged. I knew before he answered that he had come to tell me he'd joined the army.

I sat on the chair, and put the jacket over my knees.

He sat beside me. 'I thought I was due a bit of fur, for all my hard work.'

He needn't have told me he'd stolen it. I already knew.

The gas mantle chose that moment to splutter and die. In the darkness, he told me why he had decided to join up. This might be his only chance to fight in a war, an opportunity to show his patriotism. Then who knew how things would be afterwards? After a war, things were bound to be better for those who'd fought. It shouldn't take long to sort things out over there, show the Germans a bit of what for. They were nothing more than barbarians – my dad excepted.

He seemed so sure of himself that I had no heart to argue. I knew he would never see things differently. The words came out before I could stop myself. 'Frank, have you seen the casualty lists?'

'We'll make the world safe.' Frank took my hand. 'Safe for them we love.'

I remembered when I first saw Frank. I was five years old. My mother looked out of the window and saw him playing in the gas tar, runny nose, arse hanging out of his trousers. As she looked, he turned and put his nose in the air, sniffing like a little lost dog. Mam had made some soup with a bit of mutton. 'God love the poor bairn,' Mam had said. 'Fetch him in, Julia.'

Frank squeezed my hand. 'I've missed thee.'

'I've missed thee,' I said.

We turned towards each other at the same moment to say something or other, I don't know what. That's when we kissed. Without a word he took off his jacket and shoes, then my shoes, very slowly and carefully. He kissed my feet, my ankles, my calves. After that we lay side by side on the chair, kissing, and holding each other. He pressed his body against mine. I've never felt like that before. He stayed for hours and hours. It got dark and I fell asleep. When I woke, he was looking at me and kissed me again, and it was morning.

I am not going to write what we did. But I will

never be the same again.

I put the kettle on the gas ring and made us tea while Frank changed the mantle. Dad would be home soon.

Frank pulled on his shoes and coat, and gulped down his tea.

'I love thee, Julia,' he said, as we kissed by the door.

'And I love thee, Frank,' I said. But part of me seemed to be hovering above, watching, and when I heard my words, something didn't ring true.

What have I done?

Dad came in just a few minutes later. I wondered if he'd seen Frank leaving. But he had something else on his mind. His job has ended. He was not as down about it as I expected. He said the wonder is that it went on as long as it did, into the winter.

THIRTY-TWO

I now know why some people call Aunty Amy a witch. After we had eaten, she said would I come with her to take soup along to her old lodger Dorothy and her husband, as Dorothy was very near her time.

I carried the soup in the pot with two handles, draping a teacloth over it, although anyone who wanted to guess would know it was a pot of something to eat. Aunty Amy carried her birthing bag with her, 'just in case'.

We cut through the alley and past the Wheat-sheaf to where Dorothy and Cyril Pickles live, at number seventeen. As we got to the door, it opened. Cyril Pickles is a tall man, about 5ft 10in, with a ruddy face and a shock of black hair. When he stands still, as he did in the doorway, with his mouth gaping open, you don't notice his club foot.

'I were just coming for thee, Amy,' he said.

I put the soup on the fire hob, as Cyril had the kettle on the gas ring.

Aunty Amy went to the bottom of the stairs. 'Fetch mi bag up in a minute, Julia.'

I opened my mouth to say I'd go home now, but before I had chance to speak she added, 'Thah'll need to know about these things. Better sooner than later.'

Her words struck me like a lance. Did she guess about my night with Frank? Perhaps she could see something about me that others couldn't and knew that I was already pregnant, before I could know myself? I have never kept a note of when my bleeding time comes. It just does and I usually feel it coming the day before, and that's all I needed to know. Until now.

I picked up her bag and followed her upstairs where the elephantine Dorothy was lumbering about the bedroom. She turned to me and groaned. 'Don't do it, that's all I'd say. Don't ever do it, Julia.'

'Nay, you'll be singing a different tune tomorrow,' Aunty Amy said. 'You keep moving while you can.'

Dorothy gripped the washstand. She put her

hand to her back and moaned in what seemed agony. And she hadn't even started yet.

I put my hand to my belly. What if I came to this? The shame of it. Everyone would know what I'd done. And how would I manage things if I had a child to care for? I thought of Margaret's account of Clarice's worn-out sister, bairns on her apron strings, one in her belly, spilling the slop bucket in the street.

'Julia, open my bag and set't stuff out on't washstand,' Aunty Amy said.

I put the leather bag on a chair and pressed the catch. Everything was neatly wrapped and packed. I took out a bottle of antiseptic, a tin of boracic powder, dusting powder, methylated spirit, scissors, bath thermometer, Vaseline, safety pins, soap and nail brush.

'Be a love, empty that for me,' Dorothy said, kicking the piss-pot with her slippered toes.

I have never seen a pot so full. I had to bring the bucket up to tip it in. When I came back from emptying the bucket in the privy, I washed my hands at the sink.

Cyril was finishing his soup. He smacked his lips. 'Tasty. Dorothy said thah made good soup. D'you mind if I tek a drop of this next door to young Harold Wragg?'

'Course,' I said. 'It's yours. We brought it for you and Dorothy.'

Harold Wragg. The name sounded familiar, but it took a few seconds for me to realize. He was the small, skinny lad who'd taken part in attacking me and Dad all those months ago.

'What's up with him?' I asked.

'Poor lad. He were that badly beaten, they thought he'd been run over by a horse and cart. Mrs Wragg reported it to the police, and for the Wraggs to visit the cop shop, it must be serious.'

'When did it happen?'

'Let me see, it were late Wednesday last, or early Thursday. Some bugger just took hold of him when he were by't market doing his odd jobs, and let him have what for. No rhyme or reason.'

Frank's train had left Leeds on Thursday morning.

Frank had said he wanted us to have no secrets. He had asked me if I had told him the truth when I said that Harold Wragg had nothing to do with the attack. Or had I protected Harold because I felt sorry for him? I admitted I had, thinking it was water under the bridge. I said that I thought Harold a pathetic creature and he should be let alone.

I can't get rid of the picture in my mind of Frank's fist landing on Harold's face, his ribs, his stomach, and of Harold crumpling like a rag doll in the gutter. Frank shouldn't have done that. I had already felt bad, thinking I may be carrying his child. After hearing what he had done, I felt worse. I had to be sure.

'I think I know that lad,' I said. 'Let me take him the soup.'

Cyril looked up at the ceiling, silently asking me whether I wasn't needed up there.

'I'll be two minutes,' I said. 'Spoon some soup into a jar.'

Cyril took the ladle and carefully poured soup into a tin mug. For a large man, he moved gracefully and did not spill a drop.

I didn't know how I would explain to Mrs Wragg that I wanted to speak to her son, but fortunately he limped to the door himself. His face bore bruise marks, faded to yellow and green. A cut under his eye hadn't properly healed. I handed him the mug of soup. 'It's for you. Cyril next door wanted you to have this.'

His wrist was thin as a wooden spoon handle. He gripped the mug in his bony hand.

I didn't know who might be behind him, listening. I said quietly, 'This is important. I have to know. Who did this to you?'

He parted his lips, but no sound came, as if he feared to speak.

'I made the soup,' I said. 'I hope it'll do you some good. But you have to tell me. Was it Frank?' He still didn't answer me. 'Just nod or shake your head. Was it Frank Whitelock?'

He nodded.

'I didn't want him to,' I said. 'I didn't mean him to.'

He shut the door.

I hoped I wasn't carrying Frank's baby. Because I decided in that moment that Frank would never be the man for me.

Dorothy cried out as I came into the room. Her knees drawn up, she lay on her side, pushing her feet against an upright board at the bottom of the bed. She was tugging on a roller towel that was tied to the foot of the bed, her face twisted in pain.

Aunty Amy rubbed her back. I took the damp flannel and wiped the sweat from her brow, her throat and chest.

She let go of the roller towel and gripped my hand. 'I can't get reet, and I can't shift.'

'You're reet, lass,' Aunty Amy said. 'You're doing good.'

'I'm cramped. Me legs!'

I rubbed her legs. Her huge belly seemed to be moving and I thought it might burst open at any moment. Just when I thought I couldn't do it any more, Aunty Amy changed places with me and I rubbed Dorothy's back.

I don't know how long we had been like that when Dorothy let out a louder yell and said, 'It's coming.'

My instinct was to run. I stopped rubbing her back, but she didn't notice.

'I can see the head,' Aunty Amy said. 'Stop bearing down now, lass, just pant, or cry out. Let the bairn come.'

I remembered that I was to dip a piece of cotton wool into the boracic lotion, and have a piece of clean linen ready. I stood by the washstand, ready to hand them over.

Dorothy panted and cried, and then Aunty Amy held a red, slimy baby in her hands. 'It's a grand boy, Dorothy. Wipe his eyes, Julia, like I told you.'

I wiped the baby's eyelids from the nose outwards with the cotton wool. With the piece of clean linen on my little finger I cleared the mucus from its tiny mouth. I thought I would feel afraid of touching it, but I didn't.

The baby let out a cry, as if objecting to my interference. I held him as Aunty Amy tied the cord in two places, first a couple of inches from the baby's body and then close to Dorothy. She cut the cord near the baby's end and covered it with linen. Cyril stood at the door with the warm flannel. He would have handed it round without daring to look, but at the last moment he came in, and his gentle face lit up as he saw the baby.

'They're both grand,' Aunty Amy said.

'Can I hold him?' Cyril wrapped the baby in the warm flannel, and placed him in the little cot they had ready.

'Don't look at me!' Dorothy said. 'I don't want you to see me in this state.'

But he went to her and kissed her forehead.

'You get downstairs, Cyril,' Aunty Amy ordered. 'We haven't done yet.'

I went down with him, feeling I'd had enough and didn't want to see any more. But I went back later, to help bath the baby.

As we walked home, I said, 'What about Cyril's mam? Couldn't she help?'

Aunty Amy walked slowly, tired out from her work. 'Cyril's mam'll have her work cut out from tomorrow, looking after them all till Dorothy's up and about again.'

I knew my next remark would sound like a betrayal but there was no tactful way of putting it. 'Why you?' I said. 'They could afford a doctor.'

'Aye, they could. But the bugger doesn't wash his hands.'

After that neither of us spoke. I just heard the voice in my head. *That could be you, idiot. You could be pregnant.* I'm filled with dread. Frank said we would marry and he'd be glad to. But I'm too young. I don't think you can marry till you're sixteen. What have I done?

Goodnight, book.

THIRTY-THREE

Everyone hates it but I love finding my way home in November fog, scarf over my mouth. I had walked to Regent Street to deliver a eucalyptus inhalation and chest rub to a bronchial gentleman ('One part eucalyptus to twenty-five parts base oil'). I came back along Green Road, Burmantofts and Great Garden Street onto Bread Street. Silent and scary; you thank the folk who light their gas mantles and leave the blind up to give a blur of light.

While you are finding your way home from work through a thick, choking fog, you know that you can do anything in this wide world, yet at the same time you know you might never find your way through. But while it lasts it blankets out everything – war, worries, hopes and dreads.

Dad had the fire going when I got home. He had some good news. Because so many men from the slaughterhouse have joined up, they have set him on again – casual. They never knew what kind of foreigner he was and he has told them he is Belgian. That is two lots of good news because – phew! – Frank and I did not do what I thought we did. What a relief. 'If in doubt, look it up in a book' is my motto from now on. The book in question is a small, chunky volume with a soft calfskin cover and is entitled *Human Anatomy*. I found it on Aunty Amy's shelf between *Ailments of Horses* and *Flowers of the Field*. It is full of diagrams and has a whole section on human reproduction. Thank goodness I am not going to reproduce. If I did it would be by immaculate conception. Now that I can breathe again I will probably get my bleeding time. I'm sure my anxiety must have scared it away.

Something woke me. They must have rattled the letterbox. Dad has no sense of smell and, if he'd been alone, he could have died.

I went to the window, thinking the smell came from outside. The figure stood opposite by Grundy's alley, watching. Then he saw me and limped away. I only know of two men that size with a limp. One is Cyril Pickles, Dorothy's husband, the other is Clarence Laycock from Dad's work, and I am sure it was him because Cyril has an up-and-down limp and Clarence's is a drag-along-the-ground limp and it was that kind. I think it is important to write this down for possible future evidence.

The smell was like fog and kippers. I opened my bedroom door, and at the bottom of the stairs saw flames and smoke behind the outside door. Good job I hadn't emptied my piss-pot yesterday. I ran downstairs, spilling it as I went, and tossed the contents onto the burning rags. Dad's bedchair creaked as he moved and he called out to me. I stood there shivering, my bare feet and the bottom of my nighty wet, the rags on the stone floor smouldering. Dad rubbed sleep from his eyes and put an arm around me.

This time he didn't pretend that it was the work of a drunk. Dad dried my feet with the towel and tucked me up in his bedchair. He took the candle through to the doorway and fetched the mop from the cellar.

Someone had tried to burn us alive.

Dad wants to go to the police and give himself up as a German alien, and for me to move into the Dragon.

I said no. They are saying the war could be over by Christmas. We can hold out till then.

We have moved the table to the wall opposite the window, where the bureau used to be. Dad's bedchair is by the wall opposite the fire, to be out of the way should anything come through the window. He will prop the downstairs door open. I will sleep with my door open. We have filled buckets with water. Ready.

A postcard from Frank. They have not been allowed out of camp. This is his first chance to write. I know he is a poor correspondent but the fact that he will not try his hand at a letter just confirms that I have done the right thing in deciding that there will never be any future for the two of us. Because we were good friends for so long, I shall keep on writing to him. In wartime I suppose people do things they would not do otherwise. In peacetime, you could find the meanness to say hop it. He hopes I am well and thanks me for my letter. He hopes to get some leave for Christmas and has something important to ask me. If it is what I think, I shall probably have to tell him to hop it.

I knew that Margaret would be with Miss Mason today, so thought it might be a good idea to talk to her. Now that she is engaged, and since she had managed to play Thomas Turner like a fish on a rod, I thought she may have some ideas about how I could say no, kindly, to Frank. I set off for Miss Mason's High-Class Millinery establishment.

A tiny wizened newspaper-seller stood on the corner of Mabgate, calling out in a great foghorn of a voice, 'Huns shell Scarborough. Read all about Yorkshire dead.'

People were clamouring for papers. I was pushed and jostled. The papers sell out so quickly now. But I managed to buy one. The story leaped out from the paragraph headings. Scarborough, Whitby and Hartlepool had all been shelled by the German fleet. The *Derrflinger* and the *Von Der Tann* had fired hundreds of shells, killing nineteen people. More than eighty had been injured.

So many of the places that have been reported about since the beginning of the war were far away and we had never heard of them. This brought the war home.

It felt strange stepping inside Miss Mason's shop, remembering the night Frank and I robbed it. The bell I had successfully silenced the night of my robbery twanged cheerfully as I stepped inside.

Miss Mason trotted out from the back room, her face alive with hope at a prospective customer. She looked crestfallen when she saw me, but fluffed out the bow on her blouse and made some welcoming noises. She looked even thinner than when I had last seen her and her face had a greyish tinge, like tissue paper that has gone dirty after being stuffed in damp shoes.

Miss Mason always used to keep a good fire burning in winter, but when she asked me into the back room I shivered. There was a fire, with a few coals, but it was the kind of fire you knew was for show, because of a visitor. Margaret sat at the table, sipping tea. Miss Mason topped up the pot and offered me a cup. 'I'm afraid I've run out of sugar,' she said. 'There might be a scraping of honey if I swill the tea round the jar. I won't be shopping till tomorrow.'

I decided to keep the news about the bombing to myself for a few minutes. 'I prefer it without sugar,' I lied.

The tea was like hot water, with just a little colouring. As Miss Mason poured, I noticed that her wrists were skeletal.

Usually the period before Christmas was a busy time for her, with lots of ladies buying new hats. There was no sign of any hats being made.

'It seems quiet,' I said.

Miss Mason sighed and was about to say something tactful, but Margaret said, 'Between we three and the doorpost, we've given up making hats. No one has bought a hat since the outbreak of war.'

Miss Mason gave that little smile that never has the confidence to stay on her face for more than a second. 'Except you, Julia. You suited that straw hat.'

'But it's over four months since the start of the war. I don't understand.' I looked at Miss Mason. 'People come miles for one of your creations.' That's why Margaret wanted to be her apprentice.

Her pleasure in my remark seemed to bring a touch of colour to her cheeks, but only for a second. She stirred my tea, even though it had no sugar and less than a teaspoonful of milk. 'Ladies seem to think it's unpatriotic to buy a new hat during wartime. I don't know what we poor milliners shall do.'

Margaret folded a teacloth. 'People claim it won't last beyond Christmas. Let's hope we'll have a better New Year.' I recognized the teacloth as coming from the Dragon, and realized she must have brought food with her.

'And let's hope the fashions don't change too much!' Miss Mason said, 'Or I shall have a shop full of unwanted hats.'

When we left the shop, it was sleeting down, and Margaret didn't want to go with me to meet Dad from work. But when I told her the news of the bombarding of the east coast, she changed her mind and came with me. She had her umbrella and we linked arms and she held it tipped a little to keep the sleet off our faces. 'Why didn't you tell me before about the news?'

I said, 'Miss Mason seems in such a poor way. I didn't like to bring up some new calamity.' A carriage roared by and of course I was nearest the road and got my skirt and feet splashed.

Margaret said, 'She has a little put by in the Penny Bank, for a rainy day. I want to say to her, "Miss Mason, this is the rainy day." But I don't like to.'

At Dad's work, I stood by the big doors and Margaret stayed out in the street, in a shop doorway. I could see Dad finishing for the day, scrubbing at the floor with the long brush and a bucket of water, sweeping the water towards the gulley by the wall where the slurry and blood runs. Pig-face Clarence pushed past Dad and 'accidentally' knocked the bucket against his leg. Pig-face shouted at Dad. Something about having fought the Boers, and his son following in his footsteps, training at Colsterdale. Then he called to another man that Dad must have friends in high places or he wouldn't still be earning good English money and stealing good English meat.

Dad kept on sweeping. It hurt my heart to see him treated so badly. I wanted to rush in, take the brush and hit Clarence with it. But that would be the last thing Dad would want.

Once someone locked him in the ice room. Dad said it was an accident. He says I shouldn't come to meet him.

When I saw him packing up, I went off to stand with Margaret and we walked to the corner, acting as if we were just on our way. Dad seemed pleased to see us. He knew about the Germans bombarding the east coast and said that at work people were saying to him, 'How is it thah've only been a Belgian since war started?'

He says that he answers he has always been a Belgian, and he sticks to that. We walked Margaret back to the Dragon, and then Dad and I went home. He had managed to bring some offal out under his coat so I shall be making pies.

But this time just for ourselves and the Garrettys. Oh, and I suppose I shall be making one for Miss Mason.

I forgot all about Frank and his 'important question' until I got home and saw his postcard on the mantelpiece.

Thomas has written a Christmas letter to me! I do not get many letters. I shall paste this in my journal.

Dear Julia

Margaret gives me news of you and your father, though only good news, and so I hope all is well with you and that she is not being 'cheerful' for the sake of it.

As for me, my announcement of being a war correspondent was a little premature. Margaret may have told you, but we correspondents have been on 'standby' for months now, kicking our heels, waiting for permission to travel. Who knows, you may see me at Christmas. If the order doesn't come through I shall try and come home. But do not tell Margaret because I should like to surprise her, and Mother.

I have bought a fine horse, Pluto, a good-natured creature. I wish I were taking him to the Yorkshire Dales and not across stormy seas. My luggage – not exceeding the specified weight – is packed and ready. You can imagine the frustration at being on alert. Every day I wake thinking that this will be the day, and every night I go to sleep thinking, perhaps tomorrow. I suspect that the army top brass do not want interfering newspaper men getting in the way!

I know that you like poetry. Here is a copy of

Homer's Iliad. *This may seem an odd Christmas gift, but in a world at war it seems to me worth a glance. Toss it aside if it is not for you! Perhaps an up-to-date* Household Physician *would suit you better now that you are turning yourself into a herbalist – knowledge of medicine being the sister of wisdom.*

With kind regards to Mr Wood from your affectionate soon-to-be (I hope) brother-in-law.

Thomas

I have bought Thomas a pamphlet of Tom Maguire's writings, which I got from the stall in the market. Eric who runs the stall saved it for me, thinking it would be just what I would like. Dad's present is a tiger-eye tie pin. For Margaret I have bought fancy ribbons, as she is making her trousseau. For Aunty Amy, hairpins and a comb. I am going to bake a pie for Miss Mason, and some mince tarts. Bernard would like some sheet music, whatever is the latest.

It is bitterly cold out tonight. Windy, too, with smoke coming down the chimney. I have built the fire up well, as me and Aunty Amy got a bag of coal each from Dorothy's husband – an extra thank you for delivering the baby, who's to be called Robert. It seems, by all reports, that Robert is already showing signs of genius. He can recognize his mam and dad, and he gurgles in a very meaningful way. I was pleased to agree with the description of his remarkable abilities and would have agreed anyway, even if we hadn't got the free bag of coal.

The fire crackled as I set the table for me and Dad for supper. It was just the two of us. I asked him to say a Hebrew prayer. He seems to feel easier in himself if he speaks Yiddish or Hebrew, as if he has escaped into another world. A weight lifts from his shoulders. He chose a prayer that I recognized. Old Mrs Fischer gave me a book with both languages and Dad had read the Hebrew aloud to me. So I know what Dad says, even though I must write it here in English.

He stood at the table, and the flicker of the candles lit his face. He closed his eyes, seeming to be somewhere else, and said, 'The angel of rain bursts the clouds so they weep on the parched earth. May the land turn green at God's bidding. Do not keep rain from us because we have not paid our debts.'

I said, 'Dad, it's pouring down out there. Why are you praying for rain?'

He winked at me and said, 'Not that kind of rain.'

So I didn't interrupt him again. He continued. 'Part the clouds as you parted the waters and lift our desolation, for we are encircled by foes who have opened their mouths against us.'

I glanced at him. His face seemed calm and not at all as if he felt encircled by enemies.

He said, 'It is good that we should hold hope in our hearts and wait without fear for our salvation.'

The fire crackled and a coal split. The rain beat against the window. I thought of Kevin and Johnny in France, and hoped the rain wasn't pouring down on them in some trench.

Dad said, 'Lord our God who whispers to the wind to roar and the rain to pour, bless our life with plenty.'

I said 'Amen,' and we ate our bread and margarine and pickled herring.

After supper, Aunty Amy came with her new lodger, Fanny. Dad got out the cards and we played gin rummy. Fanny brought a jug of porter. I felt quite merry and said some very comical things and how we all laughed.

Sitting in bed writing. Daren't blow out the candle. Listening all the time. Dad thinks I'm sleeping. I know he's watching and waiting downstairs. Friday and Saturday nights are dangerous times. Candle guttering and threatening to die.

THIRTY-FOUR

The house is quiet. Even the fire burns silently. I sit at the table, writing by candlelight. Dad lies on his bedchair, staring at the ceiling, not moving a muscle. The only sound is my pencil scratching across the page. I am making myself slide slowly into this account because otherwise I shall write it in a rush that makes no sense.

I had better start by saying that neither of us was hurt, not physically. We have no cuts or bruises that we did not possess yesterday. All the same, after today, things will never be the same again.

I knew the meat market had closed because I recognized some of the workers who had crossed onto St Peter's Street, their shapes bulky with a parcel of something under their coats, and the smell of blood and ale on them.

It was too dark to see at first – just a group of men silhouetted under the gas lamp in the far cattle pen, nearest the big gate. Even at a distance, I knew something wasn't right about that bunch of men, something threatening seemed to come off them. My shoulders felt stiff and my arms tight at my side. I looked to see which way I would escape if they tried something on with me. Some instinct sent me towards them. Some feeling that Dad was among them. When I heard Frank's voice, it felt like a dream. Frank wasn't even in Leeds, I thought.

Closer to the cattle pen, I still couldn't make them out. That's because they were in such a huddle. The picture took shape. Two men were holding onto Dad, making him watch as the others beat up Henryk, only I couldn't see that at first because they had their backs to me. As soon as I realized someone was being hurt, I screamed at them to *Stop it, Stop it*.

Before I had finished yelling, three things happened at once.

Dad called out, 'Go home! Now! Go!'

A policeman's whistle blew.

One of the figures turned, took a step towards me, stretched out his arms and called, 'Julia!' It was Frank.

Someone ran off. Dad grabbed my hand and we ran, leaving Frank behind, fighting, I think.

As we ran, a voice called, 'They're bloody Huns.'

Another voice took up the cry as we got free

231

from the pens and ran up New York Street away from the police. The cry went up, 'Stop the Huns!'

Footsteps came behind us, clogs and boots and cries to stop us, but people let us by, not sure whether we were the chasers or the chased. We pushed into a street-seller and he cursed us as his chestnuts went flying.

Th scattering chestnuts gave us enough time to turn into Vicar Lane and the doorway of Brownlaw's chemists. The light shone on Annie's long red-gold hair as she knelt in the window, re-arranging the display for Christmas. She looked up and in a second leaped from the window.

She unbolted the shop door, let us in and directed us into the back room.

A shouting mob ran past. Later Annie told me she just kept shaking her head and shrugging her shoulders as faces pressed against the door and window panes asking had she seen the Huns.

She made us a cup of tea, saying that Mr Brownlaw had left her to lock up. He was out delivering urgent medical supplies and would not be back. We could stay as long as we wished. She would stay with us, and walk back with us. Anyone still looking would have their eyes peeled for two people, not three.

When she went back to dressing the window, Dad said, 'Why she do this for us?'

I whispered, 'Her name's Annie Garretty. She's Cissie's older sister who went away a long time ago. She must know I was Cissie's friend.'

I have just asked Dad about Henryk. It seems that poor, kind Henryk was in the wrong place at the wrong time. He had also come to meet Dad from work, to borrow a shilling to buy food. So far, like Dad, he had not been arrested with the other foreigners. I expect he has after tonight.

Dad has just tossed a coin. I asked him why. He said, 'Heads I go to the police. Let them take me away. Then you have peace.'

I put my pencil down and turned to face him. 'Tails?' I asked.

'Tails I go to work tomorrow, as if nothing happen.'

He held the coin on the back of his left hand, covered by his right palm. He looked but would not tell me whether it came up heads or tails. He can be very annoying sometimes.

'It's tails,' I said, 'because you're not making a move to put your boots on to go to Millgarth Police Station.'

He said, 'Not tonight.'

Now he is making a pot of tea. I will stop writing and slice some bread. We still have a little pickled tongue in the cellar.

Poor Henryk. If I were not such a coward I would go to the police station and ask after him. I hope they gave him something to eat.

I thanked Annie Garretty for helping us and she said that she should thank me for being such a good friend to her sister and all her family. It was her dinner break and we went to the market café for a cup of tea. I hope she and I will be friends.

(I was about to set down her story, and to say why no one in her family ever spoke of her, but something unexpected has happened and I must leave that for now.)

A loud knock on the door.

Dad won't listen to me. I always tell him to look out of the window and see who it is, but he thinks that is unmanly. As he opened the door, I swear I could hear my heart and feel the pain of it beating too fast.

For a moment I didn't recognize the voice, so educated and well-spoken. I knew it wasn't a policeman, but I pictured the bowler-hatted men who took Mr Fischer.

'Come in,' Dad said in a friendly voice.

It was Thomas Turner, a smile on his face. He brought a bunch of holly and mistletoe.

Dad was so pleased to see him that he said everything twice. 'Come in, come in. Sit down, sit down.'

Thomas sat on the tall stool by the table. I tried to straighten my hair and push this book out of sight at the same time. Then I took the holly and mistletoe from him and put it in the jam jar on the window sill. Dad seemed so eager to please that I feared he would fasten the mistletoe to the gas mantle and then Thomas might feel obliged to kiss me and I would be so embarrassed.

Dad has only met Thomas once but seemed to dance for joy at having such a well-dressed young visitor. 'Julia will pour you a cup of tea, a cup of tea.'

'I'll just give him the one cup, Dad,' I said, trying to tell him not to seem so overwhelmingly pleased. Anyone would think we never had visitors. Not that we have any like Thomas. He seemed to fill the room with his presence, but it was as if he knew that and tried to tuck himself in, sitting sideways on at the table.

'Have you seen–'

I knew Dad was going to ask if Thomas had seen Margaret. That would sound as if we were about to enquire about wedding dates. So I interrupted and said, 'The sugar? Yes it's here.'

Dad knew that I knew he hadn't intended to say sugar. He looked a little puzzled. But he took the hint, realizing that I know how we should behave. This is not because Dad is a German and a Jew, but because he is a man and a dad, and something delicate was involved concerning his elder daughter.

Thomas asked after Dad's health, and Dad confirmed that his health was tip-top.

'Have you just come from London?' Dad asked.

I frowned. There was nothing wrong with Dad asking that, but he asked with such an impressed voice, as if we never went anywhere. And Margaret and I have been to London twice, as he well knows.

Thomas smiled. 'You'll think it's odd that I've come,' he said. 'And I hope I'm not going to cause offence.'

'We're always pleased to see you,' Dad said as he sat down on his bedchair.

'The thing is,' Thomas said, taking a drink of tea, 'I called in at the newspaper offices when I got off the train. In fact, I left my suitcase there, for it to be taken over to Mother's.'

He took out a silver cigarette case and offered one to Dad.

I could see Dad was tempted, but he shook his

head. 'I'm a pipe man.'

I know that Dad refused the cigarette because he thinks saying 'I'm a pipe man' makes him sound English. He lit a taper from the fire and held it for Thomas to light his cigarette.

Thomas took a deep pull and let the smoke out slowly. 'I wanted to have a chat with my old colleagues at the *Mercury*. They're all curious as to why we war correspondents haven't been allowed to cross the Channel yet.'

Dad and I must have gone very quiet and looked worried.

Thomas leaned towards Dad and said quickly, 'It's nothing terrible, nothing to worry about. Just that the editor – because he's short-staffed – asked me to do him a good turn and call at the Bridewell to follow up a story.' Then he turned to look at me. 'I saw your friend there, Julia. Frank Whitelock.'

I felt myself take one of those breaths before you launch off into a great long, angry speech. But before I could get the words out, Thomas held up his hand. 'Please, just let me finish. The sergeant said I could use the telephone, to report back to the *Mercury* editor. I was walking along the corridor when Frank called to me.' Thomas's voice turned apologetic. 'He spoke to me through the cell door. I said I'd pass on his message to you both.'

I clenched my fists. 'I don't want to hear.' How dare Frank use Margaret's fiancé as a messenger boy.

Thomas looked at Dad with a kind and sympathetic look. 'I promised him I'd come and see you. I know how you must feel, Mr Wood.'

'No, you don't!' I heard my voice getting louder. 'How could you possibly know? They could have killed Dad. And what about Henryk? Did you see him? Has he sent a message?'

Thomas shook his head. 'I'm sorry. I was there on another story. I knew nothing about this.'

Dad said, '*Liebling*. Julia. Let the man speak.'

So I listened, feeling myself get more and more angry, as Thomas passed on Frank's message. It seems that Frank had travelled back to Leeds on the train with his new chum, Sidney. After more than a drop to drink, Sidney said he wanted to have a go at a couple of Huns his dad knew were passing themselves off as Belgians.

'Who's this Sidney's dad?' I asked.

'I believe the name was Clarence,' Thomas said. He obviously did not like having to tell this story and I began to feel bad about getting angry. So I tried to sound more friendly as I said, 'Oh, him. Pig-face Clarence Laycock.'

'Let Thomas tell the story,' Dad said softly.

'Thank you.' Thomas took another drink of tea. 'Frank wanted you to know that he had no idea one of the men was Mr Wood, not until it was too late. He swears that as soon as he realized, he turned his attention to the other man–'

'Frank attacked Henryk?' I said.

'And he wanted you to know that he hasn't mentioned your name, Mr Wood. Not to the police, not to anyone.'

'Except you,' I said.

Thomas said, 'He must know that he can trust me.'

None of us said anything for a good minute or so.

Dad sighed. He stood up, put his hand on Thomas's shoulder and said, 'Thank you.'

Then he went down into the cellar. I knew he was going for the last slice of pickled tongue. I got out the bread board, cut a slice of bread and spread it with margarine.

'No, no,' Thomas said. 'You mustn't.'

'Yes, we must,' I said. 'Dad will be hurt otherwise.'

When Dad came back up from the cellar, he said, 'Frank is not a bad lad, but trouble finds him.'

I arranged the bread and meat on the plate. 'Dad. Please. Don't say his name again. I never want to hear it, not as long as I live. He's not my friend. Not any more.'

When Thomas turned towards the table to eat the supper we had given him, he looked at home, as if sitting in our house were the most natural thing in the world. But I imagined him in his own home in Harehills, or in his father's house in London. Will he really marry Margaret? There is such a gap between them and us. If he had stayed here, it may have happened. Now I am not sure. Just because she has a ring does not mean there will be a wedding.

Thomas took out his watch and tried to hide his annoyance at the lateness of the hour. 'It's too late to call on Margaret now. I'll call on her tomorrow.' Then he thanked us as if we had given him a banquet. I felt a kind of hurt when he apologized for disturbing us. I wanted to say that he could disturb me any time. Dad took him to the door and watched him down the street.

'He is a good man,' Dad said.

But I was already pulling my shawl around my shoulders.

'Where are you going?' Dad asked.

'To tell Margaret he's back. She may want to wash her hair.'

THIRTY-FIVE

Warm and cosy from the firelight and gas mantle. Coals crackling and the tick-tock of the clock on the mantelpiece. Twelve mince pies cool on the wire tray in the centre of the table, covered with cheese cloth. The house smells of mince pies, burning coals and the fresh green of the little Christmas tree perched in the corner between the hearth and the cupboard, its tiny candles waiting to be lit (when Dad comes in). I am keeping the fire going, so as to heat the oven and get the turkey started.

I have finished reading my book. Don't feel patient enough to play Patience.

Dad said do not meet him, as Christmas Eve is a busy time and he would be late. But here we are coming up to eleven. My chest hurts when I worry about him.

It upset me that Frank came to the door tonight. I did not let him in. 'Are thah gonna leave me standing on't doorstep?' he asked, rubbing his hands, his breath making a little cloud in the cold air. 'I've come to say sorry.'

'You've said it.' I made to close the door. The fight outside the meat market flooded back to me. Men fighting. Henryk's yell of pain. Policemen's whistles. Angry voices. *Bloody Huns!*

'Please.' He gave me that lost look. 'Just give me five minutes. Then if thah wants me to go, I'll go.'

He stood at one side of the fireplace. I stood at the other, wishing I hadn't let him in. He's no friend of mine any more. He lit a smoke, telling me that he had spent two days in clink. On Boxing Day he will be travelling back to camp. He has to know that Dad and me forgive him.

I said that I forgive him, as Dad does. I heard the coldness in my voice. He flinched as I told him. 'It's over between us. You're trouble, Frank. Find a girl who doesn't mind a man with a temper.'

'I'd never turn on thee, Julia.' In the doorway, he said, 'Is thah dad at't Dragon?'

I told him that Dad had not got home from work yet, but I didn't give way, and said it very matter-of-fact.

Frank looked as if he would say something else but I didn't give him chance and shut the door.

When he left, dejected, my stomach churned. Why is it that Doing-the-Right-Thing leaves you feeling so miserable?

1 a.m.
Street noisy just now. Clogs and boots – revellers, or drunks. A girl shouting, 'Merry Christmas.'

Fire burns low. Listen for Dad's footsteps.

Silence.

I think to myself, *Put a piece of coal on the fire, then Dad'll come. Rake the ashes, then he'll come.*

I listen till my ears hurt.

I am going out to look for him.

5 a.m.

My hand shakes as I write, but I don't know what else to do. If I write simply and straightforwardly, I might know what I should do next.

Expecting the worst, I took my dolly bag with a damp cloth, bandages and ointment.

I know the way to the meat market blindfolded so did not light my lantern, not even as I walked through the cattle pens towards the big wooden doors. I put the key in the lock of the small door that's set in the door on the right. Stepping over that low threshold filled me with dread. I dared not light the lamp till I pulled the door shut behind me. My hands shook as I took the glass off the lantern. The small glow of light from the first match I struck made the pitch blackness seem even more frightening. The match burned my fingers and dropped to the stone floor. I struck another match and lit the wick. The cavernous slaughterhouse came into eerie life.

Beside me the giant time clock in its wooden frame clicked its way minute to minute with a low straining sound. Holding my lantern, I checked the time-cards. Dad had clocked off at 8p.m. Anyone could have stuck his card in the clock.

Standing in the deserted slaughterhouse, I felt as if I had entered a monstrous tomb. I imagined that a boulder might be rolled into place against the door and I would be trapped.

Dad and I once watched a cross-bred collie dog in the park. It ran in decreasing circles until it found its ball. I started to walk the length of the wall, just able to see immediately around me in the pool of light from the lantern. I heard a sound. Was someone else there? I stopped. Perhaps it had been my own echo, or the sound of my fear.

It would be hard even for the smartest dog to make circles in the semi-darkness of a huge vaulted hall. If you are not a dog, have no heightened sense of smell and all your instincts are scared out of you, it is really impossible. I took a deep breath and called, 'Dad? Dad?'

My voice echoed back from the rafters. Suddenly I was grabbed from behind. A hand on my mouth stopped my scream.

I dropped the lantern but another hand caught it.

'Julia. Shhh!'

It was Frank.

'What's thah doing here?' he asked.

My mouth was dry. I couldn't stop shaking. I asked him the same question. He said that he had been outside our house, trying to pluck up courage to knock on the door again. He had stood there for hours. When he saw me open the door, he ducked into the alley, then followed me. He wanted to make sure I stayed safe.

Holding the lantern, he cupped my elbow with his other hand. Slowly we searched the whole slaughterhouse, every corner, every gulley. We walked under the rail where the carcasses are moved through to the cooling alley. Lamp glinting, we walked between the rows of beasts.

When Frank looked at the hooks where the carcasses hung, I felt sick. I remembered the rope Dad had tied around the hook in the cellar. My legs turned weak. As if he knew what I was thinking, Frank gripped my arm more tightly. Now I know how Margaret felt before she fainted at the talk on diseases.

When we had searched the cooling alley, I could breathe again. Only one place remained. The ice room.

'No point.' Frank sounded angry. 'No one could survive in there.'

'I have to look,' I told him, crossing the bottom of the cooling alley to the door of the ice room.

'We could be trapped. That's a heavy door. If we open it and go in, we may never get out again.' He tugged my arm but I pulled away.

A pigeon had got through a broken pane in the ceiling and fluttered past me.

'You go then,' I said. 'Leave me to look.'

He sighed and handed me the lantern while he drew back the bolts.

'Hold the door,' I said quickly, stepping inside before he had chance to stop me.

I thought I was cold until I went into the ice room. The marrow in my bones turned numb. My teeth chattered. My hands shook so that I thought I would drop the lantern. If I did, Frank would come running. We would freeze to death together.

He struck a match in the doorway and called,

'Hurry up.'

Then I saw the body. It lay just to my right, curled like a baby. I swung the lantern nearer and bent down to see. I touched the shoulder. The body was as stiff as a frozen carcass. I could see the back of the head. The hair was the wrong colour. A shock of stiff fair hair. I moved round and looked at the white face, the eyes wide open. Clarence Laycock. Dad's tormentor. That's when I noticed something else. His trousers were round his knees. What I saw made me feel sick. I recognized the bone handle of Dad's butcher's steel. It had been stuck up his behind – like you would stick a pig to roast it on a spit. I grabbed it and tugged. It didn't want to come. I tugged again, then dropped it into my dolly bag and drew the strings tightly closed.

At the door Frank grabbed me and took the lantern from me. 'What?' he said.

I couldn't get the words out properly. 'Clarence,' I said. 'He's dead.'

'Let's get out!'

'Pull his trousers up.'

I couldn't see Frank's face. 'Y'what?'

I told him again, and wouldn't budge until he'd done it.

In the cellar, I washed, wire-wooled and oiled the carving steel. As I worked on it, I remembered what Dad had told me. The carving steel was a sign that once he had been an independent butcher. He had no need of it in the meat market but always wore it at his waist, like a badge of honour. Clarence Laycock had taunted him about it. What had happened? And where was Dad?

Frank said, 'If you are not sure what to do, do nowt.' But he went to search.

THIRTY-SIX

The heavy knock rapped the door. My face had that hot, tight feeling of not sleeping for so many hours, and I probably looked as stupid as I felt. I'm glad I felt tired and stupid, or I may have said the wrong things.

I don't think of policemen as looking weary. This one did. I must have looked young, though I felt a hundred years old. He asked was there a grown-up in the house. I told him I was almost sixteen.

The officer seemed to lose his tiredness as he informed me that Dad had been arrested and would be charged with theft. I heard my surprised voice say, 'My Dad? Theft? Never!'

The policeman said, 'Theft of a turkey.'

My mouth dropped open and I had all on to stop myself saying, 'Only one?' Because Dad had promised turkeys to Uncle Lloyd and Mr Shepherd at the workhouse. The policeman was probably going home two turkeys richer than when he started his shift.

My relief did not last long. The policeman told me that Dad had been taken to the Workhouse Infirmary on Beckett Street under police custody. He had a serious head injury.

'What happened to him?' I half-hoped he would tell me he had no idea. I feared he would tell me they had found Clarence Laycock's body and suspected Dad of murder.

The policeman looked at me in a way that made me feel I was a wanted criminal. He spoke like an actor saying his lines on stage. 'We believe your father sustained his injury falling off a ladder while stealing the turkey.'

I thought it best not to ask what ladder.

I rinsed my face under the tap, grabbed my shawl and ran all the way to Beckett Street in a fog of misery and uncertainty.

Mr Shepherd has a deformed leg with a foot that turns sideways since some doctor tried to mend it. I thought I'd never get to Dad. Mr Shepherd leaned on his stick and dragged himself and his slow leg across the marble-tiled floor. I wanted to rush up the stairs. He insisted on pressing the button for the lift that clanked and rattled to a shuddering stop. That lift stinks of sour food, which makes you think pigs wouldn't eat workhouse food. Holding my breath, I felt dizzy by the time I stepped out on the second floor for the men's ward.

As he opened the lift door, Mr Shepherd grunted a warning at me. He said a policeman had been guarding Dad, but it being Christmas Day and seeing how Dad was going nowhere, the policeman had gone off home.

That scared me. A turkey thief doesn't call for a guard. But police would guard a German alien. Or a suspected murderer.

When I used to take charge of cleaning that

ward for Mrs Whitelock, I hated the noise. As soon as the lift doors opened I would hear sounds of distress and fury, wheezing and groaning. Some of them weep when they think no one's paying mind. If anything, the men's ward makes worse noise than the women's.

As I approached, I heard the familiar sounds. It went quiet when the patients saw Mr Shepherd and me.

The walls of the ward are dull grey. Through the high windows the sky seemed the same smoky shade. It was like walking through a whispering, coughing fog. No one had cleaned. No one had emptied the piss-pots.

When we stopped at the bed, at first I thought it must be a mistake. But it was Dad. He looked dead. I took his hand and felt the slightest twitch of movement. There was a scared feeling to it, as if I'd startled him. I stroked his hands, trying to warm them, and said, 'Dad, it's me. Julia.'

A woman in a mouldy green dress walked unsteadily from bed to bed, cursing. I wondered why she was wandering about on the men's ward. Then I recognized her. The nurse. Not the kind of nurse I had once wanted to be and I'm glad I gave up that idea. Why should I take care of people who would put burning rags through our letterbox and break our windows and now try to kill Dad? Let them bleed, let them die, I don't care about anyone, only Dad.

Dad lay very still, his face pale and dark shadow on his chin. He likes his bonny little black moustache to be just so and I combed at it with my fingers. It had turned white. He had a huge bandage on his head, stained with blood. I wanted to smooth his white eyebrows, but was scared of hurting him. Dad's eyelids flickered. He moved his lips, and I thought he was trying to speak.

'He needs water,' I told Mr Shepherd.

Mr Shepherd dragged himself off to bring a glass of water, and this creature in the next bed croaked at me, 'What's your pa's trade?'

I turned to look at him. You get used to grotesque-looking people in there so I know how not to let my feelings show. I used to feel sorry for them when I did the floors. This one's mouth seemed squashed to one side of his purple-blue face. He was trying to look friendly.

'He's a butcher,' I said.

He said, 'Someone said it was an accident at work. Someone said a ladder, someone said a wall. What was a butcher doing up a ladder on a wall?'

As if I was supposed to know.

When I didn't answer, he said, 'Never mind, lass. They put Humpty Dumpty together again and, if you ask me, Humpty Dumpty found himself on the wrong end of a policeman's truncheon, same as your dad. They don't tell you that in the nursery rhymes.'

I whispered to Dad, whispered in his ear, telling him to get better.

Mr Shepherd came back with the water but I didn't think Dad knew the glass was at his lips so I dipped in my finger and wet his mouth.

Then Mr Shepherd straightened the name label above Dad's bed. As he leaned forward, he said, very confidentially, 'I don't suppose your dad had chance to get me a turkey?'

When I said no, he asked me not to mention the turkey to anyone else, or that Mrs Shepherd had been a customer for our pies.

Outside, the day had got lighter, a whitish sky tinged blue. I remember thinking how clean the air seemed with all the factories and mills closed for Christmas. People would be going to church to pray for peace, or, more likely, victory.

I banged on the back door at the Dragon, and threw stones at Margaret's window.

Margaret fumbled with the bolts and clunked the key in the lock. The Dragon would be the perfect hiding place for Dad, if I could just get him out of the Workhouse Infirmary. The loft where me and Bernard hid when we were little – no one ever goes up there. I went to see.

Goosebump-cold up there. I dodged cobwebs, a wasp nest and stepped around old packing cases, a broken chair and a leather portmanteau. Prints and paintings, which used to hang in the rooms and had been replaced, stood against the far wall. I moved one to see if the loose, brown-paper backings still rustled like a ghost. When we played up there, we used to take it in turns to close our eyes while one of us told a scary story and made the sounds.

The loft could be made cosy. With bed-warmers and lots of blankets Dad would be fine there. It would need a good clean and sacking on the floor to deaden the sound of his movements. Should I tell Margaret my idea?

I found her by following the sobbing sounds as I came down from the loft. Margaret, her face blotchy and wet with tears, was sitting in the dinky rocking chair.

I kept telling her that Dad would get well. Finally I think she believed me.

'Dad's not going to die,' I told her. 'He's going to pull through.'

Margaret started to cry again.

Uncle Lloyd came into the kitchen from the bar, bringing a bottle of port. He uncorked it and set two glasses on the table. I did not intend to drink fortified wine and listen to him speechifying. He talked as if there was nothing to be done. As if because Dad was under arrest, he should stay under arrest. As if, because Dad was in a bed in the Workhouse Infirmary, he should stay there. He even started on about where we should eat Christmas dinner, saying we'd best eat in the kitchen instead of the upstairs dining room. More cosy, he said. And since Kevin and Johnny are still at camp and my poor dad was where he was, then we'd be sadly diminished this year.

I persuaded Uncle to do something. He bit his lip and shook his head, but in the end he put on his big coat with the Astrakhan lining, picked up his Homburg hat and said he'd go to the police station and ask for bail. He wouldn't let me go with him.

I sat by the upstairs window in the function room where I had a good view. I watched him walk to the police station and I watched him walk back. I knew by his walk, but I ran to meet him all the same. He just shook his head.

As we came to the yard he said, 'It's not just theft of a turkey, Julia. It's the other. It's the Germany business. It was bound to come out in the end.' He pushed the back door open and said, 'Go on, you'll catch your death.'

I said, 'If they put him in prison, he'll die. If they send him to the Isle of Man with the enemy aliens, he'll die.'

In the kitchen Uncle made me sit by the fire. He sat opposite me, still wearing his coat, holding his hat on his knees. 'Your dad would want me to think about you and Margaret. I'm the one grown-up relation you have left. You must come here. I'll take care of you both. Your dad would know the law has to take its course. Especially in wartime.'

I gave up on the idea of hiding Dad in the attic at the Dragon. I got up to go but Uncle's words stopped me.

'That's not the end of it. The police need to see your and Margaret's birth certificates. I've said you're under my care now and that you're British citizens, but we had better get your birth certificates.'

He insisted on walking with me back to Bread Street. As we passed the Woolman Street flats, I saw little Sol Garretty on the balcony and I waved him down. I gave Uncle the key to our house and told him I would catch up.

'Merry Christmas, Sol,' I said, giving him a penny. 'Will you do an errand for me? Find Frank Whitelock and tell him to wait for me outside the back gate at my uncle's pub.'

In our downstairs room at Bread Street, I lifted an orange box onto the table and rummaged through for our birth certificates.

Uncle looked round the room critically. 'It's damp.' He looked into the box on the table. 'We'd better take all your papers.

'Julia?' a woman's voice called from the doorway. Mrs Hardiman stood on the bottom step. 'I'm sorry for your trouble.' She folded her arms over her pinny. 'Have I called at a bad time?' She tried to peer past me into the house to see who was there.

'My uncle,' I said.

'Clearing out, are you? Only my sister, her and her husband, they're after a house. I'd like 'em to be nearby. They'll give you five bob for your key. I don't like to ask at a time like this, but if I don't someone else will.'

'We're not moving out,' I answered quietly.

'Who is it?' Uncle called. 'Any news?'

I asked Mrs Hardiman to wait.

'It's a neighbour from across the street, Uncle. She thinks we're flitting. She's after the key for her sister.'

Uncle sighed. He looked round the room, at the blinds Mam had made, at the rug where he stood. After a long time, he said, 'You'll want to keep this rug, I daresay. A lot of work went into it. See that tweedy bit? That were a right good little coat once, in parts.'

I tried not to look. I tried not to see the mark Dad's pint pot had made on the oil cloth of the table. I went back to the door. 'I'll fetch you the key across later, Mrs Hardiman.'

She nodded, reached out a hand and touched my arm. 'Bless you, love.'

It didn't even seem like my plan. It sprang into my head fully formed as if I'd read it in a detective story. It involved helping myself to two bottles of whisky from behind the Dragon bar. One for Mr and Mrs Shepherd and one for the nurse in the mouldy dress.

It had to be Frank. I love Bernard. I love to listen to him play the piano and I think he's the best, the best McAndrew, the best piano player. But he's not brave. Uncle has him cowed and scared. I feared if Uncle shouted loud enough Bernard would always cave in. And Bernard wouldn't survive prison any more than Dad would.

But I had to tell Margaret. While Uncle interrogated bar staff about missing bottles of whisky, I got her alone at the kitchen table.

I said, 'If I don't get him out, he'll die in there, or on the way to prison.'

Margaret kept clasping and unclasping her hands and opening her mouth without managing to speak.

I told her that she hadn't had to hear the crash of a brick through our window, or cut herself as she cleared up shards of glass. She hadn't smelled burning rags through the letterbox and feared for her life. I wanted to tell her that Dad's enemy, Clarence, lay dead in the ice room. I couldn't.

Margaret, jaw clenched, intertwined her fingers and looked at them as if they'd frozen in that position. After a long time, she unclasped her fingers and set her hands on her knees. 'Mam told us to look after Dad. She must have known this day would come. We have to do it.'

'We'll need help,' I said.

Margaret frowned. 'Bernard?'

I shook my head.

Frank agreed. He worked out the times when there would be no police patrolling Beckett Street during the night. He worked out the best direction to take and said that he would tie the sacking over Solomon's hooves.

THIRTY-SEVEN

Solomon patiently let me harness him. Between us, Frank and I backed him into the shafts of the trap. It had always looked so easy when Charley did it, but it is not easy at all, especially if you are anxious and shaky, and your sister trembles and keeps saying, 'Are we doing the right thing?'

It's only late at night that you realize how much doors and gates squeak, creak and groan.

Frank took the reins. I knew that if things went wrong, he would take most blame. Boys always do, girls being thought too stupid and irresponsible to know better.

Frank tied Solomon's reigns to the workhouse railings, and we got in through the small gate that stays open for the early-morning cleaning and deliveries. The Shepherds' flat was in darkness.

I'd unlatched a window on the ground floor when I delivered the whisky to the nurse. Frank and Margaret waited while I climbed through and found my way to the first floor. There's a low light from a mantle in case of emergencies and I was glad of that, and glad that I'd worn soft shoes.

In the tiny office at the end of the ward, on her little trundle bed, the nurse slept, snoring loudly, the empty whisky bottle beside her.

Dad did not want to wake up. I took his shoulders and tried to shift him towards the edge of the bed. He was in a worse state than I thought. Maybe he would survive if I left him, and maybe he would die if I moved him.

The man with the purple face stared at me. I stared back.

'If you say you saw me, I'll say you helped me,' I said.

I went back downstairs and beckoned Frank and Margaret through the window. Frank unlaced his boots, which seemed to take an age.

We walked in a line back up the stairs to the ward.

The man with the purple face, tugging at his striped shirt for modesty, sat on Dad's bed. He'd managed to get Dad sitting up and had an arm around him. He looked at me with pleading eyes. 'Take me, too.'

I shook my head. He sighed and went back to his own bed.

Frank took Dad's shoulders. Margaret and me took his legs.

At the top of the stairs Frank stopped. He said, 'I'll slip in mi stocking feet on that marble staircase. We mun take the lift.'

Margaret started to open the lift gates before I could stop her. They had no idea how it rattles and shakes the whole building. My mouth went dry. We got into the lift and Margaret closed the gates. I pressed the ground-floor button.

Nothing has ever been as noisy as that lift clanking down from the first to the ground floor and bumping to a stop.

On the way to the open window, I feared someone would come running and shouting after us. Dad's body felt so heavy that the tendons in my arm tore and pulled. When we climbed through the window I had a picture in my mind of a policeman holding onto Solomon's harness, waiting to arrest us.

Aunty Amy had left me the key, to keep an eye on the shop and house while she visited her cousin in Skipton for Christmas. We made Dad as comfortable as we could on Aunty Amy's sofa, knowing that if we took him into our house, the police would be likely to come looking.

Dad was sleeping, or perhaps he was unconscious.

'You two skidaddle and take Solomon back,' Frank said. 'And both of you stay at Dragon. Avoid suspicion. I'll see to yer dad and get fire going. He's fair frozen.'

I sat at the table, stirring my porridge, and made myself eat a spoonful. Uncle and Bernard had already finished theirs. Margaret swallowed another mouthful.

The bowler-hatted man must have come through the main bar, let in by the cleaners. He had a policeman with him. I noticed a second policeman in the back yard, watching the house from the gate.

Uncle pushed back his chair and stood up. 'What's this?'

The man removed his hat, ignored the rest of us and spoke to Uncle. 'Permission to search the premises, Mr McAndrew?'

'Why?' Uncle asked.

The man nodded to the constable, as if permission had been granted. As the policeman left the kitchen, a look of dismay came over Margaret's face.

The man glared at her. 'Is something wrong, miss?'

She gulped. 'My room's untidy.'

'What are you looking for?' Uncle asked. 'If it's the girls' birth certificates, I took them to the inspector. It's all in order.'

The man had short grey hair and a head as broad as a bull's. He twisted his hat by its brim, watching us for our reaction as he said, 'We're looking for Joseph Wood. He has left the Workhouse Infirmary.'

'It's not possible,' Uncle said. 'He was in no fit state.'

'It is a serious breach of procedure,' the man said.

I hoped that he wouldn't tell Uncle about the inebriated workhouse overseer and nurse. I'm sure I'll never look poor Mr Shepherd in the eye again. He and the nurse will probably get into serious trouble.

After the search of the house, the questions went on a long time, each of us in turn questioned about our movements, about where Dad might have gone. I suggested Bread Street, knowing I had left our door unlocked. The police had already looked there.

Uncle snapped his fingers as the thought came to him. 'What about your next-door neighbour? He'd go to her if you lasses weren't home.'

The broad, bull-headed man's gaze went from Margaret to me and back again. We must have given something away because a look of excitement came into his eyes.

'Aunty Amy's away,' I said. 'The house is locked up.'

Bull-head pulled a key from his pocket. 'This was on the table at your house. Is this it?'

I nodded. Frank must have locked Dad in the house and left the key on our table. Idiot.

Bull-head handed me the key. 'We'll go take a look, shall we?' The walk from the Dragon to Bread Street had never seemed so long. The bowler-hatted man walked between Margaret and me. The policeman followed.

I looked at Aunty Amy's chimney, but no smoke came out of it. Frank had said he would light a fire. Perhaps he had taken Dad somewhere else.

I turned the key in the lock. The shop bell rang as we entered. The bowler-hatted man looked behind the counter and glanced around the shop. He nodded to the policeman to go into the back room while he went up the stairs. The policeman raised the blind. Aunty Amy's cat blinked at us from her spot on the sofa.

Margaret and I saw Dad's foot at the same moment, protruding from the back of the sofa. Margaret positioned herself so as to hide it,

258

holding onto the wall, as if she felt weak and needed to support herself.

'Are you all right, miss?' the policeman asked. 'Do you need to sit down?'

'I'll be all right,' Margaret said weakly. 'It's just … where is he?'

'Is there a cellar?' the policeman asked.

I nodded.

We stood motionless as he went into the cellar. Dad groaned.

After a moment the policeman came back, just as the bowler-hatted man came downstairs.

'Where is he?' Margaret said, in a panic. 'If he's not here and he's not at home, where is he?'

Bowler Hat looked at us suspiciously. He spoke sharply. 'We'll take one further look next door, shall we?'

'That's a good idea,' Margaret said, too eagerly, as if there was nothing more she wanted than to find him. 'I can't bear to think of him out on the streets in this weather, sick and ill.'

Bowler Hat spoke quietly to the policeman. 'Check every house in the street.'

At that moment Tiger leapt from the sofa, miaowed loudly and rubbed himself against my leg. I picked him up. I think I said I had to feed him.

When the policeman had gone, the look on Bowler Hat's face softened. 'Don't worry. We'll find your father.'

The door closed behind them. What state must Dad be in, lying on the floor against the damp wall?

I had just pulled the sofa away when the door

opened and I cursed myself for not locking it. But it was Frank.

'I knew they'd come,' he said. 'I watched from Grundy's alley across the street. Now they've gone, we can make him comfortable, and light a fire.'

I locked the door. Frank held Dad under the arms and nodded to me to take his feet. We lifted him onto the big chair. What if they come back? I wondered.

Reading my thoughts, Frank said, 'Don't worry. They've all Leeds to search.'

He produced a flask of brandy. I poured some into a cup and put it to Dad's lips. The brandy trickled down his chin.

Frank kindled the fire as the kettle boiled on the gas ring. Slowly, Dad got warmer, as the fire began to blaze. I filled the slipper-shaped bed-warmer with hot water and placed it by his feet.

Sitting close, I watched over him. Frank handed me a cup of tea. 'I'm meant to go back to camp tomorrow,' he said. 'But I won't go. I'll stay as long as thah needs me.'

'You've done enough,' I said. 'You can't go absent. They'd come after you.'

'I can never do enough for thee, Julia.'

'I know,' I said. 'And I thank you. But don't get on the wrong side of the army. We'll have a regiment marching down Bread Street looking for you, and that'll do no one any good.'

Dad groaned. I noticed that the bandage round his head was red with blood.

As I unwound the bandage, Frank said, 'Have a lie ready. If worst happens and they come back, say yer dad just turned up at door and fell through it. Say you were gonna come and tell 'em just as soon as yer could.'

I dabbed Dad's head with witch hazel through the matted white hair and kissed his forehead better. Aunty Amy had a couple of homemade bandages in her first-aid box and I wound a new one round and round.

Frank kissed the back of my neck. 'If I'm ever bloodied and bowed, will thah look after me?'

'You won't ever come off worst.' I smiled. It seemed that no matter how I tried to shut him out of my life, he'd be there, waiting for his moment. He'd find a crack and edge through it. I was grateful to him, but he'd done it again.

THIRTY-EIGHT

This has been the strangest Christmas, watching over Dad, keeping him warm. Margaret stayed at the Dragon, so as not to arouse Uncle's suspicions and to make excuses about where I was and what I was doing. Thomas Turner has come home for Christmas, and Uncle had invited him and his mother to supper.

I almost cried with relief when Aunty Amy came back from Skipton.

She undid her coat and said, 'What a to-do. I leave thee for a few days, and this.'

She took Dad's wrist in her hand and felt his pulse. Together we propped him a little higher with an extra cushion.

When I had told her the whole story, we sat at the table, drinking tea.

'We'll take Dad to your cousin in Skipton,' I said. 'I've worked out a plan.'

She let me go through the whole plan before saying quietly, 'Nay, lass, that won't do.'

She explained that a stranger would stick out like a sore thumb in the Yorkshire Dales. They all know each other. Besides, anti-German fever has hit them as it has everyone else.

I am never short of good ideas but the difficulty is that most ideas involve other people. For a good idea to work you need people who will say yes. Usually that would be family. I racked my brains and thought of Aunty Nora, Mam's younger sister in Ireland. Aunty Amy was not being helpful.

'You don't know her. You've never met her.'

'I have her address. She's Mam's sister. I don't have to know her.'

Aunty Amy looked thoughtful. 'Mebbe. It's another country. Your mam used to say they do things differently there. But how would you get him to the coast and across the sea?'

Dad was in no fit state for a rail journey. I knew only one person with a motor car. Not family but near enough. Thomas Turner.

I wrapped the Tom Maguire pamphlet in brown paper and drew a Christmas tree on it. Brown paper is not very good for drawing on with a pen as the nib drags up the fibres of the paper. What were meant to be fine lines smudged at the edges. I told myself that it looked well enough and that the smudges represented pine needles.

I pulled on my mother's big shawl. Aunty Amy watched me for a moment, then put her hand on my shoulder. She took the small looking-glass from the sink and showed me my face and hair. 'You're going to ask the biggest favour of your life. Look the part, girl.'

I went back next door. Our house felt cold and damp without a fire. By the sink, I washed in cold water. I combed my hair, parted it and doubled it under, tying it with a green velvet ribbon. Margaret had left me her green skirt and jacket. I changed into them. Aunty Amy was right. You have to know what it is you want and be ready to go in and get it, looking as if you mean business. I set off for the Dragon, guessing rightly that Thomas would be there.

As I hurried up the stairs to the parlour, I heard the piano and Margaret's high, clear voice, singing 'The Last Rose of Summer'. When the last note died, Thomas turned from the piano to Margaret and put his hand on her waist.

Margaret looked across and saw me. She released herself from his grip and said, 'Look who's here!'

I knew straight away that she hadn't told him I was hiding Dad. To give myself time to think, I handed Thomas his present. 'Perfect,' he said when he had unwrapped the pamphlet. 'You couldn't have brought me a better gift! But Tom Maguire's a bit radical for an accredited war correspondent.' He smiled. 'I may have to read it in secret.'

Margaret bit her lip. She knows me too well. I

would not have left Dad just to bring Thomas a Christmas gift.

'I'm so sorry to hear about your father going missing,' Thomas said.

Margaret tried to catch my eye and silence me.

I said, 'Thomas, I'm going to ask you a very big favour.'

'This sounds serious,' he smiled sympathetically.

Margaret stepped between us. 'No. Whatever it is, no.' She lowered her voice. 'We don't involve Thomas.'

He touched her arm gently. 'But darling, I am involved. I want to be.' He turned to me. 'I've already been to the police station. It's such a worry that they haven't found him yet.'

I deliberately did not look at Margaret. 'Dad's safe,' I said. 'For the present. I want you to help me take him to a safe place.'

Margaret led me to the sofa and we sat down side by side. Thomas sat in the chair opposite, watching us. I wondered whether he suspected that Margaret had not told the truth.

Margaret took my hand. 'How is he?'

I told her that he was still very poorly, but had taken some soup and a little brandy. I explained to Thomas that if he was re-arrested it would kill him. 'I want you to take us to the coast in your motor car. We'll get a boat to Ireland.'

Margaret sighed and shook her head. 'That's a mad idea. And you can't ask Thomas to take such a risk. He's one of the very few to have been chosen as an accredited war correspondent – because he's trustworthy.'

For a while none of us spoke. Thomas looked

uncomfortable but I think it was because he realized Margaret had kept our secret from him.

'I don't need you to protect me, darling.' He took Margaret's hand. 'You should have told me. You're both committing a criminal act by hiding your father. Amy, too. In normal times it would be an offence. With the Defence of the Realm Act in force it's an even graver matter.'

I felt my hopes drain away.

'Wouldn't it be better to take him back to hospital?'

'Never,' I said.

'How was I to take you to Ireland?' Thomas asked quietly. 'What was your plan?'

'In your motor car,' I said. 'We'll motor to a port. Pay a fisherman to take us across. At the other side, we'll get a horse and cart.'

'That would be a fine journey for a sick man!' Margaret shook her head at my stupidity.

'What then?' I leaped up from the sofa, feeling desperate. 'What do you suggest?'

She pulled me back down beside her. 'Be quiet. Let me think.'

'Margaret's right,' Thomas said gently. 'It's no journey for a sick man. It would be too long a journey. Besides, leaving the country would be risky. The ports are active with troop movements.'

We sat silently for a long time. A train went by outside the window. I didn't even look up. I could feel them waiting for me to give in.

Thomas got up from his chair and strode about the room. He faced the wall and smacked his hands against it. 'It might work. It just might work.'

Margaret sat very still. 'I won't let you risk your future, Thomas. This is for me and Julia to sort out.'

'How?' I asked. 'If we give him up, we're condemning him to death. You saw him.'

Margaret twisted her handkerchief in her hand. 'It's true. Even with the best of care, after all he's been through...' Her voice trailed off.

'I have an idea.' Thomas sat between us on the sofa, an arm around each of us. 'I have a house that stands empty. Elmtree House, near Garforth, by the railway track, on the Selby line. It belonged to my grandfather. Julia, I'm appointing you housekeeper. We'll take your father there.'

Margaret started to object. Thomas interrupted her. 'Margaret, you'd better stay here. If both of you girls vanish, the authorities may get suspicious.'

He told me to pack a few things. We would set off after dark, but not in the motor car. That would attract too much attention.

I packed Dad's butchery tools, wrapping each one carefully. A little shiver ran through me when I wrapped his butcher's steel. Sometime I would have to find out what happened, but not now.

I packed my pie-making stuff. Aunty Amy helped me gather blankets, pillows and rugs. She filled a basket with food, medicines and beef sheeting for bandages. I slipped this journal into the basket, along with *The Iliad* that Thomas had sent me for Christmas.

Through the window, I could make out the shape of a pony and trap. The pony tossed its head and blew puffs of steamy breath. Thomas's dog, Sheba, sat upright and important-looking on the front seat.

Even at that late hour, I thought I sensed a movement near Grundy's alley, and felt eyes watching. When I looked again there was no one. Between us, with Thomas taking most of the weight, we carried Dad into the trap. I made him as comfortable as possible, with pillows, blankets and the eiderdown from my bed. Aunty Amy brought out my bag, basket and bundles.

Once we were onto York Road, Thomas whoaed the pony to a stop, removed the sacking from its hooves and hung a lantern on the trap.

We clip-clopped along through the dark starry night. I have never seen so many bright stars. Wrapped up warm against the biting wind, I stared up at the midnight sky. Once you look, you see more and more stars, and patterns. I picked out the North Star.

'Margaret would love this,' Thomas said as he pointed out the Milky Way. 'She takes such an interest in the constellations.'

News to me. We never even see the stars from Bread Street. I didn't disillusion him.

Dad moaned a little. Every bump in the road made me anxious for him. I stayed close, warming his hands, telling him he would get well and everything would be all right.

I had nodded off when Thomas's voice brought me back to life. Ahead of us, I could see lights in the road.

'Leave the talking to me,' Thomas said. 'We're near the munitions factory.'

A soldier barked at us to halt. Sheba growled.

'Quiet, Sheba.' Thomas brought the pony to a standstill.

The soldier held a rifle. I had a vision of all of us being hauled off to prison. What would happen to Sheba? They wouldn't arrest a dog. The poor animal would be left to fend for herself.

After worrying about the dog, I worried about Thomas. Margaret was right. We'd ruin his life.

Fear got in the way of my paying attention to what was being said. I tried to make myself listen.

Thomas reached into his pocket and brought out his credentials. He explained that he was a war correspondent, briefly home on leave. Dad and I were his employees. We were to take care of his house while he was away. His reason for travelling at night, and for bringing us out at this unearthly hour, was that he would be returning to London tomorrow and needed to show us the ropes.

The soldier seemed to hesitate. He held onto Thomas's credentials as he came to take a look at me and Dad. I smiled at the soldier and pulled the blanket from Dad's sleeping face. Aunty Amy had washed him and replaced the big bandage with a smaller one. I had covered that with his hat. His eye was black and his cheek bruised, but in the dark the soldier could not see that.

Thomas jumped down from the seat, lit a cigarette and offered one to the soldier. 'I've heard my house may be requisitioned by you chaps. I want to make sure it's in tip-top shape.'

The soldier handed Thomas's identity card back to him.

'Have a good journey, sir.' He nodded to me. 'And you too, miss.'

As we went on our way, Thomas took a long drag on his smoke. 'It's a pity Margaret wasn't here to smile at him. He'd have forgotten his own name, much less wanting to know our business.'

It came out before I could stop myself. 'Good idea,' I said sarcastically. 'She could have sung the whole battalion a song and they'd have carried us the rest of the way.'

He laughed, thinking I meant it as a compliment to Margaret rather than a snipe at him.

NEW YEAR
TO
SUMMER
1915

THIRTY-NINE

The square, stone-built house stands back from the road, with stables and a horse trough to the left. In front is an overgrown cottage garden, and at the back a large neglected plot where Thomas said they used to grow vegetables and keep hens. Beyond the back field stands a small wood, and a high bank rises up where the railway line runs.

When Thomas had said to the soldier that the house might be requisitioned by the authorities, I thought it was a lie to speed us on our way. Looking round the house, I realized there could be some truth in it. It would billet soldiers, or provide accommodation for top people from the nearby munitions factory.

You go into a hall through the front door and on the right are two downstairs rooms and the same on the left. We took Dad into the big kitchen. I said I would keep to that room, so as to be warm. Thomas carried Dad on his shoulders. I was glad of that because my strength seemed to have deserted me. Twists of newspaper, wood and coal lay in the grate of the cast-iron kitchen range, soot-covered but ready to light. Thomas put a match to it.

When he saw me touch a drop of brandy to Dad's lips, Thomas said, 'It's a pity Margaret's not here. She'd be such a good nurse.'

I'm glad he went out to stable the pony, or I

might have been tempted to tell him what she's really like at the sight of blood.

Sheba went to sleep on the sofa, lying against Dad's leg.

I meant to sit in the big chair for just a few minutes, but I woke next morning to the smell of bacon frying. Thomas held a cup to Dad's lips. A drop of milk and beaten egg trickled onto Dad's chin. Thomas wiped it with his handkerchief.

'Dad!' I took his hand. He looked at me through half-closed eyes. 'You're safe,' I said. 'You're going to get better.'

'Come on,' Thomas said. 'Breakfast's ready. You need to keep up your strength.'

He set two plates on the table, with eggs and rashers of bacon. As we ate, I could see there was something on his mind. He looked across at Dad and said quietly, 'I made a mistake bringing you here. You won't manage. He's a very sick man. He'll need washing, changing. It could be months before he recovers–' He was going to say something else but stopped himself.

'I'm strong. There's nothing I can't do. Especially where Dad's concerned.'

'You're just a child.'

'I'm not a child. I'll be sixteen in April.'

He brought an iron bedstead and a mattress from upstairs. 'I'll move your dad to the bed. You can have the sofa. If he's on the bed, you'll find it easier to manoeuvre him. I'll show you how.'

I listened carefully, and watched as he showed me how to turn Dad on the bed.

'How do you know all this?' I asked.

'We did first aid at school. For a while I

hankered after studying medicine so took a bit of an interest.'

There was something very soothing about watching Thomas chop logs for us, listening to the rhythmic fall of the hatchet and the cracking of wood. As I sat there, watching through the window, I knew I would save up this memory and hold it close to me for a long time. He had left his jacket on the chair. I held it, feeling the texture of the wool, both rough and smooth at the same time. Outside, the sky seemed white enough for snow. I wished snow would fall and cut us off from the world. The three of us would stay here, until the spring. Until Dad got well.

Thomas came back inside and washed his hands at the kitchen sink. 'You know Margaret would come if she could. But it might arouse suspicion. She said that once a week she'll go to the police station, to enquire.'

For several minutes, Thomas talked about Margaret. Nothing in particular but just, it seemed to me, for the pleasure of saying her name.

Thomas has arranged with the farmer for provisions to be sent and left by the front door. I am glad he said the front door. I don't want some farmer's child looking through the back window. Dad and me are 'housekeepers'. It might look suspicious to have one housekeeper who keeps to his bed and another who does nothing but look after him.

We also have Sheba to guard us. She whimpered when she saw that she was to be left behind. Thomas explained to her that she must look after us. Sheba seemed to understand and stood beside me at the gate as the pony and trap moved away, along the lane. At the bend, Thomas turned, raised his hat and waved. Then he was gone.

Sheba spends a lot of time licking Dad's hands and sometimes his face. She sleeps at his side and keeps him warm. Sometimes Dad winces in pain. I wish I knew more. I wonder whether he might be bleeding inside. I have heard of that. At the end of the bleeding, people die.

Once he turned to me and said his sister's name: Sarah. I went along with that. I said, 'Yes, Sarah will be here soon.'

I thought of all the times I had disapproved of Dad – disliking the smell of his pipe, the way he looked so foreign, how he sometimes struggled to get his tongue around English. Now I longed for those days before everything went so wrong. I wanted that time back. I wanted it to be then, not now.

Outside is utter darkness and silence. I never knew such quiet. It is almost impossible to imagine that somewhere, far away, a war is going on.

I'm sure it was only a few months ago that Dad's hair was black. Now it is completely white. Sitting by his bed, I notice every detail about him. The pulse in his throat races. His hand flutters. I lean forward to listen to what he wants. He spoke today, in English, too. He said, 'I'm all right.'

His skin looks like wrinkled tissue paper. Deep lines run from the side of his nostrils to his jaw. He coughs and makes little moaning sounds. Other times he lies still and silent. Weak January sunlight struggles through the window and finds his face. I got up to close the curtain, but changed my mind, fearing to bring darkness to him. I could not keep the thought from taking shape: perhaps the world will turn dark for him soon enough.

No one came from the farm yesterday. No one has come today. Have they forgotten us? I fear that we will be found out. Reported. Police will come. I know I must go and see because I have just given Dad the last of the milk.

When I tapped on the farmhouse door, no one answered. I heard a shriek from inside: 'Go fetch thah father. Fast as thah can.'

The door flew open. A tiny girl aged about three rushed past me. I tried to stop her. But she had her orders and she ran, towards the fields.

A cry of pain. I followed the sounds to an upstairs room. A woman in her thirties lay on the bed. She gripped a pillow and sank her teeth into a rolled-up sheet. She looked at me in anguish and stretched out a hand. She let the sheet fall from her mouth and cried, 'I'm nearly there. Baby's coming.'

I could see the baby's head.

'Bugger said he'd be here,' she screamed.

'It's all right,' I said. 'Let it come, let the baby come. I'm with you.'

The baby squeezed its way onto her thighs and into the world. A boy, covered in blood and slippery. I grabbed a towel from the bed end and wrapped the tiny creature in it. She had set out some stuff on the washstand. I dealt with the cord. I couldn't see a piece of lint to clean the mucus from the bairn's mouth. I did it with my finger. He set up a great yell of objection.

For a moment the tiredness fled from the woman's round, cheerful face. 'He'll do,' she said proudly as she took the baby in her arms.

I went downstairs and brought up the kettle. On the washstand was an enamel basin and a jug of cold water. I washed the baby and laid him in the drawer of a dresser that had been pulled out and padded with a little homemade pillow for a mattress, sheets and a cut-down blanket.

She asked, 'Who are thee? Where's thah come from?'

'I only came for milk. I'm stopping at Elmtree House. Housekeeper.'

'Thank God thah came by.'

'Is there no doctor?'

'Old one died. Young 'un's gone to war. Me sister were supposed to be here, but I've come on early. Bairn couldn't wait to be in't world.'

I wondered how long it would be until someone came. I had to get back for Dad.

She nodded towards the baby in the drawer. 'I'll take him now.'

I lifted the helpless little creature out of the drawer, marvelling at his tiny, red, screwed-up face. 'What will you call him?'

'Herbert, after his father.' She took him from me. 'Come on, me wee farmer. Get suckling.'

A large, red-faced man with hands the size of shovels came hurrying in, the tiny child trotting after him. He was much older than the woman, old enough to be her father. He smiled at his wife and baby, and scratched his head.

'You have a baby brother,' I whispered to the little girl. 'Now will you show me where's the milk for Elmtree House?'

When I got back to the house, Dad lay on the floor. He must have clutched at a blanket because the bedding lay in a heap above and beside him.

'Dad!' I rushed to him.

'*Entschuldigen.*' His nightshirt was wet. '*Ich kann nicht–*'

Using a straight-back chair for him to hold onto, I managed to get him up. I had found a chair commode in one of the upstairs rooms.

I changed the sheets and settled Dad back into bed. He lay with his eyes closed. By the large stone sink, I rinsed the sheets. I could have done it in the cellar but wanted to stay near him. I squeezed the sheets out as best I could and put them in the tin bath with soda, to deal with later.

I have a feeling that we are over the worst, and that makes me so perfectly happy and content. When there is only one thing you can do, life is very simple and straightforward. (I suspect that this is how hermits feel when they give up the world.) Everything we could want is here. The upstairs rooms are full of blankets and woolly jumpers. There is a huge cellar full of coal. Since I delivered Baby Herbert Hopps into the world, our food from the farm contains choice items: a small cheese; brown eggs; a slice of ham. While Dad slept, I managed to go to the village and buy flour.

Each day he looks to me a little better. I have

explained to him where we are, and that we are housekeepers. But sometimes, when he wakes, he gets confused and asks me again. I would do some housekeeping, to earn our crust, but at present cannot leave him. I did take a look in the study and thought about dusting. The bookcases are locked and so I read to him from just one book, the one that Thomas gave me for Christmas. *The Iliad.*

...the horses
Rattled the empty chariots through the files of battle,
Longing for their noble drivers. But they on the ground
Lay, dearer to the vultures than to their wives.

Dad shuts his eyes. I do not know how much he understands. I picture the horses and chariots. In my mind's eye, all the horses are Solomon, with his bright, intelligent eyes. In my imagination, Solomon strikes out across the plain, spurred on by an ancient warrior. Sometimes I imagine Kevin and Johnny in their khaki, as chariot drivers. Then they are gone, dragged behind the chariots through dust and sand.

All around, his black hair
Was spread; in the dust his whole head lay,
That once-charming head; now Zeus had let his enemies
Defile it on his native soil.

As I spoke the poem to Dad, I realized that we had heard no news of the war. I had not bought a newspaper, nor talked to anyone at all about how the battles went, how long it was expected to last, how many men had died. But this poem seemed to me like news of the war.

> ...*The two-edged sword*
> *Sunk home its full length. The other, face down,*
> *Lay still, and the black blood ran out, wetting the*
> *ground.*

When I pause, Dad speaks to me, but he speaks in Yiddish. He speaks so clearly, willing me to understand. And I do. He is telling me that it does not have to be like that, it does not have to be like that at all. I think he wants me to stop reading this poem, but when I go to put the book down, he tells me to continue.

> *As when harsh misfortune strikes a man if in his*
> *own country*
> *He has killed a man, and arrives at last at someone*
> *else's door,*
> *The door of a rich man; a shudder seizes those who*
> *see him.*
> *So Achilles shuddered to see divine Priam;*
> *The others shuddered too, looking at one another.*

Pointing to his heel, Dad says, 'Achilles, Achilles!' We laugh.

His feet are white, like marble. The blue and red veins have multiplied. I wrap his feet in the blanket, with the hot brick under them.

While watching over him, I fell asleep and dreamed that Thomas came. In the dream he knew about the murder. We were in the ice room, standing over Clarence Laycock's body. 'I trusted you,' Thomas said. Clarence Laycock's ghost pointed at me. *Murderer. Murderer.* I woke wanting to ask Dad what had happened, but when I tried to talk about Christmas Eve, he looked puzzled. 'Sarah? *Was ist los?*'

'*Nichts,*' I said. '*Alles gut.*'

I have come to love this house, which has turned out to be much bigger than I first thought. It sits squat and solid, like a neat picture a child would draw when copying the description of a house from a fairy tale. Its lattice windows are lit by pale winter light. The front garden has a sundial. I have not worked out how to tell the time by it, but that is because of a lack of sun.

Carved above the door arch is the date, 1776. The long windows are dirty and do not let in much light at the front. But round the back, where we spend all our time, I have washed the kitchen windows inside and out.

In the dining room and the study at the front of the house, the fireplaces are set against the outside walls. Along the hall from those rooms, a staircase leads to the landing. Looking at the house from the back, the kitchen is on the right and a sitting room on the left. The kitchen has a large, cast-iron range against the inside wall, a sink under the window and a pantry on the opposite side to the range. There are all the usual things that belong in a kitchen but also the iron bedstead with feather mattress that Thomas brought down for Dad, and the sofa where I sleep. The parlour also has its fireplace against the inside wall and has a large, dusty sofa and plump chairs. Its real name is 'Drawing Room'. I know this because in the kitchen, above the hall door, is a glass-fronted, wooden-framed box with a set of bells that can be rung from the different rooms.

From the kitchen, a door opens, which at first I thought led only to the cellar. Now I have discovered another door. Through this door, a winding iron staircase leads to the landing, coming out by the bathroom door. This bathroom was once a bedroom. You can tell by the size, and by the fireplace. There is a sink, a lavatory and a great cast-iron bath in the centre of the room. That part is all much newer than the rest of the house. The secret door reminded me of a Thomas Hardy story where a man breaks down a door, not knowing that the girl he will fall in love with is on the other side.

After I discovered the door, I had a strange dream. I must have confused Thomas Hardy and Thomas Turner. I dreamed of Thomas, breaking down a secret door and finding me on the other side.

FORTY

One day passes very much like another. Although Thomas left me supplied with candles and oil, I use the daylight as much as I can, to save them. This means I get up with the sun and go to bed with the sun. Short days but long enough. Food is simple. We have soup. When the hens lay, Dad has a boiled egg. On Sundays I fry a rasher of bacon.

Gladys Hopps, she is the farmer's wife, has taught me how to keep hens. As a thank you for my delivering Baby Herbert Hopps, she gave me two sweet bantams. I take good care of these little creatures. Sheba believes she is their captain and escorts them about the yard. At night, I make sure they are safe in their coop, out of the grasp of foxes.

I brought more straight-back chairs from the dining room and have a row of four that lead from Dad's bed to the armchair by the fire. Once a day I encourage him to walk along this route, holding onto the backs of the chairs. If he tires, I quickly turn the next chair round, seat towards him, so that he can rest before resuming his hobble towards the fire.

Now that he is able to move about a little, I do not have to wash the sheets so often. Drying was difficult. I rescued the washing-line, which had lain unused in the yard. Simple things take such a long time. I could not find the pegs for the line, and searched and searched, until I discovered a second cellar. It annoyed me to use up precious candles for such a small thing as to find clothes pegs.

We have no calendar and I am losing track of time. A few snowdrops appeared in the garden. Crocuses followed royally, purple and gold.

Gladys Hopps brought the milk herself today. We stood by the back door and I held Baby

Herbert. As she looked at the garden, Gladys said that in the spring I should plant potatoes and vegetables. Little Mabel, who really is only three, said, 'First you turn the soil.'

'How do I do that?' I asked.

'Dig,' she said.

They knew Dad was in the kitchen, but I did not say anything about him, and they did not ask. I would have liked to show him the baby, but I am afraid Dad will give himself away. Even standing at the door, I felt anxious in case he called to me and she heard his accent.

Turning the soil sounds an easy job. It is not. The soil is hard. I found an old pair of boots. Wearing these boots, I settled the spade on the earth. Then I jumped in the air, landing on the sides of the spade and forcing it a little way into the earth. I had to do this over and over. The top of the spade slopes and my feet easily slip. I have hurt my ankle and scraped my shin. Holding a spade handle makes calluses on your hands. Each day I do a little. I have a picture in my mind of how it should look when I finish digging. A second picture in my mind would show me potatoes growing but I do not know what potatoes growing look like so that picture is a little hazy.

I rubbed the cream from the top of the milk on my red calloused hands, but it has not made a lot of difference.

I have had a letter from Margaret. As I read it aloud, Sheba sat up very straight, head cocked to one side, listening. When I had finished reading, she thumped her tail on the floor. I believe she thought the letter was to her, from Thomas. I indulged her on this and told her that Thomas asked me to pat her head, which I did.

When I read the letter to Dad, I missed out just one sentence; where Margaret says that our Bread Street furniture has been sold:

17 March 1915

Dear Julia
You will be surprised to have a letter from me in London. Yes, London! Thomas missed me so much that he begged me to come and visit him. He still cannot leave the capital because of being on stand-by for his important work. Mrs Turner would not come and of course I could not come alone. I wish you could have travelled with me. However, Miss Mason stepped in to act as my chaperone. She is a very amiable person now that I am on different social terms with her. Many of her relations live in London, so she spends much time visiting and taking tea.

I have been shopping in some of the better shops and salons. Uncle kindly gave me some money. I have not touched the money from the sale of our furniture on Bread Street. Mr Mitchell insisted that I charge my trousseau to his account. We are made a fuss of in all the fashion houses. As you can imagine, Miss Mason loves it! No one else is buying any clothes during this war. (Except yours truly!) Honestly, all the top girls in London are dressing up in uniform-type clothes and fighting over war work of one kind or another. I am sure I am a pariah among them. I wonder whether that is why Mrs Turner did not want to come. She is serving on several Leeds committees. I have promised that on my return I shall do something useful, too. As long as it does not involve dealing with sick people or smelly people – though I did not say that to Mrs T.

If they do not send Thomas to the Front soon, I am sure it will all be over and he will meet himself coming back. This war cannot go on for ever. When it is over and he returns, he wants us to marry without further delay. We would do so now but there are reasons why not. I might as well tell you that the government department that he answers to is very pleased to have bachelors for the war correspondents. I do not see why this matters as I am sure the reporters do not have to be in the thick of battles.

Honestly, I have a whole trunk of clothes to bring home and there will be much for me to pass on to you. I have not forgotten you and always I think what colours will suit you. I hope you have not lost weight, though if so, things could be taken in. Perhaps you have put on weight due to 'country living'. Do you remember that Aunty Amy always talked about 'country living'? It made me think of milk and honey.

As soon as Thomas gets his marching orders from the War Office, giving him and the other correspondents permission to travel, I shall come and see you straight away. Nothing on earth will stop me.

With all my love. Write straight back to me.

Your loving sister

Margaret xxx

I knew that Margaret had not mentioned Dad in case the letter was opened and read by someone else. I made up a couple of sentences in which she asked about him and wished him a speedy recovery.

Dad smiled. 'Your mam, she knew Margaret would be a lady. Margaret always a little lady.'

Perhaps it is because I do not have anything exciting to think about. I spent a long time today wondering what Margaret will bring for me. I hope she will bring me something yellow. I picked daffodils in the little wood near the railway line. Dad said that once you bring them in, they die. They will die anyway. It gives me pleasure to see them on the kitchen window sill. In the afternoons, the back garden catches the sun. Once I have got the garden planted, he will be able to sit outside on the bench, wrapped in his blanket, watching potatoes grow.

At least Dad was back in the present when I read the letter to him, not in some past asking for his sister. When he first wakes, or is dropping off to sleep, he speaks in Yiddish.

He was himself today, all afternoon. I would have liked to ask him about his life in Germany. And about coming to England and meeting Mam. I couldn't frame my words. When you have never asked about something, it is very hard to bring it up. He may think I believe he is dying.

Sometimes I can't sleep. I lie and look at the shadows on the ceiling. *Who killed Clarence?* I ask myself. *What happened on Christmas Eve? Was there a fight? Is that how Dad got injured? Or did the policeman hit Dad with his truncheon?*

In the daytime, I leave those questions aside. I encourage Dad to get up. He now sits in the chair every day. I place a basin on the spindly-leg table and hold it steady while he washes his own hands and face. This tires him but he likes to do it.

We keep to this room. The rest of the house could collapse and I wouldn't care. What a great housekeeper I am! Only Dad matters.

I don't know what made Thomas give me a copy of *The Iliad,* but because he did, that is what I read to Dad.

One day, after I had been out digging, I set out the straight-back chairs in a row all the way to the door. Slowly, Dad snailed his way to the doorway. He looked out at the earth and the sky, taking deep breaths. *Trying to breathe himself better,* I thought.

Later, we had soup and bread. Afterwards, by firelight and the glow of the lantern, I put on a show. I sang 'Look What Percy's Picked Up in the Park'. I recited 'Scarborough by the Sea'. I shadowboxed in the way Frank taught. Dancing back and forth, fists ready. Right hook. Left jab. I put on two bouts. In bout one, Dad watched me. In bout two, he watched my shadow on the wall.

Then he said, 'Where am I?'

I explained. Again.

Outside, tulips sway. The wind has blown them so that they look like dancers who have loosened their dresses and given up on any thought of looking spruce. Rain sleets down. I do not believe the tulips will still be standing at the end of this deluge, yet they come up smiling.

I read to Dad from *The Iliad,* which he has come to like. It may be because it is so terrible, and we are snug and warm in this one perfect room.

She ordered her bright-haired maids in the palace
To place on the fire a large tripod, preparing
A hot bath for Hector, returning from battle.
Foolish woman! Already he lay, far from hot baths,
Slain by grey-eyed Athena, who guided Achilles'
  arm.

Dad tells me, in Yiddish or German, that he wants a hot bath. He looks hopeful, *'Das heiss Bad! Ja, ja.'*

He wants a bath. How can I give him a bath? There is the tin bath. He could stand in it. But that is not what he wants. I see it in his eyes. He wants to lie in a hot bath, like in the public baths. Like in the bathroom at the Dragon.

I walk about the house. I inspect the bathroom above the kitchen. He would not be able to manage the winding stairs that lead from the kitchen. It can be reached by the main stairs, and there is a bannister to hold on to. Two pipes come from the cast-iron bath. When I turn on the taps the pipes groan and rattle. I turn them off quickly. I know it is silly, but the noise scares me. That is why I do not use the lavatory in this room. When you pull the lavatory chain it sounds as if monsters have been let loose in the ceiling above you. I imagine some ghoul will come running to get me.

I try again and turn on the tap that says H for hot. It is cold. How would we heat the water? Perhaps I could pull out the top flue in the kitchen range. Or does the magic happen from the stove in the cellar? Thomas would tell me.

I go back downstairs, holding the bannister to

try it. It might be possible to get Dad up the stairs. Especially if Margaret would come. Or Thomas.

I go back to Dad. He has fallen sideways in the chair as he sometimes does, his head to one side.

'Dad?'

I go to him to make him comfortable. I do not want him to have a crick in his neck. His head falls to the right. Gently, I take his head in my hands. I reach for a pillow to prop his head straight. His head does not want to move. I look at his neck. The pulse on his throat is still. His hand feels warm in mine. I take his wrist. I cannot always find my own pulse, much less his. I try again. I pick up his other hand. His other wrist. I put my head close to his face to feel his breath. A feather juts from the cushion. I pull it out and place it under his nostrils. Then by his mouth. The feather trembles in my hand, but not from his breath. His eyes, not closed, not open, do not see me, do not flicker.

'Dad? Dad! Dad!'

I hear him breathing. No. It is Sheba, lying under his bed.

While I have been checking the plumbing; while I have been walking down the stairs, making plans about hot water; about how I will encourage him to place one foot before the other up the stairs; while I have been working out how best to clean a dirty old cast-iron bath; while I have been doing all these things, he has left me.

I must get a doctor. But I remember something. The old doctor is dead. The younger one has gone to war. I don't know what to do. It is

291

dark outside. I can do nothing till morning. Sheba sits beside me and whimpers. She seems afraid. When she won't go to Dad, shies away from him, that is when I know for sure. The dog has told me. *Don't hope,* she says. I look at my dad. I take his hand. Too late.

I did not hold his hand, or hold him, or say goodbye or that I would miss him.

And he did not say my name or say goodbye, or say what I should do for ever without him. In this wide, war-filled world.

Dad.

I want my dad.

For a long time I am still. I sit beside him, holding him. Miracles happen. I could be wrong. I wait for him to come back to life. I wait a long time.

I pull the chair to the bed. I manage to get him on the bed. It is only now I notice how thin he has become. How his jaw juts at a sharp angle. I do two contrary things at once. I wait for him to breathe again. I put pennies on his eyes.

I know nothing. Nothing of where he came from and how and why. Now I shall never know. Can never ask.

FORTY-ONE

Farmers rise early. As soon as the sun lightened the sky, I went to the farm. Mr and Mrs Hopps were moving about in the kitchen. They thought I had come for milk. I told them, 'I think my dad has died.'

I don't know why I said *think*. Even then I was hoping it would not be true.

Mr Hopps hardly speaks.

Without speaking, they walked back with me.

'The children,' I said.

Gladys Hopps put her hand on my shoulder. 'Mabel will see to Herbert, if they wake.'

She stayed with me. Mr Hopps went somewhere, he didn't say where.

We washed Dad. Combed his hair. Put on a clean shirt.

Gladys walked out of the kitchen, along the hall. I heard her opening and closing doors. When she came back she said, 'The men will take him into the dining room. He can rest there.'

I nodded.

'Who'll come to be with you?' she asked.

I said, 'I'll write to my sister.' I took a paper and envelopes from the drawer.

She said, 'If a matter is urgent, the police will deal with it. They have a telephone at the police house.'

'I'll write,' I said. 'That's best.' I felt I should think of some explanation as to why I did not want the police but she had already forgotten about it. She watched me dip the nib in the ink and eyed me curiously as I wrote.

It did not take me long to write:

Dear Margaret
Dad died last night
In sorrow,
Julia

Gladys was looking over my shoulder at the words. I folded the paper and addressed the envelope, copying the address from Margaret's letter.

'It must be a marvellous thing, to pick up a pen and make words flow out of it,' Gladys said.

I sealed the envelope. 'I have no stamp.'

'I'll see to it. I'll take it and get a stamp and put it in the box. Come back with me.'

I was about to refuse when she said that I must stay with the children for her, while she posted my letter.

I picked up my journal and pencil to take with me. I began writing this sitting at the farmhouse table.

Now I am back here at Elmtree House. Dad lies alone in the dining room. Mr Hopps and a man called Arthur Miles came back with a coffin. On the spindly table where before I had set the enamel basin for him to wash his hands and face, I have set a tall candle to burn.

Gladys has been back and brought me food. She said, 'Poor man. Just when the summer's a-coming. To die late in the spring's a sad thing.'

She asked me to go back with her to the farm, but I said no.

I have no more to say for now. Next time I write my world will have changed for ever. For now, I shall sit with Dad while I still can. Sheba would not come near when Dad first died. Now she follows me everywhere. We sat with Dad a while ago. Sheba lay under the table, sleeping. For a moment, when she snored, I thought Dad had come to life.

Today I wanted time to go backwards. But it did not. Time for the funeral came round. Margaret had found a clock somewhere in the house and set it on the kitchen mantelpiece. Time ticked round, striking the quarter hour, like an enemy laughing in my face.

The black-plumed horse and black-draped cart carried Dad's coffin from Elmtree House to the church in the village. And the horse was Solomon, brought by Bernard.

We walked behind in the sunshine, a light breeze on our cheeks. I wanted Dad to be warmed by that sunshine, to feel the breeze and see the pale-blue sky and lightly scudding clouds. Margaret and me walked side by side. Behind us walked Bernard, Aunty Amy and Thomas. Behind them walked Mr and Mrs Hopps.

Fear and defiance. That was what I felt. Fear that even now someone would stop us. *That man, that Joseph Wood, is a wanted man. What is his true name? Josef Wald? That man should not be here. That girl, that Julia. She has the same initials, don't you see? That's guilt.*

Let anyone try. Let anyone try to stop this now.

Thomas, Bernard, Mr Hopps and Mr Miles carried Dad's coffin into the church and set it down on the trestle before the stone altar table. In the cool church with its solid pews and plain leaded windows, I thought we would be safe.

But by the pulpit, flags flew. The Union flag. St George's flag. A pendant with St George and the Dragon. In my head, I said to Dad, *It's all right, Dad. Don't be upset by the Union Jack. To hell with*

St George. You and me, we have the Dragon on our side.

Thomas must have spoken to the vicar, an ancient bespectacled man in a long black cassock. He spoke no words from the New Testament. No 'I am the Resurrection and the Life' floated on the sunlit air. I shall write down what the vicar said. Because none of it struck a wrong note. It would have been agreeable to Dad. He said:

O Lord, what is man that thou should regard him?
What is frail man that thou should notice him?
Man is like a breath;
His days are like a passing dream;
Like a flower he blooms in the morning
And in the evening fades and withers.
But the man of peace lies down in soft slumber,
For he shall live again, safe in thee;
Live where the dew of light falls across the land of
   shade.
As Joseph journeys to his long home,
Teach we poor mourners how to number our days
That wisdom may enter our hearts.
The dust returns to the earth,
But the spirit returns to God who gave it.

We sang the twenty-third Psalm, 'The Lord is My Shepherd'. I sang after my fashion. The voices that lifted me were Margaret's soprano, echoing to the vaults. Thomas's tenor, so sure and strong. Someone sang baritone, Mr Hopps, I think. I wanted everyone to sing their heart out, and they did.

Thomas had said something about his family

vault. The thought of a vault filled me with dread though I did not say so. Dad was carried from the church to the furthest part of the graveyard, away from the other graves. I was glad that he would not be in a vault, but it struck me that he might be oh so lonely over by the lichen-covered stone wall. Gently, the men lowered the coffin.

I do not remember what the vicar said at the grave. Margaret and I stood side by side, Bernard and Thomas behind us. She took my hand. So often we know what the other is thinking. In that moment I knew what was in her mind.

Dad had taught us a prayer to say for Mam. He had told us it would be just the same prayer, for a mother or a father. At the time I never imagined that we would say it for him. After the vicar sprinkled earth onto the coffin, Margaret said, 'May God watch over the soul of my dear father Joseph who has journeyed to his eternal rest.'

I joined in. 'I pledge charity in his memory and pray that his soul rest in perpetual light with the immortal souls of Abraham, Isaac, Jacob, Sarah, Rebekah, Rachel, Leah and all the holy men and women in heaven. Amen.'

We had to mean it. That word charity. I remembered Cissie and the promise she had dragged from me to take care of her brothers and sisters: *Make sure they don't clem, Julia.*

As we left the graveyard, a line from *The Iliad* came into my head. I had read it aloud to Dad only a couple of days before: *'Without respite, I mourn for you who have always been gentle.'*

As we went back into Elmtree House, Margaret

said to me, 'We still have each other. We're the Wood Sisters. We'll stick together now, Julia.'

Will we? I'm not so sure. I don't know what will become of us.

And now that I can't ask Dad, I want to know the truth. When I shut my eyes at night I sometimes see Clarence Laycock, lying dead in the ice room. I can barely bring myself to think it, but did he finally torment Dad once too often, push Dad over the edge so that in the end he fought back?

Who murdered Clarence Laycock? Because if Dad could murder, so could anyone. So could I.

FORTY-TWO

Margaret and Thomas have gone into Leeds to see Mrs Turner and so I am alone with Sheba, who is doing me the great favour of curling up with me, keeping my feet warm and trying to console me. This window seat in the study is where Thomas used to sit as a boy when he visited his grandparents. It catches the sun on this fine spring day. But I had best try and set down this morning's events in order. I blush when I think of the lies I have told.

We were sitting in the kitchen over breakfast. Thomas showed us his official papers and the tin badge of identification embossed with his name and title: war correspondent. As I looked at the khaki-covered packet of field dressings, Margaret saw that the War Office papers authorized him to act as correspondent until the end of the year, 31 December 1915. She pulled a face and told him that he had better be home in time for her birthday in September, or he'd be in trouble.

While Margaret went upstairs to re-do her hair, Thomas took me into the study. He said it was to show me a book he thought I might like to read, but now I can't remember which because I soon realized there was something worrying him.

I sat on this window seat. He pulled a chair up near me, saying that he would be glad to imagine me or Margaret sitting reading or writing there when he set off on his assignment.

He asked how I felt about staying on in his house. I told him that I was glad because the back garden is turned over and ready to plant potatoes. I would hate to have wasted my efforts. I did not say that I want to be close to Dad and tend his grave.

Thomas has a way of paying attention even when no words are spoken. I felt as if he understood my thoughts. He said that he had asked Arthur Miles (he is the man who made Dad's coffin) to mend the roof and do any work necessary to keep the property in shape.

He took an Atlas from the bookcase and pointed out where he will be going.

I had never heard of the Dardanelles. The other name for the Dardanelles is Hellespont. It is a narrow strait in north-west Turkey that connects the Aegean Sea on the west and the Sea of Marmara on the east. I love these names. I told him that I picture blue waves tipped with white; the sun rising over Marmara and setting over the Aegean. Thomas is going to set off for the Gallipoli Peninsula and we (the British, not me and Thomas) are to secure the Dardanelles from the Turks so as to support our ally, Russia. Thanks to Homer, I know more than I need to know about Greece and Troy, Hector and Priam and Achilles, but nothing about the Dardanelles. Perhaps I got the wrong impression from *The Iliad*, but I'm sure that the Greeks and Trojans only fought in one place at a time. This war is going on all over the globe. I don't understand why. I'm sure Homer would have made ten volumes of it.

I asked him was he excited about going to the Dardanelles. He said that he would rather none of this was happening. He pulled a volume from the bookcase and read a piece to me by a journalist called Mr Stead. Mr Stead exposed wrong-doing and campaigned for a better society. Thomas wanted to write that kind of journalism, because of his interest in human nature, in life. With the war, no such journalism goes on. Everyone speaks, writes and reads about the war to the exclusion of all else. All he can do is try and tell the truth to the people at home and to be a witness to the war for our generation. I felt very proud when he said 'our generation' to me, because previously he spoke to me as if I were a child.

He closed the Atlas carefully and set it down on the floor. 'There's something else, Julia. Something I need to ask you.'

I thought he was going to fire questions at me about geography. His voice scared me, as if I were expecting the rent man and was a shilling short.

I dropped my hand onto Sheba's head to stroke her. Sheba lay down and my hand dangled uselessly.

Thomas spoke quietly. 'Do you know that a man – a workmate of your father's – was found dead in the ice room when the meat market re-opened after Christmas?'

I felt my face go tight and my breath stopped somewhere at the back of my nose making me gasp. I looked out of the window, across the garden to where a shaft of sunlight fell across the sundial.

'You must tell me the truth, Julia. I deserve to know.'

I hugged my knees to myself. I didn't want the memories of that night. Didn't want Clarence Laycock's body behind my eyes. Thomas reached out and took my hand. 'Answer me.'

'I knew he was dead,' I said.

He let go of my hand. 'Was that why you were so anxious to take your dad away from Leeds?'

'No! Dad had nothing to do with that. I had to get him away, so that he could get better.'

He stood up, the chair between us, his hands gripping the top of the chair. 'No one's going to blame you, Julia. With this war, matters that would be properly looked into at other times are being set aside. I only heard about the death by chance.' He ran his hand through his hair. 'There may be a time when you're asked about this. When there's an investigation.' He waited, then said softly, 'And you must tell me. You owe me that.'

'It wasn't Dad,' I said. 'Dad didn't kill him.'

'No one's accusing. Just tell me what you know.'

I told him about Dad not coming home, about going to look for him, searching the meat market.

'You went alone at that time of night?' he asked.

'Yes.' I couldn't tell whether he believed me or not. It wasn't a lie. I had gone alone, just that Frank had followed me, without my knowing.

I realized why I couldn't mention Frank's name. Dad would not have killed Clarence. Frank would.

'Go on,' he said.

'I searched.' I remembered the shadows my lantern threw across the high walls of the cooling hall. The memory made me suddenly shiver. 'I looked in the ice room because once Dad had been locked in there. As a joke.' I heard the bitterness in my voice. 'That was when I saw the body.'

'Did you know it was Clarence Laycock?'

'Yes. I looked. I had to be sure it wasn't Dad.'

'And you didn't think you should tell anyone?'

'He was dead. I was sure of that.'

Sheba licked my hand non-stop. She stood wagging her tail and made a fuss of me, trying to make me stroke her and look at her.

'It's all right,' Thomas put a hand on my shoulder. 'I'm not blaming you. You shouldn't have had to face such horrors alone.'

I heard the question in his voice. He wanted to ask me and could not, out of loyalty to Margaret.

'Margaret doesn't know,' I said. 'I couldn't tell her. She's very squeamish.'

He looked surprised.

'I couldn't have told her. It would have given her bad dreams.'

'You poor child,' he said. 'Poor little Julia. You told no one?'

I shook my head. I hated being made to think about it again. Remembering little details. The way Frank had waited all those hours across in Grundy's alley and followed me to the meat market. How he had tried to stop me going into the ice room. Most of all I hated to think that Thomas believed Dad had killed Clarence.

'Dad would never hurt anyone,' I said. 'I'm sure he had nothing to do with it.'

'Did he ever say what happened that night?'

I heard Margaret come down the stairs. She called out.

'Try and put it behind you,' Thomas said. 'You were thinking of your father. No one as young as you should have had to bear it. But you must tell Margaret. Find the right moment, and tell her. Don't keep it to yourself.'

He changed the tone of his voice as soon as Margaret came in, asking was I sure I wouldn't join them and go to Leeds that afternoon. I could go to the station with Margaret tomorrow and wave him off for London.

Why did I say no? Not just because Margaret frowned.

I would rather stay here just a little while longer with Sheba, and make a start writing in my new notebook. The truth is I did not want to rush back to Leeds too soon. Dad would think I was deserting him before he had time to get used to the loneliness of his grave. I shall need to tell him that I intend to see how the Garrettys are managing.

I have crammed this entry into my old notebook. I shall start the new one afresh when I have something good to write.

FORTY-THREE

I have not had time to write in this book for a month. Over the past weeks we have made a thousand pork pies. Yes, one thousand. I can hardly believe it myself. We could not have managed it without the following:

my green tartan dress and cape;
Margaret's blue tartan dress and cape;
a goodly portion of the Hoppses' late pig, Chubby;
the pony and trap from Mr Miles's brother-in-law;
Dad's tip: 'People eat with their eyes';
Gregory and Sol Garretty's help.

But I had better begin at the beginning.

Wearied of being alone at Elmtree House, I caught the early-morning train to Leeds, squeezed between a stout woman with hens in a cage and an old man who smelt like a tobacco pouch and carried a sack that moved.

Aunty Amy had told me that Sarah Garretty has left school and is helping her in the shop.

Little Essie spends more time with Aunty Amy and Sarah than she does at home so I know she will thrive. I owed it to Cissie to see how the boys fared. Mrs Garretty tried not to look too pleased about the eggs I brought her saying, 'You're all but a stranger' in an accusing, sulky voice, as if I had let them down all these months.

Sol was off school as it was raining; he had caught a chill and had no boots. That didn't stop him going to fetch Gregory, though I tried to stop him because he looked pinched and half-starved.

Gregory is a boy you would describe as wiry, skinny but with overdeveloped arms from pushing a cart and heaving stuff about while running errands. When you look at Gregory's scoopy hands and long arms you can imagine him deep in the earth, cutting coal out of hard rocks like his father. At fourteen, he seems already to be the man he will become. Sol is twelve and still half-child. He is a dreamy sort of boy and I'm sure could be a scholar if he set his mind to it. His hair is reddish-gold, the colour of Annie's, though he greases it to make it dark. His eyes look as though they'd like to be blue but lack the courage and have let the colour be washed away.

I asked Gregory if he had found work. He had not.

'Would you like to try your luck in the country?' I asked, not knowing what I could do for him but feeling Cissie's presence in the room, hearing her words, *'Don't let them clem.'*

Greg's eyes widened and he grinned. 'A job?' he asked.

'Something like that,' I said. 'Working on the land.'

'Not arf. When we going?'

'Hold thah horses,' Mrs Garretty said. 'What about yon lad?' She nodded at Sol, who sat on the floor, blinking, his mouth turned down, the picture of dejection. 'If thah's tekin' the lad what can shift for hissen, thah mun tek his brother what can't.'

'I can shift!' Sol said indignantly.

'Then let's all shift together,' I said.

Margaret agreed to come and stay, too. By the time she arrived at Elmtree House the boys had taken up residence.

Sol is to start at the local school in September, if we are still here. I tried to have him accepted straight away. But the teacher said that so many children will be off during May to plant potatoes that it would not be a good time for him to begin.

Now that Gregory and Sol sleep downstairs, we girls have moved to Bedroom 3. Margaret did try Bedroom 2 on her own one night, but Bedrooms 1 and 2 are at the front of the house. She saw a cloud cross the moon above the church steeple and thought that if she was at the front of the house, ghosts would get to her first. She complained about the blackness of the sky, and an owl's melancholy and very personal tone of voice. She said that she didn't sleep a wink and, once she had made the mistake of getting into bed, was afraid to get out or call for help. Her being-chased-by-a-German dream came back, the dream she thought she had left behind in Leeds.

On the morning we were to start our potato

planting, which I found out how to do by helping the Hopps family, Annie Garretty and Bernard unexpectedly came to visit. Annie did not join in at first, on account of having worn her best dress for the day out. She sat on the bench in the sun with Margaret and watched. Annie's hair had turned a sort of rusty colour since she started her new job. With her cream dress she looked very pretty, like a daffodil.

We had emptied a sack of potatoes into a pile by the bench. Gregory and Sol sorted medium-sized ones, for planting. Bernard split the large ones so that they served as two. The small ones are not to be planted. Some of these are for our pig. (Sol insisted we call her Pinky, not that she is very pinky just now, more muddy, but that would not be much of a name.)

Sol and I lifted one bucket of spuds, and Gregory insisted on struggling with one himself. You heave your bucket along the row and bob down to place each potato in the furrow as you walk along, a foot apart.

The potatoes have to be well-covered. Fortunately Bernard picked up a spade and made a start. Annie said it looked good fun and she did not care that she had her best dress on. She would give it a go. Sheba got the wrong idea entirely and I had all on to discourage her from snuffling out the potatoes and digging them up again, her front paws going twenty to the dozen.

Bernard, Annie, Gregory and I spread earth over the potatoes. Annie and I chatted as we walked along our rows. She told me about where she works, Barnbow Munitions Factory. They have their own farm there, and are completely self-sufficient. The girls can drink as much milk as they like. Annie lowered her voice and whispered that she is saving up for her marriage to Bernard, though he has not asked her yet. If he doesn't ask soon, she'll ask him. Did I think that was a good idea? I said yes.

Coming back down the garden, I talked to Bernard. Or rather, he talked to me. I expected him to be his usual morose self, but he talked the whole time about Annie. I had to hear all over again how she spends her days at the munitions factory, but also how hard she works. How kind she is. How comical sometimes. How mysterious. She never tells him about her past, about her time with the theatrical troupe.

After they had gone, Margaret and I sat up in bed talking half the night. Margaret thinks it a bit rich that Mrs Garretty and Annie are off earning good money and leaving us to take care of two of the children; and Sarah Garretty working with Aunty Amy and lodging there. I reminded Margaret that it was my idea to bring in Gregory, and also that he and Sol have been a great help.

'Child labour!' Margaret said.

Finally, she told me what was really bothering her. She had seen Mr Miles in the village. He handed her the bill for mending the roof. 'You spent the roof money buying the pig,' she said accusingly.

I explained that Pinky was going to make our fortune. That she would have a huge litter. We would be able to pay for the mending of a dozen roofs.

'What if she dies in piglet-birth?' Margaret sighed. 'What if the piglets are still-born?'

I hadn't thought of that. I nearly said that we could still make pies of them, but that seemed a little insensitive.

Margaret wanted me to light a candle. She hates the dark. But I drew back the curtain and let moonlight into the room. It was the middle of the night before we came up with our plan. I have always wanted to have one place to sell pies, not hawk them round and round the streets. Because of what Annie had said, I thought that the gates of the munitions factory would be a good place to stand selling pies. Even when I can't see her face and she says nothing, I can tell when Margaret disagrees.

'Cough up the objections then.' I tugged at the eiderdown, as Sheba has a habit of lying on it so heavily that she drags it off my shoulder. 'Is it that you think the munitions workers are well fed enough already and won't buy pies? They'd buy them to take home.'

'It's not just that,' she said. 'You said yourself you can't get hold of flour. The munitions factory's run by the government. The government gets hold of whatever it wants. If someone supplied good pies for government workers—'

'Someone like the Wood Sisters?'

'Possibly. Well then, those suppliers might find themselves able to get all the flour they need.'

Margaret, dressed in her blue tartan, and me, dressed in my green, trotted out in the borrowed pony and trap with a baker's dozen of pork pies in a large basket covered with a snowy-white cloth. In a smaller basket, we placed half a dozen more pies, to 'oil the wheels'. There were two sentries posted at the gates of Barnbow Munitions Factory. They were pleased to find the right person for us to speak to after accepting a pork pie apiece.

Margaret did the smiling and talking to the catering manager. I wrote down the order and collected the flour from the stores.

There were no forms to fill out, except to sign for the flour. No one asked our father's place of birth or occupation. Margaret and I are business women now. That is why, in the last weeks, Gregory, Sol and I have baked a thousand pork pies. Margaret has cut out and hand-sewn for us two large white aprons each, and bakers' caps. She has also delivered the pies and written out the invoices.

Dad always said to me that 'people eat with their eyes'. Pies crusty on the outside and pink on the inside sell better than pies crusty on the outside and grey on the inside. I add bacon to the mix to make the filling pink. I have sworn the Garrettys to secrecy. I would swear Margaret to secrecy but she has not asked me about the mystery ingredient.

I should have said that the other important development in our lives is that we now have Solomon in the stables. He completes our family. He and Sheba get on famously. Gregory painted the cart red with some lead paint he found in the cellar. We were working out how best to do the lettering of 'WOOD SISTERS PIES', when Mr Miles came along the lane. He said that lettering is specialized, but he will do it for us. He said when you earn your living as a smallholder you usually have something to sell but not always the same commodity. He will letter the cart 'WOOD SISTERS', without the 'PIES'.

FORTY-FOUR

Gregory prides himself on getting the bacon just right. He and I like ours crisp. Margaret and Sol like theirs just on the turn.

This morning Sol lifted the frying pan, with sizzling bacon, from the round hole in the range. The fire showed through. Sometimes words come out before you know you're thinking something. I said to Margaret, 'Dad couldn't eat anything fried. We had soup all the time.'

She flinched as if I'd hit her. 'I couldn't come. I couldn't be here out in the wilds.' She clammed up, tightening her jaw in that way she does.

'Chicken soup,' I said. 'That was Dad's favourite.'

Margaret got up from the table saying she wasn't hungry. Both Sol and Gregory perked up, wanting her rasher of bacon. I said Sheba should have it as she was going to Leeds with us.

Margaret groaned. 'Oh, we're not taking her, are we? She pongs.'

'That's all right then,' I said. 'We'll have a carriage to ourselves.'

I was glad I'd insisted on taking Sheba. She

stepped into the train like a seasoned traveller and tucked herself close to my feet, as if helping to hide my ancient, worn-out boots, wagging her tail occasionally and smiling serenely whenever she caught my eye. I hope Margaret noticed that Sheba was less smelly than some of the other occupants of our carriage, like the wizened old woman with boils on her chin carrying a basket of apples, and the gnome-man who I swear had filled his pockets with dung.

It feels strange now to arrive back in Leeds station, with the grit, grime, smoke and noise, and people hurrying about their business. I have got used to the quiet of the country where you do not have to dodge your way across a busy road. We went to Bread Street first, to see Aunty Amy.

Her old face lit up at the sight of us. She hugged us and shook her head in admiration at how fine we looked. Little Sarah Garretty seems at home in my spot behind the counter, making a big to-do out of dusting the jars. I did have a little twinge of envy when she told me that Aunty Amy is going to send her to classes with an old gentleman who teaches botany and chemistry. But I'm glad for her. She's a plain girl compared with Annie and my dear Cissie, but good-hearted. She was the one most attached to poor little Baby Jimmy who died. I remembered passing him under the gypsy's donkey and wished we could have done more for him. But Sarah's most important news seemed to be that her mam had left the laundry and gone to work at Barnbow with Annie.

Aunty Amy turned the shop sign to closed, and

since it was dinner-time we went in the back and I brought out the pies and cake just in time for Essie, who comes there straight after school.

Bernard called round to join us and complimented us on our outfits.

When we walked with him to the Dragon, the rain squelched through my boots, so although I looked the part of a lady, I did not feel it. Bernard was on the outside, near the road, and Margaret on the inside, with me between them. She whispered that perhaps a pair of our dead aunt's shoes would fit me. My heart sank. I have worn dead people's made-over clothes a-plenty, but the thought of a dead woman's shoes sent a chill to my heart that was worse than wet feet.

Bernard held the umbrella very carefully for once. He told us that the Coliseum picture house needed a pianist. The manager had offered Bernard the job. To sit in the darkened picture house every night and make music to scare, excite and break hearts was all his joy and desire. I remember the time I saw Bernard when he was in a terrible state of misery about not being allowed into the army. Now he had turned his desire to play at the pictures into a crusade.

'War makes people anxious and low-spirited,' he said. Since his health seemed to exclude him from anything that most people consider useful, he would be making his tiny contribution by cheering people up. Also, me and Margaret would get free tickets whenever we came to Leeds.

By the main doors of the Dragon, Bernard lowered his umbrella and shook the rain from it.

'I'm going to ask Dad if he'll let me take the job at the Coliseum. Will you back me up?'

Uncle left the old barman in charge and led us into the parlour. Bernard followed. As Uncle poured glasses of fortified wine for himself, me and Margaret, he explained that things had not been going well. Publicans were blamed for everything these days, from drunken soldiers to the national shortage of hops.

Bernard passed us the postcards and letters from Kevin and Johnny, which were set out in a row on the mantelpiece. We read every one. Some of the postcards are very pretty.

As he topped up his sherry, Uncle apologized for not coming to Dad's funeral. But in the circumstances it had seemed better to stay in Leeds and keep appearances normal. There had been no more visits from the police enquiring about Joseph Wood, and he preferred to keep it that way.

I had dreaded seeing him, wondering whether he would expect an explanation of how Dad and I had ended up at Elmtree House. But he asked no questions. When he thought I was going to tell him (I wasn't), he held up his hand and said, 'I don't need to know.'

Later, as we sat down to tea, he said, 'I'll always think fondly of Joseph. The last generous thing he did was to get us that turkey for Christmas. I never even got chance to thank him.'

Margaret looked at me quickly and shook her head, warning me to close the conversation. But I had to know. I said, 'Did he bring the turkey here himself?' I stopped myself from saying that

314

we did not get a turkey, and nor did Mr Shepherd at the Workhouse Infirmary.

'He must have brought it,' Uncle said. 'It was on the kitchen table. But I didn't see him. I'd have been behind the bar. That's why I didn't get chance to thank him.'

'It doesn't matter.' Margaret passed round the cake we had brought. 'It's all behind us now.'

Bernard chose that moment. He couldn't keep the pride and hope out of his voice as he told Uncle that the manager of the Coliseum had offered him the job as pianist and had said that no one in Leeds played better when it came to judging the mood of a moving picture.

Margaret chipped in, saying that she could vouch for Bernard's perfection as an accompanist at the moving pictures. She had been there on the day that the pianist had not turned up and Bernard had stood in for him. In all his playing, Bernard had never put a note wrong.

We all waited. Bernard's skin stretched tight across his face, white on his nose and forehead, and bright pink on his cheeks. He wanted just a few words of praise from his father, some such thing as, 'No one doubts your musical ability.'

'Can you spare me, Father?' Bernard said, as if it were a very casual request. 'It would just be the evenings and some afternoons.' He bit into his slice of cake.

'Can I spare you?'

Uncle's sarcasm changed the mood in an instant. The cake turned dry in my mouth.

Uncle said that he managed without Bernard most of the time. He called him a stoop-shouldered, dim-witted, minus-a-lung, half-blind, useless great stoit. If Bernard could not fight with his brothers, he should at least have the decency to see that his place was here with his father. Bernard should get out in the bar and earn his keep. He wouldn't have his son sinking to the level of an organ-grinder's monkey, playing in some moving-picture hall, grubbing round flea pits, snuffling up to kinematograph men, offering his services here there and everywhere.

Bernard stood up and took a cigarette from the box on the mantelpiece. His hands shook. Uncle Lloyd leaped across, hit the cigarette out of Bernard's hand and sent the box flying.

The worst thing was that the anger was not real. As soon as Bernard had left the room, it was as if nothing had happened. Uncle asked Margaret to pour another cup of tea.

They hate each other. Yet Bernard won't go without permission. Why doesn't he stand up for himself?

I had a sudden thought. Perhaps that was why so many young men had gone off gaily to war, full of hope and a lust for glory. They wanted to escape from their fathers. They wanted to get away from a world that was tight and small, where nothing ever changed. Would there be no bolt-hole for Bernard?

Margaret poured tea for Uncle. I left the table and followed Bernard into the bar. He served a glass of port to the scary woman who says she can tell your future. After he had rung her cash in the till, I asked him why he did not just leave and go work at the Coliseum.

Bernard stared at me. 'I can't leave Dad. Not with Johnny and Kevin gone. That's just the way Dad is. He can't help his nature.'

I was about to say that Bernard didn't have to put up with it. In my opinion everyone can help their nature. But I realized that no matter how difficult Dad had been, I couldn't have left him. So I'm not one to talk.

Margaret interrupted me saying I must try on a pair of my aunt's shoes. Fortunately they were too tight. Margaret passed me a pair of very good galoshes, saying, 'These look new.'

A dead person's galoshes seem to me less personal and more acceptable to be passed on. But I couldn't concentrate on footwear. I kept thinking about how Dad managed to bring a turkey to the Dragon and then not make it as far as Bread Street with the other two.

'I don't understand,' I said. 'You were here that Christmas Eve. Didn't you see him?'

'No,' she said. 'If he came he must have come to the back door and just left the turkey on the table. Now, shut up about it. It's over and done with. Do the galoshes fit?'

They did.

'I'm going to see Mrs Turner.' Margaret put the other shoes back in the wardrobe. 'Are you coming?'

'No.' I didn't want to sit and talk about how badly things were going in the Dardanelles. I hated to think of Thomas there with everything going wrong and so many lives being lost.

'I'll go and see Frank's mother,' I said. 'I'll take her a pair of those shoes. It's mad that they sit in

317

the wardrobe doing nothing.'

But Mrs Whitelock wasn't in. I left the shoes next door with Dorothy Pickles, and exchanged funny faces with the baby, who's round and smiley. It's so strange to think that I helped bring him into the world. Dorothy stirred a pot of cabbage and potatoes – her and Cyril's supper.

'Thank gawd for my man's club foot. It keeps him by me.'

Then she said I mustn't tell a soul how she feels or she'll be ashamed of being so unpatriotic.

I asked Dorothy about her next-door neighbour, skinny Harold Wragg. (I have never told her that it was Frank who attacked him.) She said that Harold has joined up, even though he is not old enough.

FORTY-FIVE

Margaret has been taking piano lessons from a woman in the village. Being Sunday, we are having an easier day than usual, and Margaret is practising her scales in the parlour.

Now I have decamped to the kitchen because we just had a row. Sheba went to Margaret, I think to plead with her to stop playing, and Margaret slapped her away. Sheba, not being an easily put-off sort of dog, asked again, and Margaret kicked her. She then swore she didn't kick her but 'moved her along with her foot' because she made her miss her place in the scale. Sheba came to me with her feelings greatly hurt and now I am sitting at the kitchen table and she is under it.

I have two letters to copy into my journal, one came with Margaret's letter from Thomas, and she was a little peeved because mine was longer than hers but that was because I asked Thomas questions and he answered them.

My dear Julia

Thank you for your chatty letter. It cheers me more than you can imagine to picture the two of you and Sheba at Elmtree House. I am glad you have the Garretty boys to help you.

The best thing about the voyage to the Dardanelles were wonderful sunsets and sunrises. When you are on the ocean you feel that you are more a part of the eternal world than ever you do on land. Some mornings I stood at the prow of the ship and watched dawn break, wishing that I could paint like Turner. As it is, I sketch the ship and some of the men, but don't dare risk my charcoal to capture the sea and sky, as I should be too fearfully disappointed with my efforts.

You asked me about my horse. I am sorry to tell you that I put him out of his misery on the voyage over. It hurt me to do it and to see him brought so low. Horses and mules do not travel well, Julia. But he was a fine creature and if there is a heaven for horses he will be galloping there now.

You also asked me about how things are going here with us. I almost regret telling you to speak the truth as now I must keep to my own precepts. I had expected to be reporting on British troops taking Constantinople, but it has gone badly as you will have read in the papers. I have been ashore myself and see that no

319

intelligence officer with clear information about the terrain would have imagined success to be guaranteed or perhaps even possible. Thousands of good men have landed, only to perish on the shores – under Turkish fire or from 'natural' causes due to terrible conditions, without sufficient rations, water or shelter from the elements.

I am writing this on-board ship, anchored I won't say where. A wounded officer friend who will shortly be returning to Blighty will post this to Margaret. I must put the envelope in his hands before he is taken onto the returning ship.

I wanted to and half-believed Lloyd George's hope that we would strike a blow to end the war. That hope now seems worse than forlorn. I return to my old belief – that all blows rebound on the one who inflicts them.

Give Sheba a pat for me, and take good care of yourself and my precious Margaret.

Your friend and (I hope) future brother
Thomas

I will say one more thing before copying in my next letter. Looking through the glass-fronted bookcases in the study, I came across a second copy of *The Iliad*. It has leather binding and is printed on tissue-thin paper so the pages rustle as you turn them. At first the story seemed different, and that puzzled me. Then I realized this version had a different translator. But I recognized the main scenes. In fine pencil, someone had made notes in the margin. I'm sure that someone was Thomas at a younger age. I recognized the shape of his aitches and the slope of the hand. The notes say:

learn not to admire force;
why call a person your enemy if you have never
  met him?
learn not to scorn the unfortunate.

Exactly what Dad would have said. Exactly what I would think. Only I would add: do not kick dogs and say you are shifting them along with your foot; do not take horses on board a ship when they belong in stables, on roads and in fields.
My second letter:

Dear Julia,

I got your leter and saved it to reed till I had a few minits on my own which is not as eazy as you mite think. I red it over and over till it is not so neet and clen lookin as it came out ov the envelop. I liked heering the news. I laffed that you sed you wd put your leter through the mangel to make it fit the envelop. Things is much the same here and not a lot to tell. We wate a lot. There is a lot of doin nothin. I have met peeple from all over. Not just England Scotland Wales and I.land but all over. It meks me think the world is not as big as you imajin. It meks me think I could tek my chanse in other places never thowt of. Thank you for the pepermints. They are much apreshiated. Also the cigurets, like gold to me. The Pork Pie staid in one peice and never have I had a beter one. I wish I cud be with your for chrismas and let the New yeer in with you. I know you are not neer my mam now but you are the one what uset to read my cards to her and she will miss that as she does not like Dorothi next door to do it arf as well.
Your Frank

Is he reminding me of how he helped me last year, so that I'll feel something for him that I don't. Can't. Never will. As I read it everything floods back to me and I cannot help but ask myself: Did Frank kill Clarence? Is this the letter of a murderer? My heart says no. My head says yes, he did it.

All the same, no one ever helped me as he did. Unless it was Thomas. Frank wants me go see his mam and I will. I'll get the train and go now, and not tell Margaret where I'm going because I'm still angry with her. And she can't play the piano for toffee.

I went to see Frank's mam. I have been back for hours, sitting in the parlour, watching the fire die. I cannot properly see this page but will scribble anyway. Then it will be said.

Frank's mam stood in the doorway and stared at me, her hair sticking out every which way, looking as though she had just woken from an afternoon nap. I'd thought to ask her if the shoes from my aunt had fitted but since she was wearing them I didn't. She'd think I was reminding her of my charity, which wasn't charity at all as they weren't my shoes.

I asked could I come in.

'I expect thah's come to see it for thissen,' she said as she stood aside to let me step in.

I took it that she was being surly, as she'd had another card or a letter from Frank and I hadn t been there to read it to her.

I pulled out my letter and said, 'I can read you

this one, too, if you like.'

Even when Mr Whitelock's out, Mrs Whitelock doesn't sit in his chair. She sat on a straight-back chair and I took the stool. She listened, head on one side, as I read the letter to her.

Then she stood up and took an envelope from the mantelpiece and handed it to me.

I had to read it over and over, not believing my eyes.

It says that Frank is missing, believed dead. I can't believe it. I don't believe it.

'When did it come?' I asked.

She seemed vague, and I suppose when doesn't matter. I have forgotten the date on the letter and I meant to remember it.

Mrs Whitelock glared at me. I had offered to comb her hair, not knowing what else to do. She refused. She said that all Frank ever wanted was me to care for him and I hadn't. I said I did care for him. She snorted at me, like a horse snorts but less friendly. 'He knew.' She put the letter back on the mantelpiece. 'He knew thah was fonder of a rich toff than you was of your old pal what always stood by you.'

'No. That's wrong,' I said, knowing she meant Thomas. 'It's Margaret who's engaged to Thomas Turner.'

She sat on the straight chair again, hugging herself. 'He knew. My lad knew that he weren't the one you wanted.'

I heard myself say that I'd sent him letters, cigarettes, pork pies. She said it wasn't pork pies her lad was after, it were love. I couldn't think of anything else to say. If he wasn't loved it was she who didn't love him. I thought of Mam bringing him in off the street, wiping his nose, cleaning him up, feeding him and patching his trousers.

'I don't believe he's dead,' I said. 'I think it's a mistake.'

I hadn't realized I was crying until she said, 'Thah mun weep crocodile tears now, now he's gone.'

I've no recollection of finding my way back here. Sheba must have led me to the station, onto the train and to Elmtree House.

Margaret heard me coming in and made me tell her what was wrong. She grabbed me and put her face up close to mine. 'Did you have a premonition? Is that why you went to see Frank's mam?'

I shook my head. 'I went to get away from you. Because you're mean and cruel and you kicked Sheba.'

Then she made a huge fuss of Sheba and said no she hadn't kicked her and she couldn't help it if sometimes she lost her temper. I was the unnatural one for keeping so calm.

I don't feel calm. I feel as if all my insides have been taken out, shaken about and shoved back in any old way.

SPRING
TO
WINTER
1916

FORTY-SIX

It was my good luck to see Thomas first. But I will come to that.

March is very late for snow, but a light snow had fallen, covering the ground and the tops of the trees. The white sky promised more. I was up early as usual. Gregory and Sol had a fire blazing. Margaret said she would stay put. Propped up in bed against the lace-edged pillows, her Indian shawl with its golds, purples and indigos around her shoulders, she pushed her hair from her face. If I take her a cup of tea I always put a little something to go with it or the tea dances in her tummy. I gave her a small piece of bread. She would have preferred a biscuit, but we had none.

The good thing about an old house is that there is much to root about and find. We have spent this long winter togged out in dead people's boots, mackintoshes, sou'westers and moth-eaten matted jumpers. We little band of scare-crows – Gregory, Sol and me – trudged out of the back garden, herding Pinky and her offspring to the wood by the railway track to forage, before the ground became too deeply covered in snow.

Soon the pigs were snuffling away, very good at finding food where no one else would. Gregory and Sol threw snowballs and Sheba tried to catch them.

I heard the Leeds train on the track chugging

towards Selby more slowly than usual. When it stopped I thought something was wrong. Through the trees I saw a carriage door open, and a figure in an officer's greatcoat and cap throw down a valise then leap out. The moment I saw him, I knew. Thomas!

I called to Sheba to look and she stared at the figure for an age, barking at first as if at some stranger. Then she suddenly ran towards him.

I said to Sol, 'Go tell Margaret that Thomas is here. I'll keep him talking while she gets dressed. Run.'

Thomas had picked up his bag but he dropped it again as Sheba reached him. She leaped into his arms, licking his face. It started to snow again as Thomas came towards me. He grinned, then tipped back his head to the sky and let snow-flakes fall onto his face and into his mouth. He lowered Sheba onto the ground but she wouldn't leave him alone, running round his legs till I thought she'd trip him. When we were close to each other, he held out his hand. I took it, but he pulled me towards him and hugged me. 'Come here, little one!'

When he finally let me go, I introduced Gregory. I introduced the pigs, I introduced the wood as though Thomas had never seen it, telling him it was a good spot for the pigs to forage. Sheba padded after us, as I took his hand and tried to slow him down. I pointed out the mended roof.

'I'll take your word for it,' he said because the roof was covered in snow.

I showed him the stable and made him talk to Solomon. I asked him to fill the water bucket

from the pump, which always seems more reluctant to splash out its water when the temperature
drops.

'Water!' he said as he watched it spurt into the
bucket. 'Water, just like that!'

He wanted to go inside, but I had one more out-
building to take him to. He put his valise by the
back door and let me lead him to the shed where
we store potatoes and carrots, well wrapped in
hessian sacking against the cold. He picked up a
carrot, wiped the earth from it and bit. He ate it
slowly, shutting his eyes, and I almost expected
him to eat its dead leaves. By the time he was
done I hoped that Margaret would have made
herself presentable. (Not that Margaret ever looks
unpresentable.) He hesitated for a moment
before we left the out-house. 'How's Margaret?'

'You'll see for yourself.' I watched a snowflake
touch my sleeve and thought of a picture of a
magnified, intricate snowflake that I had seen in
a book. No two are the same.

'You mean she's here?'

I nodded.

His face glowed. There is the oddest thing
about his eyes, one is just a hint of a shade darker
than the other, as if you had stroked a child's
paintbrush across a pallet and added an extra
smudge of colour. I had never noticed that
before. In the wood, there was something like a
pain behind his eyes. Now they lit up. 'I thought
the way you were taking me all around the
houses, she must have gone. Got tired of waiting
for me.' He hugged me again. 'Oh, little Julia, I'm
such a fool!'

He strode towards the house. I dropped the hessian over the carrots, bolted the out-house door and followed his footsteps through the snow, placing my feet in his boot-prints.

I had expected Margaret to be in the kitchen. I had pictured her at the table, writing, looking up in mock surprise as Thomas came in. Or by the fire, pretending to read a book.

When I reached the house, Thomas hadn't gone inside. He stood, gazing through the parlour window, his breath steaming the pane.

A hasty fire had been lit. I guessed that Margaret had got Sol to carry a shovel of burning coals through from the kitchen. A candle flickered in a silver holder on the top of the piano. Margaret was sitting at the piano, thumping the keys, plonkety-plonking out the tune that she had practised over and over. What did sound beautiful was her high, clear voice singing 'The Last Rose of Summer'.

I could not see Thomas's face. He held onto the window sill as if for support, and gazed through the window with such intensity that I thought he might fall face first through the glass.

Margaret appeared totally absorbed in her playing.

Behind me, the hens clucked. Sol threw seed to them. 'You've fed them once,' I said.

'Margaret told me to feed them again.'

'Try to get them back in the hutch,' I said. 'There's bound to be a hungry fox around in this weather.'

FORTY-SEVEN

Thomas, Gregory and Sol built the fire at the bottom of the garden. Thomas had found some old clothes in one of the bedrooms, probably his own from years ago. He wore brown tweed trousers, a baggy shirt, and a huge jumper with sleeves that stretched beyond his hands. He had to keep pushing the sleeves back.

'It seems so disrespectful.' Margaret drew her Indian shawl tightly around her shoulders, as Thomas threw his officer's trousers onto the fire.

'I promised myself.' He poked the trouser leg with a stick. 'It was to be my reward. And damnation to the lice.'

'I'm sure there're no lice in it,' Margaret held his jacket close to her. 'Not if it's been as well-cleaned as you say.'

'The lice lay their eggs in the seams. For a day or so, after it's clean, you stop itching and think you're safe. Then a new generation of lice hatch out and torment you. I only wore it because you asked me to.'

He pushed the baggy sleeves of his jumper back over his wrists, which were much thinner than before, took the jacket from her and dropped it onto the fire, making sparks fly into the evening air.

Gregory sighed as he watched the army uniform burn. Gregory has more meat on him

331

now, but he's still a wiry little slip of a lad. I put my hand on his arm. 'By the time you're eighteen it'll be all over.' Then I said in a low voice so that the others wouldn't hear, 'Anyway, I won't let you go. You're the sorcerer's apprentice. Who else but you would have helped me magic potatoes from the ground and keep the fox from the chickens?'

Gregory took Thomas's badge from the cap. I threw the cap on the fire. Margaret shuddered. Thomas put an arm around her.

I knew that she was thinking of the wedding we saw at the church last Saturday, when the groom wore an officer's uniform.

Thomas must have guessed her thoughts, too. As we turned and walked back to the house, he said, 'I couldn't go on wearing the uniform. It was issued to me when I was war correspondent. That's over now.'

Snow began to fall again when we reached the house. We sat in the parlour, watching white flakes flutter from the dark sky, stars above shining brightly. Thomas had intended to take the evening train back to Leeds but seemed glad to be snowed in. We roasted potatoes and chestnuts in the red ashes of the fire and opened a bottle of Mrs Hopps' cider. He talked a little about some of the dispatches he had sent back from Gallipoli. With the Atlas open we made him trace the voyage and the terrain where the fighting had taken place. But he seemed reluctant to say very much. When Gregory or I asked more questions, he insisted on hearing Margaret sing again.

Sheba gave me an apologetic look, as I left

Thomas and Margaret in the parlour and went to bed. Usually she slept on my bed but she had not left his side since he came home.

I woke in the night. At first I thought it was a fox, or that an owl had pounced on some creature that let out a shriek. Then I realized that the cry had come from along the landing.

I could tell by Margaret's breathing that she was awake. Moonlight shone between the curtains. Outside, an owl hooted. I waited to see what she would do. Nothing.

'Margaret. Go see if Thomas is all right.'

'I can't go to him in the middle of the night. Idiot.'

I heard another sound. 'What if he's sleepwalking? He could hurt himself.' I lit a candle.

When I reached our door, she hissed at me to come back, but I pretended not to hear and tiptoed along the landing. Margaret slid out of bed and followed me.

The blankets lay in a tangle on the floor. As I came close Thomas shot upright, eyes wide open, but not seeing, arms waving as he swung his legs from the bed, hitting my candle so it fell from its holder and we were in the dark. 'Get down!' he called. 'Take cover!'

I ducked. Close to him, I could feel the heat off his body. Then his arms were round me and he said, 'I've got you. You're safe. I'll get you back in one piece.'

Margaret took one of his arms. I took the other. He released his hold on me as we got him back onto the bed.

'Leave him now,' Margaret ordered.

I whispered to her that one of us should stay with him.

She took my hand and led me back to our bedroom. 'Everyone has nightmares. Leave him be.'

The next morning Thomas went out with me to feed and water Solomon. We had to crack the ice on the drinking trough. While I groomed Solomon, Thomas pulled a newspaper, the *Tribunal*, from his pocket. As he read it he asked me if there had been much reporting of objections to the war, conscientious objections. But there had not, not that I knew of. He said that the No Conscription Fellowship were organizing a campaign against compulsory conscription, due to come into force in March; had I heard about that? I hadn't.

As we ate our breakfast, Gregory made some remark about the war, I can't remember what. Thomas went very still. He said, 'The waste of life is beyond anything you can imagine. And it's for territory – for empire – to make rich men richer. Millions sent to die for the economic and military interests of a privileged few.'

Margaret surprises me sometimes. She can be much quicker than me at grasping some things. She said, 'But Thomas, you're already conscripted, aren't you? You were conscripted to be a war correspondent. Just because your term ended, the conscription didn't.'

'Yes, darling,' Thomas said, 'I'm conscripted.'

Margaret smiled sadly. 'I wish you weren't. I don't want to lose you. None of us do,' she added quickly, and then blushed a little.

After all, we are all living rent-free in his house.

As Thomas went with Gregory to bring in logs, Margaret whispered to me, 'I'm going to marry him before he goes away again. It's the only way.'

Before I had chance to ask her the only way for what, he had come back inside, just as the bell from the drawing room rang. Sol gets very silly. He goes in the drawing room (which we call the parlour), the dining room or study and rings one of the bells. These are ivory push-button bells in a walnut wood surround, set one on either side of each fireplace. When the bells ring on the board in the kitchen, somebody (usually me and Sheba) has to go and pretend to see what he wants, and he gives some extravagant order. Thomas surprised him by going to see what he wanted and tickling him. Sol thinks he is grown-up, but really he is still a little boy.

Thomas asked if all the bells still worked, and he and Margaret went upstairs.

'We're in the bathroom,' she called as the bell on the board flapped down under the label 'Bedroom 4'. I had to call back that the bell was ringing. Bells rang from Bedroom 3 (our bedroom) and Bedroom 1.

I waited for the bell in Bedroom 2 to ring. It didn't. I went up the stairs, meaning to call out to them, thinking that the bell wasn't working. The door to Bedroom 2 was open and I heard Margaret's laughing, then Thomas talking very earnestly. So I didn't call out. They went quiet. I crept downstairs. They have been up there for hours.

Sol says they must have fallen asleep.

FORTY-EIGHT

The date is set. Margaret and Thomas will be married on Saturday, 8 April. I am pleased that the wedding will be in the church here. With Dad's grave so close by, I can pretend that he is a guest at the wedding.

I had already gone to bed and was in the middle of a dream when Margaret climbed in beside me. It felt like part of my dream when she said, 'Everything will be all right now that we've set the date.'

She had climbed into my bed because hers was cold and so was she. The chill off her put an end to my dreaming and I was suddenly wide awake. 'What are you bleating about? I was asleep.'

'Saturday, the eighth of April,' she said, snuggling up. 'And when we move to London, you'll come, too. No more hard work. We'll be ladies, Julia. I'll have babies – not too many – and you'll be their aunt and play with them and such-like. Aren't you pleased?'

'Yes–'

'And before you ask, yes, I love him and he loves me.' She sighed and tugged at the eiderdown, pulling it off my shoulder. 'We're going to be utterly happy together.'

She fell asleep instantly, still clutching the eiderdown. I had to try moving myself down the bed to cover my shoulders, but it also meant scrunching up, as Sheba was lying like a dog made of boulders at the bottom of the bed and I couldn't get down very far. This made it hard for me to get back to sleep so I tried to picture our future life. I am so happy that Thomas will be part of our family and I will see him all the time, every day. My question for her was not whether they loved each other. Why else would they marry? I wanted to know could we take Solomon and Sheba to London, and the hens and pigs. And of course the Garrettys. Somehow I couldn't picture it. I have not had chance to ask since, as we have been busy with wedding preparations.

Margaret's wedding dress is to be borrowed – from Miss Mason.

Miss Mason with her wizened face, blouses with a bow to hide her now-skinny chest, hands freckly with liver spots, was once upon a time engaged to be married. Not only that, but she had a dress, a satin, lacy, ribboned creation that ever since has lain in a white muslin bag, hemmed in tear-stained blanket-stitch.

I wanted to know, did Miss Mason's story resemble that of Miss Havisham in *Great Expectations?* Was she left in the lurch at the church door? Did she, on a day long ago, glide all the way down the aisle on her father's arm, glance back to see her sweetheart stride smilingly, proudly towards her, only to see nothing but dust dancing in the sunbeams that shone through the church's stained-glass windows?

Did she keep the dress because all through her long, lonely life she hoped some dandy would prance into her life and fall hopelessly in love with her? Or that her lover would return remorseful from a foreign land, arms full of bracelets and silken shawls to lay at her no-longer dainty but now calloused and corn-tormented feet.

Where Margaret used to sit, creating beautiful hats in the back room that Miss Mason calls the making room, two stout and one lean woman were cutting and sewing military caps. They stopped work, as Miss Mason and Margaret carried the dress bag from upstairs and set it on the cutting-out table. Miss Mason's hands trembled as she twittered on about the moths getting everywhere. I thought that unlikely, as the smell of camphor overpowered me. I had to pick up a half-finished military cap and fan my snitch to create a little fresh air.

Margaret clipped the bag's stitches with button scissors. Miss Mason took the corner of the sheet and peeled it back, revealing the dress to the dim light of the late March afternoon. Its first outing since 1880-something. 'It'll need dolly blueing,' she said matter-of-factly, 'to bring back its whiteness.'

Margaret stroked the white velvet ribbon threaded through the bodice and admired the antique lace panels. The dress fits beautifully. No one in our family has had a wedding dress that we know of. Mam married in her best costume. Aunty married in her best frock.

Strange that the only person we know with a wedding dress did not marry. She had made the dress herself with the help of her mother, younger sister and cousin. Her mother is long-departed but her sister and cousin married, had children and live in London. Hence the socializing when she was there with Margaret. They did not want the dress, thinking it unlucky. Margaret laughed at their superstition and said it was their loss.

Margaret had not asked why Miss Mason's marriage did not take place, telling me that it was not the kind of thing to ask unless the right moment arose. While we were upstairs sipping tea and nibbling brown bread in Miss Mason's parlour, I thought that probably the right moment never would arise and so I asked. Margaret looked daggers at me.

Miss Mason said that it was all right. It was long ago and she would be glad to see the dress worn. Her young man had fought in the first Boer War and was killed at Majuba Hill. She said, 'There couldn't be another like him.'

It made me want to cry. And to tell her that the person who broke in and stole all the hats two years ago was me. But we had other errands and my confession might have jeopardized Margaret's chance of wearing the wedding dress so I said nothing.

We went to Gelder's to buy material for my dress, although they do not have a great supply because of the war. When you ask for something, the elderly gentleman with his starched collar adjusts his ear trumpet, asks you to speak up and then says that you must know there's a war on and terrible shortages. But for Lloyd McAndrew's nieces, he's sure he can find something. And he does.

We sat at the kitchen table at the Dragon,

drinking tea and making another list. I like to keep my first list and cross items off. Margaret prefers to make a new list, which always seems longer than the one before. Uncle came in carrying a small blue bag, the kind you hand over at the bank counter with your takings.

He put it on the table on top of Margaret's list. 'I had an insurance policy on your dear father,' he said, nodding his head. 'I kept this for you, knowing that you'd need it sometime soon, that this happy day would come.'

This happy day has not come yet. I wish it would. I am sick and tired of lists, and Margaret changing her mind about things. Uncle obviously thinks no such happy day will come for me because the blue bag contained all the money from the insurance policy. I don't care. I have no intention of marrying. Not for a long time yet. If ever. If he'd given me money, I would have bought another pig.

FORTY-NINE

It all started so well. I'll make myself remember that. Thomas's mother arrived on Friday afternoon, striding along the lane from the station, gathering her skirts close, followed by an elderly, hunched railway porter, who pushed a squeaking cart containing her brown leather valise and twin maroon hat boxes.

Mrs Turner shuddered as she walked through

the front door of Elmtree House and muttered that she had dreaded this moment. Then, as if she realized we might get the wrong idea and think she meant the wedding, she said, 'This hateful house!' as though it had done her some terrible wrong in the past.

Margaret led her into the parlour, explaining that we had gone to meet the earlier train. She smiled grandly and asked what she could do to help. I went to make a pot of tea so missed Margaret's answer.

Mrs Turner took charge of the fluted white china teapot. As we sipped tea, she drew an official-looking letter from her velvet bag. 'I must take this to Thomas at the inn. It arrived this morning. You know what it is, of course.'

We did. Marching orders. Mrs Turner had wanted Thomas to contact the army before the army contacted him. Or, as the posters put it, 'Will you march too, or wait until March 2?' This was the date when the Conscription Act came into force.

'What if it tells him to report immediately?' I asked.

Mrs Turner and Margaret looked at me. They obviously hadn't thought of that. Margaret's hand shook a little, and she put her cup down.

'Don't give him it today,' I said. 'Tomorrow is soon enough. If he doesn't know, he can't go.'

So it was all my fault, the way things turned out. If I had said, 'Give him the letter *after* the wedding', everything would have turned out differently. But I'll come to that.

Margaret had prettied up Bedroom 1 for Mrs

Turner. Miss Mason occupied Bedroom 2, exclaiming over it, looking out across the front garden, being amazed that she could see the church and steeple, the tops of trees and Hopps' farmhouse. How countrified! Never had she imagined us in such grandeur! How glad and joyful to be able to see her former apprentice and now dear friend about to marry. To be able to help with Margaret's dress and to gather meadow flowers in the April morning was all Miss Mason desired. She looked a different person entirely with a gleam in her eyes and a determination in her movements.

Uncle Lloyd, Bernard and Aunty Amy were to come the following morning. Margaret worried about this. What if the train service was disrupted? Who would give her away if Uncle was delayed?

I was up well before dawn and woke sleepy Gregory and Sol. They lit the fire and put the kettle on while I went out to see Solomon.

Solomon whinnied and stamped his hooves in greeting. He knew it was a special morning, as I'd told him all about it. I plaited blue and white ribbons in his mane and tail. No horse has ever looked finer. Gregory spread the covers we'd chosen over the seat of the cart.

I was glad to have an errand later. Margaret was sitting at the dressing table in our room, combing her hair. She handed me the official army letter and asked me to take it to Thomas at the Green Dragon. She said that it wasn't fair to hold onto it and give it to him during the wedding breakfast.

Thomas was dressed in his dark suit, looking tremendously smart. He said he was glad to have a visit from me as he had been up for hours and didn't know what to do with himself. The innkeeper had sent up a tray but he couldn't eat a thing. I'd be doing him a great favour if I ate a slice of toast. So I did, glad of the peace and quiet after the madness of everyone dashing about getting ready. I was curious to meet his best man, who popped his ginger head around the door. His freckles made him look young, until he came in and I saw close up that he was about thirty. He shook hands with me, patted Thomas on the back and said he would leave us to chat and be back to walk Thomas to the church shortly.

I got Thomas to tell me all about the best man, Derek. Thomas teased me and said that I had probably read too many novels where the best man fell in love with the bridesmaid, but that really Derek was far too old for me.

We then got so absorbed in talking about dragons, because of the name of the inn probably, that I almost forgot why I'd come. Thomas said that George wasn't the only destroyer of dragons. St Philip slayed a huge one at Hierapolis and St Martha killed a terrible dragon at Aix-la-Chapelle, which I wouldn't have known how to spell before this war. That's when I remembered the letter I'd come to deliver.

He opened the envelope carefully and read the letter slowly.

'What's the matter?' I asked, fearing he would be in hot water because we hadn't given him the letter yesterday.

He handed it to me without a word. I saw that he had a whole week before he was due to report. That was all right then.

He seemed to sink into his chair for a moment, then took a deep breath and was himself again. 'They'll give me no quarter, Julia. I'm not a religious objector. I'm a political objector. I compromised myself by agreeing to War Office conditions – playing the part of the trusty war correspondent. I thought I could find ways round the censorship, the rules, the regs. Now I'll look like a coward, a conchy.'

'We know you're not a coward,' I said. Though I don't know how we knew.

'With Margaret by my side–' He didn't finish the sentence, but dropped the official letter and envelope into the fire.

'Does Margaret know you're going to refuse?' I spoke so quietly that I thought he hadn't heard me at first.

'I told her I would do my duty. I told her I would follow my conscience. She'll understand.'

When I got back to Elmtree House, Uncle was pacing the front path looking out for me. He scolded me for being so late, and not even in my bridesmaid's dress. Everyone had gone to church, he said. I knew this because I had passed them as I ran up the lane, pretending not to see the dirty look from Mrs Turner, the sorrowful shake of Miss Mason's puzzled head and the big wink from Bernard. It wasn't my fault if Margaret had given me an errand.

Margaret was in our room. I dashed in and pulled off my skirt and blouse. She helped me on with my dress, smoothed my hair and gave me the posy of wild flowers that Miss Mason had picked.

Neither of us spoke. I hoped she wouldn't ask me what Thomas had said. I had been gone too long to pretend that I had just put the letter in his hands and left.

Uncle called up the stairs, with that deliberate patience in his voice. Then he cursed at Sheba, who had seized her moment, rubbed herself against his black trousers and left her hair all over his trouser legs. I called Sheba upstairs, patted the bed and told her to rest there till we all got back. Margaret, so serene, so sedate, walked onto the landing. She headed for the main stairs even though we generally used the back stairs. Sheba ran out and down the stairs ahead of us.

I walked behind Margaret, holding her train as if she were a queen, and thinking that no queen had ever looked more beautiful.

Uncle stood at the bottom of the stairs, looking at her with admiration. As we walked down the stairs, taking care with our dresses, she muttered quietly to me, 'What's Thomas's conscription date?'

I told her that it was next week.

She smiled, and I thought that she must be glad they would have a whole week together. I also knew that I should tell her the truth. I kept quiet.

'What did he say?'

I said, 'He's not going. He threw the letter on the fire.'

On the third step from the bottom she stopped. Uncle held out his hand to her.

By the gate, Gregory, dressed in his cut-down dark suit, sat in the decorated cart, holding Solomon's reigns. Birds were singing in the trees. A robin watched us from the hedgerow. Uncle helped Margaret up, and then me, saying that he would walk on ahead, and meet us by the church gate.

'Wait, Uncle!' Margaret's voice trilled high and clear. The birds stopped singing. 'Uncle, I'm not going to marry Thomas. He won't do his duty. He's burned his conscription letter.'

After the first silent shock, Uncle had a lot to say. A fine time to call off a wedding. Couldn't this have been sorted out sooner? Of course Thomas would go. Margaret was having wedding jitters.

But Margaret was adamant. 'I fooled myself into thinking that when the call came, he would go. He burned the letter, Uncle. Tell him, Julia!'

I tried to nod but my body seemed to have stopped working.

Margaret started to cry. 'I can't stand by a man who won't fight for his country.'

Uncle pulled out a handkerchief.

Her tears turned to sobs. 'Not when Kevin and Johnny and everyone else are out there, prepared to make the sacrifice.'

At the mention of his sons' names, Uncle finally nodded agreement. 'You're foolish to have left it to this moment. But better late than a lifetime of regret. I'll go tell him.'

'Don't leave me, Uncle. Take me home. Let Julia tell him, it'll come better from her. She saw him burn the letter.'

346

Uncle always does what Margaret asks.

Gregory climbed down from the cart. Uncle took his place.

I walked along the lane, behind the cart, glad to have Gregory beside me. I hoped Margaret would change her mind and Solomon would stop at the church gates. But he trotted past the church towards the Leeds road.

My shoes have soft soles but Gregory sounded like a tap dancer as we walked across the threshold onto the stone flags of the church aisle.

Thomas turned to glimpse Margaret. He saw me. For a moment he did not seem to grasp it. He turned away, then back again. I must have shook my head or raised my hands, or made some gesture or look that told him. He looked at me and then past me with a kind of despairing disbelief. If I live to be a hundred I shall never forget the disappointment on his face and the misery that seemed to float in waves along the aisle.

'Don't feel sorry for a conchy coward,' Gregory whispered, but he whispered loudly. Bernard, Aunty Amy and Miss Mason turned to look. Knowing they would all go to Elmtree House, I set off for the Green Dragon to wait for Thomas and his best man. I would have to try and explain.

FIFTY

A chamber in the Town Hall had been set aside. Stiff white paper arrows fixed on wooden stands guided visitors up the wide staircase and along the marble corridors. Mrs Turner needed no guiding. Full steam ahead, her black-gloved hand assaulting the brass bannister and the polished rails on the landing, she marched towards the committee room. Bowing from his stiff shoulders, an aged, uniformed usher swung open the heavy polished door for her.

Margaret says that everyone at the Town Hall knows Mrs Turner, as she sits on so many wartime committees. She is mortified to have to appear at her own son's tribunal for a ruling on his claim for conscientious objection to war service.

We all stood, as the three tribunal committee men filed in and took their places behind the long table: an army captain; a small round ball of a man who looked very much like the picture house manager at the Coliseum; and a familiar figure that at first I couldn't place. He wore round, owl-like glasses that magnified his prominent eyes. He looked up after fussily arranging his pencil and papers. Mr Brownlaw. Godfrey Brownlaw, the chemist, who had trapped Annie Garretty like a fly in amber and kept her prisoner in his window, her long tresses flowing, buoying up the sales of

348

Feather's Supreme Hair Lotion. He nodded a slight greeting to Mrs Turner, and I thought he looked a little embarrassed. The chairman came in last. Then we sat down.

They tried to make us laugh. Perhaps they thought they were on the stage at the City Varieties. A young man with a stammer and a black eye was escorted in. He tried to explain to the tribunal that his widowed mother could not run their farm without him. He had promised his father on his deathbed that he would take care of his mother. That was his reason for conscientiously objecting to army service.

The chairman shook his head as if at an imbecile. He explained to the objector that there would be no farm if the Huns overran Britain. There would be no mother to take care of either. Case dismissed.

The next man gave his name as Claude Shuttleworth and explained that there had been a mistake.

'A mistake?' the chairman said. 'I suppose by "mistake" you refer to the fact of your having been sent conscription papers?'

Titters from Messrs Brownlaw and the round man. Stony-faced silence from the captain. But there had been a mistake. Claude Shuttleworth had been arrested for non-compliance while visiting his sister in Leeds, but he had a letter from Lord Netherton, to confirm that he was Master of Hounds for Lord Netherton's hunt and therefore exempt from conscription, as were all men who worked in hunting.

The chairman whispered to the others. Mr

Claude Shuttleworth was sent on his way, with a warning to stay in the country and not visit his sister in Leeds where the finer points of such exemptions were not properly understood. More mirth.

Thomas was brought in between two policemen. He had lost weight but stood proudly and answered in a clear voice when the chairman demanded his name, and whether he knew why he was there.

Thomas said that he was there because hundreds of thousands of men's lives had been thrown away. A government previously measured and sane wanted more lives to hurl into the abyss. He had seen men sent to certain death in small boats to land on a beach where they were mown down.

The captain interrupted and asked had Mr Turner watched from the safety of his war correspondent's position, and made notes as men died?

Thomas answered that he had been with the men and shared their defeat and exhaustion, so that the world might know of their experience. If people on the Home Front truly knew what was happening, they would withdraw their support from the government. He started to say that war turned the mind crimson.

The chairman tapped his hammer and demanded that Thomas answer questions as put, and not make speeches. He was not in Parliament and never would be. What would he do if a Hun were to ... he coughed and looked round the room as he thought of a way to re-phrase his question. Godfrey Brownlaw whispered in the chairman's ear. The chairman whispered back and Mr Brownlaw posed the question.

'What would you do, sir, if a Hun were to attack your fiancée?'

I thought he hadn't seen me till that moment. Thomas looked in my direction for the first time. 'I have no fiancée,' he said quietly.

'I wonder why that should be,' Godfrey Brownlaw said, leaving time for a ripple of tittering laughter. 'Let us make this a rhetorical question. If you *had* a fiancée, and a Hun were to attack her, what would you do?'

'I would come between them,' Thomas said. 'Put myself between them and try to reason with the man.'

Sarcastically, Godfrey Brownlaw repeated the words. 'Come between them. Try to reason. With a Hun, sir?'

I didn't know I was going to speak. We had been told not to. The words just came out. 'That's exactly what he would do,' I called. 'That's exactly what he did when a drunken English ape turned nasty with me outside this very building when my sister had given a rousing speech for the vote. He stood between us and when that ape landed a punch, Mr Turner still tried to reason with him.'

Two ushers leaped on me. They thought it would be easy to drag me out. It would have been if I'd cooperated and let myself be taken. But I did my party trick. I made myself heavy and refused to budge. It took three of them in the end to get me outside into the corridor, and the roughest of the three was Mrs Turner. As they manhandled

351

me into the corridor, I called at the top of my voice, 'There's neither English nor German, Christian, Turk or Jew, only humankind.' They frogmarched me to the top of the stairs. I pulled free. 'I'll walk. I've seen enough.'

'You stupid girl.' Mrs Turner pushed her face close to mine. 'I suppose you think that was helpful!'

'It was true!' I tried not to let them see that I was shaking. The ushers had taken hold of my arms again, one of them digging his bony fingers into my flesh as hard as he could.

Mrs Turner's breath burned my cheek. 'Chalk and cheese, you and your sister. You're lucky this is a free country and you're an unimportant slip of a slut, or you'd be up for treason.'

She turned and strode back to the tribunal room, as the ushers marched me downstairs. All the fight had slid out of me because as they dragged me away from Thomas, I knew. When I saw him standing there, all alone, I knew.

I love him.

As we got to the side door, I felt like running, just to be away from there – and away from my feelings. A voice in my head told me that I'd let Thomas down. I should have stayed quiet and heard the worst.

As the ushers pushed me into the street I almost fell into a young woman in a crumpled linen suit carrying a document bag. The ushers apologized to her and disappeared back into the building.

A Scots voice said, 'You're Margaret Wood's sister, aren't you?' It was Jean. I remembered her from Mrs Turner's house, from Margaret's Votes for Women group. What she said sounded to me like an accusation. Margaret Wood's sister. The one who put paid to the marriage by saying the wrong thing.

'Give me five minutes,' Jean said, 'to take these documents to my boss. He's due in court and left them behind in the office. Wait for me on the other side of the Headrow.' She didn't pause for an answer.

As I waited on the windy corner, I had time to kick myself for being thrown out of the tribunal and not learning Thomas's fate.

Jean caught my eye as she nipped between two carriages to cross the Headrow. I turned and walked slowly towards the station, letting her catch up with me.

'Were you here for Thomas Turner's appearance?' she asked.

I nodded.

'He's been committed to prison,' she said.

'Which prison?'

'I expect it will be Armley Gaol, or it could be the Bridewell.' She looked at me curiously.

I felt myself blush. I felt that she could hear the words in my head. *I love Thomas. I love him.*

'I want to visit him,' I said.

She shook her head. 'They won't let you. Believe me, I know.' After a moment she took my hand. 'Come on. I have to go back to work but I'm going to walk you down to the Dragon. Is that where Margaret is?'

I nodded.

'You shouldn't be on your own. I know she

jilted him, but she'll want to know the outcome. Go and tell her.'

I explained that I had to get back to Elmtree House for the animals.

'They'll survive,' she said. 'Go and see Margaret.'

We sat in the window seat of the Dragon parlour. Margaret listened while I gave an account of the tribunal. She didn't even call me an idiot for intervening, just said that I was lucky not to be arrested and charged, and that I may have Mr Brownlaw to thank for that because he's a friend of Uncle's. I asked did she still love Thomas, but a train went by just at that moment and she didn't hear me.

When it was quiet she said, 'Any man who doesn't fight won't be able to hold up his head after the war. He'll be a figure of derision, a funkhole Cuthbert. Thomas might be strong enough to stand for that. I'm not.'

She walked me back to the station and we didn't exchange one word. At the barrier, she leaned forward for me to kiss her cheek. She didn't kiss me. Does she believe I betrayed her?

On the journey back to Garforth, the train seemed to hum out, *Does she know? Does she know?*

I am back at Elmtree House, where Thomas said the Garrettys and I can stay as long as we like. I feel utterly wretched. I thought that when I fell in love it would be wonderful. Now I have to ask myself, did I deliberately get in the way of Margaret and Thomas marrying because I care for him? I search my conscience, asking whether I could have done anything differently on that day I delivered the letter. Perhaps if I had said to Margaret that she should marry him and talk about principles afterwards, she would have listened to me.

It is so hopeless. He adores Margaret. When he came back to the Green Dragon from the church, his best man walking silently beside him, he saw me waiting there. He couldn't speak. He took the flower from his buttonhole and crushed it in his hand. He adores her and always will. He could never love me.

FIFTY-ONE

I used to hide this book because of protecting Dad. I hid it under the loose floorboard in Bedroom 3. Now I hide it behind the bookcase in the study. The Garrettys don't think twice about my going in there because I sit in the window seat to read and write. It is no longer just my journal that I hide, but the records of the No Conscription Fellowship.

Our government has many enemies: Germany; Austria; Turkey; the Irish rebels of Easter week; the Independent Labour Party; the National Council of Civil Liberties; Socialists; Pacifists; and me.

Thomas would say that if you use force, you beget force. That if once your country can force you to kill, it will forever be able to say kill, like ordering a dog to kill a rabbit. The *Tribunal* and

355

the *Herald* make more sense to me than all the other newspapers put together. I read late at night when Gregory and Sol are sleeping. Once if an Englishman killed a German or a German killed an Englishman, they would have been tried for murder. Now the authorities that would have tried them say, 'Kill. Kill. Kill.' It is beyond my understanding that there cannot be another way to solve a conflict.

When Jean's letter came I thought she was being kind after seeing me so upset on the day of the tribunal.

Dear Julia

I am still working at my typewriter in the legal office but I have Sundays to myself. It would be very nice to take a train to Garforth and come along to where you are this Sunday afternoon and have a cup of tea with you. (Don't go to any trouble.)

I trust this will be convenient as I have not left you time to say no!

Your friend, I hope
Jean Mackie

That was how it began.

I made a seedcake in honour of our visitor. After we had drunk tea and eaten the last crumb of cake, Gregory and Sol made an excuse to leave. They make themselves useful to Mr Hopps, and in turn he has lent them shot guns and taught them to shoot crows and rabbits.

Jean asked to see the wood. I felt as proud of the primroses and wild violets as if I'd planted them myself! We walked through the cool, shady

356

wood onto the bank. The sun thought about putting in an appearance as we found a spot where we could sit without crushing flowers.

I waited, knowing that she had something to say.

Jean stretched her legs and admired her well-polished, black-buttoned shoes. 'Have you heard of the No Conscription Fellowship?'

I had. The *Herald* and the *Tribunal* had printed accounts by Fenner Brockway of the opposition to conscription.

'The leadership's being prosecuted for publishing a pamphlet against the Conscription Act.' She pulled a leaflet from her skirt pocket called 'REPEAL THE ACT'.

Beyond the wood, near the Hopps' farm, a shot rang out. A black crow fell from the washed-out sky.

I took the leaflet. 'Is this for me?'

'If you want it.'

I said that I would like to read it.

'Do you have somewhere safe to keep it? It's mild stuff in my view, but the government puts it on a par with dynamite.'

I folded the leaflet and slid it into my skirt pocket. 'I'll keep it safe.'

'Some of the women I met through the suffrage movement are involved, supporting conscientious objectors. There's a Fellowship organization, publishing the newssheet that keeps members up-to-date with developments. Violet Tillard has been sent to prison for refusing to tell the police the name of the printer. Everyone who's connected with the committee has had their house turned upside-down in the search for the records.'

'Records?'

'There's an index card – name, occupation, address, family contact – for all conscientious objectors in the country. A network of supporters gather information, such as the outcome of local tribunals and appeals tribunals.'

'You mean like Thomas, being sent to prison?'

'We keep track of what happens to objectors. Some are allowed an exemption certificate, say on religious grounds, for Quakers – if the tribunal's sympathetic. Which they rarely are. The tribunals make up their own rules. Some objectors take up non-combatant duties, or work in labour camps.'

'Is there more news about Thomas?' I tried to make myself sound calm, though I could feel my heart banging in my chest.

'He was taken to London under military police escort to have his case heard again at the central tribunal. It's because he'd already worn an officer's uniform as war correspondent. Apparently he distinguished himself at Gallipoli. Brought wounded men back to the boats. The top brass tried their best to turn him round, make him into an officer.'

'And?'

'He's in gaol. One of the men in Pentonville Prison got word out – names. Thomas's was among them.'

'Why Pentonville?'

Jean absent-mindedly pulled up a blade of grass and ran her fingers along it. The grass cut her and she gave a little cry of annoyance then sucked her finger. 'Julia, don't expect any of this to make sense. It doesn't.'

We were quiet for a long time, until she said, 'The records, the card records. I have them.'

'Where?'

'Safe, I hope. But I have the only copy. The Fellowship would like there to be another set. I've started copying out the cards but it's a long job. When I've copied them – or when someone's helped me copy them – that other person could keep that extra set.'

'Store them?'

'They're updated all the time. We notify the families about where their men are, say which prison they've been sent to. If there's a legal issue, such as men being sent out of the country without anyone knowing, we have someone who'll take it up in Parliament.'

I waited for her to ask me if I would keep the records. She did not ask. Nearby a woodpecker tap-tapped at a tree. (Why is it you can hear woodpeckers but they always seem to be out of view?)

'I'll do it,' I said.

'Thanks.'

Another shot rang out, silencing the woodpecker. This time I saw no crow fall. Perhaps Gregory had shot a rabbit.

'I have the cards with me,' she said. 'Is there somewhere in the house we could make a start – and I've a huge piece of terrible knitting we can throw over what we're doing if the boys come in.'

I know it is perverse because they are the details

of men going through the most awful experiences, but I enjoyed filling out the record cards. It made me feel that I was doing something useful. The card for L.G., who refused on religious grounds and was told that the Old Testament was full of killing. D.M., a socialist and anti-imperialist, who was not listened to at all and exemption refused. V.H., who had an exemption certificate that was torn up by the recruiting officer.

We also finished knitting a scarf, which I have sent to cousin Kevin in France, with a note saying one for Johnny is underway.

It is most peculiar to feel that I am living two lives. On Tuesday morning, Gregory and me trundled our cart to the munitions factory, piled high with pies for their canteen. When Gregory asked me wouldn't I rather be in there with his sister, making munitions, it made me realize that I am as much a part of the war effort as those who make bullets for rifles or shot for machine guns.

FIFTY-TWO

Thomas managed to smuggle out a letter and I am the one he wrote to! Before I set off to find Jean Mackie and tell her I have heard from him, I shall enter the details onto his No Conscription Fellowship index card and copy his letter into my book. It is written from Felixstowe Prison. On

the back he has listed the names of other conscientious objectors imprisoned with him.

Dear Julia
I chuckled all the way to prison after your brave
words at the tribunal and only hope you did not find
yourself in hot water on my account. My second
tribunal appearance and interviews since move from
persuasive to bullying.
Long and hard I struggled to know what I should
do. The absolutist position draws me. No more war.
No more truck with war. I am refusing to let my mind
turn to blood-lust scarlet, fearing that if we all give
way to violent solutions, that will colour the thoughts
and feelings of generations to come. The absolutists are
the real heroes but I cannot do it. It may be that in my
heart and soul I am more afraid of a bullet through
the brain or a bayonet in the belly than other men. Yet
the thought of killing is worse than the thought of
being killed. I am willing to serve with the Red Cross
or Friends Ambulance Brigade, but the powers-that-
be want me back in officer uniform.
Don't fear for me. Take care of you and yours.
Your good friend
Thomas

P.S. I hope at some future time Margaret may see that
I am not a coward, and do not make my choice lightly
or easily. On that day, perhaps her heart will warm
towards me again. I am not a man to change his love
as he changes his shirt. Never will she lose her place in
my heart.

We sat in the market café. Jean Mackie nursed

361

her cup of tea and flicked ash from her cigarette into the brass ashtray. I passed her a battered copy of *Great Expectations*, containing the list of names held at Felixstowe.

She pushed a magazine across the table to me. 'There's a knitting pattern in there you might like to try.'

'Thanks.' The cover showed a smiling soldier wearing a matching knitted scarf and gloves. The information for me to update my cards would be somewhere in the magazine. I slid it into my bag.

When we were in the bustle of the outside market, I risked telling her that Thomas had said he wanted to join the Friends Ambulance Brigade.

Jean spoke without thinking, not like her at all, but she voiced my thoughts: 'If he'd explained that to your Margaret, she might have married him.'

She had just missed a tram. I waited with her at the terminus where the trams turn round below St Peter's Church. Discarded tickets blew along the ground. You can see this spot from the Dragon windows, and I wondered whether Margaret might look out to see what kind of evening it was. Perhaps she would see me standing there.

'Julia, something's happened since Thomas wrote that letter to you. I didn't want to risk saying it to you earlier with people about. One of the letters I've given you – it's from a man who was in Felixstowe prison with Thomas. He threw the letter from a train as he and the other prisoners were being taken to France under military orders. They've been told they'll face a firing squad if they go on refusing the uniform.'

I leaned into the tram stop for support, feeling my knees grow weak. 'Why didn't you tell me before?'

'Because I knew how you'd take it. Take some deep breaths, Julia. You look faint.'

'I'm all right. But what will happen to them?'

'Fenner Brockway will make sure it's taken up in Parliament. He's planning to go to France. Anyone in the least influential who might take up the men's cause will be contacted.'

'Thomas's godfather, Mr Mitchell,' I said. 'He's influential. He won't want Thomas to end up with a bullet in his head for his principles.'

'Who is he?'

I told her, and that I'd write to him.

'No!' she said adamantly. 'Leave it to someone else to write. Don't forget you have a wider duty now, to keep the confidences secret for the sake of the No Conscription Fellowship. If we're found out, then the work will be put in jeopardy. Tell me, and I'll make sure he's contacted.'

'What about Margaret, and Thomas's mother, shouldn't they know?'

Jean shook her head. 'You don't seem to realize, Julia, that we're fighting a war, too. We have two weapons: the pen, not the sword; and secrecy. Tell no one. Leave it to Mr Mitchell to tell Mrs Turner. Don't do anything that might lead the authorities back to you.'

As I watched Jean hitch her skirt and clamber onto the tram, I thought that if there wasn't a war on, I'd probably wonder if she was happy, spending her days typewriting away in her law office for a funny old man, her evenings in a room at the top of a house in Harehills where she lodged with a widow and her daughters. I'd wonder if she were lonely. But happy and lonely don't seem to matter too much just now. I might just as well wonder where she hid her set of No Conscription Fellowship cards. I'd never know.

She called to me from the step of the tram, 'Go in and see your Margaret. I would if I had a sister!'

I didn't notice until I got closer that the shutters were up at the Dragon, and draped in black. I'd read about airship attacks on London, and the black-out there. Did Uncle expect an attack on Leeds?

I let myself in the back door. Cynthia, the stout cook, stood at the kitchen table peeling carrots and moaning, her eyes streaming. A chopped onion sat on the board. A long strand of grey hair escaped from her hair-netted bun and draped itself over her shoulder. She is the only person I know who keeps dandruff in every inch of her hair, not just the scalp. She threw her head back and moaned piteously, scattering the carrots with dandruff disguised as salt. 'O gawd, little Julia. You always was one for knowing.'

Since I had been credited with 'knowing', I was reluctant to give up my reputation by asking what was wrong.

Always on the look-out for scraps for the pigs, I eyed the carrot peelings and looked for something to wrap them in. I picked up a newspaper from the chair.

'That's it. You read it. Only thank God your uncle got the telegram first.'

To have twin cousins always seemed to be some kind of magical occurrence. To have twins like Kevin and Johnny who were utterly perfect and grew up to be sought after by every girl was tedious and annoying. To have twins for your cousins who died on the same day in the same battle seemed unreal. Kevin and John McAndrew. Their names in black on white.

All the breath went out of me.

That is a stupid thing to say. The breath did not go out of me. It is still here. I just felt that it did. The breath went out of them, far away, days ago, at the Battle of the Somme.

Bernard sat across the window seat in the parlour, his legs drawn up, his body leaned onto his legs. Margaret lay on the chaise longue, one leg on the floor like an anchor. She looked up when I came in and opened her arms to me. We said nothing. Just held each other. I started to cry. But I felt treacherous, knowing I wasn't crying for them but for us.

Bernard turned to look at me with dead eyes. 'Why them? The glorious Kevin and Johnny,' he said. 'That's what everyone will say. Why not Bernard, the useless article?'

I went over to him and put my hand on his bony shoulder blade. 'No one will say that.' I didn't add that it would have been difficult for him to die in a battle when he hadn't left Leeds.

Determined to be inconsolable, he shrugged so as to rid himself of my hand. He hates anyone to touch him.

I tapped on Uncle's door. It was open a little way so I went in. He was fully dressed but half-sitting half-lying on his bed.

'Uncle?'

'Julia!'

I went across to him. 'It's terrible. I never thought... I suppose I thought they were indestructible.'

'You're good girls, in your different ways. You and Margaret. The boys were fond of you two.'

After a long time, he said, 'She mustn't put off her wedding because of this. Life must go on.'

I wondered how to remind him that she had jilted Thomas at the church, when he already knew. By way of presenting the facts to him, I started by saying, 'This has been a terrible strain for you, Uncle—'

'Even so. The date's set. If it were imminent that would be a different matter. I don't know how I'd walk her down the aisle. Or do you say up? I never remember which is up and which is down, referring to aisles and weddings. But I've ten days to pull myself together.'

You'd think that living behind and above a public house there would always be a drop of brandy to hand. That is not the case. Uncle had a jug of water and a basin on his washstand, and a bottle of holy water on his dresser.

'Would you like a cup of tea?' I asked. 'And a drop of rum?'

'That's the thing,' he said. 'Tea and rum. Tea and rum all round.'

Back in the parlour, Bernard held to his position on the window seat. Margaret sat beside him on the piano stool, looking at him sorrowfully. She had taken his hand and he had not snatched it away.

I announced Uncle's confusion and how he thought Margaret should not put off her wedding and seemed not to understand that she already had, weeks ago.

'Oh, not that wedding,' Margaret said. 'Not the wedding to Thomas Turner.'

'What other wedding is there?' I asked, forgetting about my promise of tea and rum.

Margaret turned in my direction and stretched out her legs. 'Do you remember meeting Godfrey Brownlaw?'

My face must have showed that I did remember Godfrey Brownlaw, but she continued as if my shocked, twitching facial muscles had not commented unfavourably on the podgy chemist.

'He's a widow, with two boys, and has the chemist's shop on Vicar Lane.'

I pictured his protruding eyes, soft white hands and self-satisfied smirk.

'He was on the tribunal,' I said. 'He stuck the knife in Thomas.'

'The tribunal was very fair,' Margaret said. 'You could have been thrown in gaol for contempt, with that outburst of yours. If Mrs Turner hadn't stood up for you, you would have been charged.'

'Huh! Is that what she said? And you, how can you jilt Thomas and take up with an old man?'

'He's thirty-eight and eligible to be called up. It's unlikely because of his occupation but they seem to be calling up everyone.'

Bernard more than winced. His body jerked in a little spasm-like movement. I expected him to make some mean joke about himself, such as the authorities would even get round to him in the end, when everyone else was dead. But he said nothing, which seemed even worse.

It was my turn to drop like a sack of coal onto the chaise longue. 'Margaret, when were you going to tell me about this wedding?'

Margaret waved her hand in the direction of the escritoire. 'I'd already written to you. Just what with everything I hadn't posted it.'

'You want me to come then?'

'Of course. You'll be my bridesmaid. We already have the dresses and everything.'

That's when I remembered. Tea and rum. Rum and tea.

Bernard left the room, saying he'd make a pot of tea and open a bottle of rum.

I couldn't think what to say. She stared at a train passing by outside the window. After a long time, when I heard Bernard on the stairs again, I said, 'Do you love Godfrey Brownlaw?'

She sighed. 'It's ridiculous to think that there is only one man for one woman. Dad could have married someone else. So could Mam. Godfrey is a kind man. He has two delightful, motherless boys. They all adore me.'

I stared at Margaret in disbelief, feeling that I might explode.

'Don't look at me like that,' she said. 'There are things that you do not understand. I pray you never will.'

FIFTY-THREE

I would go mad at the thought of Margaret's wedding if I had time. I try not to think about it, and am keeping busy. Working with Gregory and Sol, taking care of the pigs and hens, baking pies, trekking to and from the munitions factory with our cart. (We never did get Solomon back from the Dragon.) Sol has a real talent for growing things, and Mrs Hopps gives him lots of tips.

Late at night, when the boys are sleeping, I work on the No Conscription Fellowship records. There has not been a newsletter for some time, so Jean and I put one together. She found an elderly printer, willing to produce it if she took the copies back from him straight away. I have addressed envelopes to half the people on the membership list, printing in block letters to disguise my handwriting. We will divide up the envelopes and post them from different places. Jean has decided to take the train to Manchester to post hers from different boxes. I still have to think about where to post my copies.

It amused me to read in the *Tribunal* that government agents are trying to find the 'Information Bureau' that keeps records for every conscientious objector and the tribunals and court cases. When I met Jean in the market café, she nicknamed me 'Information' and I called her 'Bureau.'

'Here's a cup of tea, Information.'

'Thanks, Bureau!'

I had a sad letter to write today to the family of a man who died while working as forced labour in a quarry in the Dales. He was an absolutist who would not do any work that contributed to the war effort but was sent to work in a danger-ous part of the quarry without food or water. He collapsed, was sent back and then did not jump out of the way of falling rocks.

It is in the papers about the conscientious objectors from Felixstowe being taken to France and condemned to death. Thomas and the others are to be brought home. So they are safe for now. The worry is what may happen next.

FIFTY-FOUR

In years to come this day will be just a date and not even a memory. So I take it as my duty to my sister Margaret Wood to tell of this her wedding day as best and as clearly as I can. Without malice.

A glorious hot day. Everything a frenzy of activity at the Dragon. Uncle Lloyd and I are never easy in each other's company. He always tries to get me running around doing some job or errand, forgetting I'm not a child at his beck and call. I hate looking for a person's collar studs. You'll find one that looks perfectly satisfactory but a front stud was wanted, not a back stud. I had enough on helping Bernard – holding the glass for him while he brushed his hair, knotting his tie for him when his nimble fingers turned to thumbs.

Miss Mason helped Margaret beautifully. She excels at fussiness. Margaret wore Miss Mason's 'Miss Havisham' dress. Again. I wore my blue satin bridesmaid dress. Again. I would not have minded this wedding failing.

I brought Thomas's letter, wondering whether Margaret might change her mind if I showed it to her. In the end I didn't. He has joined the Friends Ambulance Brigade and will cross the Channel this week. At least now we will be able to write to each other.

Uncle, Margaret and I trotted along to the church, with Solomon once more decked out in his finery but this time drawing a fancy carriage painted in scarlet and gold leaf, and with leather upholstered seats. Godfrey Brownlaw would have preferred a horse of his own choosing but Margaret knew how much it meant to me to have my lovely Solomon wearing his ribbon trimmings and silver star.

Aunty Amy wore the shawl her merchant navy nephew Malcolm had brought back from India. She clutched it for dear life. Aunty Amy has a face like a stone statue that never shows too much pleasure or pain, but I said, 'What's wrong?' Some old eyes look as if nothing could shock or surprise but hers had changed, like some new hurt had danced there and then stopped mid-leap, leaving her pupils wide-open and her irises frozen. Did she know something about Godfrey Brownlaw that we didn't? Nothing would surprise me. I felt a surge of hope that I'd be at a wedding where when the question came 'Does anyone know of any impediment as to why this man and this woman should not be joined in holy matrimony?' the answer would be 'Yes!' Aunty Amy would tell some foul secret revealing how Godfrey Brown-law had murdered his first wife.

But it wasn't that at all. She had meant to keep quiet until after the wedding but as I had asked, she told me. Malcolm's ship has been sunk, and all on board are feared lost. I'm not to tell Margaret. Not today.

It felt unreal standing in the church and writing my name in the book as witness. I had practised my signature so it looked flourishing and un-familiar. In future years I will be able to deny it if the need arises.

Outside the church, Bernard took photographs with the Brownie that Mr Fischer had asked his daughter-in-law, Sophie, to send to me, wrapped in muslin and brown paper, before he was taken to the Isle of Man to be interned with the other aliens.

We went back to the Dragon afterwards. I had impressively, but with bad grace, supplied pork pies, chickens and a ham.

We sat at the huge oak table in the lodge room above the vaults bar. Uncle Lloyd must have called in a lot of favours for the wedding recep-tion. Someone had been saving butter and sugar for the cake. With a war on, Uncle's too fly to show off. He wanted just family, but Margaret invited some of her suffragette friends.

Bernard played musical hall songs: 'My Old

372

Man Said Follow the Van' and 'The Man Who Broke the Bank at Monte Carlo'.

Brownlaw's two little boys seemed very shy, and were dressed up like miniature waiters. I can see why Margaret took to Ernest and Edward. They're polite little chaps and obviously totally smitten by Margaret.

Miss Mason and Aunty Amy urged Margaret to sing. Bernard hush-hushed everyone and wouldn't play till there was total silence for her. Margaret is usually pale but she was all flushed and pink like the bacon I add to the pork pies. She still takes me by surprise sometimes though I know her so well. She reminded me of the old Margaret at the suffragette meetings. There was a little round of applause, then Margaret held up her hand and began to make a speech.

She told a story that I'd forgotten. She said when she and I were little, there was a knock on our door one afternoon. It was Margaret's friend, little Clarice from the Wheatsheaf. She'd come to ask our mam to give a song at a wedding reception, because she had a beautiful voice. Mam took off her apron, combed her hair and went down the street.

Margaret paused for a moment, and everyone gazed at her while she smoothed her dress. I thought she wouldn't go on, that she'd lose her nerve. She took a deep breath. She said, 'Julia and me were supposed to stay indoors till Mam came back. But we held hands and followed Mam down Bread Street, through the alley onto Wheat Street. We stood outside the Wheatsheaf and listened to Mam sing the song that I'm going to sing now.' Then she whispered to Bernard and he began to play 'Under the Shade of the Old Apple Tree'.

There was a kind of sigh in the room when she began, then no one made a sound. You could feel the silence around her voice. I glared at Godfrey Brownlaw but he couldn't take his eyes off Margaret. Perhaps I'm wrong. If he loves her that much it must be all right.

Margaret had invited everyone from the suffrage group, so Mrs Turner sailed about the room, avoiding me. I had just cut two slices of cake for Edward and Ernest when I turned and bumped straight into her and the slices of cake jumped off the plate and landed again as if I'd successfully tossed pancakes, which I never manage.

Mrs Turner glowered at me. 'It won't wash in a court of law,' she muttered viciously. 'And you're not eighteen yet by a long chalk.'

What on earth was she yapping on about? I could have asked her. But she seemed to think I knew. Given that the last time I saw her was at the tribunal when she tried to murder me, I felt like punching her. For Margaret's sake I kept calm. Margaret says that when conversational situations become tricky, facts and figures help – because no one can usually check them, especially if you make them up. Numbers change the tone of any argument or conversation, according to Margaret.

'I'll be eighteen in eight months,' I said calmly. 'Now if you'll excuse me, I have two slices of cake on two small plates for two small boys, aged nine years and three months, and ten years and two months. Respectively.'

The numbers were not impressive and had the disadvantage of being true, but it did get me out of the situation with only one more half-hearted attack from Mrs Turner. 'There's nothing respectable about you, young lady. Or respectful either.'

Jean Mackie stood in a corner, eating a pork pie. She complimented me on my dress. Margaret and Godfrey were dancing a waltz. I said, 'The last time I saw Margaret dancing it was the tango – with Thomas Turner. I don't suppose Godfrey Brownlaw can tango.'

We started to giggle, as if I'd said something else.

Jean said, 'You'd be surprised what old men can do.' She laughed, but it was the kind of laugh you think might turn into something else.

She didn't want to stay, so I wrapped her a slice of cake to take home and walked her to the door. Her voice as we said goodbye came out flat and tired. 'Margaret did the right thing, marrying an old man. There'll be no young men left in the world.'

I asked her had she lost someone. I think those were my silly words, which sounded too much like misplacing a pen or losing your way in a wood.

'My brother,' she said, 'on the Somme. The day after your Kevin and Johnny. And my fiancé. Last year.'

I hadn't even known she had a fiancé and a brother. I had always thought of her in connection with the typewriter. I suppose because I envied her that typewriter, even if it did produce legal documents and solicitor's letters. Most of our meetings, we'd talked business – the No Conscription Fellowship. She had never left an opening to talk about anything else.

'It was good of you to come then,' I said, hating the stiffness in my voice. I walked her to the end of Peter Street.

'What else am I to do with myself?' She looked at me as if she expected an answer, but I didn't know what to say.

'Do you have another brother?'

'Yes, two more. But I had just the one fiancé,' she said with a wry little smile.

There is nothing more to say about the reception. Margaret and Godfrey were taken by Solomon, Charley driving, to the station to board a train for Ilkley where they will spend two nights in a hotel.

I am staying at the Dragon in the room that was Margaret's, and now that I have stopped writing, in the early hours of the morning, I feel utterly desolate. My sister has gone. We are not the Wood Sisters any more. She says we are, but she is Mrs Godfrey Brownlaw.

It is the morning after the wedding, at which I didn't cry. Now I can't stop crying. I'm alone in the kitchen at the Dragon and have set the kettle to boil, but it's as if I watch someone else do such things. Later I will have to get the train back to Garforth, as though nothing has happened.

Such a dream I woke from. A whinnying call.

Solomon galloping across muddy trenches, slithering and sliding and trying to get up. Me and Thomas Turner helped him because Aunty Amy said we had to ride bareback to Malcolm's merchant ship, which was stuck in seaweed on the Aegean. I saw the ship, with Dad waving from the prow, just out of reach and not able to hear me. Solomon slithered again. We were somehow in the wrong country, on the way to a railway station where Kevin and Johnny waited for Frank to arrive on the next train. When I woke I was crying.

The morning light edged round the blind. I threw on my clothes and ran downstairs. There had been a whinnying. Solomon had said good-bye.

Poor Solomon. I was too late. Charley never comes in the house or he might have rushed to find me and tell me. He is not good with words but knew he'd let me down.

An army sergeant came for Solomon at eight o'clock this morning when I was half-asleep and half-awake. They call it requisitioned. I call it stealing. I call it a disaster. They've taken him for the war, not even asking his name. I didn't get chance to say goodbye. All I could do was take Solomon's white wedding ribbons, just left dangling from the hook in his stall. I held them, and I cried. I don't think I'll ever stop.

FIFTY-FIVE

I used to long to be on the train. Now I seem to be on it all the time, but the same old line taking me from Leeds to Elmtree House, Elmtree House to Leeds. I am known to the train driver and guard as the girl with the dog, because Sheba comes with me. She sits up straight and alert, as if she knows some people might object to her and she wants to prove that she is on her best behaviour.

As I cross the Marsh Lane Bridge, I look through the train window into the Dragon parlour. Sometimes the curtains are closed. Or the room is empty. Once I saw Bernard hunched up in the window seat, and another time with his back to me, sitting on the piano stool. Nobody ever looks back and waves to me as I used to wave to the people on the train.

I still like to look at strangers and make guesses about their lives. What is the attraction of strangers, people we'll never see again?

Aunty Amy says that as you get older, everyone looks familiar. Walking through the market, she says that she's known all these people before, or their mothers or fathers.

She says the only thing poor people have to pass on is their knowledge. Ask and people will be glad to tell you what they know. I suppose that's why she drove me and Margaret mad, demanding that we shut our eyes, smell an English apple and tell her its name. I can be bullied into shutting my eyes and telling you which is the Cox's Pippin, Worcester Permain and Bramley.

Of course, some people have much more than knowledge to pass on, but it is not usually to a person who has nothing. Money finds its way home. That is why I am surprised at what happened.

The letter had asked me to call at a solicitor's office on Park Row. I have read about expectations and surprise legacies. But I feared a summons to answer questions regarding the disappearance – and mysterious re-appearance – of my late father, and the possible connection between him and the late Clarence Laycock, slaughterhouse man, dead under mysterious circumstances. I did not connect the letter from Mr Underend, solicitor, with Mrs Turner's nasty remarks to me on the day of Margaret's wedding.

Wearing the fur jacket Frank had made for me, I strode from the station to Park Row, trying to look like the innocent daughter of an innocent man. Heads turned. Innocents do not wear fur. I thought about taking the jacket off, turning it inside out and hanging it over my arm. No. Brazen it out. Having a dog helps me to feel safe and apart. But I worried, too. What if I was to be questioned and held in custody? Would some kindly solicitor's clerk or police constable take Sheba to Margaret for safe-keeping? Would Gregory and Sol manage to take care of things at Elmtree House without me?

It is puzzling when you open a door and there are only stairs and no downstairs room. A board indicated that Underend & Co resided on the first floor.

I let go of Sheba's lead, and she galloped up the stairs ahead of me. As I followed, I wondered whether a downstairs room might be reached by a secret staircase. Perhaps Jean Mackie works in such a building and hides her copy of the No Conscription Fellowship records in a secret compartment in a secret cupboard in a secret room in a secret office, on a floor reached by a secret stairway, and not in her attic room in Harehills where the landlady lives downstairs.

Mr Underend's large, egg-shaped face made me want to ask if his favourite nursery rhyme had been 'Humpty Dumpty'. He met me with a jovial nod and a chubbily tight handshake. Waving me into a choice of chairs, he waited until I sat down before taking his own chair again.

He stared at me greedily, waiting for my coat to fall open. I pulled it tight and glared back.

Not a preliminary to a murder enquiry. His client Thomas Turner, currently serving with the Friends Ambulance Brigade in France, has instructed him to authorize me to have tenure in his house until the cessation of hostilities and in the event of his death to inherit the house.

After he had told me that and asked me to sign a paper, he said that there was money for the house's upkeep and he was authorized to give me a payment.

I told him I didn't need any money for upkeep. He looked disappointed.

'What are you wearing under that coat?' he asked.

I stared at him. He turned a shade of pink.

'Only it's so warm in here, with the fire. I just wondered–'

I could hear a typewriter clattering in another room and footsteps on the stairs. I stood up to go. He stood up, too, his mouth dropping open, his chubby cheeks wobbling as he shook his head from side to side.

A pair of large female hands shoved me back into the chair. Mrs Turner loomed over me. 'Hussy. No decent girl of your age and station wears a fur coat. You're no better than you should be and a damn sight worse.'

'Mrs Turner, you promised.' Mr Underend spluttered and spat. 'Confidentiality, my dear Mrs Turner.'

Sheba growled and made for Mrs Turner's ankles.

I grabbed Sheba's lead, dodged Mrs Turner, who tripped over Sheba and saved herself by grabbing the chair. I dashed for the stairs. She ran after and I could feel her wishing to push me down as she yelled after me, 'Fallen woman? You will be!'

If you are slim and in charge of a frightened dog that is trying to be brave, it is not a good idea to argue with an angry, hefty woman who is behind you at the top of a narrow staircase. Sheba and I legged it.

As we hurried along the street, she called after me, 'I'll have you investigated. Thomas'll find out the truth. I'll get you, and that damn yappy dog, too.'

She was still calling after me as I walked up

Park Row. 'You'll never have him. Does your sister think she can cast him aside and toss him to you as if he's a velvet-clad boy doll?'

As we outran her, I remembered that I had always wanted a velvet-clad boy doll after reading a story about one when I was seven. The velvet-suited boy doll in the story had been abandoned and found in the gutter by a poor girl who loved him and restored him to glory. He bore no resemblance to Thomas. I wondered whether Mrs Turner had read the same story.

Being halfway back to the station, I decided to give Jean and Harehills a miss. I did not want to bump into Mrs Turner again.

As the train crossed Marsh Lane Bridge, I glanced in at the Dragon parlour. Bernard sat on the piano stool, his back to me. I imagined the songs of Schubert. I imagined a day – was it so very long ago? – when I had a dad, a mam, a sister, handsome twin cousins and my favourite cousin, who played the piano like an angel plays a harp, and who did not then hate himself and only hunched his shoulders in a normal sort of way.

On the return journey, Sheba did not sit up to attention. She lay down in an exhausted fashion and shut her eyes, pretending to sleep.

Only then did I take in what the solicitor had said. I have tenure of Elmtree House. If Thomas dies, his house will come to me.

If Thomas dies, there is no sense or meaning or purpose in the world.

I have space on this page to copy in Thomas's letter.

Dear Julia

I received your letter and your thanks for my 'kindness' in giving you some security at Elmtree House. I am glad to think of you and the Garrettys there, making good use of the place – and taking care of Sheba for me. It keeps me sane to know I have some small stake in normality, not that any of our lives can be normal as long as this war continues.

I had a horse ambulance until yesterday, and a fine horse, too. It is heart-breaking to see how young so many of these boys are and to think that the soldiers who were the army of 1914 are now entirely gone. We patch up those who can be patched up and send them back. I can't tell you how that feels.

If you think it's the right thing to do, please give Mr and Mrs Godfrey Brownlaw my good wishes. I truly wish them every happiness.

Thanks for the cigarettes and chocolate. You are very kind.

Yours as ever
Thomas

FIFTY-SIX

I approached Margaret's house carrying foxgloves and campion, a decent-sized pork pie, a china trinket box from me, a set of tortoiseshell combs from the Garrettys and a sense of dread in case Mrs Turner had been invited. Sheba picked up my anxieties and licked my hand encouragingly.

Margaret flung the door open. Before I had time to wish her happy birthday she announced, 'Godfrey doesn't like dogs. But he's at work now so we won't worry.'

Of course, Sheba's not just any dog. I would defy even the most insensitive dog-hater to dislike her. Godfrey's sons appeared at the top of the stairs, very smartly done-up and wearing brown-paper crowns. I remembered which was Edward, the eldest, and Ernest, the youngest, because the little one looked so earnest. It must please Margaret greatly to have little page boys to dress up in celebration for her day. They rushed down the stairs and made a great fuss of Sheba. 'Can we take her in the garden?' Ernest asked.

'It's *may* we take her,' Edward corrected him gently.

'You'd better ask Sheba,' I told them. 'She's a dog with a mind of her own.'

Sheba agreed to go with them. From the window Margaret and I watched them playing. Once in a while, they would look towards Margaret and wave. I had to praise the birthday cards the boys had made for her. Their gift, a china lady in a crinoline, which they had saved up their pocket money to buy, had pride of place in the centre of the mantelpiece.

'They think she looks like me,' Margaret said approvingly.

After ten minutes we were called outside to watch Sheba perform a trick Edward and Ernest had taught her – jumping over a stick that they took it in turns to hold.

'Aren't they wonderful?' she said to me, as I

carried a tray to the table in the garden. 'Such energy and so good-natured. They're clever little boys, too. It's the first time I've known children who aren't half-starved and ill-educated. This is the life I wanted, Julia. You can just feel the difference, can't you?'

I could. And in Margaret, too. She seemed at ease in her new garden. Her hands were always smooth but, as she poured tea, I saw that she had buffed and manicured her fingernails. Each one was perfectly shaped, with a neat half-moon.

'Who's coming to the party?' I asked, expecting her to reel off everyone we had ever known who might bring a card and a present, and make a fuss of her.

'Godfrey wants it to be just us,' she said. 'I suppose he's right, what with the war and everything.' She sighed as if she didn't think he was right at all. 'We're going out to see a moving picture tonight. That's his treat.'

She called the boys over. 'Your father won't be in till later so we'll have our own little party now.'

'H-e-l-l-o! Who was going to start without m-e-e?' The voice sang out from the dining-room window, and a minute later he appeared, even podgier than I remembered him, wearing a paper hat, twisting his whiskers around his fingers and dancing down the garden. He lifted Margaret from her chair, gathered her into his arms and covered her cheeks and forehead with wet kisses. 'My sweet birthday girl!'

Edward and Ernest looked thoughtfully at the table. Sheba, who had been making a den in the middle of a snowberry bush at the bottom of the garden, suddenly realized that she had not been giving her flock full attention, and made up for it by charging at Godfrey, barking fiercely, and politely offering to savage him. I calmed her down.

'Good evening, Father,' Edward and Ernest said flatly.

'It's afternoon!' snapped Godfrey. 'Good afternoon!'

'Good afternoon, Father,' they said in unison.

'Is this your dog, Julia?' Godfrey squinted against the sunlight.

He knew very well that Sheba's mine. 'Unless Margaret wants her for her birthday,' I said. 'I'm taking care of her for Thomas Turner.' I wanted to add, *You know. Thomas Turner, the 'coward' who's out serving on the Western Front. Treated abominably by your damn tribunal. Thomas Turner, the man Margaret should have married.* But simply saying his name did the trick.

Godfrey glared. The sun went behind a cloud. Margaret shivered. Edward ran indoors to get her wrap.

'Scotch tea parties are always best,' Godfrey beamed.

'Why do you call it a Scotch party, Father?' Ernest asked.

But Godfrey had picked up Margaret's serviette and was placing it on her lap very slowly and carefully.

Edward answered his brother. 'It's because it's just family. You don't go to a lot of expense. Scotch people are careful with their money.'

'But not as careful as Yorkshire men,' Margaret said.

'You won't say that when you see what I've bought you, darling.' Godfrey kissed her wrist and the inside of her arm.

Margaret freed herself and poured tea. 'So, what are we all going to see at the Rialto tonight?' she asked.

'That's just for you and me, dearest,' Godfrey said. 'I thought I told you that. I'm sure Edward and Ernest will want to stay here with their new aunt – and her dog,' he managed to sound almost civil about Sheba, 'and let Mother and Father have an evening out together. Just the two of us.'

'That'll be grand,' I said quickly, but not as quickly as Edward and Ernest. The boys seemed very willing to forego the moving pictures for the pleasure of my company. Strange lads.

Only Margaret looked forlorn.

When we had finished our birthday tea, Godfrey led Margaret into the house to give her her present.

I played ball with the boys and Sheba. Edward missed the ball and stood looking through the dining-room window at Margaret and Godfrey. Godfrey fastened a necklace at her throat then buried his head in her hair. Margaret waved to Edward. Godfrey closed the curtains.

They did not come out for an age. When they did, Margaret looked flushed and unhappy. She had damped down and combed her hair. Godfrey helped her into her coat and said it was time to set off for the picture house.

I gave them time to catch the tram then said to the boys, 'Come on! We're going to the pictures, too!'

We caught the next tram and ran all the way to the Coliseum. 'They won't let a dog in,' Edward said.

Our luck was in. Bernard had managed to escape Uncle Lloyd for the evening and was playing the piano. Mr Diddle, the manager, gave us free seats on the front row. Sheba watched intently for a while then gave up and went to sleep, lying across my feet so that I wouldn't be able to sneak off without her. As if I would.

The boys now hold me in awe as the aunt who can get them *and* Sheba into the moving pictures for nothing. I wanted to tell them I am not their aunt. I am Julia, just Julia. But they are taken with the idea of having an aunt. (Godfrey is an only child – no surprise that his parents thought one like him was enough – and his late wife had no sisters so I am a unique item for them.)

Margaret and Godfrey must have gone out for supper because we got back before them and the boys rushed up to bed out of the way. I went to bed, too, but to write my journal.

My room was next door to Margaret and Godfrey, and I wish it hadn't been. I will gloss over some of the sounds I heard but must record Margaret's distress.

She hardly ever raises her voice except to sing, but she did tonight. I heard almost every word of his side of the argument and a good deal of her side. Godfrey has decided to send the boys to boarding school so that he and Margaret can be alone together.

'They're my family, too!' she yelled at him. 'I must have a say.'

I don't know what happened after that, but it went very quiet, except for Margaret's sobbing.

The next morning, when the boys were at school, we sat at the deal table in the kitchen. She leaned forward, her head on her arms. When I finally roused her into confiding in me, she told me that the boys are to go to a school in York. It was recommended by Mrs Turner, who sits on a committee with Godfrey. 'I don't know how I'll survive without those two little boys to keep me going.'

I said everything I could to try and console her. That she'd see the boys at weekends. Holidays. Perhaps Godfrey would change his mind.

She shook her head sadly. 'Do you know, I sometimes shut my eyes and try to pretend that Godfrey is Thomas. Don't ever tell anyone. Swear.'

'Does it work?' I asked.

'Not really.' She sighed. 'Thomas is always in my thoughts. If I forget his voice, all I have to do is say, "Hello, you", and it comes back to me.'

I had planned to get the late-morning train back, but she asked me to stay a little longer, and go to the doctor with her.

'Are you ill?' I asked.

'No. I need him to tell me something I already know.'

I sat in the waiting room, looking at a copy of *Punch,* while she had her consultation with Dr Sinson. When it was over and he walked her to the door he said, 'Congratulations again, Mrs Brownlaw. Mr Brownlaw is a very lucky man. But you should have come so much sooner.'

Sheba slid from under my chair, and we followed Margaret outside into the bright September day. On the street we stood for a moment under a copper beech. A leaf fell onto her hair. 'I'm going to be a mother,' she said quietly. 'What do you say to that?'

I picked the leaf from her hair and put it in my pocket. 'That's wonderful.'

When she had nothing else to say, I asked her had she thought of a name. (I hoped she would call a boy after Dad, or a girl after me.)

'Thomas,' she said defiantly, as if expecting me to contradict her.

Thomas is a nicer name than Godfrey, in my opinion, but I don't think Godfrey will be very pleased about it. I thought it best not to say anything. I reminded her of the meeting before the war, in London, when she sang the suffragette song by Charlotte Perkins Gilman and said that she would call her daughter Charlotte. She reckoned not to remember the evening, or the song.

FIFTY-SEVEN

In the dream, thunder and lightning. The earth opened. I saw mud, trenches, the living and the dead. Men. Horses. Solomon, always Solomon, struggling to stand. I reached out to take his reins.

The thunder in my dream turned to a thumping on the front door. When there is a knock on the door at that time on a December morning, you have to think the worst.

I slipped out of bed, fear hurting my chest. I walked along the landing to Bedroom 1 and looked out of the window. A huge black bicycle lay on its side on the path. A female figure stepped back from the door. I saw a turbaned head, which tilted back. Annie Garretty.

When they knew it was their sister, the boys got the fire going straight away. Annie sat shivering in the chair, too cold to speak. I made her get into the downstairs bed, still warm from Gregory and Sol, while we made tea.

'There's been an explosion at the factory,' she whispered.

Sol went very still. 'Where's Mam?'

'That's why I've been so long,' Annie said. 'I waited and waited. I hoped they'd find her.'

No one spoke. We all looked at Annie.

'Mam was in the room where the explosion was. No one came out alive. We're not supposed to say. We were told not to speak of it.'

I got the brandy from the cupboard and poured some into their cups of tea.

Annie told us that just after her shift started, there was a terrible explosion in Room 42 where girls were filling shells. Normally she would have been in that room but had been sent to the packing room to help them catch up. 'Dozens of girls were killed.'

'Mam,' Sol said. 'Won't we see Mam again?'

They'd all gone thin and small-looking. No one cried. I made them get back into bed, Sol and Gregory at the bottom of the bed. I heated up potato cakes on the fire and spread them with pork dripping. I topped up the teapot and gave more tea and brandy.

'Don't any of you move all day,' I said. 'Just rest. All of you rest.' After they'd eaten the potato cakes, I said, 'Go to sleep now. It'll be best to sleep.'

The boys did. Or at least they lay there with their eyes closed.

Annie followed me into the yard. My routine in the mornings is so familiar that I don't need to think. Hens. Pigs. Goat.

'I'll go back to Leeds,' I said. 'Your Sarah and Essie will have to know.' The mean thing was that I also wanted to visit Uncle, Aunty Amy and Margaret, who all save peelings and scraps for the pigs. 'You stay here with the boys and rest. Aunty Amy and I will take care of the girls.'

When we went back inside, she said could she get into my bed, as she thought she'd toss and turn and needed to be on her own.

As I tucked her in, she started to talk and talk, but not about the explosion. She said she would have to tell me from the beginning – because everything led up to how she felt at this moment.

When Annie was seven, her friend, a bigger girl called Eleanor Gomersal, got some money from somewhere she shouldn't. And she asked Mrs Garretty if she could take Annie to the pictures at the Miners' Institute in South Accommodation Road. Eleanor told her mam that Annie's mam had paid for their tickets. The following week Eleanor got more money and took Annie to the Empire.

Annie got scared when people began to stamp

and boo and throw things at the funny man on the stage because he forgot what he was meant to be saying. That was when Annie realized that people on stage did not make it up as they went along. The next turn made everything all right because it was an acted story about a family everything went wrong for. A wicked man had evil designs. This made Annie and Eleanor forget to breathe. The parts were played by a man, a woman and a boy and their movements were almost like dancing. Even when the actors did not speak, Annie and Eleanor understood their fear, joy and despair. When the show ended, the two girls went to the stage door and asked to join the acting troupe. It was Eleanor's idea and she thought they would probably be turned away, but they might just be given free tickets for the following week. They had both decided that the make-believe world was so much better than everyday life.

Annie was astonished and a little afraid when the wicked man, who was really the manager of the theatrical troupe, said she could join. The sad woman, who was his wife and not really sad, went to see Annie's mam. She explained that they could do with a girl, if she could be taught, and especially a child of Annie's beauty.

A monthly figure was agreed, to be sent to Annie's mam, who asked Annie again was she sure. Annie was not sure, but yes seemed to be the right answer.

For Annie, what followed was like sleep-walking. She didn't quite hear what was said to her through the strangeness. The strangeness of people and places, the smell of steam trains, wicker baskets, grease-paint in damp dressing rooms, mothballs and old costumes. After leaving home and her family, she thought she was no longer real. And she sleep-walked, not even thinking whether there would be any coming out at another side, meeting her old self again, being real as she had been real when she played in the streets. She did not know why what she did was called play-acting. For her there was no play in it and it did not feel like acting either. It was something she did out of a part of herself she knew nothing about, somewhere in herself where she found something. That was what Stuart and Estelle Lee had seen in her. That was how they knew she must come with them. They were disappointed that she could not sing and told her it was a pity. If they said it was a pity she knew it must be so, but had no feelings about it. The only feeling she had was sometimes an odd curiosity about herself She wondered whether it was the same for others, this feeling of distance, of sleep-walking. But when she looked at the others smiling and chatting, she thought it was not the same for them.

Because she never felt fully awake, she never went fully to sleep either. At night she stared at each new darkness until her own eyes got dark and her cheeks hollow. No one was anything but kind to her, as long as she played her parts. But no one tried to reach her either, as they did not know she had gone away.

When her performance lacked lustre – Estelle's word – because of her tiredness, Annie was given something to help her sleep. When this worked too well, she was given something to help her wake.

Sometimes a person tried to come close to her in ways she didn't like. She knew then how Eleanor Gomersal had got the money to pay for them to go to the pictures at the Miners' Institute, and to the Empire. When someone came close to her in that way, she simply said, 'I'll tell Estelle.'

Everyone was afraid of Estelle.

In this way, years passed.

When she was too old to play a child, Estelle and Stuart tried to teach Annie how to be a sister, a sweetheart or a mother. She tried to find what they wanted inside herself but it was not there, not in her. Estelle shook her. Stuart shouted. They seemed to want to make her cry.

They came back to Leeds, to the Theatre Royal, and said, not unkindly, goodbye. They said more than that, but she could not remember what else.

At first the family was glad to see her. With the money Estelle and Stuart gave her, Annie saw to it that all the children got new shoes. Then her dad said she was no better than she ought to be. She should go, and go quickly, and no one should speak her name again. It was as if there was a shame to her coming home. That was why no one in the family spoke of her, not even Cissie, who was my friend (and I had thought Cissie told me everything). Annie was meant to be the one in the family who had gone away. To come back was to go against what had become natural.

For some time, things were hard for her and she would not say more, only that she could not remember everything. It was too much to remember.

I said, 'All that's past now. All that was a long

time ago.'

One day she could not stop shivering. She had not slept or eaten. With the little money she had left she went to a chemist's shop to find something to put her right, so that she would feel well and earn her living somehow.

She went into Brownlaw's shop. He turned the sign to closed, took her into the back of the shop and sat her down on a spindly chair near the counter where he did his measuring and mixing.

'Who are you?' he had asked, putting his chubby face close to hers, his protruding eyes looking for clues. 'What do you want?'

He gave her the medicine she needed to feel calm, to feel better. That was how she came to be sitting on the chair in his shop window, advertising hair lotion. That was how she came by the room she used to live in, in Chapeltown.

I knew she was only telling me part of the story, perhaps because Godfrey Brownlaw had married Margaret. I knew if I asked questions, Annie would tell me nothing more. But I had to ask.

'Were you sorry when he married Margaret?'

She finished off the brandy. 'I was glad.'

I didn't see what any of that had to do with the explosion. 'Don't you see?' she asked, as she pulled the eiderdown to her chin. 'I've always let my mam down. I've never done the right thing. I've never been in the right place. I should have been in Room 42, not her.' She said, 'I didn't tell it properly. I didn't make you understand.'

I thought I understood as much as I needed. But there was more.

'I want you to go ask Mr Brownlaw for something to help me. He'll know what to give you. I know it's a lot to ask.'

'No, it's not,' I said. 'I'll just ask him for the medicine that Annie Garretty takes.'

NEW YEAR
TO
WINTER
1918

FIFTY-EIGHT

Fortunately I was able to leave Gregory and Sol in charge at Elmtree House and come here to be with Margaret and my baby niece. I have had so little time to write, but as Margaret rests and dozes and the baby sleeps, I sit in the wicker chair by the window in the pale January light.

Margaret woke earlier. She lay back on her pillows, her hair flowing out like Ophelia drowning. She said that she was too tired to nurse a biting baby. It hurts and wearies her. How can she say the little one bites when she has no teeth? Margaret may want to rise in the world but we are not the aristocracy yet. No wet nurse will take over my niece. I threatened that I would leave if she didn't at least feed Charlotte. She agreed, but said, 'Stop calling the baby Charlotte. Her name is Thomasina.'

Godfrey suggests names of his own as he walks across the landing muttering, 'Rose, Violet, Daisy–'

It worries me the way Margaret moons about and has not left her bed for two weeks, though Aunty Amy says Margaret needs her rest. Margaret fixes on things that upset her. Their window-cleaner was killed on the Somme. She looks at the tiny rain streaks on the window pane. There's a white-grey bird dropping and an odd purple smudge, like a bruise. She told me that

401

the last time the window-cleaner came to be paid she had no change and he said to leave it till next time. There was no next time. She knows he had children, but not where he lived. I said I would ask the neighbours. But no one ever knows where window-cleaners live.

Godfrey didn't like my being here at first, especially with Sheba, but he has learned to put up with it. When he tip-toed to the door and put his head round, Margaret shut her eyes immediately, pretending to sleep.

He beckoned me to come downstairs. 'What a time to bring a babe into the world, Julia.' All the way down the stairs, he kept his hand on the bannister and walked sedately like an old man, which I suppose he is. 'The German U-Boats have been at it again. We've lost two million tons of shipping. There's only three or four weeks' supply of food in the country. What have I done, adding a girl to the population?'

I stood on his heels twice before we reached the hall, which was piled with supplies in boxes.

'I've been waiting for a delivery of bandages and medicines – that's why I'm late. I got half what I'd expected and I won't be able to fill my order. It's for the hospital in the park.'

I helped him carry boxes out to the back seat of the motor car. Sheba ran in and out with us and I'm sure would have helped if she could.

Godfrey shivered. 'Put your coat on!' he said, wrapping his muffler round his throat. 'Don't be walking in and out like that. You'll catch your death.'

When we'd loaded all the boxes he asked me

would I like to come. Sheba stood nearby, wagging her tail. He knows I take her to the park in the late afternoon. 'Oh, all right,' he said. 'Bring the dog.'

That suited me very well, as I'd be able to leave him to order the hospital staff about while I went for a run with Sheba.

I don't know why I always forget how he drives. Margaret says it's because I'm an optimist and I expect him to improve. He doesn't. We mounted the pavements as we turned corners. He said that turning right gave him no difficulty but on left-turns the kerb, according to him, is placed for the convenience of pedestrians and horse-drawn carriages, not motorized transportation. The left-turn through the wide hospital gates was fine, in fact, but the swerve right to the hospital entrance seemed to take him by surprise. We hurtled towards the wall of the raised flowerbed. I lurched forward, gripping Sheba tightly as we walloped into the stone wall.

'Damn wall,' he said. 'Landscaping chappies don't take account of modern-age drivers.'

'It's not too badly damaged,' I said, leaping out. 'Sheba and I'll walk home – she needs the exercise.'

I don't think he heard me. He was too busy examining the front of his motor car.

I raced Sheba across the hard ground to our favourite willow tree. A few soldiers, distinguished by their blue hospital trousers, walked the paths.

This morning Margaret was out of bed, sitting in the chair, for the first time since giving birth. She

403

sat in her rocking chair, brushing her hair, her cheeks bright pink. Baby Charlotte lay in the cot, watching her mother.

When she had finished brushing her hair, Margaret started to read a book and then another, marking the pages. She asked me for a sheet of paper and a pencil. I tore a page from the centre of this journal, which I thought was very good of me. I left her writing and went to make some tea.

When I went back her eyes were very bright and her face even more flushed. I wondered whether she had a temperature. She took a sip of tea and pulled a face, which I thought was a bit much since I'd given her my spoonful of sugar as well as her own.

She took another sip of tea. 'I want you to bring me a reasonable quantity of hemlock,' she said in a quiet, determined way, as if she was demanding another spoonful of sugar.

I didn't know what to say at first. Then I gabbled on and on. Margaret must not consider for one moment taking her life. Things might seem bad now, but nothing is for ever. Once the baby stopped demanding to be breast-fed, she'd feel better. Once the war ended, she'd feel better.

'The hemlock's not for me, you silly fool,' she said.

I felt as if I would explode. I stood over the cot and said, 'If you don't want this baby, I'll have her.'

'Not for the baby!' she said. 'It's for Godfrey. I'm going to kill Godfrey.'

She set her tea down and picked up her pencil.

I watched her writing. I've heard of women turning peculiar after having a baby but I'd never expected Margaret to go funny. Was she having me on?

'What's Godfrey done?' I asked.

'This morning was the last straw. He recommended I slid a small sliver of soap up my bottom to keep me regular.'

I couldn't help it. I know I shouldn't have laughed.

She took no notice of my laughter. 'How dare he be so, so personal?'

'Because he's your husband, I suppose.'

'Huh! He wants to get back into bed with me, Julia. He hints about all the women who've given him the eye, women who'd have thought him a good catch. So I'm supposed to feel fortunate? Julia, get me that henbane and get it soon.'

'Hemlock or henbane?' I asked.

'I don't care. Whichever works best.'

I put my hand on Margaret's forehead to check whether she was running a temperature.

'If I have a temperature, it's because he makes my blood boil. Can you imagine fifty more years of that man?'

I made the mistake of querying whether he would live that long.

'He boasts that his father lived to the age of eighty-nine and his grandfather to ninety. Here.' She passed me the sheet of paper. 'I made a few notes from one of Godfrey's books. It shouldn't be too difficult.'

She had written:

Hemlock

Common names: poison parsley, poison root, spotted parsley, water hemlock, water parsley, winter fern.

Medicinal part: the herb.

Description: found in waste places and moist soil. White or yellow-white taproot produces hollow, spotted stem, fine leaflets like vanes of a feather. June to August, large clusters of small white flowers. Seeds grey-green to greyish brown.

Properties and uses: dangerously poisonous plant sometimes used for sedation. In classical times, a standard method of executing convicted criminals. Socrates most famous example. Poisoning has occurred when: a) seeds mistaken for anise; b) leaves mistaken for parsley; c) root mistaken for parsnip; d) hollow stem used to make a whistle and blow a tune.

She was watching me with a mad look in her eye. 'If you knew what he was like, you wouldn't hesitate.'

The baby started to cry. 'Come on, Charlotte, my little sweetheart.' I picked her up and handed her to Margaret.

'You'll do it,' Margaret said as she put the baby to her breast.

I decided not to argue. 'I'll see,' I said. 'I'll think about it.'

'Good.' She looked happier than she had in a long time. 'Come on, little one, you suck to your heart's content. Your real daddy will be back from the war soon and we'll live happily ever after.'

I wanted to say, 'Margaret, do you think you've

gone mad since Charlotte was born?' But I don't think a mad person knows they have gone mad. She was smiling and stroking the baby gently as she spoke.

'Women are great users of poison, Julia. I've read about it. Sometimes it might have been deliberate, sometimes a mistake. I'd probably get off if it was found out.'

Would she? I'm not so sure. Perhaps she's right. Everyone knows how easily the 'weaker sex' can make mistakes. A person could easily mash up parsnips, carrots and a portion of hemlock root. They could make a whistle of a hemlock stem and give it to a chap for his birthday; whisk up a refreshing anise drink of hemlock seeds and soda water, or add an infusion of deadly nightshade to a warming hipflask of neat whisky. Obviously you would have to know the man, but what husband is going to suspect an act of kindness from his wife?

I left Sheba with Margaret, with strict instructions to guard her and Charlotte, and put my coat on. I decided to see whether Aunty Amy could supply a remedy for what I hoped would be short-term insanity, but before that I needed to find Godfrey.

It seemed uncanny that Margaret had reminded me of Ophelia. Hemlock was what Hamlet's uncle used to poison Hamlet's father – pouring it in his ear. The ghost told Hamlet that it coursed through him swift as quicksilver.

Godfrey agreed to meet me in Hitchens Café in fifteen minutes, when his assistant had come back from her dinner break. An elderly waitress showed me to a table in the corner. 'There's not much on,' she said, slapping a menu on the table.

I ordered two slices of what I hoped would resemble cake and a pot of tea for two. 'I'm waiting for someone, so could you delay my order for ten minutes, please?'

I took out a cigarette. That was one advantage of being related to Godfrey, he seemed to be able to get his hands on smokes easily enough.

The waitress came back when she saw that I couldn't find a match. She took a packet of matches from her apron pocket and handed it to me. 'You were waiting for someone,' she said. 'Only they might not get through. Army's cordoned off town centre. Checking papers – looking for conchies and cowards. There's one in here, if you ask me.'

She nodded to the corner. I turned round to follow her glance at the chap with his head bent, pencil in his hand. 'That's my cousin,' I told the waitress. I called to him and he came over, bringing some music paper. The waitress gave him a dirty look. Bernard pretended not to notice.

'I've been composing – a song for the new addition to the family. Ode to – what's her name?'

'Charlotte.'

He wrote the name at the top of the sheet, ran his finger along the notes on the page, di-do-di-dumming the tune. 'You'll have to help me on the words since you've seen more of her than I have.'

'I can't think about a song just now, Bernard. I'm worried about Margaret. She's not herself.'

'In what way not herself?'

I thought it best not to go into too much detail.

'She's having bad dreams,' I said, missing out that she was having these dreams while wide awake.

Bernard slid the sheet music into his briefcase. 'Murderous dreams?' he asked.

'How did you guess?'

'There's something I ought to have told you.' He blew a smoke-ring across the table.

I hate it when someone teaspoons out information when what you need is a great draught of explanation.

Bernard tapped his fingers on the table as if he might get a tune from the cloth. 'Do you remember that awful Christmas?'

I nodded.

'When we got a turkey at the Dragon and you didn't? And your dad got arrested and ended up in the Workhouse Infirmary?'

I waited.

'The thing is, Julia, about what happened that night–'

Godfrey's falsetto voice interrupted the conversation. He stood in the café doorway. Everyone turned to look at the chubby man with an army officer on either side of him. Godfrey spoke to the whole café. 'I have attested! Not only am I local volunteer organizer for the civilian motor corps, I am in a necessary occupation, supplying hospitals. I am thirty-nine years old, a married man with three children.'

He whisked papers from his pocket and flourished them to the tallest officer.

'Bernard, ignore them,' I said. 'Get on with the story. It's important.'

Bernard pushed back his chair, shot to attention and called across to the officers. 'Bernard McAndrew! Reporting for duty.'

'Bernard, sit down! You were telling me about that Christmas. About Margaret. About Dad.'

The officers marched over.

'My cousin has an exemption,' I said to the one that looked most human. 'On health grounds.'

'It was a condition that's cleared up,' Bernard said solemnly.

'Bernard, not even you can grow a second lung,' I said.

'If you'd like to come with us, sir,' the human officer said.

The inhuman one raised his eyebrows and shook his head at me, which just goes to show that you can't judge by appearances.

Bernard grinned at me, whipped the music from his case and handed it to me. Clutching his music case, he marched off, keeping pace with the officers. At the door he turned back and gave me our salute.

Godfrey took Bernard's seat, with his back to everyone else in the café, no doubt thinking they were judging him, suspecting him of forged papers.

'Who's Charlotte?' Godfrey said, reading the inscription at the top of the sheet of music.

'Your daughter.'

'Oh, is that what Margaret's decided? Well, that's not so bad, but it's still a sort of boy's name, isn't it? Charles, Charlotte. What was she after before? Georgina, something like that. George, Georgina. I blame the suffragettes for all that.'

I didn't remind him that Margaret's choice had been Thomasina, for Thomas Turner.

The waitress slammed the teapot on the table. She had forgotten the cake.

'I prefer Daisy,' Godfrey said as he watched me lift the teapot lid and stir the weak brew, 'but I can get used to Charlotte. I'll go back to the registrar this afternoon.' Being magnanimous seemed to restore his spirits.

'Godfrey, I'm worried about Margaret. She's not herself.'

'No! She's the little mother now!'

'I think if she and I could go away somewhere, for a rest, taking the baby, of course. A change of scene, something like that.'

'I can't possibly leave my post,' Godfrey said loudly, perhaps hoping some of his critics in the café would hear. 'All the hospitals need supplies. Someone has to co-ordinate that and make the hard choices of sorting needs from wants.'

'You needn't come, Godfrey. I'll take care of Margaret.'

'Oh no. I won't hear of it. Margaret and I have vowed never to spend a night apart, and I won't break that vow. She is the light of my life, Julia.'

I stubbed my cigarette. 'Lights can go out, Godfrey.'

When I look back on these pages, it appears that I have stayed in Leeds for weeks on end. That is not true. I have been back and forth to Elmtree House, as I feel responsible for Gregory and Sol, but they get on very well there. I am sad that we do not presently bake pies for the munitions

411

factory, due to a shortage of flour, but that has made life easier in other ways. Staying with Margaret gives me more time to write my journal, and to meet with Jean and exchange information for the No Conscription Fellowship record cards. When will Margaret get better? Aunty Amy has given me oatmeal (like gold dust just now) with instructions to make porridge for Margaret's breakfast. She also supplied me with basil leaves, saying, 'Basil tea lifts the spirits.'

It's worth a try. Whenever I go out shopping Margaret gives me a meaningful look, intending for me to buy hemlock. I am glad she has not confided in anyone else or she would be locked up.

FIFTY-NINE

I long for the days when I wished for something to happen. I am sitting in the window seat at Elmtree House writing this on Easter Sunday afternoon, having been to church this morning. I do not usually go to church but when we heard the peal of the church bells breaking through the quiet of the morning, Sarah, Essie and I decided to go. The girls have come for the Easter weekend, to visit their brothers. We made Sheba stay in the kitchen with the boys. Gregory says that the bells toll long enough for a person to stroll from the next village, which is a bit of an exaggeration but we knew we would be there in time.

We hurried along the lane and through the church gate. Lots of other people had the same idea. We slipped in at the back of the church, just edging in on the last pew. Even from there the heavy scent of flowers made me feel I must be in heaven. Mrs Miles and some other ladies do the church flowers on Saturday evening. By Sunday, going into the church is like shutting your eyes and sticking your snitch into a bouquet. Even if you don't shut your eyes, you feel as though you have because your sense of smell drowns out every other feeling until you get used to it. I don't know the names of all the flowers. Except the daffodils, of course. They always remind me of my days out with Frank at Roundhay Park.

I prayed for Frank. There has been no more news since he was reported missing feared dead and, although we should never give up hope, it has been a long time now. I prayed for God to keep Thomas safe. He should have married Margaret a year ago yesterday in that very church. I asked Sarah to say a prayer for Bernard because I am too angry with him for just going off like that when there was no need. I would not usually have mentioned Margaret in my prayers, as she can take care of herself without divine intervention. But since she has been so strange, I thought I had better.

The vicar tried to be cheerful and encourage people to hope. I suppose that is his job. Though he did say that life could be hard to bear when so many from the village won't return, but that Christ carried his cross and had risen again on the third day. The vicar thought that in the third

413

year of the war, we should take courage and hope from that message.

After the service, Sarah and Essie went back to the house before me to make sure Gregory and Sol didn't hunt the painted eggs before we gave the little Hopps children time to find one apiece.

I went to have a word with Dad. The daffodils have made a fine show on his grave and seemed alive in the breeze that blew across the churchyard. I tugged a few blades of grass from the earth with my fingers and dug at a couple of weeds with a flat-edged pebble. Over the past two years, whenever I saw a small roundish white rock, I would pick it up and put it in my pocket. Now his grave has an oval necklace of white stone. He would like it. I asked him today, 'Did you know that you would be in my heart for ever?' I think he did know. I told him that I would come and see him next Sunday on my birthday, which sounded as if I was hinting for a present. Who knows? Maybe he will arrange something for me.

When I came back, Jean swung on the gate, smiling. 'Wonderful to get away from Leeds for a day,' she said.

Sarah and Gregory had collected the two Hopps children. Everyone was waiting for me so that we could start the painted egg hunt. I had hidden eggs in the outside oven, one under the horse trough for little Herbert and a brightly spotted egg on top of the sundial for Mabel because it is the right height for her. Jean found the oven egg and one Sol had hidden in the hen hutch. We all laughed and felt very cheerful.

Gregory and Sol hunted an egg apiece then went shooting rabbits with Mr Hopps. They have come up with a way of re-using the pellets. Who would have thought such little townies would become country boys?

Jean could not believe her luck that she would be taking two eggs home with her, saying that would be her dinners planned for Monday and Tuesday.

Mabel and Herbert carried their eggs home carefully, Sarah and Essie going with them. I suspect Mabel will be disappointed that the eggs are coloured only on the outside. I am sure she has got it into her head that they are decorated all the way through.

When we were alone, Jean and I sat at the table in the study. I had set a vase of flowers at the end of the table, picked that morning. Somehow it made our task more bearable. Just in case anyone came in, we had our usual multi-coloured piece of knitting – a blanket on two sets of needles – ready to cover our records.

She dictated information for the cards and I wrote. We have both used up all our ink so had to use pencil. I have an indelible pencil, so for letters to the wives and parents of conscientious objectors, I licked the point to make the writing more respectful-looking. But when Jean caught sight of my blue tongue, she fetched an eggcup of water for me to dip the pencil in. We discussed whether to put a P.S. apologizing for the pencil but decided against it because the recipients will know we are minus ink, and it would trivialize what can be very serious letters. I wrote to the

M.P. George Lansbury, passing on the request of a woman whose conscientious objector husband died in prison. She wanted to have the death investigated.

It is the kind of work that leaves you with all sorts of feelings. After we had hidden the records away and Jean had tucked the letters in the pouch she wears tied at her waist under her skirt, we even picked up our blanket and did a few rows of stocking-stitch. She had red wool from an old cardigan; I had black from one of the moth-eaten jumpers I found upstairs. I have become adept at neat knots since there are breaks in the yarn where moths have banqueted. We had as many feelings about the No Conscription Fellowship work as there are stitches on a row. Sometimes I feel guilty at doing so little and doing it secretly when others are being pilloried, driven mad or dying for their beliefs. Jean said that we should be proud to be doing something anyway. She is full of gloom that this utterly pointless war goes on and on, but hopeful, because they are brave, courageous people willing to go against the tide of opinion. It seems to me now, from the mood of people in church this morning, that if we were to turn the clock back to 1914, people would not be so willing to be dragged into war.

I admire Jean more than I admire myself. I came to my opinions because of Dad being German and an internationalist. She came to her opinions because she has a good head on her shoulders. She wished that Margaret could be here and would share our views, and asked me what swayed Margaret, who could have gone either way but followed the Mrs Pankhurst and Mrs Turner line. I said that you sometimes don't know those closest to you as well as you thought because they can change without bothering to tell you and you are left looking at the same person, you think, and it is someone different.

We did more knitting than expected, but it has not turned into a blanket yet. 'Who's it to be for?' Jean asked.

I said it should be for Thomas Turner. She agreed.

SIXTY

Margaret thinks she set the events in motion. But it was my fault, in all sorts of ways. I should have argued more strongly against her plan to poison Godfrey.

I had better put this down in order or it will make no sense when I come back to it.

Once a week I go to Margaret's to help in whatever way I can. When I got back with this week's shopping, Margaret walked slowly downstairs. She spied the basket I had set on the table and started to root through it. 'Hemlock root! I thought you'd never find any. You're a genius, Julia.'

The thought of poisoning Godfrey seemed to lift her spirits. She hadn't smiled in weeks. 'Now you must leave this to me. If there's any blame to be taken, I'll bear it.'

She chopped, boiled and sang. She mashed,

salted, peppered and used her ration of butter. When Godfrey came home, she topped off her creation with three slices of hard-boiled eggs and set the plate in front of him.

'Julia and I had our tea earlier, darling,' she said.

Godfrey picked up his knife and fork and tried his food. 'Delicious!'

'You see, Julia,' he said, as Margaret retreated upstairs, 'I knew she'd come round of her own accord in her own good time.'

I watched him eat.

As he set his dirty plate on the draining board, I said, 'You're a model husband, Godfrey.' I rinsed the plate under the tap. 'But I'm sure I was right earlier about Margaret needing a change of scene.'

'Be a good girl and give me a hand.' He wiped his full lips on the towel and burped. 'I have a delivery to make. Not only are the poor chaps at Chapel Allerton Hospital deficient in various limbs, but some have hernias. The trusses are in the hall. We're chock-a-block at the shop.'

I helped him take the boxes of splints, bandages and lint out to the car. We piled them high on the back seat. As I straightened them, he brought the crate of trusses from the hall and plonked it on top.

I said, 'There's too much for you to take in one journey, Godfrey, can't you leave some of it?'

'Too much? Too much? When our boys are giving their lives? I can't do too much, Julia. I can't do enough. None of us will ever do enough. Now you stay by the front door and watch that lot in case some blighter comes and takes a fancy to it. I'll go up and tell Margaret I'm going.'

Godfrey was gone a suspiciously long time. He came downstairs smiling and adjusting his clothing. He picked up the clothes brush, brushing off Sheba's hairs from trousers and sleeves, handing the brush to me to do the back of his jacket.

I walked to the motor with him, trying to think of a tactful way to say to leave Margaret alone, just a little bit.

The motor let itself be coaxed into starting and set off jerkily, gathering speed, bumping over the cobbled street. I saw it so clearly I almost felt I could have reached out and prevented the accident. Of course I couldn't.

The motor dislodged a loose cobble that flew up and bounced on the front of the car. Godfrey swerved and came to a halt. The crate of trusses shot forwards and caught him sharply on the back of the neck. The motor car spun wildly, spluttering and rattling as it smashed into the garden wall of number nineteen.

I ran to the motor car.

Godfrey leaned over the steering wheel very still, his head at an impossible angle. I reached for his hand to take his pulse. As I touched him he fell sideways against me. Utterly lifeless.

A small crowd gathered. I turned to a lady who looked like an infant-school teacher, very neat and contained. 'Would you fetch a policeman?' I asked.

She said number fourteen with the green curtains had a telephonic line connection on the premises. She would make an emergency call straight away.

Margaret's elderly next-door neighbour, a retired draper, hobbled up, wearing a smoking jacket and funny little hat. 'This is no sight for ladies and young people. Leave this to me. I was at Ladysmith.'

I climbed in the passenger seat. 'He's my brother-in-law. I'm staying with him.'

Godfrey would have wanted me to guard the medical supplies and make sure that they reached their destination safely. Poor Godfrey.

I didn't leave him until the police came.

Margaret had gone back to bed and was nodding off. I took her a cup of tea. I seem to spend a lot of time making tea with rum, or tea with brandy.

She pulled a face when she tasted the rum and a second later knew something was up. 'What's wrong?' The colour left her cheeks. 'Have I killed him? Has the hemlock run its deadly course?'

I thought I'd better clear that up first. 'It was a parsnip,' I said. 'You gave him mashed carrot and parsnip.'

'Liar.' She took another sip of tea. 'But it's a good story. We'll stick to that. He's dead, isn't he?'

'Yes.'

'Oh my gawd, what have I done?'

'Nothing. You've done nothing. You can't murder someone with boiled parsnip, even a very woody parsnip.'

Slowly and patiently, I explained about the cobbles, the crate of trusses and the broken neck.

'Aunty Amy doesn't sell hemlock. I wouldn't have known where to get it even if I'd wanted to.'

Charlotte woke up and started to cry. I picked her up and shushed her, walking her round the room.

Margaret looked at me accusingly. 'Why did you let me think it was hemlock?'

'I don't know. You seemed so desperate to … to do something.'

There was a loud knock on the door.

'That'll be the police,' I said.

'Will you deal with them? Tell them I'm nursing my baby.'

'No. You'll have to speak to them. You're the widow.'

We went downstairs.

The police officer looked very old and I thought he must have come out of retirement. He explained that a post-mortem would be undertaken because of the nature of the accident, to ascertain cause of death. A youngish woman police officer with severe hair and ink on her fingers wrote down everything I said. I described the accident.

Margaret sat half-stupefied, closing her eyes so as not to go dizzy and faint. I knew she was thinking that she had wished Godfrey dead.

The young woman officer did not write down my 'If only Godfrey had placed the trusses on the floor of the car.'

Neither of us can sleep. I didn't want to climb into Godfrey's side of the bed beside Margaret but she looked so upset and so afraid. She isn't asleep and isn't complaining that I am writing by candlelight.

She says that in the morning we must go to York and bring Edward and Ernest home from school.

SIXTY-ONE

Margaret wore a hat with a heavy black veil. She dabbed a small lace hanky at her snitch, then tucked it in her pocket and took Ernest and Edward by the hand. I held Charlotte, who was so good and took a great interest in the flowers.

The school head boy had come back with us on the train when Margaret had gone to break the news to the boys. He had returned for the funeral. Ronald, a tall, lean, blond lad with a strong jaw and changeable blue-grey eyes that made me think of the sea. He stood behind them, a hand on either boy's shoulder. It must be a good school to have someone come along and care for the boys in that way.

As we walked back through the cemetery, I took Baby Charlotte to see the daffodils on Tom Maguire's grave. 'He's a poet,' I whispered to her. 'And when you're older, you'll be a poet, too.'

Uncle Lloyd had insisted that we go back to the Dragon. I'm so glad that we were in the upstairs parlour and not in the function room where Margaret and Godfrey's wedding reception took place. A trestle table had been set up for a sit-down breakfast.

As the one man in uniform at the table, Bernard sat tall and proud, his head so high that the egg spoon seemed to travel a long way to reach his mouth. His joy in himself and his uniform almost put me off my boiled egg, except that I was hungry.

Mrs Turner pounced on Margaret, condoling and fussing over the baby. 'What's her name?'

I wanted to re-stake my claim for the name Charlotte, and dreaded Margaret saying, 'Thomasina.'

'Daisy,' Margaret said, explaining that Godfrey had chosen and registered the name.

Poor Godfrey. His one last act of defiance. But to me she will always be Charlotte, the name she was promised before she was conceived, when Margaret was still in her right mind.

'We'll carry it on,' I heard Mrs Turner say to Margaret grandly before turning her attentions to Uncle. 'We'll carry it on together.'

I asked Margaret what they would carry on. Between them, they will keep up Godfrey's motor transport responsibilities and the delivery of supplies to hospitals. Both Mrs Turner and Margaret have learned to drive, which I envy them. Though since it was Godfrey who taught Margaret, the enterprise makes me a little uneasy.

Edward asked me if he and Ernest would have to go back to school in York. Could they not stay at home and take care of their step-mama and baby sister? The head boy frowned and said that now was not a time to be bringing up such a question. I said that it was a very good time, and to ask Margaret that evening. I hoped it would give her something to think about. Ernest whispered to me, asking me where Sheba was. I promised he'd see her soon.

I felt sorry for the little chaps but needed to catch Bernard's eye. He sets out for France after this leave and if he won't tell me what he knows I think I shall burst.

Annie Garretty was sympathizing with Margaret over her loss and enquiring whether Godfrey had been insured, when I pulled Bernard away.

'What happened on Dad's last Christmas Eve, Bernard? If you know something, you must tell me.'

Bernard put on his puzzled look. If he'd been a stage character he'd have opened his eyes wide, parted his lips and shook his head in feigned ignorance.

I'm sure I would have got something out of him but Margaret was staring at us.

The skin over his nose and cheeks tightened. 'Honestly, Julia, I don't remember saying anything.' His ears turned pink.

I stopped myself from accusing him of lying. 'The Christmas turkey. How was it that Dad brought one to you and not to anyone else, yet you didn't see him?'

Bernard said that there must have been some misunderstanding. He had no recollection of that time, or of a turkey. Misunderstandings happened all the time. After all, he said, I had told all and sundry that the baby was called Charlotte when her name was Daisy. I gave up, which is probably what he wanted me to do.

Given that the last time Mrs Turner spoke to me it was to offer to shove me down a flight of stairs at the solicitor's, and choke Sheba with her own lead, it seemed a bit rich that she came over smiling as if none of that had ever happened. She has heard what wonders I perform in supplying a nutritious meal one day a week at the munitions factory, all from my own produce (meaning shot and snared rabbits, the occasional poached deer, turnips, potatoes and onions). Mrs Turner explained that she now presides on the School Board and that Meals for the Bairns has become a top priority. If I could see my way to supplying just one big pot of stew for one school each week – well, every little helped. There would be payment, of course, though perhaps not as much as the government paid. I said I'd see what I could do.

It pleased me that I would be able to write to Thomas and tell him that I had seen his mother. He would be glad about that.

I asked Margaret if she would be writing to him but she said what a question, on the day of her husband's funeral and she in mourning. 'You write to him. You tell him.'

My feelings when she said that puzzled me so much that I felt sort of dizzy. I sat in the window seat. What would be worse: Margaret getting Thomas back; Thomas falling in love with some stranger; or his not coming back at all?

Margaret sat beside me. 'I did love Godfrey at first, Julia. But you can't know what it was like to live with him. Of course I'm sorry he's dead. But it's not my fault. And if you ever tell anyone

425

about that bloody hemlock parsnip!'

I told her that I hadn't been thinking about that.

'Well then, a penny for them.'

But I was saved from answering. Little Ernest came and leaned against Margaret. She took his hand. Ronald, the Greek-god head boy walked over with Edward.

Margaret flashed him a sad smile as she twisted the Whitby jet ring on her finger – it was a little too big. 'Ronald, you'd be doing me a service if you'd bring the boys home very shortly.'

'Of course, Mrs Brownlaw.'

Margaret turned to me. 'Julia, bring the baby and come with me.' She hurried us out of the room. 'Damn, damn, damn. There's milk oozing out of my breasts. I feel such a fool.'

The reason I love Margaret, and the reason she drives me mad and I sometimes hate her, is that she always puts on such a brave face, like some warrior queen. All she has ever wanted is to get on well in the world. You should not have to be a warrior queen to achieve that, but perhaps she is right. The peculiar thing about her is that she doesn't know she does it. She believes she is all serenity, a lily of the field, and can just 'be'. I am the one who strives. For the first time, as we dashed along the landing to the blue room, Margaret folding her arms around her chest, I realized that in some ways we are very much alike.

SIXTY-TWO

My body aches from lifting our potatoes from the ground. Gregory and Sol laugh at me for wearing shabby leather gloves. They enjoy the job. In the end I took over the stacking in the shed and left them to do the lifting. The potatoes must be stored carefully to make sure they keep well.

But though I dream of spuds and of drowning in spuds, I won't write more about them. Not when I want to give an account of Bernard's wedding at St Patrick's Church last Saturday. Bernard, proud finally to be in the Leeds Pals, wore his uniform, of course. Annie wore a dark, expensive costume, which had belonged to the first Mrs Brownlaw, and she carried a spray of roses. I witnessed their signatures, along with dapper Mr Diddle the picture house manager. (Bernard described him to Uncle as a 'business man' because he did not want Uncle turning nasty about kinematographic connections.)

Margaret stayed at home with her boys and the baby. 'I know we're not in the Victorian age now,' she said, 'but it's too soon for me to be seen dancing at a wedding.'

She has brought a phonograph, and the boys and their friend Ronald come home every weekend and play records in the drawing room. Margaret is teaching them all to dance, to take their minds off the loss of their father. She has promised them they can come home to Leeds at the end of term and be day school boys again.

Though St Patrick's is a few minutes' walk from the Dragon, for sentimental reasons, Bernard insisted we have the wedding tea in Hitchens Café, where he was first swept into the army by the recruiters. The wind whipped us along the Lower Headrow towards the café. Bernard sat by the big mirror. Every now and then, when he thought no one was looking, he stole a glance at himself and Annie, as if he could not believe his luck.

'She's not just marrying me because she'll get the widow's pension if I die, you know,' he whispered to me after the toasts.

'Idiot! Of course not. She loves you!'

Poor Bernard. I wish he held a better opinion of himself.

I tried once more to get him to tell me if he knew what happened that Christmas Eve when Dad was taken into custody. To encourage him to speak, I admitted that I had discovered Clarence's body in the ice room. I didn't mention anything about Dad's butcher's steel. 'Bernard, I can't bear not knowing whether Dad had anything to do with Clarence's death. You'd want to know if it was your father.'

Bernard straightened his tie. 'If it was my dad, I would wonder. But not your dad. Not gentle Uncle Joe.'

'Please, Bernard, tell me.'

'Sorry, Julia. Nothing to declare.'

Annie drew him away from me, whispering in his ear and making him laugh.

As Uncle and I walked them to the station, the wind had whipped itself into a frenzy, and we didn't speak from the effort of fighting the wind and holding onto our hats.

'Give my regards to Scarborough,' Uncle shouted over the din of the station platform as he shook hands with Bernard and Annie. He had booked them into a hotel, as a wedding present.

The train chugged away from the platform. Bernard leaned out of the window, waving.

Uncle said, 'She'll be an asset in the Dragon, that lass. Finally Bernard's done something right.'

'In marrying Annie, yes. Not in joining up.'

'Oh, he'll pull through, lass.' Uncle took my arm companionably, and I wondered for a moment whether he thought I was Margaret. 'Creaking gates always last longest. God takes the best first, so Bernard's a while to go yet.'

'Bernard is the best in my book,' I said. 'He has music in his heart and soul, and I'm right sorry he's going to war.'

'Then we'll have to agree to differ, Julia.'

I find that a useful little phrase. I told it to Jean when we met in her room the next day to work on the No Conscription Fellowship records.

It surprised me that though Jean is so untidy herself her room is neat and ordered. She has a bed, a table, one rattan chair and a four-legged stool stacked high with books. She says that the room has to be tidy because it's so small.

Uncle's little phrase got us through the afternoon.

She'd say, 'Mr Prime Minister, Generals Julia

429

and Jean agree to differ with you.'

I'd say, 'White-Feather-Givers of England, Jean and Julia agree to differ.'

We agreed to differ with the newspapers, the Germans, the Austrians and every warlike man or god, including the characters in *The Iliad*. I told her the story of *The Iliad* while we took a pause after filling the record cards of a conscientious objector who had died in prison.

When we had finished our work, we walked to Margaret's together, where I had left Sheba with Edward and Ernest, as Jean's landlady doesn't allow pets, except her own.

We all strolled to Potternewton Park. I pushed Daisy's pram.

As we walked through the main gates, I thought of poor Godfrey delivering his supplies. The stone wall he crashed into has been mended and the skid marks have gone from the flags.

Edward set stumps in the ground for cricket. I tossed a coin for first bat, and he went in to bat. Margaret bowled and the rest of us fielded, except for Daisy who slept.

When Edward had scored fifteen runs, I noticed that a few soldiers in their blue hospital uniforms had come out and were walking about the grounds. Edward whacked the ball and set off running. I heard a cry, and turned to see Jean collide with a soldier, whose crutch flew into the air and landed by a tree. The soldier had caught Edward out.

Edward's face! Of course the poor man realized straight away he shouldn't have done it. 'Ouch! My mistake, batsman.'

He and Jean helped each other up, and Edward retrieved the crutch. Ernest went in to bat, I bowled, and Margaret and Edward fielded.

Jean and the soldier sat the game out on a bench and I noticed that she took out her newly knitted scarf and gave it to him.

'He's a Scot,' Edward whispered to me as he dashed over to beat me to the ball. 'So I expect they'll like each other.'

When we walked home, Jean said, 'I know you're dying to ask. We exchanged addresses, but it means nothing. Soldiers are always looking for some new girl to write to them.' But she looked pleased.

'I bet he doesn't know you agree to differ on the war,' I said.

'He agrees to differ himself!'

We laughed. I glanced at Margaret quickly to see whether she felt left out, but Edward and Ernest were talking to her about their school sports day.

SIXTY-THREE

We are in the fifth year of this unending war. For a long time everything has felt non-stop and unreal.

I have a dream where I am running in front of a tram that has the destination 'DEPOT' on the front. It chases me into a tramshed that turns into the cooling alley of the meat market, hung with carcasses. I cover my eyes and keep on running, out of the tramshed. It's the cooling alley *and* the tramshed, and I bump against bodies, not knowing whether they are men or beasts. The tram pursues me and this time the destination says 'TERMINUS'. I run along the track ceaselessly, trying to reach a stop, terrified by the darkness all around me. I lose the tracks and myself down dark alleys where doors open and the arms of the troubled dead reach out to claim me.

The dream started after I got Thomas's letter telling me he won't be coming home:

Dear Julia

It cheers me to hear that Elmtree House has proved such a lifesaver to you and yours. Something good came out of something bad. I place a lot of store on that and hope it can be true on a grander scale.

I have belatedly written to Margaret expressing my condolences for her loss. I do not know whether it was the 'correct' thing to do but my heart nagged at me for not doing it before now.

From the ashes of this conflict perhaps we shall create a better world. It's what I intend to do if I live through it. There are Quaker chaps here with so much faith I sometimes wish I could have a dab of it. We tend our soldiers, of course, but the civilians fend for themselves. Some of us are talking about what we can do over here after the war.

Since I do not believe that as a 'funk-hole Cuthbert' I shall be welcome in England after the war, perhaps I can do some good here when that time comes.

With kind regards
Thomas

Bernard's letter didn't help either. What is it about me that no one feels they have to 'put on a brave face'?

Dear Julia

Thanks for your letter which I have read several times. Annie has written too, but you know she is not the best letter-writer in the world as she says herself, and so as I read I ask her a dozen questions and if thoughts travel across the English Channel, she will lie awake with my question marks playing a tune in her brain.

It must be a relief for Margaret that Godfrey Brownlaw insured himself so well. (Was Annie hinting at me when she reported that?) At least Brownlaw's was a quick death in the familiarity of his own back street. He must not have known what hit him (i.e. a box of trusses). Don't ever tell the Brownlaw boys what items of surgical relief killed their father. It will make them think that life is not just cruel but a cruel joke, and they will find that out for themselves soon enough.

I watch my fingers with great pity as they move across this page. It sounds like a madman's thought but I would rather die myself than see my hands destroyed. You think we did some digging that day when we covered the potatoes in your garden. Compared with our exertions here, it was like scattering moonbeams. The earth goes deeper than the oldest gravedigger imagines. My dearest hope is that I shall be able to play my musical composition to little Charlotte one of these days, even though her name is now Daisy. In fact, I believe my little ditty will suit a

433

Daisy better.

Last week, when I was off-duty for a couple of hours, I came across a well-tuned piano amid ruins, a house collapsed around it. Julia, imagine sitting in the window seat in the Dragon parlour, shutting your eyes and opening them to find the walls gone. You are suspended by a single floorboard. When you look out to see a train passing, the window isn't there. The railway bridge has collapsed and the train tracks tumbled hundreds of feet into the earth, broken and sticking out at strange angles. That will give you a little inkling of what it is like here.

I must stop now. Pass it on that I keep my spirits up and am very well indeed.

With love and kind regards to all
Your cousin
Bernard

P. S. I do not like to ask you this as I know you are the one that has to find everything out and you have too much of a sense of responsibility. (I never told you that before.) Do this for me. Find out – tactfully – if Annie is in a delicate condition. I do not know whether she hints in her letters or is referring to indigestion. Do not say I told you to do this or she may think I will be disappointed if I am wrong.

SIXTY-FOUR

I am taking care of Margaret. She woke and asked me to open the window, though the doctor has said she must be kept warm. Some people believe that when they die, the window must be open for their soul to float free. I do not ever remember Margaret believing this so hope it is only that she is tired of the stench of eucalyptus, Friar's Balsam and black treacle.

It's a beautiful clear day and the leaves should not have fallen yet, but the north wind has blown all day long, swirling leaves onto the path and into the street. I had to replace the window-stopper, and used one of Godfrey's old socks.

All round the room I have placed dishes of water to moisten the atmosphere. Margaret complains when I change the poultice on her back that leaning forward exhausts her and the poultice on her front hurts.

While she slept I went to the kitchen to stir the chicken soup. I miss Daisy since she has gone to stay with Miss Mason until Margaret gets better. We are taking all sorts of precautions though it could be that this is a waste of time since we are ignorant of how this dreadful plague catches hold.

While I stirred the soup, the telephone rang, and as Mrs Bell who comes in to help every day will not touch it, I had to leave the soup and pick up the receiver. Mrs Turner said that she has some news that would cheer Margaret. I asked was it about Thomas. The wrong thing to say, of course. And it was not.

I tried to put her off but she insisted that she would come and give the news in person, convinced that it would aid dear Margaret's recovery. She is even more ignorant than I am about the treatment and cure of influenza. If good news is a medicine, she should tour the hospitals, informing ill patients that they have been left a legacy, awarded the freedom of the city or been given a tortoiseshell kitten. The lame would walk and the sick dance their way to health through the joy of good tidings.

Margaret took such a small amount of soup. 'You have some, Julia,' she said, sounding worn-out. Her arms lay thin and limp against the bedclothes.

I set the soup on the dressing table, covering it with a serviette for later.

When the doorbell rang, I called down from the window for Mrs Turner to come up.

Margaret shook her head to say that she wanted no visitors. I explained that Mrs Turner wanted to see her and that she had some good news. Straight away I could have bitten off my tongue. Margaret's eyes lit up. 'Thomas?' she asked.

'Not Thomas. But he's safe. I had a letter. I'll read it to you when she's gone.'

Mrs Turner plodded heavily up the stairs. I have hung a damp sheet in the doorway to stop the movement of germs, and tried to keep her near the sheet. 'Mrs Turner, I'm sure Margaret would feel better if you stayed in the doorway. She's afraid of passing it on.'

Mrs Turner turned her smile on me in a way that made me feel sure she knew something to my disadvantage. 'It's you young people who are most likely to catch it,' she said cheerfully.

A small basket of Worcester Permains hung from her arm, a newspaper on top. She set down the apples on the bedside table. 'From my garden. Margaret, dear, I know you won't feel up to eating an apple as such, but perhaps stewed with a drop of cream from the top of the milk.'

'Thank you,' Margaret said, making an effort to keep her eyes open.

Mrs Turner produced her newspaper and announced, 'There's talk of an armistice.'

We knew that already. Talk, talk, talk.

'But this is the news I've brought for you.' She put on her spectacles and ran a finger down the page of the newspaper. 'Listen to this. It's from the Parliamentary Bill that will finally give women emancipation: "A woman shall not be disqualified by sex or marriage for being elected to or sitting or voting as a Member of the Commons House of Parliament." We've won, my dear, we've won.'

I thought Margaret hadn't taken it in, or didn't care. But her eyes filled with tears. Slowly, a tear rolled down her cheek.

'We were right, Margaret. Right to fight, and right to support the war effort. We've got our reward. Thanks to us, future generations of women will be able to vote. There'll be women in Parliament.'

More tears rolled down Margaret's cheeks. I

wanted to tell the silly old baggage to sling her hook, but she went on.

'Don't be sad, my dear.' She took Margaret's hand. 'I know you paid a high price, giving up that son of mine for your principles. But you did the right thing. If you hadn't brought him up short, I think he may have refused any part of the war effort and ended up in prison or faced a firing squad.'

I wanted to hit her. I wanted to tell her that Thomas did just that, along with a lot of good, brave men. I gave Margaret her handkerchief. 'Margaret needs her rest now,' I said.

Margaret spoke in a calm, polite voice. 'Thank you for coming, Mrs Turner. I'm glad to hear the news. But it all seems such a long time ago.' She closed her eyes.

Mrs Turner kissed her cheek. 'Goodbye, my dear.'

I walked Mrs Turner downstairs. I only offered her a cup of tea because there was a scream building up inside me and I had to say something to keep it down.

She watched me critically as I warmed the china teapot. 'Poor Margaret. First losing her husband and now being struck so low with this terrible scourge. You have had the doctor to her?'

'Yes.' If I hadn't been using both hands to make the tea I would have torn a few lumps of my hair out because I could see what kind of conversation it was going to be. A nosy-parker conversation. I was right.

'I noticed her poor husband's chemist shop is still open for business. I expect Margaret will be selling out, when she's well.'

I was torn between wanting to keep her guessing, and the desire to boast about how silly old fools were not the only ones who could carry on 'business as usual during hostilities'. I said, 'Godfrey has two sons. They're still young but may want to carry on the business.'

She looked surprised. 'I notice you have your Wood Sisters Beer Shampoo in the window, and lots of herbal remedies, not at all like Mr Brownlaw kept the window. And of course, one would wonder who was the chemist.'

'You must step inside and see who's the chemist.' I poured her tea. 'Don't let me spoil the surprise.'

She obviously doesn't know that we have the kind services of an ancient, long-retired pharmacist, Aunty Amy, as manager, and Sarah Garretty behind the counter, learning the trade.

I swear Mrs Turner can't make up her mind whether we are ruthless racketeers with secret hordes, or incompetent, uppity lasses who've got beyond their station in life. Well, I hope we have.

When she left she said that she'd pray for Margaret. I'm glad she's not going to pray for me. I have come to the conclusion that if there is a god he is a devil who likes to torment the human race.

I carried a jug of hot water upstairs and poured it into the basin for Margaret to inhale.

'I haven't the strength,' she whispered.

'You must,' I said. 'For Daisy, and the boys.'

'They'll be better off without me.'

'No, they wouldn't. And we're the Wood

Sisters, don't forget. It wouldn't work with just one.'

It wasn't funny, but she laughed. The laugh hurt, and turned into a cough.

After she had inhaled for a couple of moments, I got her to take a warm drink and an aspirin.

I need her to get better. I want to know what is in the envelope she has in her top drawer, hidden under her handkerchiefs and marked 'Julia, not to be opened until my death'. I don't want her to die. I couldn't bear to lose her and to be left alone. She has driven me mad sometimes but I would not exchange her for any other sister.

Her voice sounded hoarse. 'I'm no good to them. What kind of mother kills?'

'Kills what?' I tucked the eiderdown round her tightly.

'Two men.'

'Go to sleep, Margaret, you're imagining things.'

'No. Godfrey. I killed Godfrey.'

'You didn't kill him. It was an accident.'

I heard Dr Manning wheeze into the hallway, coughing and spluttering. 'Where's the spitoon?' he barked.

Mrs Bell answered that we did not keep a spitoon. A few seconds later, I heard her say, 'Well I never', and guessed that the doctor had spat on the beautiful mosaic-tiled hall floor.

He clattered up the stairs, steel caps to his boots that made him sound like a clog-dancer warming up. An ancient, stooping man with a graveyard face, he gives off an air of it being all your fault if you are ill. He was a great friend of Godfrey's.

He took Margaret's temperature and asked about her bowel movements. After which he turned to me accusingly and said that I was not sweating Margaret sufficiently. He suspected I was missing the aspirin, which I assured him I was not. He said the bed-warmers were not sufficiently hot and there needed to be more of them. He believes in the efficacy of lard as the food providing most warmth. Sick as she is, Margaret pulled a face behind his back. I had to try hard not to laugh.

I was also taken to task for opening the window. 'The patient does not need fresh air. She needs warmth.'

On the landing he shook his head. 'When I saw her last, it looked like a mild case. I'm afraid it has become more severe. You need to ensure she inhales or the inflamed mucous surfaces will worsen.'

Mrs Bell stood at the bottom of the stairs, paying a lot of attention to the umbrella stand. As I closed the vestibule door behind the doctor, she said, 'I didn't clean up his mucky spit in case he did it again on the way down.'

After he had gone I made up more of the recipe he recommended:

Salicylate of soda: 2 drams
Bicarbonate of potash: 2 drams
Carbonate of ammonia:36 grains
Compound infusion of gentian concentrated:
  2 drams
Water: 6ozs

One tablespoonful to be taken every four hours.

She must also inhale from half a pint of hot water, with five drops of pine oil, or the same amount of tincture of aconite root.

Margaret's temperature has raged all night. We have kept a fire burning in the room and a kettle boiling. As the oven bricks cool, I heat them again. I top up the hot water in the steel foot-warmer that's shaped like a slipper. I scalded my hand because I am so tired and clumsy.

As I sat in the chair by her bed, I remembered taking care of Dad and the madness of reading *The Iliad* to him. She couldn't sleep. I said, 'In *The Iliad,* the characters are given descriptions, such as Hector, tamer of horses, Odysseus, never at a loss. We had names for ourselves, too. You were Margaret, singer of songs. Dad was sometimes Joseph, smoker of Virginia tobacco. Bernard, player of tunes. Uncle Lloyd, server of pints.'

'And you?'

'Everything. We had the most titles. Julia, keeper of the journal. Julia, baker of pies. Margaret, creator of hats. Margaret, turner of heads.'

She whispered, 'Margaret, slayer of men.' She grabbed my wrist. 'I need something to live for, Julia. My life is empty without him.'

I thought that was a bit rich given that she'd intended to poison Godfrey.

'No,' she said, 'not Godfrey. Thomas. He's the love of my life, Julia. Do you think he still cares for me? If not, I might as well die.'

'What about Daisy? And the boys.'

'I'd be a useless shell. You'd be a better mother to them than me.'

I picked up my journal and looked for the page

where I had pasted Thomas's letter from long ago, where he said he would always love her. Of course it wasn't in this journal. It was in the one with the blue and purple cover that Aunty Amy's nephew Malcolm brought from Venice. So I pretended to find it. I knew the words by heart. I read the sentence to her where he said that he would always love her.

'Say it again,' she said. 'Say it again. Say it again.'

Over and over I said the words to her.

'Julia, you're crying. You're the best sister. No one ever had a better sister.'

She fell asleep, smiling.

I do believe she has come through the worst. Her cough had been dry and wracking, since the beginning of her sickness. At about four o'clock this morning, she coughed stuff from her chest. She said that eased her and took a drink of cold tea. Now she is sleeping peacefully. I will refill the kettle, then I will try and sleep myself, though the least little noise wakes me.

She has come through.

I woke this morning and Margaret was smiling. She has asked to see Daisy, and says that she is feeling much better. I said I would fetch Daisy tomorrow.

'Fetch her now,' she said. 'I'm better.' She fell asleep again.

Little Daisy curled up beside her mother. They both slept soundly for hours. When she woke, Margaret said, 'He mustn't stay in France. When the war ends, you'll go and fetch him for me.'

That was when I knew she was better. I never swear, but I did then. I was whacked and there she was, lying there, looking like the heroine of an opera, a beautiful baby, her own house and a secret in her drawer.

'I'm buggered if I'll fetch him,' I said. I pulled the letter from the drawer. 'What's this,' I said. 'What were you going to say that you couldn't say to my face?'

'Take it,' she said. 'But don't open it. Don't open it unless you are feeling very strong.'

I was about to tear it open when the look on her face stopped me. She held out her hand. 'Not yet,' she said. 'Give it back.'

SIXTY-FIVE

The war is over. For the rest of my life if anyone mentions the end of the war, I shall always think of a winter morning and washing on the line, frozen.

I would never have left out washing overnight on Bread Street. People would have complained about walking into it. At Elmtree House there's no one but ourselves so it didn't matter. My skirt and Gregory's shirt and trousers had frozen on the line and felt like stone. The next morning nothing was dry. I stood there wondering whether it would rain.

I heard a great booming sound like a circus cannon. Sheba barked and dashed about the yard. I glanced up at the sky, wondering whether it was

444

one of those airships.

Sol said, 'That bang'll burst the clouds. It's going to pelt it down.'

He held the basket while I unpegged the damp clothes.

Gregory wobbled round from the front of the house on a large black bike that didn't belong to him. He careered towards us, crashed into the horse trough and took a hard tumble. He sat up and rubbed his knee. 'The war's over. That was a firework. I saw the police sergeant come out from his house and fire it off as a signal.'

I helped him up. He'd bumped his nose and scraped his hand.

Just then the church bells started to peal. We said nothing, just stood there as frozen as the clothes were on the line.

Then Sol punched the air and grinned. 'There'll be right celebrations in Leeds tonight.'

The bells chimed on and on.

Gregory propped the bike against the wall. 'It's not fair. I didn't get chance to fight.'

Gregory and Sol caught the train to Leeds to find their sisters and join in the armistice celebrations. I reminded them that Annie won't feel like celebrating since she had received news of Bernard's death, but they are sure everyone will be going mad with joy.

I'm tucked up in the downstairs bed in the kitchen at Elmtree House. The fire's low but Sheba snuggles by my feet. I have a pillow under my knees and the leisure to write undisturbed. I am hugely relieved that the war is over. If I could

445

get past the sorrow, I might feel some joy. But I think about those who will never come home. Frank. All my cousins. Aunty Amy's Malcolm. Jean's fiancé and brother. My own dad, as much a casualty as any soldier. Even Godfrey! And of all the others across the world, their sisters, wives and mothers.

Most of all I think about Bernard. I couldn't bring myself to write about him before. When Uncle showed me the letter, I pretended to read it but couldn't make myself focus on the words. I pictured him, his eyes dimming. Did he see Annie and send her a last thought, or did he die with a raging hurt that his piano would never again come to life for him? I'm glad I'm here alone as I don't feel like celebrating.

Being here at Elmtree House has been a kind of adventure. Now I shall have to go back to something and I don't know what. Perhaps I am destined to be the looker-on in Margaret's life, while she brings up her children. Without this house I won't be able to provide for the Garrettys, but I expect now they are big enough to provide for themselves. Probably Annie will give them work at the Dragon if they want it. They like to be with Mr Hopps on the farm, but I can't see them spending their lives as farm labourers.

I had better stay here for now, for the sake of the hens, the goat and the pigs. This morning Pinky and I had a grunting conversation and she let me scratch the back of her neck. Sheba pushed her way in, so I had to scratch her back, too. Neither of them offered to scratch mine.

I walked up to the farm for milk, wondering how

many more times I would do this, since the house was mine only for the duration of the war. Misty, silver-white cobwebs balanced delicately on the hawthorn bushes. Icicles jutted from the Hopps' barn roof. Gladys was upstairs with the children. She called for me to help myself. I took a drink of milk from the jug while it was still warm.

In the study, I took the No Conscription Fellowship records and on every card for every conscientious objector I wrote: '11 November 1918, Armistice'.

Now the night's dark and the candle's low. I don't know what made me suddenly feel like dancing. I wound the gramophone and played the tango that Margaret and Thomas danced to. The music wound round inside my brain, and I made up a song as well as a dance. The words of the song wondered what Thomas is doing tonight and when he will come home.

SIXTY-SIX

I am writing this sitting up in bed in the early morning.

As the dull days tumble towards Christmas, sometimes I wake in the night with that same question. I want to hunt out the policeman who came to the door in the early hours of Christmas Day 1914 and ask, 'Was it you? Did you seize Dad when you saw his sack and found turkeys? Did you hit him round the head with your truncheon when words in broken English rolled off his tongue?'

When I have lain awake too long, swirled with questions, I try to lull myself to sleep with a kind of litany.

Odysseus, never at a loss. Hector, tamer of horses. Joseph, slayer of beasts. Margaret, singer of songs. Daisy, child without fear. Bernard, player of sweet music. Amy, kind healer of ailments. Uncle Lloyd, sharp puller of pints. Kevin and Johnny, charmers of ladies. Mrs Turner, fiercest of females. Cissie, best of all friends. Annie, maker of make-believe. Godfrey, driver of motor car. Edward, keeper of cricket bat. Ernest, adorer of his new mammy. Sheba, cleverest of dogs. Pinky, chubbiest of pigs. Julia, hoarder of words. Frank, boxer of shadows. Miss Mason, imbiber of fortified wine. Thomas, man of peace.

Mostly I say the litany in my head but sometimes aloud, which Sheba likes, especially when I come to her and Thomas's names.

Gregory and Sol have not come back to Elmtree House. They stayed in Leeds with Annie and Uncle Lloyd to help at the Dragon. Cellermen not farm boys, bartenders not smallholders.

I tend the animals alone and my days have a sameness shaped around creatures that talk to me without words and Sheba, who likes to walk the lonely fields and lanes. It somehow comforts me to know it has always been like this for us humans, a hard life and cold winters, but so lovely to be in the world and part of it.

Yesterday morning I went to collect the milk. Mrs Hopps had scalded her hand with steam from the kettle. I tore up beef sheeting to make a bandage for her. She asked how old I am now. When I told her nineteen, she said, 'You won't be stopping here much longer.'

I have not thought what I will do. The long winter seems to have frozen my brain. I do not even read much but sit in the evenings and watch the fire.

I saw them as I walked back across the fields with Sheba. Margaret, bumping along the dirt lane with Daisy in a perambulator. Mrs Turner, clutching her skirts, stepping around a puddle.

When we went inside, Mrs Turner filled the doorway and snarled, 'Well, my dear, you have made my son's house cosy.'

A feeling of dread ran through me. She knew the terms of my tenure at Elmtree House. For the duration of the war. Had she come to evict me?

They had brought a loaf of bread and expected eggs, not knowing that hens will not oblige year round according to the number of visitors. I thinned soup with milk and water, and added another potato and carrot.

'I know we haven't always seen eye to eye, my dear,' Mrs Turner said as she sat at the kitchen table, viciously tearing off a small portion of her bread. 'But my son told me you've been his loyal correspondent through thick and thin. I need him to come home. It's not as if he did nothing in the war. He wasn't a cowardy custard altogether.'

I felt myself go red and uncomfortable. 'Mrs Turner, if you knew what some conscientious objectors went through, you wouldn't call them cowardy custards.' I wanted to recite chapter and verse. Tell her of the objectors who had been crucified to the wire, gone insane in prison, faced death rather than wear a uniform and fire a bullet. But the No Conscription Fellowship habit of secrecy kept me silent.

'I'm sure you're right, my dear,' she said through gritted teeth. 'But now it's time for Thomas to come home. He's being stubborn, saying that he'll stay in France with this War Victims Relief business. We're all war victims. He needs to start again. His godfather, Mr Mitchell, has a post for him, and I should like him to take it.'

They looked at me as if I could produce Thomas from the cellar. Sheba looked at me and pounded her tail on the flagged floor.

'What can I write that you can't write yourself?' I asked.

Why should he come back? The woman he loved had jilted him and married someone else. If I could never forget that, how could he? When he walked past the church or drank a glass of ale in the inn where he spent what was to have been the evening of his wedding, he would remember.

'He's my only son, my one and only.' Mrs Turner tidied a strand of grey hair back into her bun. She slapped a railway ticket on the table. 'I want you to go to France and bring him back. Mr Mitchell will make arrangements for you from the London end. And before you say you can't speak French, the younger Miss Reeves has written out ten useful phrases and their phonetic pronunciation.'

'No!' I said.

'Don't answer yet,' Margaret said, ignoring the fact that I just had. She double-wrapped herself and Daisy in shawls and took my arm. 'Let's take Daisy to the wood. She'd like to see a robin red-breast.'

Mrs Turner called after us, 'Bring back some holly and ivy.' She handed me the bone-handled carving knife.

Margaret let me carry Daisy across the frosted, bumpy ground. She said, 'Don't mind Mrs Turner; tact never was her strong point. But you can see how badly she wants her poor boy back. He must have gone through sheer hell. They all did. It can't do him any good to stay over there. He needs to start his life again.'

'Why me?'

Apparently Mrs Turner thinks I'm the one he'd listen to. It would be a humiliation for Mrs Turner to go, as she has already written and begged him to return, and he ignores her request. She believes that because I am an outsider, it would not be a humiliation for me, and Margaret agrees.

The robin redbreast obligingly appeared, head cocked to one side, its gaze directed at us. I pointed to it and Daisy seemed happy enough but wanted to get down and explore. Not a good idea with holly bushes and tree roots, but she insisted. The two of us circled her, limiting her explorations.

'And *I* want you to go,' Margaret said quietly, as Daisy tripped, started to complain and pulled herself back into a standing position by clinging to my skirt and leg. 'I love him.'

'You go then.'

'I can't. Not when I jilted him.' She grabbed my wrists so hard that she hurt me and I couldn't break free. 'Bring him back and then I'll make him fall in love with me again. Daisy needs a father.'

I kicked her on the shin to make her let go of me. 'She's got a picture of Godfrey on the sideboard, that's more than a lot of bairns will have.'

She lifted her skirt and rubbed her shin. 'Why did you kick me?'

Daisy tripped again and this time started to cry. I picked her up. Her strong little hands tested my nose to see whether it could be pulled off. It felt as if she was joining in with her mother to torment me.

Tears filled Margaret's eyes. I thrust Daisy back at her.

'Too late,' I said. 'You had your chance with Thomas.' I turned to go back to the house.

'Wait! I've something to tell you. You have to understand why I couldn't marry him.'

Something in her voice stopped me. We sat down on a damp tree trunk under the beady eye of a thrush. The story did not come out as evenly as I will set it down. Daisy had to be watched. Margaret took a long time to get to the heart of it. I had to listen to how she had taken it much harder than me when Mam died and how I hadn't even understood or remembered that a baby brother died, too. So I shall leave out a great deal, and all my interruptions or agreements, such as when she swore me to secrecy. And why, when we got the chance to fatten turkeys at Elmtree House two years ago, she wouldn't let me do it, and why the very thought of turkeys made her ill. This is the gist of what she said:

'Before I gave birth, I knew what a terrible risk it can be. Poor Mam. I thought, *What if I don't come through?* That's why I wrote the letter you saw in the drawer. The letter was still there when I got that terrible sickness and you nursed me better. But that wasn't the first letter. The very first was after that Christmas Eve when I knew what I'd done. You must swear to keep this secret. Never let anyone else know what I am going to tell you.

'You remember that I'd moved into the Dragon and you were still at home. Dad promised Uncle a turkey. I wanted to make a good impression on Uncle since I was living there free and he had given me spending money.'

This was the first I'd heard of spending money.

She said, 'I had the oven ready for the bird and Dad had not fetched it by eight o'clock on Christmas Eve, so I went to meet him. I got all the way to the meat market and through the yard to that little door set in the big doors. Just one gas light was lit. By the big clock, a tall man slid his time card into the slot, and another card, too. I knew from the way he turned his head towards me that something was wrong, even before I heard the banging and the yelling.

'I remember thinking, Julia should be here; she'd scream, "Dad!" and would know what to do. So I screamed, "Dad!" just as you would have done. I rushed to where the sounds came from, all the way across that huge place. The man at the clocking-out machine came after me, yelling at me to skidaddle, sling my hook. I kept yelling,

"Dad, Dad!" so he would keep banging and I would know where to go. I reached a huge door with a heavy handle that I couldn't budge. The man was behind me. He set his lantern down and he grabbed me, grabbing my breasts and hair, and shoving me against the door. He pulled at my clothes, tearing my skirt and drawers. The strength came from somewhere and I moved the handle. The door swung inwards as the man pushed me against it, into a room colder than an iceberg. I saw Dad, his hair and moustache frozen. He staggered towards me. The man shoved him back and Dad fell. I ran to him. I can't remember what the man said. Something like now there would be two of us found after Christmas and that everyone would know the Hun and his daughter had been there to steal and got what they deserved. Dad called him Clarence and said he'd had his fun, now let us all go home.'

Daisy had found a little den in a bush and popped in and out as Margaret spoke. All the while she peek-a-booed we smiled at her and clapped hands as Margaret told the story.

'Clarence obviously meant us both to be found dead in the ice room. We would have been, too, but he intended to have his way with me first. That was his undoing. Dad was in no fit state to do anything, but being Dad he had had the foresight to kick something towards me.

'It was a turkey. I picked it up by its neck and it was frozen solid. I remember thinking of the oven, ready and waiting for it at the Dragon, and what a nuisance that it was frozen. At the same time I knew that Dad and I could meet the most horrible death and how unjust that was when I never used to go to the meat market and you always did and were his favourite, and if he wanted to die with anyone nearby it would be you, not me. I swung the fowl at Clarence. I believe I hit the back of his knees first, or perhaps his private parts. Because he was taller than me, I only hit his head after his legs buckled. He was dead, Julia.'

I asked her about Dad's butcher's steel that I'd found in the ice room near Clarence.

She shook her head. 'I remember leaving the frozen turkey by Clarence, so that whoever found him would think that he'd gone in there to steal and had slipped.'

She looked puzzled for a moment, then her face cleared. 'Perhaps he grabbed it, to force his way out. But I'm sure he was dead.'

'You – or someone – shoved it up his bum,' I said.

Her mouth opened wide. 'Oh my god. Did I?' She looked as if she would faint.

'And you left it there. If anyone else had found him–'

She stared at me. '*You* found him? I didn't know.'

Daisy grew tired of playing peek-a-boo and came to sit on Margaret's knee.

'What about Bernard?' I asked. 'He knew something was up.'

'He'd come after me,' Margaret said, 'guessing where I'd gone. You know what Uncle was like for going on at him, telling him not to let his cousin go out into the dark alone. Bernard took Dad into the Madman for a drink of brandy to warm

455

him through. I took one turkey home – fortunately unfrozen – and left the other with Dad, in his sack, for Mr Shepherd. After all, it didn't matter if you and Dad didn't have a turkey. You could have eaten with us at the Dragon.'

'You took the turkey home? You didn't think to go to the police?'

'No! No more than you did. You know how scared we were, expecting Dad to be picked up any time. How could I? He would have been blamed. So would I. We could have hung, Julia.'

She started to shiver. I put my arm around her, and so did Daisy, kissing her mother on the cheek.

'I didn't mean to kill him, Julia. It was him or us. Before Dad died, I wrote a confession, to say that I killed Mr Laycock while protecting myself and my father from his violence, just in case the police caught up with Dad.'

It had grown dark. We walked back towards the house, guided by the oil lamp in the kitchen window. Daisy had fallen asleep on my shoulder. I still didn't know what happened to Dad. Margaret said that Bernard told her he had tried to talk Dad out of delivering the turkey to the Shepherds, saying he was in no fit state, but Dad had insisted. So it was true that he only had one turkey on him when he was 'arrested', or whatever happened to him. I'll never know.

I asked her why she had told me now.

'Julia, I want you to bring Thomas back. Don't you understand why I couldn't marry him when I knew for sure he wouldn't join the army, when he said he couldn't allow himself to kill? I *had* killed. How could I stand by a man who kept the opposite principles? I would have given myself away. I can't put it properly into words but I couldn't, just couldn't. But now it's over. We're all starting again. Will you do it? Bring him back, or at least try.'

'I can't,' I said. 'And I can't put it properly into words either.'

'Please, Julia. Think about it.'

Mrs Turner must have been watching and flung the door open.

'Well?' she said. 'Where's my holly and ivy?'

SIXTY-SEVEN

Daisy's smiling face on Christmas morning! Edward had carved her a small wooden boat. Ernest gave her a toy dog. At least, I think it was a dog, but with a head like a seal, no ears and no tail. It had belonged to him when he was small. He had sponged it clean and tied a velvet ribbon around its neck. Margaret made her a dress of green velvet. My present was a tiny winter garden in the lid of a jar. I made it from mosses, acorns, twigs and white cotton to represent frost.

During Christmas dinner Ernest worried about the animals at Elmtree House. I had to tell him that I had led the goat and pig to Mrs Hopps, who would take care of them, and that chickens did not mind being left alone as long as someone came to feed them. Mabel would do that.

After dinner I walked to the park with the boys, Daisy and Sheba. I wished I had brought the perambulator, as Daisy got tired and had to be carried. Edward hoisted her on his shoulder in the park but didn't want to be seen carrying an infant on the way back.

At the garden gate I handed her back to Edward and they ran across the garden with Sheba giving chase.

I went inside first, quietly as I thought Margaret might be taking a nap. I hung my coat in the hall and walked towards the kitchen. The drawing-room door stood open and I saw Margaret under the mistletoe, her back to me, a man's hands on her waist and a head turned down to hers. They stood like that for a long time and I turned away feeling dizzy and confused. At first I thought I'd seen a vision of a Christmas past: Margaret with Godfrey. But this male head had too much hair to be Godfrey.

'Look who's here!' It was Edward's voice in the hall.

'Ronald!' Ernest cried.

It was the head boy from their school.

Later, I said to Margaret, 'I saw you. He's years younger than you. He's a boy.'

'He's not a boy. Don't you know he's articled to Mr Underend and studying to be a solicitor?'

'You were kissing him.'

'Just a Christmas kiss, that's all.'

All through the mince pies and cups of tea, Ronald told us stories of legal wrangles and strange criminal cases. They all seemed to be entranced by him, except me, Daisy and Sheba.

I took Daisy to bed and I think for once she was glad of the peace and quiet of her cot. Sheba lay beside me while I told Daisy a story. I told her how once trees fell down, buildings lay in ruins and all the people were unhappy because a great dragon had laid waste to the land. But when the dragon was killed the people decided to plant the trees again, to build the houses, to grow the crops they needed and find more cows and goats for milk. Ernest came in for the end of the story but by then Daisy slept.

'Are you talking about France?' Ernest asked.

'Yes.'

'Where will they find the animals again? How will they make everything as it was before? I've seen the pictures. There's nothing left.'

'It'll take a long time, I expect. But there's a peace conference. For once people are concentrating on making a better world.'

'Ma said that you might go there. That you know someone who's helping to re-build France and that his mother thinks it's time he came home.'

That's when I knew I would go. Ernest looked alarmed when I said I had a train ticket to London and that a Mr Mitchell would arrange my passage the rest of the way.

'What about Sheba?'

Sheba pricked up her ears.

'I'll take her with me.'

His little face! Perhaps he's right that France would be no place for a dog. There'll be no food for her, and she might end up in a pot herself.

I'll be so sad to leave her, but he has promised to take good care of her until I come home.

SPRING
1919

SIXTY-EIGHT

I have a khaki-coloured rucksack that was Godfrey's and a tapestry bag that belonged to the first Mrs Brownlaw. Under my skirt, I wear a substantial money belt made of unbleached linen, with cash to cover my expenses and return tickets for myself and Thomas, if we choose to use them.

There is something wonderful about leaving England, even when a person is seasick going from Dover to Calais. I know it is probably wrong to feel joyful and exhilarated, but I do. As we left the white cliffs behind, I felt like a warrior, a warrior for love.

When I arrived in Calais, a British soldier walked me to this lodging, which he assured me was a 'respectable house'. I half-hoped it might not be respectable. (By the sound of drunken English singing now coming through the ceiling from the bar downstairs, I am not entirely sure that it is.) The soldier had a word with the buxom lady owner, who looked me up and down in a way that made me wonder whether I might be whisked off in the night as part of the white slave trade.

I am writing this in a cobwebby loft room that smells of garlic and straw. The room has bare floorboards and straw mattresses – two of them occupied by sleeping females, one of them snoring intermittently in a way that reminds me of the hoot of the Selby train as it approaches Garforth.

In the morning I am to take a train for Arras. The soldier said it is lucky that the railway lines were secured for the British troops. So far things have gone easier for me than expected. It is about 65 miles to Arras and I feared I may have to cadge lifts or even walk, which I could do because I have stout boots that I imagine were just the kind of boots Tess wore in *Tess of the d'Urbervilles.*

The landlady refused to understand when I asked for a candle, so I must stop writing now. I shall sleep with the rucksack as my pillow, and the tapestry bag in my arms.

As I stepped off the train in Arras, two children clutched at my skirt, asking for pennies and food. I took out Thomas's photograph and showed it to them. The girl, small, her hair tucked under a scarf, painfully thin and with an ancient little face, took my hand, asking me to go with her. Her name was Ann-Marie.

We walked through a strangely quiet cobbled street. White dust clung to my boots and skirt. I tried out one of the phrases I had learned and asked the girl where she lived. She pointed down below the ground and I saw that someone was coming up stone steps from what must have been a tunnel or a cellar.

I knew we were in the heart of the town, but it was missing. We skirted round a line of people clearing fallen masonry and rubble, passing the rubble brick by brick, stone by stone, along the human chain to four men with hammers and chisels who chipped the bricks and stones straight and stacked them neatly by the side of the road.

We walked along the cobbled street past a shop front without windows, past what must have been a picture house. Part of a torn poster advertising a film fluttered across the road. A bent old man poked about in the debris, gathering pieces of metal to put in his sack. He kicked at the rubbish, trying not to bend unless he found a worthwhile piece.

The wind blew and the whole sky seemed full of white dust, which filled my nostrils and made my eyes smart.

I showed Ann-Marie the photograph again, thinking she had misunderstood me. She tugged my hand, and came out with a long explanation that I didn't understand. We reached a field and I looked for a farmhouse, or any house at all, but saw nothing but a few tents.

She waved her arm at a great stretch of fields where the ground lay bumpy and uneven, clay and soil mixed where the earth had been dug over. It was dotted with crosses. Hundreds of roughly made wooden crosses. 'Tommy,' she said. 'Here lie Tommy.'

So many. I hadn't thought there could be so many.

To think I had come here with such joy and expectation. I had not thought to come to a burial ground, to come all this way to see the resting place of so many British soldiers, and Thomas's grave.

I showed her the photo again. 'Are you sure?'

'Yes,' she said. 'Tommy. Here.'

As I walked through the field of crosses, I forgot about the little girl, until she stumbled and fell. She sat on a mound of earth looking at her grazed knee. I sat beside her and kissed it better. I gave her a hunk of bread and cheese from my bag. It disappeared into her clothes and she thanked me many times before running off.

Some crosses were carved with names and numbers or had a tag attached. Others had no markings. I read the names, looking for Thomas Turner, looking for Kevin, John or Bernard McAndrew. Looking for Frank. It made me feel dizzy to walk among them. I felt myself staggering across the huge bumpy field until I had to go, had to turn and half-walk half-run from there.

Back in the town, I felt I must find someone, the Red Cross or army headquarters, and make proper enquiries. But I couldn't get my bearings, couldn't see where I should ask, or even think what the words would be. Sense tells me he's alive. We've heard from him. Yet with so much death, what can I say? How can I ask for him? *I'm looking for a man who I didn't think was dead but so many are – he surely can't have stayed alive.*

I found my way barred by the human chain, each person passing a piece of rubble to the next. As I moved to excuse my way through, someone handed me a boulder. I set my tapestry bag on the ground and took the boulder, then a stone, and another.

Because of the dusty, grey-white sky I did not know whether it was afternoon or evening when we stopped and people walked away, leaving me standing in the centre of the street. I looked for my tapestry bag but it was gone. I still had the rucksack on my back. Only the men tapping the stones clean stayed at their post. Then the noise stopped and two birds circled overhead before flying towards the field. Everything was silent, as if the village had gone to sleep.

It was the way he moved, laying down his hammer, raising his head. It was the angle of his shoulder under his dark jacket covered in white dust. I walked towards him. I didn't call out, but he turned towards me.

The haversack thump thumped against my back, my skirt suddenly got in the way, too much blue plaid material wrapping itself round my legs. He grabbed me and hugged me. 'Julia!'

That was a relief. I'd worn Margaret's costume because mine was in a sorry state and hers practically new. But I'd worried since leaving Leeds station that he'd see me from a distance and expect me to be Margaret, and I would have to pretend not to notice the disappointment in his eyes.

We walked back to the edge of the town where the tents are, close to the burial ground. I didn't tell him about thinking him dead, but told him I had seen the giant graveyard. No graveyard should be so big and hold so many who are young.

'That's nothing,' he said quietly. 'No one from home has the least idea.'

One of his friends had a fire going and was boiling a pot of something or other that looked like nettles. I took off my rucksack. Although most of my food had been in the tapestry bag, I had a few things in my rucksack – provisions from Elmtree House, so that he would know all was well there. Two potatoes, a carrot, a turnip and some smoked bacon. He laughed as he held a turnip in one hand and a potato in the other. 'You grew these?'

'In your garden,' I said.

Mrs Hopps had sent a cheese. We feasted. He wanted to know all the news from home.

When we had eaten, his friends walked back into town to take up their work with the clearing of rubble. We sat draped in blankets by the smoking fire.

'I wish I knew how to send smoke signals,' I said. 'I'd signal to all at home that you're well.'

He smiled. 'Would they care?'

'Of course.'

I told him all about Margaret and Daisy. I told him about his mother's work on the School Board, about Annie Garretty being at the munitions factory when it blew up, and about Bernard, who barely had time in France to thump out a tune on a found piano before he was killed. I told him about Margaret almost dying of influenza. I might have told him she wanted to see him again, but he leaned forward to push a stick onto the fire and his fringe fell down over his face and I wanted so much to lean across and stroke his hair.

He turned and looked at me, his steady grey eyes curious and happy. He smiled at me and for a moment the pain and hurt I'd seen in his eyes earlier flickered away. 'Your letters kept me sane.'

I didn't know what to say. I mumbled something.

'Why have you come, Julia?'

Why had I come? Because Margaret wanted him back. Because his mother felt old and lonely and had sent me to fetch him. Because Sheba pricked up her ears whenever she heard a man's footsteps in the lane, and then sighed and shut her eyes to hide her disappointment when it wasn't her master. Because the war was over and it was time for people to go home.

Because I loved him.

'I've come to help in the reconstruction of France,' I said. The wind changed and the smoke from the fire blew into my eyes. 'I read about the War Victims Relief in the No Conscription Fellowship newsletter.'

He looked surprised. I had never mentioned the Fellowship work in my letters to him for fear of giving away information to the censors.

I told him about Jean and how we had kept the records all through the war when the authorities had tried so hard to find them.

He told me that he had helped distribute food supplies sent by the Canadians. Beyond the city, farms still stood and he had helped to clear a well. As soon as the next shipment of food arrived, he'd go to Calais again.

'Have you really come to work with the Relief?' he asked. 'And why Arras?'

I thought of saying that I'd seen a picture of Arras from before the war, which was true. But I gave myself away, not in what I said but in how it came out. 'Because you're here, Thomas.'

And he knew. For a long time we sat by the fire, saying nothing. He reached out and took my hand.

'You're cold.' He put his arms around me.

We got to our feet and walked back to the village, and all the way he kept his arm around me. I felt so happy.

'Has it been hard for you?' he asked.

'Yes.'

And though I hadn't told him, he said, 'They shouldn't have sent you.'

'I wanted to come.'

'You don't have to re-build Arras.'

'Since I'm here I might as well,' I said.

For the rest of that day, I stood in the human chain and passed stones along to the next person in the line, and the stones ended with Thomas and the other men, who chipped away and stacked the bricks and stones neatly, ready to re-use when the time came. Maybe this was how I would spend my life now, in a foreign country, not understanding the language.

Though I couldn't see him I was conscious of him there, just a few yards from me, and I thought that this was the craziest time in my life.

When we stopped in the evening, we stepped through a doorway without a door under a lintel that leaned at a strange angle, into a café with a makeshift roof made of corrugated iron. We took seats at a round table. A woman with gap teeth appeared from somewhere below ground, carrying a jug of wine, which she poured for us.

'Don't look so surprised,' Thomas whispered. 'Arras has a warren of cellars and tunnels. People left during the worst of the bombardments; now they're returning and living underground. I can't bear to be underground. That's why I'm in the tent.'

He reached across the table and took my hand. I tried not to think of Margaret, but I could see her hovering over his shoulder like a disembodied spirit.

I said, 'Margaret would have written, but what with marrying and having a baby and–'

He let go of my hand. 'I did write her a note of condolence. I don't know whether she received it.'

A stooped, elderly waiter brought two dishes of thin stew. A piece of gristle floated on top. I had seen no animals since arriving in the village, none at all.

Thomas picked up his spoon. 'If you get past the gristle, you'll find it's all right.'

I don't think I would have asked if it hadn't been for the second glass of wine.

'You once said you'd love Margaret for ever,' I said.

'She once said the same to me.' I must have frowned or looked disapproving. 'Julia, there'll never be another Margaret. She's one of a kind.'

'So you still love her?'

'There's a line from Blake. I think it's "Songs of Innocence". Something like: "And we are put on earth a little space, that we may learn to bear the beams of love." It's strange that when so many have gone, it makes the beams of love harder to bear for the ones who are left. Everything's different now. Even the way we love feels different, it has a sharper edge and there's a bit missing. But it's still love. And it's what I feel for you, and I think you feel for me.'

'You love me?' My voice sounded so loud. I thought everyone must have heard me. The stooped man, the gap-toothed woman, the elderly Jewish man at the next table, the little girl Ann-Marie peering through the doorway at us. The whole of Arras above and below ground. Margaret on the other side of the Channel probably.

I couldn't betray her and say she loved him. 'What about Margaret? You love Margaret.'

He fished a crumb of broken cork from his wine glass. 'That was a long time ago.'

I knew exactly how long ago it was: the date of Daisy's birth, add on nine months. My mouth felt dry. I pictured him hitching her up onto the stone lion at the Town Hall when she was to give her suffragette speech on that sunny Sunday in 1914. I remembered his breath steaming the window when he came home from the Dardanelles and gazed at her through the window of Elmtree House while she played the piano, badly, and sang, magnificently. I remembered his words: 'I am not a man to change his love as he changes his shirt.'

He leaned towards me. 'I know it seems mad. And sudden. But one thing this war has taught me, it's to value the time we have. I want to be with you. When I saw you, glimpsed you in the street in that outfit, the colour, the swing of the skirt, for a moment I thought of Margaret. When I saw it was you, grown-up and covered in brick dust, I felt such joy. Margaret would never have come here, she would never in her wildest dreams have sought me out, much less crossed the Channel and claimed to be re-building Arras.'

I smacked his arm. 'Don't mock me!'

He grabbed my wrist and kissed the palm of my hand. 'I'm not mocking. I love you. I want to marry you. What do you say?'

I can't remember how much longer we talked, or whether it was the next day or the day after that, in the café again, when I finally said, 'I would like that.' He did not give me chance to add, a *'but'*. He leaned over and kissed me, then turned to the little Jewish man sitting alone at the next table and asked him to make a toast for us. The old man stood up and crossed painfully from his table to ours. After he had raised his glass, he spoke to me in Yiddish, telling me I'd made the right choice.

I thought if Dad were listening in another dimension he might appreciate hearing the announcement of my marriage in his own tongue.

I had spent each night underground since arriving in Arras. That starry night I said, 'I don't want to stay in cellars tonight. I've been too much alone.'

We lay together, holding each other all night, not wanting to let go. It's so cold in a tent in winter. Thomas said he had expected never to be warm again, to be warm when so many were cold for ever.

We stayed as close as the two halves of a wishbone.

On the human chain the next day, I felt I'd be torn in two not having him beside me. The old Jewish man, Isaac, stood next to me and talked to me in Yiddish. When he did, I cried. I cried because Dad will never see me married or know how my life will be. I cried because I thought last night may turn out to be an illusion. I knew I must tell Margaret first.

That evening, when we sat by our fire outside the tent, the number of stars multiplied every time we looked at the dark sky. We made love so slowly at first, and I kissed his shoulders and his eyelids. He stroked me all over saying, 'Julia, my own Julia.'

In the night a dog barked somewhere, beyond the fields of graves. I opened my eyes, knowing it was time to go home.

He was looking at me. 'Not yet. We'll marry here. Just you and me.'

I shook my head. 'We must do it properly. Tell Margaret. Tell your mother. And there's something else you should know.'

'What?'

I shook my head. 'You'll find out when we go home.'

It would be up to Margaret to tell him the truth about Daisy.

I let myself in the back gate. Sheba gave a bark before bounding towards me, twisting herself around my legs, barking 'Where've you been?' I explained everything to her, until she stopped barking.

Margaret was sitting on the chair in her front room, balancing Daisy on her lap. The fire burned brightly. She sang:

Daisy, Daisy, give me your answer do.
I'm half crazy all for the love of you.

It won't be a stylish marriage,
We can't afford a carriage.
But you'll look sweet sat upon the seat
Of a bicycle made for two.

After we had put Daisy to bed, I said, 'Thomas is back. We ... he and I ... we came back together and...'

She pretended not to understand and made me finish. She said, 'I always thought you had a bit of a moony spot for him. But I didn't think you had it in you to snatch him from under my nose.'

'It's not like that,' I said.

She had given me a glass of something sweet and red, not port wine or sherry. I don't know what it was. It made my cheeks hot. I felt blotches coming out on my neck as I heard the outside door slam.

She put down her glass. 'There's Ronald and the boys.'

The three of them came rushing in, making a fuss of me, and full of the story of a moving picture they had been to see. Eventually, Ronald ushered Edward and Ernest away, saying meaningfully, 'I'm sure your stepmother and aunt have things to talk about.'

I waited until he had closed the door. 'You and the head boy?' I asked.

She tutted. 'Stop calling him the head boy. I've told you before. He's articled in a solicitor's office.'

'He seems pretty much articled here, too.' The sticky red drink on an empty stomach had made me dizzy. I held onto the sofa arm.

'You wouldn't understand,' she said. 'I'm not sure if I do myself. You see, he had nothing to do with the war. He just missed it. You only have to look at him – his smiling face. His eyes have not one jot of distress. You could gaze into his eyes for hours and see no pain. He's jolly. He's a happy young man, and he makes me feel glad.'

'But ... you sent me to fetch Thomas.'

She picked up a shoe belonging to Daisy. 'Well, then, you've got something to thank me for.'

I spotted the other little shoe across the room and retrieved it. 'Isn't there something you'd better tell Thomas? Isn't there something he should know?' I asked.

'Oh, for goodness' sake! Spit it out. You mean Daisy.'

'Yes.'

'Sit down, Julia. Listen carefully.' She took the other shoe from me. 'You can do too much telling. Some things are best left unsaid.'

'But such a secret–'

'There is no secret,' Margaret said firmly. 'There are only secrets if people tell them. You've got something into your head, that's all.'

She picked up a silver-framed photograph from the sideboard and handed it to me. I gazed at Godfrey, his hand on Margaret's shoulder as she sat in the photographer's straight-back chair, Baby Daisy on her lap.

'Take a good look, Julia. Take a good look at the late Mr Godfrey Brownlaw, his wife, Mrs Godfrey Brownlaw, and their daughter, Daisy.'

I stared at the photograph. 'That's right,' she said, setting down the little shoes neatly by the door. 'Stare at it until you believe it.'

I handed the photo back to her and watched her place it on the sideboard, slightly more off-centre than it had been before. She said, 'And now I'm going to telephone Mrs Turner and ask her and Thomas round to supper.'

'Do you think that's a good idea?' I asked. I dreaded the thought of Mrs Turner. I could hear her saying, 'That girl's drunk. Again.'

Margaret thought for a moment. 'No. Probably not a good idea. The invitation should come from you. You know where the telephone is.'

'It's your house, not mine.'

She looked round the sumptuous room. 'Yes, it is,' she said in a pleased voice as if she had never thought of that before. 'But you're my sister and so you're entitled to telephone and invite them.' She took my arm and led me into the hall. 'We're the Wood Sisters. We always stuck together, and we always will.'

I felt slightly unsteady as I walked through the dark hall towards the telephone. I turned back to Margaret, ready to say something else, I'm not sure what. Something about the past, something about how if you start to tell it differently...

She didn't let me get my words out. 'Julia, our past is what we say it is. Our future is what we'll make it. Trust me. I got us the vote, didn't I?'

This Large Print Book for the partially sighted, who cannot read normal print, is published under the auspices of

THE ULVERSCROFT FOUNDATION